THE
PEMBLETON
MYTH

THE PEMBLETON MYTH

PRUE PHILLIPSON

KNOX ROBINSON
PUBLISHING
London & Atlanta

KNOX ROBINSON
PUBLISHING

34 New House
67-68 Hatton Garden
London, EC1N 8JY
&
3104 Briarcliff Rd NE 98414
Atlanta, Georgia 30345

ISBN PB 978-1-910282-90-8

Typeset in Bembo

Printed in the United States of America and the United Kingdom.

www.knoxrobinsonpublishing.com

CONTENTS

The Pembleton Myth

A novel set in one day in the late 1950's in the imaginary northern town of Midcaster and county of Northshire, in the days when Planning was young.

The Planning Department

County Planning Officer – **Quentin Bird**
His Secretary – **Miss James**
Deputy County Planning Officer – **Derek Lister**
Chief Assistant County Planning Officer – **Ron Foggart**

Section Heads

Architecture	Development Plan	Administration	Development Control	
			East Area	West Area
Hugh Cole	Unnamed	**Leonard King**	**Harry Wade**	**Paul Pembleton**

Planning Assistants		Chief Admin. Assistant	Assistant Area Planning Officer	
Gordon Harris	**Ken Myers**	**Jocelyn Smeed**	**Roger Weston**	**Neville Ca**
John Pennyman	& others	Typists		

Draughtsmen	Switchboard Girl	Draughtsmen
Bill **Tony**	**Miriam**	**Hine** **White**
	Office Boy	
	Cyril	

County Surveyor – **Dowland.** Deputy C.S. – **Amberly**. An Assistant – **Arnold Walla**

District Surveyor **Wilf Mason**   District Councillor **George Cranston**

Family Members **Eleanor, Cathy & John Pembleton, Lorna Ann Foggart, Lena Carr, Barbara & Dorothy Bird, Hazel Wade, Shirley Lister, Hilde, Hugh's girl, Christopher King**.

Applicants: **Matthew and Jane Hodge** and her mother, **Mrs Pawson**.
Professor Tom Smith and others.

1

THE EARLY HOURS

Midcaster was getting up on a September Thursday in the late 1950's, a little tired of the heatwave that was into its second week.

County Hall, looming along one side of a square overlooking the river Bryn, was wearing a skirt of fog round its lower storeys. Opposite it a statue of a 1914 sailor pointed east along the river to the sea. He was mysterious in the fog, almost alive.

From Floor 3 he was invisible. Here, outside the Planning Office windows, the top layer of fog shifted and thickened and shifted again. The cranes and warehouses on the far bank of the river where the town of Barton rose appeared one minute and the next were engulfed in a claustrophobic greyness. But there was no one in the office looking out. Desks, files, drawings, waited as last night's cleaners had left them.

Eleanor, Paul Pembleton's wife, opened an eye and saw her husband standing at the bedroom window, a tall shape, perfectly still, contemplating their long front garden. He was wearing his light tweed jacket which meant he was going round the rural western half of the county, his area. How could he want to exchange that for the streets of London? Yet the letter offering him the job would probably come today. Nothing in his posture suggested he was thinking of it.

"A delicate watercolour entitled 'Fading leaves'," he said.

She hoisted herself up and wormed her feet into her slippers.

"Look at those knobbly veins. I'm a real mess this pregnancy."

He looked round and gave her his swift, devastating smile. "*I* don't mind them."

She joined him at the window. "Oh, it's another of those shy days. Too hot later. Why is there a kitchen chair on the lawn?"

"Cathy ate her breakfast there an hour ago." He swung round, grabbed her bra off the bed and wound it round her neck. "Clothe thyself. It's past eight."

It was typical of him to alternate apparent languor with swift movement.

1

She listened. There was not a sound. "Is John up too?"

"John walked in here at six wearing only his new school cap. He's downstairs, uniformed to the eyebrows, clutching his pencil box and shoe bag. Cathy's reading."

She shook away the sleep. "I was having a wish-fulfilment dream about London. The letter was all in capitals but it said 'Regret your application was unsuccessful . . .'"

She set off along the passage and down the three steps to the bathroom. He followed. He sat on the bathroom stool, stretching an arm along the towel rail. His legs trailed over most of the floor. He said nothing and she felt obliged to rush on.

"I love this house. I love leafy Newmont. It's not pretty-pretty. It has long back lanes with cats and dustbins. And everyone lives here from college dons to bus conductors." With her toothbrush in her mouth this came out amid spit and splutter.

"You liked our first flat in Islington. Plenty of cats and dustbins."

"And smog for the new baby's lungs. We'll have to go miles out and pay five thousand for a semi when we have this solid terraced house, long garden and trees!"

"Your Mother can baby-sit if we're not too far from Windsor." He was mischievously quoting her one point in favour.

Back in the bedroom he flung himself on the bed, hands cupped under his head, while she dressed in a navy maternity skirt and matching smock with white polka dots.

"Why do wives get the jitters worst?" he asked rhetorically. "Hazel Wade will be feeling like this about Harry."

Eleanor snapped on white popper beads and saw him in the mirror utterly relaxed. She thought, how can he, with his quicksilver temperament, be so calm, not knowing. She said, "Hazel should know now. Harry will have phoned from Morlton after the interview. But their kids are grown-up and married. They're free."

His face was long and mobile but only his eyebrows twitched now. "I've mastered the job. And Ron Foggart's rearing his ugly head. Hugh Cole goes at the end of next week and they haven't filled his post. Foggart's suggesting dividing Hugh's Section between the Areas. A clumsy arrangement."

She clipped on round white earrings. "You're overworked now."

"Talking of Hugh Cole" – he sat up as if the other subject was now closed – "you wouldn't go to *his* party but what about Westhill one evening? At least the Listers have chairs for everyone."

"Derek and Shirley? Have they asked us?"

"I've a hunch Derek will start talking about 'a little do at my place. Do the right thing by old Hugh.'" Paul gave a perfect imitation of the Deputy's rich warm voice.

"He's OK but his wife terrifies me."

He laughed. "I think of her as a homely sort of person."

"Yes, if you mean she's as well-groomed as their home. It makes her seem phoney." She faced him but only added, "Will I be a credit to John?"

He stood up. "Yes, you have a clean scrubbed look."

"And *you've* got your county clothes on. Are you going round the Area? D'you want sandwiches?"

"I'm going out *after* lunch. Sites to visit round Wanwick."

"Wanwick Moor on a day like this! You won't get that in London."

"It's not picnicking by the Falls of Wann. I have to cope with *people*." He picked up his keys, small change and a packet with two cigarettes in.

Feet clattered down the attic stair. "I'm having another breakfast. I'm starving."

Paul called out, "Cathy, it's scandalous how much you feed that tapeworm of yours." Shrieks of laughter answered him.

Amidst it all a pitiful voice squeaked, "Mummy, have I missed school?"

"That poor little lamb!" Eleanor pushed out of the room past Paul. It was easy for him to joke but bringing up children was a serious business and moving them all three hundred miles to London was a fearful thought.

Four streets away, in a house Paul and Eleanor had never been invited to, lived Ron Foggart, the Chief Assistant Planning Officer. It had a sign: The Lorna Ann Guest House and Lorna Ann was Foggart's sister whom no one at the office had ever met.

Foggart opened the inner door with the sailing ships in stained glass and then the solid green-painted outer door. He lifted in the milk crate and set it down next to the china rabbit. He straightened up, looking along the street, seeing nothing but area railings, leather-leaved shrubs and boarding house signs. He took a deep, satisfied breath, enjoying the absence of people.

"Damp, damp. There's damp in the air." An old man came downstairs. "This talk of heat-waves. There's no escaping the date. October next. My chest hates winter."

Foggart said, "Good morning, Mr Price" and went into the kitchen. His own weakness was stomach.

The two gas stoves were going full blast for the guests' breakfasts. Betty, who lived in, stood over them, her face grim. If he asked her to boil him an egg she'd do it but he hated to nourish her sense of martyrdom. He had to endure anyway her sighs and groans when putting up his lunch in the lull between cooking and washing up.

"He's wanting his bait again," she'd say to Lorna Ann. "Beck and call, that's me."

He wondered sometimes what position Betty thought he had – some sort of clerk perhaps. When he had his name in the paper: "Mr R. Foggart, Chief Assistant Planning Officer, representing the County Planning Department ..." she never saw it. She only read the lives of film stars. Lorna Ann wouldn't draw attention to it. She resented the success he'd made of his profession, though they both knew it was through cunning and opportunism, not ability. Her own career in the theatre had been a failure. That was why she wanted her name up outside the house in illuminated letters. LORNA ANN.

To the guests he was Lorna Ann's brother, little Ronnie, an appendage. They saw a small hollow-chested, middle-aged man, weasel-faced, hook-nosed, with thinning black hair streaked across his head. For him living here was like living on the edge of a world. He *could* buy a house, rent a furnished flat. But where was the sense? There was a roof here, food of a kind, sometimes a little colour from the life of the boarding house.

Eight-twenty. He could go soon. He liked being early at work. He scanned Betty's back. Even the stiff bow of her apron defied him.

She glanced round. "Don't say you want off. Mrs Ede's not down yet. She has the lot. Porridge, bacon and eggs, toast and tea."

"Do my sandwiches before she comes down then."

Betty faced him, porridge spoon in hand. "Oh no, Mr Foggart. I does me breakfasts, then I does your bait. There's no two ways about it."

"I'll do it myself." He was dancing with impatience now to get to the office. His latest scheme was churning in his brain like the creation of an artist.

Betty's eyes opened wide. "Oh no, Mr Foggart. No one else is going to monkey around in *my* kitchen."

He picked up the paper and walked through to the private sitting room. If he could undermine Pembleton, the archetypal Oxford man . . . Perhaps that cocky new assistant of his, Neville Carr, would get into hot water and make trouble for the Western Area. . .

He jumped up and went into the kitchen to see if there was tea left in any of the teapots. Betty was spreading a smear of fish-paste on thick white bread. "Mrs Ede was bilious in the night. Not eating today. Here, they're finished."

She pushed the sandwiches down into a brown paper bag and thrust it at him.

The Chief Assistant took his lunch and went out with a small secret smile to his car. He would make a cup of tea at the office. The thought pleased him.

Neville Carr, Paul Pembleton's assistant, lived in Bosworth Crescent in the Old Town. He and his wife Lena had one vast rambling attic room and a store cupboard made into a bathroom. Across the road they had a share of a private garden. Gates and railings had gone in the war. Blown newspapers clung round the grimy privet bushes. Lying in bed he could see through the dormer window a square of early morning glow gilding the tips of beech twigs above the fog.

"You could imagine you were in the country."

Lena said, "Who wants to?" She could keep it up like this all day.

He thought, Damn, I'll have to stay in the office today. Pembleton's doing site visits after lunch. He was out all day yesterday too. "Lena," he said, "we should get up early and walk round the city before it wakes. Marvellous atmosphere."

"Don't let me stop you," she said.

Her garish beauty that had captivated him when they met at university was now so overlaid with a scowl of boredom that he could hardly bear to look at her. Some days she dragged herself from the bed to the table and drank coffee, her large painter's hands clutched round the black and red striped mug. Or she might stay in bed till he'd gone.

When he put on his office suit he found she was dressed too, in a red smock over purple slacks. With her long yellow hair the effect was bizarre. But in the corner, unused since they'd come to Midcaster six months ago, was her easel and some canvasses.

"You're going to paint! That's great."

"But I need colour. I'm in my vulgar phase. Gauguin. Van Gogh. What's out there? Grey mist, sooty stone. And not a face I know."

He made the coffee, a little touched that she was appealing for sympathy.

"You moaned when you had your job that you never had time to paint." He put two slices of bread under the grill to toast. "It's your fault if you know nobody. Anyway you've met the Pembletons."

She snorted. "They had us and we had them. She's having a baby so that'll finish it. We missed Hugh Cole's party because you fixed that wretched trip to Scotland."

He'd planned the weekend to jolt her out of this but she'd found fault with everything. He ate his toast and drank his coffee in silence. When he got up to put on his motorcycling gloves he said, "You could call on Mrs Pembleton."

She let her long thick hair hang forward till it brushed the breadcrumbs on the board. She knew how this revolted him. "You want me to have a baby, don't you?"

"Don't start on that at ten to nine in the morning."

"God!" she hooted. "Tell Paul, you're sorry you're late. We were starting a baby."

He made a frantic gesture with his gloved hand. "Will you stop it and say goodbye for once? Some couples actually kiss, did you know?"

"Do they now? Does Paul Pembleton kiss that drab hulk of a wife of his?"

He took a stride to the door. "I've never been late in six months."

That provoked the devil in her. She leapt between him and the door, spreading her arms. "Will Paul go mad? Will you have that guilty look like a choirboy caught eating sweets in the sermon? They have pink and white faces and hair like a little mat on top. Paul Pembleton's hair grows from his forehead and shapes itself rounds his head."

"Why d'you keep talking about Pembleton?" he yelled at her.

She was off guard. "You mentioned him first." Then the devil was back. She reached up her hands to press down his hair. "A mat. That's it."

There was a second when he could have hit her. She knew it and pulled back her hands. He never had, ever. She'd married him because he was gentle and because her father had been a man who believed in corporal punishment. So Neville had a vow with himself never to be violent with her. But his gentleness was familiar to her now and contemptible. She would goad and goad him. His mother used to say, "In this world goodness provokes evil." He'd never understood it till he'd been married to Lena. He tried to take her in his arms but an idea had come to her and she stood transfixed.

He said, "I'll be home to lunch. He's going to Wanwick. I won't get any site visits."

"Come on then. Kiss me."

She was full of suppressed excitement as if she'd made a sudden plan. He put his lips to hers, then went quickly out of the room and down the stairs. The cathedral clock struck nine.

Miss Smeed, the Chief Administrative Assistant, put on the tunic she had made out of an old coat. Worn over a beige blouse in summer and a brown jersey in winter, it was serviceable for the office. At the neck where the stitching was poor she pinned a bronze brooch in the shape of a leaf.

In the mirror she could see beyond the red-tiled roofs of Barton a haze of blue distance. Up here on the steep southern bank of the Bryn she was well above the fog. Looking into that western distance she could imagine the moors where the Bryn rose. In a file on her desk was an application from a Matthew Hodge of Old Mill Farm near Blattingford. She would send it in today with other new applications from the western half of the county and Mr Pembleton would go and see the farmer and discuss it. The names stayed in her mind but her senses struggled for the smell of the farmyard, the bleating of sheep, the purple of the heather. Sometimes when Mr Pembleton had been out to such places and returned to the office she noticed mud on his shoes and she pictured him striding about the site for a cattle court. She noticed everything about him, which bow tie or fancy waistcoat he was wearing for an office day or his country clothes.

If only he wasn't so quick-witted, so self-assured, so – *invulnerable* –! But Mr Foggart could be making trouble for him and she had seen the merest flicker of irritability in Mr Pembleton lately. Of course he was awaiting a reply from the London County Council about a job application so he must be on tenterhooks. She liked to think of him on tenterhooks. But if he got the job –?

She went to the window, her eyes on the smudge of the far hills. The Council might give her early retirement in a few years. She would take a bus to Blattingford and Wanwick and all the other places he visited. A pilgrimage in his footsteps. Surely her parents and Aunt Lil would have died by then. If he was still about she would work as long as the Council let her. She left her bed to air while she went to do the breakfast trays. She saw Aunt Lil had stuck her chamber-pot outside her bedroom door.

She was glad Mr Pembleton couldn't see her life. The high point of the day was walking down through Barton to the Bryn bridges and over to County Hall, nearer and nearer to Mr Pembleton. The low point was the journey home every evening. It had to be raining hard for her to take a bus.

At first light on Wanwick Moor there was mist only in the hollows and in the valley bottom round Blattingford. Old Mill Farm had a pocket to itself beneath the scoop of the hillside. When Matthew Hodge opened the kitchen door he could see only an arm's length in front of him but he came out into the farmyard. Jane heard the door. She heard him softly greeting Jess, the sheepdog. She thought, he's up earlier than ever these days. He can't bear to be in the house since Mother came.

Matthew climbed the sheep-track that went up behind the old barn. The ground was baked hard with the long dry spell. Against his boots the heather, beaded all over with mist, was still brittle. He could feel the presence of sheep above and around him, could sense their awareness of the dog, but they were quiet. Jess too was subdued. It was the uncanny silence of the mist and the half-light.

All at once they were out into the clear air. Jess bounded ahead as if released. Matthew stood still. Above him the crest of the hill was sharp in the paling light but there was no colour yet in the tips of the bracken. He climbed again till he came to a boulder where he sat down and looked back across the valley. White fleeces of mist curled here and there in the enclosing hills like the one cocooning the farm below him. There was a quality about the light that made him hold his breath. It would be another perfect day.

He thought, I'll have to go into Wanwick and see George Cranston about the bungalow. I hate that enclosed heat of brick and stone but I must know when he can get his builders started. For my own peace of mind – and for Jane's sake – I must get the old woman out from under my roof.

Jess came and lay at his feet. She looked up into his face, cocking one ear like a question mark. He tickled her long muzzle. To stay here with Jess and the sheep and the heather and the wide sky and speak to no human soul – that was his idea of a perfect day.

But soon he could hear the clash of churns from the direction of the byre and the subdued voices of Sykes and Reeve. They'd be saying, "Not like him to miss milking."

Over the hills to the west the sky was pink, reflecting the rising sun. If only he could trust George Cranston . . . Jane said, "Cranston will do a favour for an old school friend but if something bigger comes along he'll take his men off Mother's bungalow at once." Jane was nervous of people though she saw to the heart of them. But Cranston was on the Council and could do them harm if he was offended. Peggy, Jane's friend who was married to Wilfred Mason, the District Surveyor, had said, "It'll get past the local council with Cranston ready to build it. Then it'll go to County Planning – that's Pembleton for this area. *He's* all right. Wilf likes him and he was super when I started up Westways. The things people said about the Home – the children were nut-cases, they'd terrorise the village! It was great to talk to a reasonable man like Pembleton."

Jane had reported Peggy's phone call word for word in her faithful way. Matthew was impatient now to meet Pembleton but in his heart he loathed that any man should tell him what he could do on his own land, with his own life. If he had the skills he would build a home for his mother-in-law with his bare hands down by the curve in the road where he couldn't see it and no one should be able to say him nay.

In an hour the sun would have sucked up all the mist. Mooing and shuffling came from the byre. He stood up. Jess sprang to her feet, alert. As he strode down the hill he noted where the dry-stone wall needed mending. There was quiet pleasure awaiting him there. He thought, there are few people I care for. Not to have about me. Peggy was tolerable. "Straight as a dye," Jane called her. "Her masterful manner puts you off but she has to be tough to run that Home." Mason – the man she'd married to everyone's surprise – stammered and couldn't look you in the eye, but Jane said he was all right too. Honest and kind. But to Matthew people were devious, the old woman in there most of all.

He went in and found Jane and her mother in the kitchen.

Jane said, "Mother *would* come down. She heard you go out."

Mrs Pawson said, "I'm wakened every day with the milking anyway."

"She'll be quieter" – Matthew addressed Jane – "in the bungalow."

The old woman snapped, "Quiet as the grave. Is that it?" She went to the basket chair in the corner and sat down. She lived in that chair. If she was going to start coming to it as early as this there wouldn't be any hour of the day that was safe from her.

He muttered to Jane, "I'll go into Wanwick . . see Cranston . ."

Her mother caught the word. "Wanwick? It's not market day."

Jane said, "I could phone Peggy. Wilf was at the meeting."

"You're trying to keep me in the dark. Both of you."

He said, "I'll see Cranston myself." He opened the back door.

"There's tea made," Jane said quickly. He shook his head.

"Oh let him shut the door, girl. The mist's getting in."

He pulled it behind him and walked over to the byre. It felt like shutting a door in someone else's house.

In his architect designed house in Rufton, Midcaster's one de luxe suburb, Quentin Bird, the County Planning Officer, slept. His wife, Barbara, lying beside his portly shape, harried him with sleepless eyes. Round and pink, his face was cuddled into the pillow like a baby's. On the bedside table were his spectacles folded in their case.

Downstairs, his unmarried daughter Dorothy selected a brown egg for his breakfast. White ones, he always said, looked unhealthy.

A tall, big-boned handsome girl, she stood at the kitchen window, her eyes looking at the landscaped garden but her mind seeing only the massive frame and towering curly head of Roger Weston, Assistant Area Planning Officer for the East Area, who hadn't rung her since her last satiric sketch in the local paper – 'clodhopping farmer at nightclub.' It was true she had taken him to the newly-opened *Demon King* in Castle Street and his *father* was a farmer but . . . oh it was a curse being a writer!

She glanced at the clock. In three minutes she would wake Daddy. He would be at the office at nine-fifteen. At some point in the day he might *see,* even *speak* to Roger. She ate some cornflakes and, unaware, watched a chaffinch on the lawn.

When she tapped at her parents' door her mother's voice said, "You needn't have bothered. I've been looking at the clock for two hours."

Quarter of an hour later her father upended his empty eggshell so that it looked like a new egg and put it carefully to one side. "Another half minute. Just half a minute and it would have been quite perfect."

"I'm sure it had four," Dorothy said.

Her mother stopped in the middle of pouring the tea. "I saw you go down and fill the bird-bath up."

Dorothy snarled, "I didn't *over*cook it. That *proves* I timed it."

Bird said, "Now now, in the interests of accuracy – hardly *proves* it, does it? Myself, I find it better to *be* there. The same with toast."

"All this about an egg!"

"No, my dear, the egg is not important. The principle of order and precision is. There is a best way to do every job."

Dorothy put her elbows emphatically on the table. "You couldn't keep that up in real life. Take planning. If you tell me things are perfect at the office I just won't believe you."

Her mother sighed. "Dorothy, don't start philosophical discussions at breakfast."

Quentin Bird looked at his watch. Time was still favourable. "Alas, Dorothy," he admonished her, "I wouldn't ask you to believe it. Compromise is inevitable. If we all had logical minds – and *large* minds to see the general good behind our own interests –"

"You know I've had a bad night," his wife said.

"So in fact you're betraying your ideals all the time." Dorothy stood up and gathered the eggcups together.

He reproached her mildly. "'Betraying' is an emotional word and 'all the time' is a gross exaggeration." He looked at his watch again. "Take office administration for example. In that field I can have almost entirely my own way —"

"I hope you've got *that* perfect then." She wondered if he knew how her mind ran on Roger Weston whenever the office was mentioned.

"Ah but the ingredients change. Personnel come and go. Mr Wade and Mr Pembleton, the two Area Planning Officers, may both leaving. And more work comes in. One must keep an open mind. A tidier way may present itself."

Her mother said, "I wish you wouldn't start Daddy thinking about things. If he reorganises the office we'll never get away for our holiday. You're all right, Dorothy, you've had one. Ours is late this year, don't forget."

"Oh yes, taking the Sunday School kids to camp. That was terrific."

"You could have said no when the vicar asked you."

Bird finished his last cup of tea and rose to his feet. "As a matter of fact a scheme for reorganising the office is being mooted now."

"You see, I knew this would happen if we didn't get our holiday in early."

Barbara Bird put a plate on a tray and sat back exhausted.

"You've heard me speak of Mr Foggart," he said to Dorothy.

"The one who never comes to office parties? Your number three. Chief Planning Assistant. What's he done? Jumped off Old Town Bridge?"

Bird went into the hall and fetched his grey trilby and rolled umbrella. "Chief Assistant Planning Officer. And please don't say such extravagant things, Dorothy. It is he who is suggesting some changes."

"Oh I thought *you* initiated everything."

He picked up his briefcase, walked round the table and gave his wife a peck on her forehead. "I hope," he said to Dorothy, "I'd listen if the *office boy* had improvements to suggest. And now," he looked at his watch, "it's time for me to go. It occurs to me that Mr Wade will be in the train at this very moment returning from Morlton. If he's been successful there that will mean a new Section Head for the East Area."

My Roger could succeed him, Dorothy thought instantly. He's not new and raw like that Neville Carr in West Area. She made her father meet her eye.

He smiled at her with consummate neutrality. "Yes, the moment may be propitious for other changes. Possibly. We shall see."

She followed him to the garage, itching to hear Roger's name spoken – but he wasn't *her* Roger any more, damn her idiocy. She said, "I think Harry Wade has the kindest and *saddest* face I've ever seen. I hope he *has* got the Morlton job."

Bird inserted his round body into the car. "For *his* sake I rather hope not. Morlton is an up and coming County Borough and Harry has been in one place too long to adapt well. We shall see. The doors, thank you, dear."

When Dorothy went back into the house she saw her mother had picked up the local newspaper, her eyes drifting from headline to headline.

Dorothy said, "Daddy is extraordinary. I bet he knows them all at the office through and through. X-ray eyes. He really is right for his job, don't you think so?"

Her mother looked over the paper. "Yes, he does fuss over little things. You poor darling with that egg! Never mind, it's a lovely day. We'll sit in the garden. You shall sunbathe and I shall go to sleep." She went back to the paper.

"I work," said Dorothy. "I'm a writer." Her mother nodded, reading.

Harry Wade was perspiring as the sun beat in through the train window. He took his spectacles off and wiped them. He counted six telegraph poles and looked at his watch. Not quite nine! Only half an hour since Morlton and still three hours to go to Midcaster. If he went out into the corridor he knew he would have a smoke. He'd promised Hazel he would give it up. "Oh Harry," she'd said on Tuesday, when he'd bought a packet at Midcaster station. "One or two," he'd pleaded, "just before the interview – to settle my nerves."

Actually he hadn't been nervous, not more than usual before addressing an audience. When he saw the other candidates in the waiting room he became quite calm, amused even. They were all younger than himself and had that quick, keyed-up look of Paul Pembleton. Of course Toplady would want a vigorous young Deputy to help build up a new City Planning

Department in Morlton. Harry felt quite detached from it all by the time they called him in.

It was now that he needed a smoke. Even in a job he was used to he could get flustered. People said, "Harry's got a flap on." Juggling many things at once might be meat and drink to Paul Pembleton but *his* favourite way of working was slow and steady. Hazel often said, "I like Paul. They're a nice family the Pembletons, but it's hard luck on you, pet, having him as your opposite number."

Toplady was the Pembleton type. Intellectual. Not the chummy hearty type like Derek Lister, so how on earth had Toplady picked *him*? Now he went over everyone in the office, wondering who might be sorry to see him go. There weren't many people who listened to anyone's troubles. At least he did that well.

A lady leaned across and tapped his knee. "This is a *non*-smoking carriage."

"Good gracious!" He looked at the cigarette between his fingers. "I'm so sorry."

He stepped out into the corridor. An embankment, a signal station and a scrap-yard went past the window. How dreary the Midlands were! He'd nip straight round to the office when he got in. They'd sit up all right. First time he'd ever surprised them. First time he'd surprised Hazel. On the phone she'd said over and over, "I can't believe it, pet." And she'd asked, "Morlton isn't all steel works, is it? Some nice suburbs?" Then the pips had gone. "Tell me tomorrow, pet. I *can't* believe it!"

If she'd only said, "Congratulations!" or "How clever of you!"

He watched a woman pegging nappies on a line. Smoke from a factory chimney sagged over the washing like a grey woolly caterpillar. Hazel would have been fretting all night. Would the sideboard fit into the new house? What about the children coming to visit with the babies? He let down the window and tossed the cigarette onto the rails. I bet she's never been to bed. I bet she's turning out the attics.

In Westhill there was a breeze. The morning had the smell of autumn. Westhill had no trees. It was high and new and raw and climbed up the hill above the village of Brynbank by the river. Derek Lister, the Deputy County Planning Officer, had the best-designed house in Westhill, below the crest of the hill and facing south across the valley.

He exclaimed, "It's thick down there again." He was doing his exercises at the open window. "I warned Hugh Cole not to buy that cottage in Brynbank." He took a deep breath and did a knees-bend. "As a scout I was always told not to camp in a hollow."

His wife said, "Do you need to do that when you play so much golf?"

"Look, Shirley, if I didn't take care I'd run to fat."

She joined him at the window combing her newly-permed hair.

"Yes, you can't see Brynbank at all. Well, poor Hugh won't have many more fogs to put up with. Is it next week or the one after he goes to Africa?"

"Poor Hugh's champing at the bit. He packed in serious work days ago."

She said, "None of you realises Hugh Cole is a desperately lonely little man. I wish we'd had him here more often." She was staring at the spot where, normally, she could see the chimney of his cottage.

Derek Lister pulled on his shirt. "You will harp on this lonely genius idea. You met all his Bohemian friends at that party of his."

"But he doesn't *belong* to them" – she paused, making up her eyes – "any more than he does to you, the Establishment."

"He had a good laugh anyway, mixing up the two halves of his life."

"Of course he did." She giggled suddenly, laying her smooth ringed fingers on his sleeve. "Mrs Bird blinking at the bearded artists drinking out of bottles! The only one of you who was at ease was Paul Pembleton."

"Rubbish. I was at ease. You were at ease."

"I wasn't. That hairy sculptor was breathing beer all over me. But Paul looks at ease anywhere. And of course he was the only married man there without his wife."

"I should hope so too. She's expecting a baby soon. I wouldn't let you –"

He had the grace to stop. Pity he'd blundered to start with. She dusted her shoulders vigorously with the clothes brush.

He felt about for the right thing to say. All he managed was, "Well, how about a send-off for Hugh here, instead of the usual office thing?"

She said, "All right. It'll have to be tomorrow week. That's golf free."

Because she was so groomed and composed he bustled his way downstairs. "OK. I'll fix it. And goodness! Harry Wade might be next – though they'll be crazy at Morlton if they appoint *him*. I'd be sorry to lose Paul though if he gets the London job." He talked himself into the dining room. "Got to be early," he called to her. "Bird's got his teeth into a crazy notion of Foggart's. The only work I'll get done will be after hours."

"You'll be late home then." She cut him a grapefruit and carried it in. "Harry Wade's a sweetie," she said and went back to the kitchen to take down the mug she kept for Mrs Ball, the charwoman. They had lent her to Hugh Cole last week to help after his party and she was intrigued to know what had happened. If Mrs Ball was in a talkative mood she would stay in and potter and not bother to arrange coffee with a friend in town.

Derek, watching through the open door her neat movements and passive face, decided she'd forgotten the mention of babies.

Down the hill in Brynbank, Hugh Cole, head of the Architectural Section, adjusted himself to the sound of knocking and went to sleep again.

After a few moments the window was pushed up and a girl with a long plait climbed in. When she was standing over him, holding a covered plate, he opened one eye. "Ugh, sausages again."

She put the plate down and looked at him unsmiling. She was German and new to the Village. It was only a month since she'd come to live with the sculptor next door. Hugh had tried to win her from the sculptor who was dirty and untalented, but she said, "That is not a proposition. You can't take me to Africa." She compromised by bringing him breakfast whenever the sculptor got up early to work.

She said, "Sausages! Is that all to say? Not good morning nice day?"

He sat up. "It's not nice. It's foggy. That damp shut-in silence –"

He disappeared under the bedclothes but she embedded her fingers in his mop of hair and hauled hard. He came up shrieking.

She said, "You have an office to go to."

He tugged her onto the bed by her long plait. "And you have a repressed desire to be the wife of a nine to five man."

"You take their money." It was what the sculptor said. "Prostituting art."

She pulled her plait out of his grasp as if it had been old rope.

He got up, his slight boyish body naked as a babe and went into the bathroom.

She called, "Can I come to more goodbye parties?"

"Not at the office – if the swine give me one. Bring me my clothes."

"I not see your friends again?" She shouted over the splashing of his shower. "I liked the tall thin one – like an actor."

"Paul Pembleton. His whole life is an act. I'm ready."

She carried in his suit on a hanger, holding it while he put on his shirt and pants. "That is – how you say – a pose – to bear office work."

"Bear it! It's his favourite role." He pulled on his trousers – dark grey and neatly pressed. "To me this is fancy dress but he's in it to the hilt. On the phone, dictating a letter, redesigning a lay-out all at the same time."

"No no. He was relaxed, detached. And he *talked* – not chatter."

"It's not incompatible, Hilde. Where's my tie? I want my old school tie."

She didn't move. "He not care about those things. He was sane."

He pushed past her and found the tie looped over his briefcase. He faced her. "I'll have you know Paul is getting less sane every day. It'll engulf him yet. The paper world." She shook her head. "God, what's he got that knocks you women over like ninepins."

She said, "Your sausages will be cold," and went out slamming the door. The fog swallowed up her footsteps instantly.

Sadly in the silence he took the sausages and carried them into the kitchen. "Dead slugs." He dropped them in the bin. "If I tell Paul what she said it'll feed his vanity." He switched on the kettle. But he *would* tell Paul every word, almost certainly, and more.

At quarter to nine Paul Pembleton kissed Eleanor in the doorway to the garage.

She loved this spot because she never ceased to marvel that a man like Paul should kiss his wife every morning before leaving for the office.

Today she held him a moment. "The letter might come second post." She felt tears pricking. "If only we could stay here till the baby's bigger."

He prodded her smock. "It's big enough now in all conscience."

"We could do without more money. You're lord of your own area."

"I wouldn't mind a job where I'm not so outrageously busy all the time."

She followed him into the garage. "Give Neville more to do. Don't hog the work to feed the Pembleton Myth."

This was a private joke between them. Today she saw to her dismay that it struck him seriously.

"Neville's made a bad mistake. It won't come to light in my time but I'm damned if he's going to make any more." He tested the tyre pressures.

Eleanor was agog for details but Cathy came dashing through.

"I'll open the door, Daddy." She yanked it up.

"Run or you'll be late," Eleanor said.

"I'm like lightning." Like Paul she could turn from stillness to violent energy in a moment. She had his lanky figure too, pale face and brain as sharp as a needle.

"Mummy, am *I* late?" John appeared behind her. Seeing him so absurd and small in his uniform made Eleanor gulp again. Paul began easing the estate car out into the back lane.

He called, "I'll tell you about it tonight," and to John, "Give my compliments to Mr Garnett."

When he'd gone Eleanor gave John her sudden vivid smile. Over the years she'd copied this from Paul. He kept you guessing with his straight look under ironical brows and then the smile came, quick and warm. With Paul it was gone in a moment like a lapse but Eleanor let it linger.

She took John's hand. "Come on, darling. The back way's quicker."

The lane was cobbled and down one side was the high wall of a nursing home. A horse-chestnut grew in the wall and John loved to stroke it, calling it his elephant's trunk. When the blossom fell he said, "My elephant's cried pink tears." Now he sniffed, "Bye, elephant," and Eleanor thought, he's as bewildered as I was on my first day at school. He needs my love as I need Paul's. Cathy is so much tougher.

John said, "What did Daddy say I had to give to Mr Garnett?"

She thought, Is Paul all right? The last few weeks he has seemed less buoyant after a hectic day. We're both thirty-seven. Can he keep the *Myth* going into his forties? There was a little excitement in the thought. Everyone should be vulnerable in some way.

"Mummy, what have I to give to Mr Garnett? I've only got my pencil-box and shoe-bag and we're nearly there."

She squeezed his hand. Cathy was always saying, "You know, Mummy, half the things we ask you you simply don't answer."

"Just one of Daddy's little jokes, my poppet."

"Daddy makes lots of jokes. I don't know when they are and when they aren't."

"Neither do I, darling. Here we are."

The traffic lights had failed at the junction with Lavender Terrace. A policeman was sorting out the chaos. Derek Lister, with his right arm out of the car window, drummed his fingers on the roof. When there was no fog he drove down to Brynbank and along by the river to the Old Town. It was longer but less subject to hold-ups. And when he passed Hugh Cole's cottage he tooted his horn and watched in his driving mirror for Hugh's M.G. to appear, a red blob of speed, and they raced to the office.

"You're mad," Shirley said. "One of these days there'll be an accident." Well, with the fog down there he was taking the top road and what a mess he had landed in!

Harry Wade's house was down there, in Lavender Terrace. Poor Harry, trailing to Morlton on a fool's errand! Then as if his thought had created her, he saw Hazel, Harry's wife standing at the edge of the pavement, looking first at the policeman and then at the stationary cars. On one arm she had a string bag of vegetables and a coil of rope. In the other hand she was holding a slatted orange box. The policeman caught her eye and waved her across. She grabbed her box and ran forward. As she passed the bonnet of Derek's car she turned and looked at him. Her face came alive. She called something and brandished the coil of rope, laughing. She tried to raise the orange box so he could see it better. A car hooted then and she scuttled to the other pavement. Lister's lane was given the go-ahead and he let in the clutch.

Extraordinary! Her pantomime could only mean Harry had got the job. She was so excited she'd been out already getting packing equipment. Shops opened early there.

He had to brake again. He swore out loud. He had wanted to be as early at the office as Ron Foggart. He would say, "What's the idea of going over my head to Bird with this scheme of yours?" His anger overflowed from Foggart to the world in general. Why the hell didn't the man in front get a move on now the jam was clearing? Harry Wade – a Deputy! And Hazel a Deputy's wife! She'd look good turning up for a civic function wearing that headscarf and old coat like a tent. Great big-boned creature, half a head taller than Harry. They looked like a comic turn when they went out together.

He drove a hundred yards in second gear. Stupid antiquated roads. He thought, if a post of City Planning Officer of Midcaster is created I'll go for it and there'll be no room for Foggarts creeping into high places. It's staff changes that have stirred him up – Hugh Cole going, Pembleton waiting to hear from London. And Harry Wade –!

He put his foot down and overtook a bus. If only Quentin Bird wasn't so damn scrupulous. "Don't pre-judge, Derek," he was always saying. "We must keep an open mind." Lister longed to reply, "It's also possible, Quentin, to learn from experience." Only he didn't call him Quentin, anyway. Absurd name. Bird had said, "You're welcome to call me Quentin – outside the office." Blast him. Surely he could have stopped having an open mind about *Foggart* after all these years.

Lister turned into River Street, heading for the car park, and slid the Zephyr alongside Foggart's Consul. He didn't see Paul's new estate car but he'd be here by nine and he was the man to see first. Bird had seen him and Harry on Tuesday before Harry left for Morlton and had said, "One point against the scheme, Derek, is that both the A.P.O.'s are against it. They might have been condemning it out of hand because Foggart originated it. But we must look at it – all of us – with an open mind."

The fog was lifting. The sun was a pale disc above the river. When he got up the steps to the Square he could see the statue of the sailor quite plainly. He felt suddenly cheerful at the prospect of a battle.

Hugh Cole pointed the scarlet nose of his M.G. into the fog and put his foot down. "Lister's getting cowardly in his old age. Must have taken the top road." He always talked out loud when he was driving.

He began to sing, "I am a road-hog in the fog, in the fog," to the tune of 'There is a tavern in the town.' "I know this road like the back of my hand." He looked down at the back of his hand just out of interest. "Funny, I wouldn't have known it, not in a crowd."

He changed down for the sharp bend fifty yards ahead. There was a steep hill too, after the corner, where the road plunged down towards the river to get round a spur. "I can feel my way along this road." Suddenly, round the corner, he had to. There was a fog pocket here as thick as a blanket. He put up a hand to shield his face. When it yielded all round him it felt as if he'd crashed into a wall of foam rubber.

He stopped and got out, shaking. He wanted to ward it off with his arms. It smelt too, not just damp but acrid. Of course, the new power station across the river! "This spot will be a death-trap all winter and I'll be on the Equator, sweltering. If I get past here, now, everything will happen as it's planned. A week next Monday I'll be on the boat and they'll all be going to the office as usual. God damnit, they've got to miss me, the swine."

He stood in the road, clinging to the car. "I wouldn't find it again if I moved." Then he heard sounds. A large vehicle was grinding up the hill in bottom gear. Shouts of "Hi there!" or something like it suggested a man was walking in front.

Hugh tried to shout, "Mind my car!" His voice came out in a thin croak. A huge thickening of the fog loomed up. It must be a double-decker bus. He abandoned his car, took three blind strides towards the nearside verge and fell into the ditch.

The bus ground slowly on. "It never even knew my car was there. I don't exist for other people." He dragged himself shivering out of the ditch. Wet grass had dripped all over him. He couldn't find his car. There were tears on his cheeks as there always had been as a child when things went wrong. Then he walked right into the bumper, banging his shin-bone. He held his leg, weeping. When it eased he got into the car. If the bus had got through this fog pocket he could, only he hadn't a conductor to walk in front.

When he let in the clutch he knew if he didn't guess the bend right at the bottom he would ease the car over the bank into the river. He felt the ground levelling out round the craggy spur. He pulled the wheel over to the left. The gradient steepened. "I've got it right. I've got it right!" Visibility increased and at the same moment there was a crunch. The car stopped, jammed against the rock. Above him the crag rose into the fog.

A cyclist who had been hesitating on the verge of the fog pocket like a swimmer on a cold day, came over, wheeling his bike. Hugh got out, trembling.

The cyclist asked, "How did you come to be over here?"

"Didn't fancy ending up in the river. I over steered round the bend."

"How did you know there *was* a bend?"

Hugh was giggling now. "Luckily," he said, "I know the road."

"How far is it as bad as this?"

"Just in the dip. Look, I'll get in and back off but give me a bit of a shove will you. I've got to sell this car. I don't want to make it any worse."

When he'd got the car straight he got out again. He needed to talk some more.

The cyclist asked, "What's that smell?" He kept sniffing the air.

"The power station across the river. We'll get this whenever there's a fog now."

"Ay they wouldn't think of that, would they? There's my Dad. Set his heart on a bungalow in the country to retire to. Will they let him have it? Not on your life. But they can put power stations wherever they like."

"Yes," said Hugh. "One wonders sometimes who *they* are."

"I was going to look at Brynbank. I heard it's pretty for so near the city and they'll let you build where there's houses already. But if the road's like this I'll not go."

"You wouldn't like Brynbank," Hugh said. "Funny types live there now. Your Dad would be a fish out of water. They're all artists and foreigners. Weird goings on."

"Oh well, I'll forget it. Glad I met you." The cyclist set off back to town.

Hugh commanded himself, "Follow that bike." Accelerating rapidly he overtook it. The bike wobbled in surprise. "This isn't fog like that back there," and he began to sing, "Road-hog in the fog" again. A Zephyr in his driving mirror made him think of Lister but it was the wrong colour. And the Deputy would be safe at his desk by now. He raced the Zephyr just for the hell of it till it dawned on him it was a police car. He was pulled over.

"Driving licence please. Endorsed already eh?"

"Please notice the name. There are plenty of Coles but only one De Beaumont Cole. I had a French grandmother."

"I can believe it."

When he was allowed to drive on he said aloud, "They'll watch the ports and maybe I'll never get away."

The car park behind County Hall was full but he slipped in near the exit, blocking the way out for several cars one of which he noticed was Paul's. "He'll curse me if he's going out today. He's always in such a rush these days." Lifting his briefcase out of the car he remembered the caricatures of Foggart he'd done the night before. He could have an amusing half hour showing them to his assistants, Gordon and Penny. Relating his adventures on the way would fill up more time. But first he would have some hot coffee. He skipped up the steps to the square, thumbed his nose at the sailor and darted in under the portico of County Hall.

When Matthew Hodge went off to Wanwick he left the kitchen door open. Mrs Pawson, hunched in the basket chair, shivered. Jane closed the door, saying, "It's going to be hot, Mother. The mist's lifting. Matthew hates to shut the house off from his farm."

"*His!* If his father hadn't put up the money you'd still be at Beckbridge living off your in-laws. He's had everything fall into his lap, your Matthew."

Jane smacked the brown teapot down onto the table. "How *can* you say that? He worked like a slave on his father's farm. So did I. You know what a big place it is."

"Oh ay. You did more for them than you ever did for me."

"And Mr Hodge only lent *half* the money. Matthew saved for years for the rest. His heart wasn't in crops. It was always animals. You've seen how he is with animals."

"Pity I'm not one then."

Jane flung open the door and swept some crumbs out over the step. On an impulse she came right out and shut the door. The black hen ran up, clucking throatily to itself. Jane stood a moment looking down into the valley. The sun had sucked up the mist from the lower fields. The other way behind the cow byre rose the hummocky flank of the moor. For all she was city-bread she loved the moor. It was a kinder isolation than she had known as a child in the tall terrace house in Rose Street, Midcaster.

She walked to the field gate, the hens clucking after her. Now she could see down to Blattingford with its chestnut trees and the top of the Old Mill. That was the view her mother would have, lush and very English. She thought, if she hasn't her fire lit on a winter's morning I can walk down and see how she is. I can make it pretty for her on that knoll above the road, with stone steps and a wrought iron gate and a little rock garden. I want to make her happy in her old age. She never made me happy but I must do it for her.

She took a deep breath of the hill air and went in again to her mother and smiled at her. "It's so lovely. Why don't you sit outside later?"

"On the muck heap I suppose?" her mother said.

Matthew parked the car in Wanwick market place and walked round to the old Cattle Market. A sign on huge wooden legs said 'Cranston and Son. Builders.'

Cranston's red Vauxhall was sliding to a stop beneath the sign.

"Matt, you old devil!" he gasped, easing his bulk out of the car.

Matthew thought, he's forty-five, same as I am. Looks fifty-five.

"I wanted to ask about the bungalow plans. Did they go through?"

Cranston shouted at his workmen repairing a wall, "Get a move on. I want you on the Dunford job next."

Matthew asked again, "Did my plans pass at the Council meeting? Friday, wasn't it?"

Cranston let out a bellow of a laugh. "Course the plans are through. I've got the members in the palm of my hand."

Matthew said, "If we've got their permission why can't we go ahead now?" He knew why from Jane's talk with Peggy Mason, but he had to have things confirmed.

Cranston spat on the ground. "Planners! If it wasn't for them I'd have my men on your bungalow today."

"Why don't they take the local council's word for it?"

Cranston bellowed again. "*Our* word! We only live here. If we've approved something they'll be scratching their heads to see how to turn it down."

"Can you give me a date, George?"

"Man, I don't blame you being in a rush. I've met your mother-in-law. You're wise to put her down the hill where she can't get at you."

"She's in my boy's room. He'll be home at the end of term."

Cranston put one foot carefully in front of the other and studied them.

"They'll have had the application in Midcaster since Monday. It'll take them till now to file it. Then someone'll put it on the A.P.O.'s desk. The Area Planning Officer you understand." Matthew thought, how George is loving this! "If *he* likes it he could get it on this month's agenda – Area Committee

Meeting – week on Monday. *I'll* hear as soon as the notice of approval gets back to Mason. Three weeks if there's no snags."

Matthew felt his jaw tighten. "What snags might there be, George?"

Cranston began a laugh which ended in a snort. "They'll find some! The A.P.O.'ll look at the site – Pembleton – or his assistant – lad called Carter or something. Don't let *him* bully you. Looks like an overgrown boy-scout but he's a young fire-eater. Came to see my new garage and called me an obstinate old man! Hang it, I mayn't have your secret of eternal youth –" He eyed Matthew's lean body and curly hair –"but I'm damned if I'm old! But Pembleton – huh – try rattling *him*!"

"If he's reasonable I can talk to him. Tell me the snags, George."

Cranston burst out, "Access – that's one. Mason's a wet rag but he knows how their minds work up at the County. Said access could be dodgy."

"We don't want a garage of course."

"Man, that's not the point. If she had a car could she get it out on the road?"

Matthew looked up at the sky, bright blue now with heat beginning to seep down.

He muttered, "That's not sense. She's not going to start driving at seventy-one."

Cranston spat again. Then he laughed. "You don't want to think you're up against a senseless machine, eh Matt?" He turned to speak to his men.

Matthew said, "I'm holding you up. I've some shopping to do for Jane." He turned on his heel.

"Give her my love, Matt." Cranston's laugh exploded out of him. "Always had a soft spot for your Jane. And if you have any trouble with the Planners let me know and I'll settle the bastards."

Matthew scarcely turned his head. He should never have come to Wanwick. He should never have involved Cranston. If Pembleton was a civilised man there was hope. Surely he would see what it was like to have a poisonous viper on the farm.

2

THE WORKING MORNING

Paul Pembleton came out of the lift at top speed. Opposite him the clock on the wall above the County Planning Officer's door said two minutes past nine.

Flashing past Lister's room which was next to Bird's Paul heard his name called. Lister was lounging at his desk watching the door. He had an unlit cigarette in his hand.

He said, "You move so fast I'd have missed you if I'd stopped to strike a match."

Paul saw the room like a stage set with the doorway as the proscenium arch. He imagined the directions. 'The colours – sunshine yellow and tan – express the vigorous personality of the man at the desk. He is a square man with a big face and a thick head of hair.' Actually, the colours were fortuitous. All the north-facing rooms in County Hall were yellow and tan, except Bird's. He'd had his redone in two tones of grey with a fitted carpet the colour of red wine. It was, at least, dignified.

Paul thought of the next stage direction: 'In the doorway appears a tall man who wears his hair a little long. He has an intelligent face.'

Lister said, "Well, come on in and shut the door. *You* can spare a minute if I can."

Paul sat down and accepted a cigarette. This was going to be about Foggart's new scheme. A pity. The less things were talked about the better. Silence acted on them like a brake. Lister leant across to give him a light. He was a man whose lighter always worked. For a moment while Paul inhaled, their hands were close together. Paul saw them in a film shot before the camera tracks back to show the faces – Lister's big and square, thick brown hairs encroaching across the back of them like weeds, his own long-fingered, the sort of hands, Eleanor said, a surgeon might have, sensitive but powerful.

Lister said, "What d'you know about Ron's latest?"

"Only what Bird told Harry and me on Tuesday. Putting Architecture under the two Areas."

"I wasn't consulted till yesterday."

"Bird's working up from the small fry. He'll consult himself last of all."

"I gather you and Harry don't go for the idea. Bird seems to fancy it."

"If Ron's sold him this he could sell him anything."

"No, no. Be fair, Paul. The old man's only after efficiency −"

Paul swung round in his chair. He was in now, jolted off the sidelines.

"Efficiency! *You* haven't fallen for it, Derek, for goodness' sake? It's the most screwy, cock-eyed, lunatic −"

The Deputy sat smiling at him like a friendly bloodhound. Odd how they'd reversed roles all of a sudden.

"All right," Paul laughed. He knew what Derek thought of dramatics in anyone but himself. "All right, here are my reasons." He told off his points very fast, his fingers flickering under Lister's nose. "First. What's the aim of all this? Hugh Cole's leaving and they haven't got a replacement yet. So Foggart puts it to Bird that it'll be tidy to divide Hugh's Section between the Areas. But the work doesn't divide out evenly. Weeks go by when I don't send Hugh a single piece of work, but he and Gordon and Penny may be up to the eyes in something for Harry."

"And sometimes it's the other way round?"

"Could be of course. In theory." They smiled at each other briefly.

"Point two. What do they think Cole's been doing for five years? Sweet Fanny Adams?"

"Well, he does his best to give that impression."

"Ay, but Bird's not going to hand back to Establishment a post of Hugh's grade and say we don't need it. That would be the road to Departmental suicide."

"Oh yes. He'll have to keep it in the office somehow."

"Point three. The Architectural Section does a lot of Development Plan work. It would be a nuisance if the Plan boys had to come in and borrow Gordon and Penny from us every time they wanted them. Tell Bird that. Tell him it'll be *untidy*."

"Yes, that's a point certainly."

"What I really want to know is what's in it for Foggart? His schemes are always to bring himself more power, more money or both."

"He's thinking of three areas −"

"I smell an outsize rat."

"To spread the work you know." Lister sounded bogusly casual. "Take a bit from your area and a bit from Harry's and make a central one. It'll be a smallish area, sort of lozenge-shaped. He had it drawn out on a sketch map Bird showed me. It'll contain the big developments though – the sites for new factories and the proposed motorway."

"Everything that gets reported in the national press. So Foggart's offered himself for the job, has he?"

Lister shook his head in despair. "You're too quick, Paul. I wasn't supposed to be telling you that. In any event Bird's story is that he offered it to Foggart."

"Oh of course." Paul stood up and hooked his hands onto the desk, like claws. Leaning his weight on them and hunching his shoulders he drew his brows together and looked down at Lister. This was Foggart's well known vulture pose. Paul achieved it so perfectly that he seemed physically to resemble Foggart when he spoke. "Mr Bird, you're going to say a new area needs a new man, an experienced man who knows the area and can handle appeals, a man of sufficient seniority to represent the County in important negotiations. Well, Mr Bird?"

Paul snapped out of the pose, sat down, crossed his legs, clasped his hands on them and cocked his head slightly on one side. To Lister he assumed instantly the plump trim shape and round bespectacled face of the County Planning Officer. "Now, Ron, old boy," he said, in the high edgy voice Bird used when he was not fully in command of a situation. "Now Ron, I couldn't expect *you* to take on a job like that." Paul smiled, relaxed and without altering his attitude was himself again.

"Oh God," Lister said, wiping his eyes, "why d'you waste your talents in Local Government?" His face was red and his eyes creased with laughter.

Paul said, "Well, I wouldn't like to see Foggart with a finger in Development Control, would you, Derek?"

"Would I hell! I've been fuming about it all the way to the office."

Paul smiled. It was well known that Lister, a most genial man, became a monster of irritability at the wheel of a car. Paul could imagine him coming in from Westhill in the rush hour on a foggy morning.

Lister went on, "Incidentally, I saw Hazel Wade. She tried to signal something. Might have been saying Harry had got the job. She was carrying some rope and one of those crate things."

"It 'ud be like her to start packing up the minute Harry phoned. It'll be the eighth wonder of the world if he has. It'll give Foggart more ammunition though."

"How's that?"

"New man appointed. Unfamiliar with the County probably. Good excuse for dividing the Areas into three. Give the new man fewer applications to deal with."

"Ay, might be a new man in your place too. You've not heard from London yet?"

"No."

"You haven't an inkling?"

"Derek, I honestly don't know. I might hear later today."

"Well, it's a nuisance this uncertainty. Place has been pretty quiet for a while."

Paul drew slowly on his cigarette. "Not for me it hasn't, the last six months since Neville Carr came."

"Neville Carr? Isn't he OK?" The Deputy liked to have people taped. "He must be better than Gerry Toms you had before."

"Gerry was a happy idiot and knew his limitations. Neville – well, I only mention it so you know I won't mind if he's quietly removed from my Area in the reshuffle."

Lister waved his arms about. "I can't arrange that. *He's* not likely to be affected. I must say I'm surprised though. Truth is I suppose you and he are too much alike."

"We're *what*!" Maybe to him, Paul thought, Neville and I are intellectuals and of course non-golfers. That would be enough.

Derek waved it away. "All I want to establish are some positive facts to go to Bird with. You've told him yourself you don't want the Architectural Section under you and Harry. What about the three Areas?"

"I don't mind that. Every year there are more applications. It's time the County was split three ways." Paul was ready to go. He and Lister could usually get through all they wanted to say during one cigarette. He stubbed it out and stood up. "Important reservation: I'd rather keep the status quo than see Foggart with an Area."

Lister said warily, "Of course he'd have to be Chief A.P.O. as well."

Paul stopped in his tracks. "*Chief* A.P.O?"

Lister said in a placatory tone, "Supervisory was the word Bird used. As you said, we've got to keep the post in the department. Ron couldn't go *down* in the world."

Paul exploded, "If Bird gives Foggart any say in *my* Area I'll leave anyway. I'd rather sell vacuum cleaners than ask him whenever I want to make a decision."

Lister held up one hand. "Keep your voice down. The old man's in." He looked at his watch. "Ay, nine-fifteen, on the dot. Listen, Paul, all you've got to do is lie low for a few days. If I can put it to Bird that he'll be throwing a spanner in a smooth-running machine maybe he'll think again. So just keep out of the limelight, will you?"

"If I can and still fight this scheme."

"I'll do the fighting, tooth and nail."

"Beak and claw." Paul said, thinking of Foggart's vulture pose.

Lister had to laugh. Then he gave a sort of salute of dismissal and Paul got himself out of the room.

In the corridor he found Ron Foggart passing rapidly to his own room the other side of Lister's. He was wearing his haggard early morning face. Paul saw the thin black hair brushed in streaks across his balding head.

"Morning, Ron," he said pleasantly.

Foggart looked at him and at the Deputy's door. "Too much talk going on."

Paul said, "It's usually quicker to say things than send memos."

Foggart gave him one of his burning looks. It changed to surprise at something behind Paul. They had heard the lift. Out of it erupted Hugh Cole.

"Boys, boys! I've been at the door of death." Anyone did as an audience for Hugh Cole. Foggart looked at him with distaste.

"Death by drowning?" Paul asked.

"All kinds of death." They would have had the whole story but the County Planning Officer's door opened. Bird's head appeared, round and precise like a clock face.

"Cole! What's the matter with you? You're wet!"

Hugh bowed. "As long as my jokes aren't, sir, I can bear it."

"Have you had an accident?"

"All but. You might have had the press round for my obituary. Body of distinguished architect found in river."

Bird regarded him unbelievingly. "I think you'd better get dried. If you have no work to do before you leave us, I suggest you tidy your office. When you're quite recovered of course." His head withdrew as if pulled by a string.

Foggart said, "Huh." He turned the handle of his office door. "I want to see you later. I've been to your room already."

"I think I shall be at home," Hugh said. "You haven't a spare suit, have you, Ron. You're the only person in the office as small as me." Foggart went in and shut his door.

Hugh said to Paul, "Funny, you'd think he'd have a pair of pyjamas. Doesn't he *sleep* at the office? With his head on the original Development Plan?"

Paul said, "Yes, the cleaners come and cover him over with dead files."

Cole guffawed. They had reached the end of the passage where three doors led off, straight ahead into Control, right to Architecture and left to Plan.

He said, "Come in a minute. I did some marvellous Foggart caricatures last night. And you haven't heard what happened this morning on the road."

Paul shook his head. "Lunchtime maybe —"

"You're always too busy these days."

Paul smiled. "There are more applications. Did nobody tell you?"

Cole exclaimed, "God, Paul, don't you hate your job?" He seemed to expect an answer, but then he laughed. "Hilde reckons you only endure it by play-acting."

"Hilde?"

"My woman. The sausage girl."

"The German one? What's she talking about? She's never seen me at the office. We only met once — at your party."

"It was enough for her. And what are you looking so narked about? She fell for you, hook, line and sinker."

"Huh — as Ron Foggart would say."

"And to you. Well, my boys will be agog for their daily entertainment. Don't send anyone to see me, I may be undressed."

"I wouldn't anyway. I have the office image too close to my heart."

"Look after your own image," was Cole's parting shot. "The Pembleton Myth has been looking a little ragged lately."

Paul stared at the closed door. The Pembleton Myth was his own private joke – his and Eleanor's. Hadn't she said something this morning about it – "feeding the Myth"? And here was Hugh Cole with the same expression as if it were common talk in the office. He felt exposed. For a second he hesitated outside the door to Control. His arrival there each morning was, normally, like a tornado – both doors flung back. Today he pushed one door gently and slipped in.

Miss Smeed had been at her desk in Admin. since twenty to nine. She had walked fast down the steep stretch of West Bank to Old Town Bridge. She liked looking down at the river as she walked. It was a bit of nature, the river, even though, past Midcaster, it was dragging a load of oil, sewage and detergent foam. When, like today, you couldn't see it for the fog it could be any early morning valley anywhere. That was the advantage of leaving before eight thirty. The shops were still shuttered and Barton streets were quiet enough to be mountain sides and herself a young shepherd, his plaid over his shoulder and the breeze in his hair.

"Morning, Miss Smeed." Roger Weston, Harry Wade's assistant, was walking into County Hall at the same time as herself.

"Well Roger." He was a nice boy, very big and broad with a tower of curly hair making him almost a giant. "You're early. Is it the Agenda again?" In the East Area they were always in a scramble getting applications ready for the Agenda.

"I'm still on my own. Harry Wade won't be back till lunchtime."

"Oh Morlton of course! His interview. Fancy me forgetting."

They were in the lift now. He seemed to fill it. She remembered his picture had been in the paper when the rugby season had begun. He played forward for the County and had just been made captain.

"Well, well," she said, "if Mr Wade's successful – dear me, the office won't seem the same without him."

Weston laughed. His laugh, like his voice, was very deep. "He'll be with us till he retires." Odd how positive he was for a young man. She liked his way of speaking, slow and firm, and his country voice made her think of hills and farms. He came from the western depths of the County, way out even beyond Old Mill Farm where Mr Matthew Hodge lived. Of course he had a flat in town but his father was one of the few big farmers of those parts, well off and a local councillor. That was why Roger had been given the East Area – to avoid embarrassment.

As they came out of the lift at the third floor she said quickly, "Wouldn't it be funny though if we lost both the Area Planning Officers at once."

Again the rounded, positive reply: "Pembleton's more likely to get to London than Wade to get to Morlton."

"Oh I don't know." She felt herself flushing up. She *would* do this – bring him into the conversation and then blush like a girl. The corridor was dim, thank goodness.

She carried her paper bag of sandwiches into Admin. and put them on her desk. Roger thundered off to Control – six foot three and fifteen stones of solid bone and muscle, the paper had said. Well, a nice boy and the only one in sight if Mr Pembleton left – unless she went back to Mr Lister.

She began checking through some files. Two months ago Mr Pembleton had asked her, "Miss Smeed, how thoroughly do you check the files?" She was floored. She'd stumbled and hesitated. What did he mean, how thoroughly? "I check the consultations have been done." "Do you read the letters?" "The letters? Oh dear, Mr Pembleton, that's the technical side." "Quite right," he'd said and that was all. He'd given her one of those sudden smiles of his that came and went in a flash. She supposed it was to reassure her but the memory harassed her as the Agenda came round again.

Mr Foggart came in suddenly. "Mr King not in yet?"

"It's not *nine*, Mr Foggart. I'll ask him to come through as soon as –"

"I'll come back."

She read through some more of Mr Pembleton's recommendations. He could write faster than anyone she knew – whole sentences without lifting pen from paper. "There you are, Miss Smeed," he'd say, "just dot the i's and cross the t's."

The typists began to drift in.

"Ee yes, it was dead thick when I got up. I thought there'd be no buses."

"You couldn't see across our street."

"It's going to get hot though. I put me sun-top underneath. Look."

Miss Smeed said, "You've already got a lovely tan, Sandra." She was forever paying them little compliments like that but they only giggled and looked embarrassed.

The doors swung and closed. It must be Mr King. Girls always came in with a flurry of chatter. She didn't look up. Leonard King, her Chief, was the one man in the office she really detested. He gives me the creeps, she would tell herself. It was the only explanation that seemed to justify her feelings which were quite unchristian.

There was a reaction among the typists. She had to look up. Mr King was being followed into his office by a small boy. Sandra giggled. The boy turned at the door, stared at them with a deadpan face, the double of Mr King's and stuck out his tongue.

"Ee, did you see that?"

"The cheeky monkey!"

"Must be his boy. Spit'n image."

"Why's he not at school?"

"I can't stick small boys."

Poor little mite, thought Miss Smeed. Must feel lost and strange in this big place.

His father was taking no notice of him at all. He was having his read of the paper which was how he spent the first twenty minutes of every morning.

She picked up a typed sheet and went and tapped at his door.

"Oh come in, Jos, don't knock." He had abbreviated her name to Jos when she'd told him it was Jocelyn. "I don't call anyone Miss or Mr. You can call me Len." She didn't of course and he was the only person in the office who didn't call her Miss Smeed.

She held out the paper. "Would you just look this over, Mr King. Hello, pet. It's the standard request for Time Extension. I've suggested some small emendations. Oh and Mr Foggart said he wanted to see you."

"He'll come back."

"Yes, he said he would. I don't think you should do that, pet –"

The boy was fiddling with papers on the desk.

Mr King said, "Oh let him. I have to keep him amused today somehow."

"But, Mr King, he's muddling up the Enforcement Orders with the Ministry circulars. You see, pet, Daddy's work – he *is* your son, Mr King?" The boy was grinning.

"Oh ay, the wife can't do with him at home. Fed up."

"Hasn't your school term started yet then, darling?" The boy squeezed up his slit of a mouth and said nothing.

Mr King took the paper from her hand and glanced at it. "What's different here?"

"I've amended the wording to make it sound" – she hesitated – "a little more courteous. It's always worried me. Of course it's only a suggestion."

He gave it her back. "Take it as passed." Her unanswered question to the boy seemed to register. "Answer the lady, can't you?"

The boy turned on him venomously. "Mum said to keep me mouth shut."

Miss Smeed put her hand to her leaf brooch, lining it up with the edge of her tunic, her fingers shaking. She backed towards the door. "I didn't mean to pry."

King glanced up and grinned. "You see what he's like, Jos."

She fled back to her desk.

Foggart was restless. He wanted to be stirring things up, spreading rumours. You couldn't do that through little notes. You had to go and see people, drop hints. In an atmosphere of speculation things were inclined to come to a head. Bird, especially, had a horror of tittle-tattle. "We must put this straight," he would say. "There has been talk." And then a decision which might have been put off would be taken that day. Foggart had a feeling this might be one of those days. If he could just push things along . . .

He would try Leonard King again.

Admin. looked bright and busy, painted like all the South-facing rooms in egg-shell blue and white. Foggart looked up and down the room, pleased that a few mirrors and powder compacts whisked out of sight at his entrance.

As he stepped up to Leonard King's office he saw a boy's face staring like a moon through the glass, a pancake face, a small copy of the Admin. Officer's.

He walked in, glared at the boy, and demanded of Leonard King, "The Quarterly Reports are due, aren't they?"

"Hello, Ron. Quarterly Reports. Could be."

"They're to be sent off a week before the Committee Meeting in future. Day before is no good at all." He was staring at the boy as if to detect the reason for his presence without having to ask for it.

King flipped his mail about. The boy did the same with some papers the other side of the desk. A few fell to the floor.

"Is this your boy?" Foggart said. "He shouldn't be here you know."

"Oh he's been ill. Not supposed to go to school yet."

Foggart's eyebrows rose. Leonard King had no sense of the fitness of anything.

He snapped at the boy. "What was the matter with you?" The boy grinned.

"Well?" Foggart said to King.

King shrugged his shoulders. "Go on, tell him," he said to the boy.

"Chicken pox. Look, I've still got some spots," and he turned his head to show some on his neck.

Foggart recoiled. "Chicken pox!"

"The other two have got it now," Leonard King said. "The little 'uns. The wife's sick of coping with this one too."

"The infection!" Foggart gasped. "He'll spread it round."

"Oh adults don't get it. Not so much."

"Man, it's ten times worse in adults. It can come as shingles. You'll have to take him home. At once."

King shrugged. "He's not infectious now, Ron. I shouldn't worry about it."

"Why's he not at school then?"

"The doc said not to send him till all the scabs are off."

"There you are. The scabs." Foggart shuddered.

King was sitting there, still grinning. "Come off it, Ron. He won't stir out of here all day. Now what's this about the Quarterly Reports. They'll never do them any sooner. None of 'em. Whose orders is this?"

"Mine. About the boy —"

"That's new isn't it?"

"It won't do any harm to anticipate new arrangements."

"Oh. Is that supposed to mean anything?"

The typists nearest the door were listening. This was how Foggart had meant it to be. Keep them agog with rumours. But his mind was on the boy again.

He said sharply, "If I catch *him* wandering about – you'd better take him home at lunchtime." He walked out shutting the glass door carefully. He saw Miss Smeed half rising from her desk in the main office.

"Oh Mr Foggart –" She was putting together a file on her desk. "It's the Appeal case you were wanting."

"Bring it to me later. But Miss Smeed," – he stepped up and laid his hands on the edge of her desk – "don't go in there if you can help it. I wouldn't like to see you go down with shingles. A man in our – a man I know got it last year. Very nasty."

When he'd gone the typists burst into cries of "Chicken pox! You won't catch me going near him."

Miss Smeed thought, no one likes Mr Foggart but that was considerate of him. It's Mr King I can't stand. No wonder the boy is cheeky. No discipline.

"I tell you," Hugh Cole said for the twentieth time, "if I didn't know that road like the back of my hand I'd be in the river now. Have you ever had to feel with the wheels of your car, Gordon, Penny? I tell you, they'd have been dragging the river for me now."

Gordon Harris, smoothing his beard, watched his chief with interest. Cole was normally too quick-thinking to repeat himself. This told Harris that for once he'd been shaken to the depths, depths which a chap like Pennyman would never guess at. Cole had been near death and under the chatter he was imagining what drowning would have been like. Harris saw he was shivering. He had taken off his damp jacket and the north-facing room was cold for shirtsleeves but it wasn't only that.

"Come on, Hugh," Harris said, "let's see these drawings you did last night."

"Ah surely, surely." Cole drew them from his briefcase. All showed a little man with an outsize nose, protruding ears, a long scraggy neck and startling eyes. Three were just roughed in but the fourth was finished to the last detail and showed him perched on his desk, his body proportioned like a vulture's, hands clawing the desk, little feet stuck out in the air behind him like tail feathers. Pennyman hooted and the two draughtsmen, who had come over from their desks under the window, chuckled happily.

The door opened and Foggart, on the prowl round the different departments, walked in. The draughtsmen shuffled to their desks, obscuring his view long enough for Harris to lay a map over the drawings. Pennyman giggled like a guilty schoolboy.

Hugh greeted Foggart with glee. "Ron, where are my spare clothes. I'm still wet."

Foggart cast a disgusted look round the room. "Have you got the revised factory design ready for this afternoon's meeting?"

Cole said, "Factory! Factory!" and dashed round the room snatching at drawings and throwing them down again.

.Foggart stood waiting like a grenade about to explode a mere yard from the table where the map sheet covered his caricatures. Pennyman leant over the map and peered at it through his large spectacles.

Cole, finding something that gave him an idea, exclaimed, "Ah it's the plastics factory you're talking about. It makes plastics so the front elevation is a single polythene sheet. No doors or windows. One touch of a button and it's up and over. Tucks in under the roof. Think of the light and air for the workers. Viewed from the main road the impact will be tremendous. You don't need drawings. What, you must have drawings?" – Foggart hadn't spoken – "There you are then." Cole handed him a plain card.

Pennyman, unable to move away, was in agonies of suppressed laughter. Harris and his beard were quietly shaking in his corner. The two draughtsmen were leaning off their stools, eyes goggling, not sure what was going on.

Foggart stared at the card, speechless.

Cole snatched back his hand. "Oh well, if you don't like it –" He tore the card in two. "My God, the work I put into that design." He threw the pieces into the wastepaper basket with a groan, then giggled at Pennyman. "Where the hell are the *real* drawings?"

Pennyman shrugged his shoulders and giggled back.

Foggart glowered at them both and at the shambles of a room. "I don't know how you can ever find anything in this place." He made a grab at the map so suddenly that the corner Pennyman was leaning on was torn away. "You haven't looked under here." The map fell on the floor.

Pennyman immediately turned his back and walked over to Harris. Neither of them dared to look at Foggart's face.

Cole burst out laughing louder than ever. "Rather good, rather good, don't you think?" Foggart said nothing. His hands shook as he pushed the drawings to one side. He lifted up some sheets of designs from the jumble of papers underneath.

"You see, they're here." His voice was higher and harsher than usual. "You'd better be at the meeting when this man comes. Three p.m."

Cole put his hands in his pocket and did a little jig. "Of course we won't get him to agree to those. Their place is in an architectural review. But I'll come and talk to him." He hopped to the door like a mop-headed puppet.

Foggart didn't follow him. He looked round the room again and focused on Harris and Pennyman. He said icily, "I wonder how this firm will get on under its new management." His voice was under control again.

Cole danced back to the middle of the room again. "Good God, Bird hasn't appointed someone without consulting *me*?"

Foggart looked in his direction without looking at him. A muscle in his cheek was twitching. "I don't know what you may have heard. There've been too many rumours. I'd be obliged if you'd discourage any talk till an announcement is made."

His eyes were drawn to the table again. The head in the large drawing peeped out from the shuffled papers, with its ghastly staring eyes, beak of a nose and ears like sails. He swung on his heel and rushed from the room.

Cole said, bubbling with laughter, "Penny, you idiot, why didn't you sit on it?"

"Well, he didn't *say* anything."

Harris snapped, "What could he possibly say?"

Cole and Pennyman looked at him with interest and giggled some more.

Pennyman said, "But Hugh, what did he mean about your job? Bill and Tony heard everything. He raised his voice specially."

One of the draughtsman called across the room, "Did Mr Foggart mean he's taking over here himself?"

Cole clapped his hands with glee. "By Jove, yes. That's it. Of course Foggart couldn't design a dog-kennel but he'll be here in an executive capacity. You poor sods!"

He dashed into the glass cubicle – his private office as Section Head. Piles of designs overflowed desk and chairs.

"I suppose he'll *use* this place. The day I leave I'll put a notice on the door: 'Under New Management' and stick all the caricatures round the walls."

Harris smoothing his beard muttered to Pennyman, "Sometimes he goes too far."

"Hugh?" Pennyman said. "Get away. Would you rather have Foggart?"

Foggart hid himself in his own room to recover. He knew how Bird had come to appoint Cole five years before. A professor friend of his had said, "If you want to put Northshire on the map start a Design Section and put this first class young architect in charge of it. He won a travelling scholarship to the States. When he comes back, grab him." Bird had asked his name. "Hugh Cole. De Beaumont Cole actually but he makes rather a joke of that part." That had won Bird round. Foggart had seen him showing distinguished visitors a model of one of Cole's layouts for a Development Area. "It's made to the design of De Beaumont Cole whom we are fortunate to have on our staff." What could *he* do with a name like Ron Foggart? But revenge would come – on Cole, and on Lister and Pembleton plotting to thwart his scheme. He rubbed his palms together. "I'll have the Bird eating out of my hand before the day's out."

Roger Weston had worked for fifteen minutes before anyone else came into the Development Control Office. Once or twice he looked up at Harry Wade's empty cubicle. The conviction that he should be there drove him through his work like a secret source of power. People drifted in after nine but nothing broke his concentration.

Neville Carr came in, late, his mat of hair flattened from the pressure of his crash helmet, cheeks red with haste. He looked first at the glass cubicle of his chief but it was empty. He expelled a long breath, took out a handkerchief and wiped his forehead.

To reach his own desk he had to pass Weston's and he stopped with his hands on it, saying in a grumbling voice, "*You* look as if you've been here since the early hours."

Weston said, "Yes, Neville, early for this place." He withdrew into his cocoon.

"Is Mr Pembleton coming in this morning, d'you know?" one of the draughtsman asked Neville.

Hine, the longer and thinner one, looked up. "He's with Mr Lister. Saw him go in as soon as he arrived. Mr Lister *called* him in."

Neville said to Roger in a low voice, "It's to do with the Areas, don't you think? All these conferences. Pembleton and Wade had a meeting with Bird on Tuesday afternoon. D'you think they're planning another Area? There's too much for two really."

"We manage."

Neville reddened. He said baldly, "Would *you* apply for it if they did make one?"

Roger completed a sentence in the file in front of him and said without turning his head, "Of course. And I'll apply for Harry's job if he goes."

Neville gazed across at the two empty glass cubicles on the opposite wall. "I wish I had a chance if Pembleton goes."

Roger thought, I suppose he's got money troubles. What does he expect only six months into his first job?

He watched as Neville prowled restlessly round the office. He remembered Dorothy Bird writing a satirical piece about the concept of the elements as the basis of character. He had told her, "Neville, my opposite number in the West Area, would call me earth and himself fire, when really he's just rather brash and childish." She had laughed and said, "I don't know *him* but you are certainly not earth. Solid yes but fire on the rugby pitch. Maybe I'd call Derek Lister earth and Paul Pembleton fire."

Roger turned back to his work, suddenly devastated that he had broken with Dorothy. Neville settled down. The office was silent.

This was the moment when Paul Pembleton slipped quietly in. His entrance generally broke into a hubbub and shook up the whole scene. This time everyone stared as if the gentle opening of the door had made them expect someone else.

He laughed. "What? Have we granted permission for a power station in the National Park?" The tension eased. He went into his private office and shut his door. Because of the half-glazed sides he by no means disappeared from sight. Roger had once heard him say to Harry Wade. "We're like ruddy goldfish in here."

Paul was aware of all eyes looking for him to seize a file, call for Neville to go through the Agenda and pick up the phone to dial an applicant, all simultaneously, so he sat perfectly still for a full minute. After the talk with Lister and Hugh Cole joking about the Pembleton Myth he would put off working with Neville Carr for as long as possible. Neville would make heavy weather of the rumours flying about and would ply him with questions. Paul thought briefly of his own son John who also took life too earnestly. He wondered how the poor solemn little lad was surviving the first hour of school.

Eleanor was walking in at the back door when she heard the phone ringing. She set down her basket among the breakfast things and floundered through to the hall.

"Midcaster 6704. Mrs Pembleton speaking."

"Oh dear, you're out of breath. Have I made you run?"

Eleanor was better at voices than faces but she had to search about for this one.

"It's Hazel Wade, isn't it?"

"Such news, Eleanor! But how are you? Not too long now till the baby – I'm sorry you had to hurry to the phone."

"I took John to school. It's his first day."

"Never in the world! That little pet! But how about this, Eleanor? Harry's got the job. Deputy at Morlton! What d'you think? I'm still gasping."

Eleanor said everything she could, but there was something in Hazel's voice, a high-pitched note as if she were trying not to cry.

"I've been up all night. I turned out the attic – all the boys' reports –" Eleanor drew up the stool she kept near the phone. Hazel had to get this off her chest. She'd had a shock – "and I saw Derek Lister. I waved at him in the middle of the road. Really I hope he didn't understand. He had a hot and bothered look driving to work in the rush hour."

Eleanor asked, "Didn't you want him to know?" But she guessed why – Harry would be at the office by lunchtime Paul had said. It was his big surprise – like a child.

Hazel said, "You're the first person I've told, properly I mean."

Eleanor was delighted. She had never felt one of an in-crowd yet Hazel had picked her as principal confidant.

Hazel answered her thought. "I always feel with not playing golf that I can never quite get through to Shirley Lister." Then she was off on another tack. "Eleanor, I'm a selfish pig – I've never asked – has Paul heard from London?"

"No," said Eleanor, the suspense coming back like a sickness. "Not yet."

"And it's much worse for you with the baby coming and the children at school. How will you manage?"

Eleanor went patiently over their plans. The baby should be born before Paul had worked his notice. Her mother would come and stay while Paul looked for a house. "I hope we'll sell this quickly and then we can spend Christmas together at Windsor. It'll be a squash but Mother won't mind. The children will have to start new schools of course."

"Men are mad," Hazel said. "Harry only did it out of bravado. People kept saying, your family have left, you won't want that big house. Why stay in Midcaster?"

Eleanor wanted to defend Paul. He had said for the last two years that in Local Government you must move for wide experience. And the baby hadn't been planned. But Hazel went on. "My boys *would* go down south. Harry told them about the new industries here but they married south-country girls and babies arrived. They'll never come back."

Eleanor laughed. "I'm south-country and *I* came. I love the county – Beckbridge, Cottle, Wanwick Moor." She was naming the places Paul was likely to see today.

This upset Hazel again. "Yes, and what's it like round Morlton? I mean, Morlton. I've never been there in my life. I shan't know a soul."

"Listen, Hazel, Harry couldn't go on working as an A.P.O till he retired. It's a wearing job. The Agenda coming round every month. As a Deputy he'll be able to delegate, only handle what he wants to, go in a bit later in the morning –"

Hazel's voice came sadly down the line. "But will he be able to *do* the job?"

"With his experience?"

"Eleanor, he still worries about *this* job. You don't know, married to a man like Paul who can keep abreast of six things at once and shed it all like a skin when he leaves the office." Ah, the myth, Eleanor thought. "But Harry!

They *know* him here. Dear old Harry. One of his flaps. But in a strange place –! A Deputy has to *be* somebody. People respect Derek Lister despite his outbursts and riding roughshod over people. But what'll they make of Harry? I couldn't bear to see him unhappy."

Eleanor thought, she really is crying now. "Hazel, love, Harry's the dearest person I've ever known. He must be the only one in the office whom everyone likes. You'll have a streetful of friends before you've been in Morlton a month. You always welcomed everyone new here." But the boot would be on the other foot in Morlton. She wished she could be sure for Hazel's sake.

"Ah, but you're charitable. To the younger generation we're old has-beens. Look at the Carrs. They only came to us once. After that they made excuses. You should have seen the way Neville looked round our cream walls and flowered chairs. He said Lena had decorated their flat herself – strong colours. You've seen it perhaps. She's supposed to be an artist. *I* don't know. She came in a loose pink dress with long trailing hair –"

Eleanor laughed out loud. "Hazel, they're quite impossible, the Carrs. They don't get on with each other never mind other people."

"Don't they? Perhaps I'm not very observant."

"She was cross at being dragged up north. She did commercial art in London while he was gathering extra qualifications. And they missed a year in America because the fellowship he won was for unmarried students only. She blamed him for that too."

Eleanor felt a little guilty. She thought Lena a lost and friendless soul. And she had a tenderness for her when she recalled how the girl had been unable to take her eyes off Paul for those two whole evenings and how utterly indifferent to her Paul had been.

Hazel said, "Well if the poor child was upset because of the move I for one should understand now. I'll ask them round before we leave. Of course we must have everyone. You and Paul especially. I haven't seen you since – was it the cricket match in June?"

The Planning Department had an annual cricket match against The Surveyors. Derek Lister whipped the team up and had been very put out when Neville Carr refused point blank, saying he had no intention of making himself ridiculous. So Lena had missed seeing Paul run through the Surveyor's with some deceptive slow bowling and Roger Weston knock up a beefy fifty in the Planning Office's winning score. Eleanor regretted that they would miss in London the intimacy, the sheer fun of a small department.

Hazel was saying, "What did Paul think of Hugh Cole's party the other day?"

Eleanor laughed. "He said it was a riot." He had said plenty more but Eleanor couldn't lay bare his character the way Hazel did with Harry. He had said, "The Village set made me feel ancient. They'd have been smoking hemp if we, the Establishment, hadn't been there and they were as unable to manage their drink as poor Harry."

Hazel, who seemed to be uncannily echoing her thoughts, said, "Our dear Roger had to drive us home. Harry wouldn't trust himself."

Eleanor remembered that Hazel mothered Roger Weston during the week. His bachelor flat was near Lavender Terrace and he went there for supper once or twice a week. On Saturdays they watched him play rugby before he went home to his father's farm and on Sundays Hazel took home-baked cakes or pies to his flat ready for his return.

"There's one of the younger generation who thinks the world of you," she said.

"Roger. Yes. I'll miss Roger."

She's determined to be depressed, thought Eleanor. She said, "You'll be nearer your boys in Morlton, not more than three hours' drive."

Surprisingly Hazel began to laugh. "Oh my dear you've tried everything. But I am better now. At least we're not going to Africa like Hugh Cole. What must *he* feel like?"

Eleanor wasn't going to start on *him*. Her first free morning for five years was being frittered away. She murmured that the milk was on the doorstep in the sun and Hazel cried, "Go get it, pet. You've done me a power of good."

Eleanor plodded to the door. She couldn't help being wrung out by people. The haze had cleared. The milk bottles felt warm. It was ten o'clock. In two hours the lunchtime post was due. Would there be a letter from London?

Mrs Bird peered from her deckchair at her daughter's brown curves and then up at the neighbours' windows to make sure that the cherry tree hid them from sight.

"You might just as well have nothing on as that bikini."

Dorothy had a notebook and pencil on the rug with her. Every now and then she stabbed the pencil into the grass, thinking.

"How did your father and I produce such a great strapping lass as you?"

Dorothy rolled over on her back. "This rectangle of grass is my office and if you want to come in please knock." She wriggled onto her front again and began writing fast.

Mrs Bird shifted about. In the daytime she could usually sleep without difficulty but the sight of Dorothy's hurrying pencil unnerved her. Quentin viewed the articles with tolerant amusement, so long as her pseudonym was not penetrated by anyone at the office. The affair of Roger Weston had nearly scuppered that.

"You lost Roger Weston with that writing of yours," she said the minute he came into her mind. Dorothy didn't look round. "If you hadn't done that sketch about a farmer at a nightclub he would have asked you out again."

"Talk away, talk away," Dorothy muttered into her rug.

"You always used to say men were never big enough for you. You should have grabbed Roger as soon as you could."

Dorothy jabbed her pencil into the grass again. "Mother! Didn't I throw myself at him at the first Christmas party he attended? I invited him to badminton. He didn't play badminton so we went swimming. All this with Daddy getting het-up about keeping romance out of the office. You think I wanted such a great hunk of manhood to pass me by?" She yanked a dandelion out of the grass.

"But why you had to ask him to a nightclub and then tell him it was you who wrote that stupid article —"

"It wasn't stupid. It was funny."

"He didn't have to *know* though. Why did he have to know?"

Dorothy got to her feet, clutching her notebook to her midriff. With the other hand she dragged the corner of the rug over one shoulder like a highlander's plaid. Towering six feet tall she glared down at her mother. "He rang me up when he saw the paper. He asked me so I told him. That was that." She began to stalk off across the grass.

"Oh dear," Mrs Bird said, "don't go so far. I can't sleep if you're far away."

Dorothy went, over by the rose beds. After a few restless minutes her mother followed, floundering with the deckchair across the lawn. Dorothy who had relied on her laziness was quite astonished.

"I'm not going to talk, dear, really I'm not. I only thought you might sometimes want to talk about *him*. No, I'm not starting again. This one seems to be going well. You've turned a page. Who's in the dock this time?"

Dorothy had a gleam in her eye. "It's about Hugh Cole's party. You and Daddy told me what it was like and my imagination will do the rest."

Her mother put her hands up to her face. "You can't –!"

"I can and I will," Dorothy said. "It's hilarious."

Shirley Lister was still in two minds about her day. It might be too hot for coffee in town with a friend. It all depended on Mrs Ball being willing to tell her what had happened at Hugh Cole's bungalow the day after the party. So far Mrs Ball had arrived, hung up her hat and coat and said, "Seeing it's a fortnight since I was here I'd better get cracking upstairs." This was the only allusion to her not being at Westhill last week.

Shirley put the kettle on. That would bring her back to the kitchen.

When Mrs Ball smelt tea brewing she left her armaments – scouring paste, polish, window-cleaning liquid and disinfectant – on the landing and came down. Shirley often said to Derek, "She brought up six children in a two-up, two-down colliery house but she accepts that we live on our own in a detached four-bedroom mansion that must be cleaned immaculately right through once a week." "You pay her, don't you?" he said.

As soon as she sat down, filling out her flowered overall like a skin that had grown with her, Mrs Ball took on an air of relaxation.

"You didn't mind the message about Mr Cole last week?" Shirley asked. "I hope you didn't find the work too heavy."

"Heavy! It was nothing when they got out from under me feet. Strewn all over the floor they was at nine in the morning. Mr Cole stepped among them as if they was so many mats laid there."

"I'm afraid you'd find him rather a comedian."

"He's a gentleman," Mrs Ball cried stoutly. "A real gentleman." Shirley raised her eyebrows but Mrs Ball was warming to her subject. "Ay when he was dressed for work he woke them all up and gave them their orders. One to make me a cup o' tea. One to clear the empties outside and the two girls to dry up for me."

"Girls! Two of them were still there in the morning?"

"Oh ay, you don't know the half of what goes on in Brynbank."

Mrs Ball always assumes, Shirley thought, that I was born yesterday. Maybe in her eyes I've never begun living. Once I grumbled about the trials of marriage because of Derek's long hours at the office. She said, "Marriage! You don't know what marriage is."

"I like a bit of old-fashioned courtesy," she went on now. "It was beautiful what he said. 'I want you to pay every attention to this lady. Every attention.'"

Shirley giggled. "And did they?"

"I didn't bother to find out. When he'd gone I shooed them away. Most of them live in the Village. I soon got cracking on me own. It's a canny bungalow when you can see it for muck."

Shirley wanted to keep her talking. "Any more titbits from the Village?"

"Well, there was a funny thing happened yesterday." Mrs Ball finished her tea and got up to clean the gas stove. "A notice went round asking if anyone would like an unwanted baby."

The sunshine outside looked suddenly sick. That was the funny thing, was it?

"Ay, there's this sculpturer – you know, one of these characters that carves stones with holes through them. Lives next door to Mr Cole."

Shirley slipped on rubber gloves, laid a newspaper on the table and began to polish her silver tea-set. "I know. He has a beard. A big man."

"Well, he hitched up with this German girl when he was studying over there."

"Yes, she was at the party." Shirley recalled her stolid Teutonic face and thick plait of hair.

"Ay well, she followed him back to England. You can guess why."

Shirley thought, everyone gets babies. Everyone else.

"She came as an au pair but the family had to send her to one of these unmarried homes when it got conspicuous. Seemingly she wrote and told her mother as soon as it was born and she came over hot foot. If it had been one of mine" – Mrs Ball made a crushing stroke with her scouring pad – "but this lass just dumps the baby in her mother's lap and comes up here and joins her sculpturer. That was a month ago. Now yesterday she gets a letter from her mother saying she can't stay in England any longer and to come and fetch the baby. But oh no. The sculpturer has an idea for a new work – a big one – and he's got to go to India to do it. Look at temples and starving people."

Too vigorously Shirley squirted a blob of silver polish in a creamy pool on the newspaper. "Of all the ridiculous –"

Mrs Ball paused and looked round, brandishing a Brillo pad. "Ah but a gorgeous marble building with a Oxfam figure on the steps. Picture of human progress you know."

Shirley felt small and humiliated. She asked abruptly, "The girl wants to go with him I suppose?"

"Oh that's it. Cool as can be, bless you. She hoped *I'd* take the baby."

Shirley put her hands over her face. "Oh no no no."

"Ay." Mrs Ball beamed, delighted. "I said I'd done bringing up kids and I've telt mine when they start that they needn't come and dump them on me. But the girl says, 'You go to some nice houses, Mrs Ball. Bags of brass. *They'd* know what to do with one.'" She laughed at this sally, eying Shirley sideways.

Shirley bent over the teapot. I'm the villain of the piece in her eyes. That handsome, virile Mr Lister, he could father a dozen hefty lads. My God, I don't think.

Mrs Ball ventured a still more explosive laugh. "Imagine a little brat running about here, knocking over your ornaments and trying on your make-up."

Shirley drove the polishing cloth round and round the teapot lid. "As it happens," she burst out, "Mr Lister and I *have* discussed adoption." She regretted it at once.

Mrs Ball cried, "By, that would be a chance for the poor little mite." And then with unusual delicacy she faced Shirley. "I'd not have joked about it if I'd known there was any question of you really –"

Shirley smiled, slid off her stool and screwed up the newspaper. "That's all right, Mrs Ball. I've heard of people adopting and then having their own baby soon after. Right, I'll make sure all's tidy for you hoovering upstairs. By the way, what *is* the baby?" It was dangerous ground, like asking the make of a car you had no intention of buying.

"It's a boy."

It would be. Derek always said, when she reproached him over his refusal to see a doctor, "You know I want a son and you keep putting off adoption." He wouldn't believe it was the giving birth she yearned for. "Get one at six weeks and you escape pregnancy and the worst time of babyhood. And giving up golf." If she said she didn't give a damn about golf he wouldn't believe that either, since she'd been picked for the County Ladies and was one up on him. He didn't know what it was like to be a woman, that was all.

Mrs Ball had put all the clean parts back into the gas stove. She hesitated with her hand to the appliances cupboard where the Hoover lived. "They're not working class, you know. The girl's father's a lawyer. It's not everyone can go abroad for a month's holiday like her Mam did. Of course *their* friends don't know about the baby. Disgrace and all that. Very respectable people the Germans. Funny when you think how they tret the Jews. And the sculpturer's father's a vicar. Church on one side and the law on the other. And then the young ones go off the rails, but you can't hold that against the baby. It weighed ten pounds at birth. Of course they're both hefty – and dark-haired too, like Mr Lister."

"Does the sculptor *want* the girl to go with him to India?"

Mrs Ball drew out the Hoover. "That's a thing I couldn't say. She'll have a good body on her for drawing but as it's starving people he's after that's not much use."

"She must love him, following him all over the place."

"I'd say she'd go with anyone who asked her."

"Yes." Shirley recalled her wandering eyes at the party when the collar and tie beings were introduced to her. She had eyed Roger Weston's massive frame and Derek's square jaw but she had finished up with the tall, lean Pembleton and sat at his feet most of the evening.

"Where else has she got to go?" Mrs Ball said. "Her family won't have her back."

Shirley washed her gloves in the sink and said brightly, "That's the mess these people get into, isn't it?"

She swept past Mrs Ball and ran up to their bedroom where there was a bedside phone. I could phone Derek now and tell him. Her mouth was dry.

First she twitched the curtains straight and looked down over the valley. The cooling towers of the new power station were silver in the sunshine. Further west the valley wound into the hills. She could take the Mini and drive up there and spend the rest of this sun-filled day on the moors. But what was the point?

She picked up the phone.

Matthew Hodge drove home to Old Mill Farm over the treeless curve of Wanwick Moor. It was two years since he had first driven this way with Jane murmuring, "Our first home on our own," and now, with the old woman there, he couldn't feel any happiness in coming back to the place.

When he had walked with Jane round the neglected cow-byre and had seen the sheep tracks threading their way up the slope of the moor he had murmured, "Animals, animals, Jane. Our own animals." Jane had paid a duty visit to her parents in Midcaster while he had made the place at least habitable.

He had never known a woman to prey on others as Jane's mother did. She had lived on her son, Jane's only brother, until he was killed at El Alamein. Then her husband suffered under her and so did Jane when she could get at her.

His own mother was a powerful woman as strong and independent as a mountain. She needed nobody. She had treated Jane in the twelve years of their married life with her as a child. "Now go and mix the hen food. Have you set the men's tea?" Jane was afraid of her but devoted to her with an awe-struck devotion since the night of their son's birth.

It was the worst January they'd had there and the midwife hadn't been able to get through the snowdrifts till morning. His mother had delivered the baby with her own hands. "No one on earth could have done better," Jane always said, "I was so tense."

It was the only time Matthew could recall that his mother had ever laughed with him. She had handed him the baby rolled up like a white cylinder in old linen. Her face was wet with sweat and so was the cloth she had bound round her hair. "My God," she said, "a cow drops them a sight easier than that, but I'd rather have a grandson than a calf. By the Lord, he'll make a strong one this. Look at the limbs on him. It's me and your Dad he'll favour, not you and Jane. You were a nervy, sickly child, God knows why. You'd better call him Martin after your Dad."

In the long galling years that followed he saw his father finding in Martin the son he had tried but failed to be himself. His father said, "He works hard, sleeps deep and eats like a horse. That's the way a boy should be." Matthew and Jane were both bad sleepers. Their sufferings drew them together.

He looked at the sheep on the moor. All had his own markings. Martin had helped him do them in the holidays. He'd been at boarding school since he was nine and loved it. He could have travelled into Midcaster as other country children did but Jane's mother was there. Jane said, "She'll get hold of him and make him stay with her all week." Matthew agreed to the boarding school though it set them back in their savings for their own farm. If it hadn't been for his father's bumper harvest three years before and his burst of generosity for Old Mill Farm they'd still have been at Beckbridge.

He turned the car onto the farm track and drew up to open the gate. The joy of these two years, till six weeks ago, had been too great. There had always been an ache of fear that it couldn't last. Jane had been sick with delight at being in a home of her own at last, but pitifully unsure of herself and amazed at his confidence in buying the stock. He didn't like dealing with people but he knew a good beast and people could tell that he knew. The farm was paying its way now. Next year there might have been spare money for improvements – if it hadn't been for Jane's father's death.

As he closed the gate it squeaked slightly. He fetched the oil-can from the boot of the car and oiled the hinge. He tried to keep it up, the pride in his property, but the zest had gone out of it. Having the old woman there was like a blight.

As he drove up to the farmhouse he found himself grinding his teeth. He knew he did this sometimes and it frightened him. He had done it as a child when a big boy at the village school had caught a bird and begun to tear out its feathers. Matthew had leapt on him, desperate to rend him to pieces. The other children, scared by his ferocity, had fetched the teacher. He never forgot coming to himself and seeing the bruises on the boy's face. One terrible day he'd begun on his own son. Martin had made a paper boat and the collie pup had chewed it to a pulp. Matthew had seen Martin give the dog a vicious kick. If Jane hadn't come out into the farmyard and sharply called his name he would have beaten the boy insensible. These were things it wasn't safe to think about. Every day he wished the old woman dead.

When he walked into the kitchen he found Jane in tears and her mother hunched in the basket chair as he'd left her, but wearing a look now both sly and defiant.

He put his arm round Jane's shoulders. "What's up?"

"It's Mother. She tried to kill herself."

"She . . ." He stared at the old woman in disbelief. She looked rooted in the corner. It was impossible to imagine she'd ever left it. "How?"

Jane seemed to take courage from his presence. "Her left wrist. See."

She turned back the cuff of her black wool dress. The wrist was bandaged thickly. Mrs Pawson sat still with her eyes on Matthew's face and a tight grin on her lips.

"You mean . . .?"

"Yes. The bread-knife. I'd gone out with the washing basket. She thought she'd have all the time while I hung the things up but I'd left the pegs. I was back in a second. When I saw – ! But it wasn't a deep cut. It didn't need the doctor. Oh Matthew!"

Matthew gripped her hand. "Mrs Pawson, you're a wicked old woman."

Jane cried, "No, she's frightened, lonely. It's still the shock from Father going."

The old woman spoke at last, her voice weak and husky. "See what he calls me, Jane, after all these years – Mrs Pawson."

"There," Jane pleaded softly to him, "that hurts. She wants you to say Mother."

He thought, I believe in civilised behaviour but this old woman has forfeited all that. He turned and spoke to Jane as if she wasn't there and the rudeness was all too easy.

"She'd never have killed herself. She wanted to frighten you."

Mrs Pawson reared up out of her chair. "Wouldn't I? Wouldn't I?" she screamed.

Matthew took her by the shoulders and heard Jane yell his name. He sat her mother firmly back in the chair and hissed at her, "The pegs are dead opposite you on that hook. You knew fine well Jane would be back at once."

Jane drew him away. "She wouldn't notice. You're making her out something she isn't. Truly we must try kindness. Call her Mother. Give her a kiss."

Matthew slipped his arm from her grasp. She had asked him something quite impossible. He walked out into the farmyard and shut the door firmly behind him.

Later, when Jane had persuaded her mother to rest in bed, she found Matthew at the broken wall. He laid down the stone he was lifting and looked her full in the face.

"You don't honestly believe she'd have cut an artery. Let herself bleed?"

"Oh I don't know. I don't think she knows herself. But she was so wretched this morning, talking about the bungalow . . ."

"The bungalow? She should be pleased about it. Why isn't she pleased?"

"Maybe we've rushed it too much. We should have made her feel wanted *here*."

"She's in Martin's room. He'll be home at Christmas."

"He can have the sofa. The bungalow couldn't be built by then anyway."

"Why not? It must be." He was clenching his teeth. "Cranston said he'd put his men onto it as soon as the plans are approved. He ought to build it in two months."

"You saw Cranston then? When will we get planning permission?"

As Matthew told her it all she doubted Cranston's good faith. "We'll talk to Mr Pembleton calmly. If Cranston loathes him he must be a good man – as Peggy said."

Matthew was looking down the valley over the rich meadows. "It's my land, my money. Why do we have to talk to anyone?"

She searched his face. "You know the law. You're too reasonable to question it."

Matthew lifted his head to gaze down the hill again. "I think I'll come back to finish this. I want to go down and look at those bullocks. Sykes wasn't happy about two of them yesterday."

"Oh Matthew, stay close by." She stood with her arms hanging limp. "Please."

"She won't try anything again. You know if you'd got the doctor it might have been a step to getting her certified." He threw this out casually as he turned to set off.

"Certified! You can't mean that!"

"I'd rather something happened to *her* than to my two bullocks."

"Oh Matthew!" She put her hands to her face but checked the gesture and let them fall. "No, that's right. Be honest. Go and look at the bullocks." She was near to tears.

He said, "Your apron's coming undone." And he strode off down the hill.

She began fumbling at the strings. Only her jutting hipbones were holding the apron up. She thought, I'm torn apart between him and Mother. I'm a skeleton.

As she went in to make her mother a cup of tea she was thinking, certified! Aren't we all a little mad? Am I sane? Is Matthew? Who do I know that's totally sane?

Then the doorbell rang and there on the doorstep was the answer – Peggy Mason.

"Oh Peggy. Come in. Am I glad to see you!"

Peggy was in her nurse's uniform, so she must be relieving the regular district nurse. She said, "I was at a scald in Blattingford so I looked in to see how things were."

"You'll have a cup of tea?" Jane took her through to the kitchen.

"Ay I will. It's getting hot and I'm always thirsty driving. You look worried, pet."

"It's the bungalow. Matthew's already been to Wanwick this morning and George Cranston says there may be trouble over the site. It's preying on our minds so."

"Oh ay, Wilf told me Pembleton probably wouldn't like it."

"Oh Peggy –"

"You just make the tea and don't worry. I had no use for officials myself one time. Slowing things up, stopping people doing what they wanted with their own money."

Jane paused with the kettle poised over the teapot. "That's what Matthew said. His own money, his own land."

Peggy said, "Yes, and before I started on Westways I'd have had nothing to say on the other side. But there *is* another side. Money's a privilege. The land is everyone's heritage. We can't abuse our share of it. Look at the slums –"

"Of course, *slums*."

"Ay, but look at ribbon development strung along main roads so people back their cars into the traffic. It's worth folks studying the best way to plan things."

Jane poured a cup for her mother. "I'll just take this up. But you know, Peggy, I wonder if you'd have seen it like that if the planners hadn't let you have Westways, or if you hadn't married a district surveyor."

Peggy guffawed. "You could have an atom of truth there, my pet. Your mother's all right, is she?"

Jane, hearing hurried shuffling noises as she opened the kitchen door, said quickly, "Oh yes." But she knew her mother had been listening on the landing. Peggy had a loud, penetrating voice. She went particularly slowly up the stairs.

"Here's a cup of tea," she announced, brightly.

Her mother, arranging herself under the counterpane, cried, "That Peggy's here again. Everyone in the country's nosey. I don't think it'll suit me, the country."

"You couldn't have stayed in Rose Terrace. They're pulling it down."

"Ay, your precious planners. Nothing wrong with it. All those rooms and two attics. You could keep yourself to yourself there."

Jane had loathed the high backyard walls and her mother bolting the door the minute she got in from school. "You're in now, I've got you. You can't get out."

"Well there's your tea." She set it on the chest of drawers and went back to Peggy, as her mother muttered, "You'd rather talk to her than me."

Peggy said, "There's something more, isn't there, Jane? You look washed out."

"I'll tell you," Jane said, yearning for the relief. "As a friend not a nurse?"

"Surely," Peggy laughed, and pulling out her hatpin, she yanked off her hat. "There, I've shed the nurse. It's never a baby is it?"

Jane told her what her mother had done that morning.

"Ay, I thought you were safe from babies. Not to worry. She won't do it again."

"Peggy, talk softly. She gets up and sits on the stairs."

"Well, she's naughty, but I'll whisper."

"But why would she do it?"

"Get attention of course."

"But I give her lots of attention."

"Matthew's then. You should have seen the things some of my girls at Westways did just to get noticed. Half of them weren't retarded at all, just never been noticed."

Jane drank her tea in nervous gulps. If only she could take things in her stride, like Peggy. If only Matthew could. But her mother's demands for attention were unending.

"He was so happy," she said. "I could see him smoothing out, looking younger, till Mother came. But we ought to be able to cope with it, both of us. *You* would."

Peggy filled up her teacup again. "Ah well, Jane, I've been lucky in my life."

"Lucky! Oh Peggy you make me ashamed." Jane recalled that Peggy had lost her parents in an air raid and her fiancé just at the end of the war. She spent years in India as a medical missionary till she fell ill herself. When she came back she worked in a London Children's Home but was warned to seek country air. So she came north to her home county and put her savings into Westways which was a derelict mansion then. That was when Mr Pembleton spoke at a local protest meeting on behalf of her plan for a home for abandoned children. She met Mason, too, the district surveyor, a widower with four children, and simply took over the family. That was the sort of woman she was.

"Ay lucky," she said. "I haven't just had one life. I've had lots. And not many gets four kids when they're nearly fifty."

Jane thought, do they suffer, the Peggys of this world? No, that's wicked – of course they do – but in that tight, drawn, eaten-up way that Matthew suffers? She said, "Peggy, if you were me, would you inflict this on your husband?"

"You're asking the wrong question, Jane. You've no choice, have you? She's got nobody but you. I know it's hard. You'd set your hearts on getting away on your own."

"Is that where we were wrong? Setting our hearts. One should be ready for anything. You always were."

"Like I said, I had lots of chances." Peggy got up and put on her hat. "I've a lacerated hand in Wanwick, two hospital after-cares in Fawley and a crushed toe in Dunford. I ought to do those before lunch."

"Oh I'm sorry." Then she said in an urgent whisper, "Matthew said Mother ought to be certified. What if he asked the doctor without telling me?"

Peggy stuck in the hatpin. "He can't today because Dr Andrews is in Midcaster himself seeing Mr Pembleton about *his* new house. They're knocking down his old cottage for a road improvement." She burst into a roar of laughter. "Ah Jane, you and Matthew. You need to laugh a bit more."

It was nine-thirty and the office day had genuinely begun. In the Development Control room, Paul Pembleton sat back and stretched his legs, letting his hands hang by the side of his chair. The sun's heat pressed in through the big windows. All he could see, half turning his head, was a hazy sky, the blue masked by Midcaster's smoke pall. Why was he sitting in this little glass box high above the river? He laid his fingertips on his closed lids. He'd been up too early. Six o'clock. It wasn't civilised.

He called, "Hine, open a window, will you? I'm half asleep in here. Thanks."

He wanted to be out, up the Wann Valley and on the moors. But there was the morning to get through, everything for the Agenda and the zest had gone out of acting the Myth. He must call Neville in but felt suddenly his old dread of encounter. Only Eleanor and his sister knew he could still feel the sensation that had been almost a sickness with him as a boy – the moment of meeting someone before you spoke. Eleanor understood because she had been intensely shy herself and she still fiddled with her beads or twirled her wedding ring round when she talked to people. At seventeen he had set himself to conquer his dread and had started smoking. At the same age he had found he could make his school fellows laugh with his gift of mimicry, his teachers had seen in him flashes of brilliance and he had mastered his cunning spin bowling. He didn't meet Eleanor till his student days after national service, when she was already teaching. By that time he had perfected his pose of sardonic detachment. Perhaps it was because she saw through it and loved what was underneath that he had also fallen in love with her.

He looked across at Neville who was working with that frowning intensity that had put Paul off the first week he'd been in the office. Paul remembered saying to Harry Wade, "This lad's bright, but I feel as if everything I do is being scrutinised through a microscope. Harry had said, "He's only learning the job." "It's indecent to do it so blatantly." "Give him plenty of rope then. Send him out on his own." That was what Harry had done almost from the word go with Roger Weston. He'd been lucky.

What maddened Paul was that Neville, who bridled if told anything twice, had made an inexcusable gaffe in a simple procedure. It was buried in a filing cupboard now but Paul was sure that if he'd pointed it out to Neville on the day he'd discovered it Neville would have wanted action at once and it would have been all over the office. Foggart's nose for such things would certainly have sniffed it out. When Paul had sounded Miss Smeed over how much she checked, she had become het-up and anxious. It was best to let it lie. And if I'm not telling Neville, Paul thought, I must stop thinking about it every time I see him.

He called, "OK, Neville, come over and let's go through this new stuff."

Neville pushed back his chair. His face was red. Perhaps he was hot too. As he came across the room Paul knew it was still there, this business of encounter, this stepping out from 'I myself alone' to 'I face to face with you.' It wasn't fear any more, not in an every day situation like this, but still a sharp awareness.

Neville took the spare chair, drawing it round close to Paul's. He picked up the first of the new applications and read, "'Blattingford.' Well, I've never been *there*."

Paul said, "We've only had four applications from there in *my* time. This is just north of the village. It can't be more than six miles from Wanwick. I might have time to pop over the moor and look at it this afternoon."

He was going to put the file straight into his brief case but Neville was holding the edge of it. "They'll not get away with this. It's a hundred and fifty yards from the farm and half a mile from the village. Access is at a steep bend in a narrow road."

"So I observe," Paul said.

"They don't even claim it's for a farmhand. It's for the owner's mother-in-law."

Paul leant back in his chair. "You would say then that Mr Hodge's application does not conform with County Council policy on development in rural areas."

"Of course it doesn't –" Neville began, then looked at him sideways. Paul gave him one of his flashing smiles so he wouldn't know whether he was being laughed at or put at his ease. He relinquished the file at once and Paul slid it into his briefcase.

A barge on the river hooted thinly. Paul picked up the next file. What an artificial situation this was! "Alterations to a shop front," he said cheerfully. "Rather nice that." He gave it to Neville. "Check it when you're next in Axton. I think we can give them that. See it gets on the Agenda by Monday."

The next file was a fat one. "Not this old thing again!"

Neville looked in it to see what was new. "It's a letter from the Ministry of Works Estate Surveyor." He read out, "I confirm the contents of my previous letter and would be grateful for the final views of the County Planning Officer on the whole matter."

Paul threw back his head and laughed. "Poor man's forgotten what we said at the meeting. He's a little chap, bald as an egg and the same shape. Some Trog must have found the file at the back of a cupboard and asked him what to do. He'd say, 'Write guardedly to the Planning people and find out what's happening'. So he did."

"I think it's scandalous the way these things drag on."

Paul shut the file with a click and tossed it at him. "Go through it and see what they need to know. If you draft a letter I'll sign it before I go out." He picked up the next file. "This one's in the wrong pile. I was at Leeburn recently and dealt with it." He was talking at top speed now.

Neville said, "A letter about it came through from Admin. while you were out."

Paul read it and grabbed the phone. "Get me Mr Leigh of Leigh and Watt." He could feel it coming on – the Myth. There was a stimulus in having his mind on several things at once but the fun was showing everyone else how well he could do it. He reached to the shelf above his desk and handed a file to Neville. "That's the electricity line at Cottle. It came Monday. I'll pass there this afternoon. Sketch me out an alternative to the Board's line. You'll find the Transformer can go in behind the pub." The phone rang.

The switchboard girl said, "Mr Leigh isn't in yet. I said to ring you as soon as he is. Was that right?" She had a low voice, a little husky, which went with her beauty queen face, dark red hair and luxurious figure. Paul had heard her breathe seductively down the phone, "Good morning, County Planning Department. Can I help you?" Unfortunately office procedure was new to her all the time. So far Paul had never allowed her to irritate him. He looked at his watch.

"Miriam, I have a meeting at ten."

"Oh yes," she purred. "They said he'd be in any minute."

He gave Neville another of his smiles. "These ruddy architects in private practice. Ten to ten and not in yet. I suppose we'd be the same."

Neville said, "You'll want this underground – after it leaves the Transformer?"

"Of course. It's trailing round right in front of Cottle Castle. Where it's under the cottage eaves you can leave it. Here's the motor mower shed at that miners' welfare club at Bentley. How far did you get with that?"

"I told them to put it next to their Sports Pavilion."

"They've probably built the damn thing already. See what the trouble is." The phone rang. "Mr Leigh to speak to you."

Paul said carefully, "Miriam, show the people for my meeting into the *small* Committee room when they come. Got that. OK. Put Mr Leigh on."

He pointed to his watch and then to his desk diary. Neville nodded and went to get the file. At least he was quick on the uptake. Paul said into the phone, "I have your letter, Mr Leigh. You write of a new access onto the A road from your client's land. If you recall our meeting . . . No, I can only recommend the Committee to approve it if your client combines his access with Mr Pepper's. He's perfectly agreeable . . . There was no bus in Pepper's front garden yesterday . . . Certainly, if he's using his premises to park a commercial vehicle it will be looked into." He rang off.

Neville put the file into his hands. "It's turned ten, Mr Pembleton."

The phone buzzed again. "It's a Mr Mason," Miriam said. "I held him for you."

"D'you mean the Wanwick District Surveyor?"

"Shall I ask him?"

Paul swore under his breath. "Has anyone arrived for my meeting yet?"

"Three of them. I showed them into the Small Committee Room." They might be the three bears, Paul thought, for all she'd notice.

"Tell Mr Mason I'll ring him back in half an hour."

Paul tucked the file under his arm. He said to Neville, "Can you get on with the files for the Agenda before you do anything else? I'd like to sign as many as I can this morning before Admin. start flapping."

He got himself out of the room but immediately the panelled corridor erupted. The mop-headed figure of Hugh Cole popped out of the door to Architecture. Paul tried to get ahead with his long strides, but Cole danced before him like a skiff before a liner.

"Well, did you know," he chortled, "I've got a replacement."

Paul said, "Another rumour?"

"Ah but I had this from the horse's mouth." Cole's voice was penetrating. His laugh exploded. "I should have said *vulture's* mouth. It's Ron Foggart."

"For God's sake, hush." But it was too late. Bird's door opened and he stood, owlish in his tortoiseshell spectacles, slightly inclined forwards, like a puppet.

"I was in my inner office, gentlemen. My *inner* office." He was using his high-pitched embarrassed voice. "Disturbed. Oh distinctly disturbed. The Deputy and I are in conference. Definitely too loud, gentlemen." He rocked on his heels and waved his plump little arms at them. "Section heads, you see. Section Heads." He turned to go in again, muttering something like "undergraduate quality about those two." He shut the door.

Paul seized Hugh's arm and propelled him along till they were clear of The Nest as Bird's office was always called.

"You bloody fool. Some of us have to go on working here after next week."

Cole was still laughing but at half-volume. "Wouldn't the old man have made a marvellous schoolmaster? O Lord, I'll miss this place."

They were outside the Committee Room door. "D'you mind not making a scene here? I have a meeting –"

"It's news about Foggart though, isn't it? He as good as told me so himself. Listen, we had the most marvellous bit of Foggart-baiting in my room this morning."

"For Christ's sake!" Paul shook off Hugh's hand on his arm.

Hugh stared at him. His cheeky schoolboy face was blank with surprise. "Holy Smoke, you really are mad at me. I thought it was one of your acts."

"It was and it wasn't. Now, scram, please. I don't want to be borne into my meeting on a gale of laughter."

He had already turned the handle of the door before he realised he had no idea what this meeting was about. It could have been mud huts at Timbuktu. For a second it was like a dream where you go on stage not knowing a word of your part. He glanced at the file he was carrying. Oh yes, Dr Andrews. Site for a house at Fawley. If he managed things well this could be wrapped up in quarter of an hour. He switched on his official bearing and walked in.

Hugh Cole wandered back along the corridor looking for someone to talk to. Lister popped out of Bird's office and said, "Hugh!"

Cole pretended to duck. "It's the Deputy Headmaster. Where's your cane?"

"Stop acting the fool for five minutes and come into my room."

"*I'm* not the one who's acting. You should have seen Paul square his shoulders and march into his meeting every inch a planning officer."

"Paul's always put on a display like that."

"Ah but he wasn't laughing at himself. That laddy's been overworking."

"Look, shut the door will you. I've got something to tell you which I'm not supposed to be telling anyone. The old man would have a fit."

"I'm honoured." Cole held out a flash cigarette case. "South Street jewel raid."

"I'm only telling you to stop you spouting silly rumours." Lister took a cigarette.

"I'm only handing round fags to make sure you give me a going-away present."

"Quits," the Deputy said. "Now shut up and listen."

The Small Committee Room was an intimidating room. Leather-upholstered chairs stood to attention at a long narrow table down the centre of which marched a line of metal ashtrays. At the end by the door was a chair with black wooden arms.

A swift glance at the group chatting by the window showed Paul that the County Surveyor's Department was not yet represented. Good, he'd start without him.

"I do apologise for keeping you waiting, gentlemen." He drew out the chair with arms and held out his hand to the only man he didn't recognise. "Dr Andrews I presume."

Dr Andrew's architect, Mr Benson, an overripe, florid-cheeked character, murmured to his client, "Mr Pembleton."

They all approached, disturbing the ranks of leather chairs, and sat down. The doctor had eager eyes and looked nervous. The other two were Peters, a young flabby man, new to the County Architect's Department, and Smales, a swarthy police inspector. Paul handed round a copy of a plan and deliberately addressed his opening remarks to Dr Andrews.

"I'm sure Mr Benson has made clear to you why three departments of the County Council as well as the police are involved in your application. This plan shows the County Surveyor's new road widening scheme and the site for the new police house. Mr Wallace from County Surveyor's will be along any minute, but we can all look at this meanwhile. The area marked in blue would be the site of your house –"

"Just a minute, Mr Pembleton," the Inspector said, "I thought that's what we were here to discuss. Whether it's feasible. The land hasn't been allocated like this, has it?"

Paul allowed him one of his swift smiles. "I had these plans prepared in my department to show a possible arrangement of the whole site."

The Inspector murmured. "I see. A basis for discussion. Very well."

"Perhaps you would comment on the site in the light of your usual requirements."

Smales, making delaying noises, drew on a pair of rimless spectacles and examined the plan carefully. "We've had larger sites –"

"And smaller," Paul said. "A village constable hasn't time for a huge garden."

Smales went on painstakingly, "I see no reason why this shouldn't –" He looked at Peters, the young architect.

Paul too fixed him with a straight gaze, "Mr Peters, can you say whether the site will satisfy the County Architect?"

Before he could answer there was a slight tap on the door. A weedy sad little man with large hands came deprecatingly in.

"So sorry, Mr Pembleton, I was held up."

Paul's sharp ears heard Mr Benson, more florid than ever in the heat from the windows, mutter to the doctor, "*He's* come from the floor above. *You've* come twenty miles." Paul was also aware that the doctor was casting anxious medical eyes at his architect from time to time as if fearing that a coronary might be about to carry him off.

Paul introduced Mr Wallace from the County Surveyor's Department. He knew him to be a friend of Foggart's from way back when they were articled clerks together. He handed him a plan.

Wallace sat down and stared at it. "I hardly realised," he began hoarsely and then cleared his throat. He seemed breathless. "I hardly realised things had got to this stage."

Paul said emphatically, "We had to have something to go on. Inspector Smales and Mr Peters agree that as far as their departments are concerned the site for the police house is adequate."

Peters made a small noise, as Paul expected, and he turned to him with his most vivid smile. "I beg your pardon, Mr Peters, you hadn't expressed an opinion yet."

Peters lifted his podgy hands two inches off the table and lowered them again.

"I don't see why it shouldn't do –" He looked at the Inspector and laughed.

Wallace cut in, "I think the Planning Department is rushing things. The County Council, which is the landowner, has not yet authorised any division of the land."

Paul briskly slapped his hand on the plan. "We're clearing your improvement lines easily. And you will recall that the demolition of the doctor's rented cottage – to accommodate this new road lay-out – is precisely why he needs a new house."

Wallace croaked, "This is a black spot we're improving. We don't want a lot of new accesses."

The Inspector leant across the table. "*We* don't need a garage you know."

Good, Paul thought, he dislikes Wallace. I'll get the doctor his house.

"You need standing area. Must have standing area," Wallace said.

Paul decided to lop off this budding argument by addressing the doctor again.

"Perhaps Dr Andrews would tell us whether he's satisfied with the proposed site before we proceed further."

The doctor looked at Benson who sat up in his chair beaming. "I never doubted two houses could be got comfortably on this site. The frontage is limited certainly and of course Dr Andrews requires a garage but it can be done. I made some rough sketches allowing the police house more land than you show here and it's quite practicable."

There was some more chatter about details but Paul smiled round at them all. "If there are no further obstacles then, gentlemen, the County Council can be advised to sell this site to Dr Andrews."

Wallace cleared his throat. Benson chipped in first. "You'll want an outline site plan for this area, from us, won't you, Mr Pembleton?"

"Yes. If I get it by Monday it can go on this month's agenda. I'll recommend that outline permission be granted to that area surplus to the County Council's requirements for a police house and to the County Surveyor's road improvements. Right?"

Dr Andrew at last opened his lips, "I don't know how to thank you —"

Wallace's voice interrupted, like the croak of the bad fairy at the party. "I'll have to work out our access requirements. Let you have them in writing."

Paul barely glanced in his direction. "I'm sure Mr Benson will co-operate with Mr Peters and Inspector Smales to make the best use of the land available."

Everyone made agreeable noises while Wallace sat there, mouth slightly open, gazing at the ceiling as if he'd heard nothing.

"Well, gentlemen," Paul looked at his watch and stood up, "if no one has any further observations to make —"

They all got to their feet and the doctor, clutching his copy of the plan, seemed to want to thank him some more but Wallace had pushed his way forward, "You'll send me up the outline application when you get it."

"You could work out your access requirements now — from this plan."

Wallace looked at the plan derisively and at the doctor who was reluctantly following Mr Benson out of the room. "Huh, this has no official status" — he spoke loud enough for the doctor to hear. "It's just a piece of paper." He stumped out after the others.

Returning past Lister's door Paul saw that it was open and the Deputy was standing in the centre of his emerald green rug like a large man balancing on a small raft.

"I thought that was your meeting breaking up. Smart work."

Paul was surprised to see Hugh Cole sitting in the visitor's chair.

Hugh said, "I've had my six of the best. Now it's your turn."

"You've worked that joke to death." Lister made no bones of his impatience. "It was unlucky timing though, as far as the old man is concerned."

"I know," Paul smiled. "You told me to keep out of the limelight. But good God, what could he have heard? We might have been talking about anything."

Lister said, "Bird's got ears for these things. Hugh's laugh and then Foggart's name. He looked at me and said 'Someone's been talking,' and made for the door."

"So he thinks you told me about you-know-what and I must have told Hugh. It hasn't done either of us any good." Paul looked at Hugh who jumped up and bowed.

"I've been honoured with Mr Lister's confidence while you were busy."

Paul shrugged, "Why not? It's Foggart who likes his schemes under cover."

Hugh nodded vigorously. "Absolutely. Like when you turn over a stone, all the slimy things run back to their holes."

"No, damn it," the Deputy said, trying to regain command of the situation, "we've got to keep up some sort of front. Senior officers and all that. We don't want our every move to be the subject of gossip among typists and draughtsmen."

"They are already," Hugh said. "You're out of touch, Derek."

Paul was inclined to laugh too. He was warm and relaxed after his meeting, with the little doctor's grateful smiles fresh before his eyes. But Lister's face went red with anger.

Paul said quickly, "Derek's right, Hugh. This time it's Foggart's own game, to get tongues wagging, so Bird will feel compelled to act. You'd better disabuse your chaps."

Cole sprang to attention and saluted. "I go." Then he cocked his head on one side. "But if my section's split between three Control Areas and Foggart's Chief A.P.O he *will* be their boss, though I don't know how anyone can divide Harris and Penny into three."

Lister growled, "Do the best you can. You won't have problems like this to deal with much longer."

"Ah yes. Back to pure architecture. No longer one of THEM. Will you forget – when I'm gone" – he produced a choking sob – "that you are THEM? I met a cyclist this morning after my dramatic escape from death. He said, did I know that THEY can put power stations wherever they like but won't let his old Dad build a cottage in the country? I nearly confessed, 'I also am one of THEM. Throw me in the river if you like, but deep inside, under the paper layers is a human soul who, if it had a wife and children, would go home to them at five o'clock like any decent citizen. But I was a coward. I said, 'Ah who are THEY? Who indeed?'" He saw Lister open his mouth to interrupt. "All right, neither the time nor the place. I go to spread the veil of silence on my men."

Lister leant back with a sharp release of breath. "He's getting to be a buffoon."

Paul thought, he's still angry. He looked at his watch. "Someone's ringing me at half past."

"You've got five minutes. I didn't call you in to listen to Cole. I've had the crazy idea of giving him a send-off at our place. You and Eleanor would come, wouldn't you?"

"Thanks, Derek, yes." Didn't Eleanor say, 'I'm terrified of his wife'? He got up.

"Sit down, man. That was just by the way. It's this wretched Areas business. If Bird sees you today for God's sake play it cool. He's wavering."

Paul too felt a surge of anger. "Bird's intelligent. He's seen Ron with an Area."

The Deputy spread his hands. "They were younger then. Planning was younger. A lot of our criticism is hindsight. Ron can put up a good show. The knottier Appeal cases. He shuts up like a clam and admits nothing. Bird approves of that."

"For heaven's sake! *You're* not wavering, are you? Ron's a lazy inefficient bastard." What had happened to Lister since he'd been set for a tooth and nail fight only an hour before? "On day-to-day applications he'd antagonise people right and left. You got Foggart pushed up to Number Three where he could do least harm at the last reshuffle. Just throw another job at him."

Lister's reaction was now so sudden it looked as if the shot was too near the mark.

He rose from his seat, a bull roused and blazing. "By God," he said with a tone he'd never used to Paul before, "nobody tells *me* what to do —"

What he would have said next, how he would have climbed down, because he couldn't keep that up, not with me, Paul thought, would never be known. The phone rang, pushing its insistent buzz into the conversation as if to spare them further embarrassment.

Paul stood up at once. He was shaken. It felt like a punch. He said, "I'll go."

Derek snatched up the phone and barked, "Lister here." He wouldn't look at Paul.

As he closed the door Paul heard him say in a puzzled, quieter voice, "My wife?" and then wearily, "Well, go on, girl, put her through."

Hugh Cole was lying in wait for Paul round the corner. "My men have taken an oath of silence on the Development Plan. What have you hatched with Derek?"

"Nothing. Someone's ringing me at half past. I'm late now."

"What's up? If *you* forget he's the Deputy *he* won't. You can't presume on the natural geniality of the man. He's not on the golf course now."

It was true. You were friendly with a chap for years. One minute he was inviting you to his house and then — "I've got to get on, Hugh." He tried to pass by.

Cole shook his absurd head sadly. "The coils in Control are deadly. You can't shed the Man from the Council. I hate to see you go under like the rest."

The door to Control opened and a vaguely female figure blew towards them.

"Oh Mr Pembleton, *there* you are."

"Look out, the Smeed," murmured Cole and vanished into his room.

"I knew your meeting was over, but we didn't know where — after that — and Mr Carr has Mr Mason waiting on the phone. Will you want me about eleven-fifteen?"

"No, now," Paul said. "There are letters to go off. We'll manage it all at once." He smiled. "We generally do." Poor Miss Smeed. She loved him to act the Myth. But after Lister's fury and Hugh's uncanny insight it wouldn't come easily.

He waved Miss Smeed in front of him into Control again. The back of her neck had a masculine look, coarse and red as if newly scrubbed. Her blouse was white and lacy against it over the top of her tunic. Soon she'd be back to jumpers. Eleanor always said, "Is Miss Smeed into the woollies yet?" It was one of the first signs of autumn.

All this went through his mind as they crossed the room to his glass cubicle. He couldn't escape this cursed over-awareness of people. There was Weston hunched at his desk, his great hands, more happy with a rugby ball, gripping a ballpoint pen. Neville was half out of the cubicle, holding the phone for him. Hine and the other draughtsman were listening to Pennyman – what was *he* doing here? So much for Cole's veil of silence.

Before he took the phone from Neville he drew the Fawley Corner file from under his arm and gave it to Miss Smeed. "We should get the outline plan for this by Monday. Expedite anything to do with this application. Dr Andrews, Fawley Corner. Remember?"

Miss Smeed nodded, clutching it to her tunic. "Give her a task," he told Eleanor, "and she gets down to it like a starved man to a feast." Eleanor had said, "She *is* starved."

He took the phone from Neville and said pleasantly, "Good morning, Mason." He covered up the mouthpiece as soon as he'd said it and pushed two more files at Miss Smeed. "Look at that one, will you? We'll have to tell him to submit access details." Mason was talking about bathroom extensions at Little Capgate. His stammer was giving him trouble over the initial C. Paul liked him. Not all the District Surveyors took the same interest in the planning side of their work. "And in this one, Miss Smeed," Paul said, "we've got to consult the Water Board . . ." He saw her settle in the visitor's chair and start scribbling in her notepad. He sat down and stretched his legs under the desk. "Yes, Little Capgate," he said into the phone. "Bathroom extensions?"

It was about Hugh Cole," Shirley's voice said, as serene as the square of blue sky Derek could see outside. "Have you asked him yet about the party?"

"Party! Huh. No."

"I've rung at an awkward moment, Derek? Haven't I?"

Her voice was so clear, as if she were sitting across the room from him. Funny, she knew better than to ring him at the office as a rule.

"Any moment would be awkward today."

"It is definitely Friday next week we're having the party?" she said next, as cheerful as ever. "I think that's the best day. Will you tell them any time after eight?"

"*I'm* not inviting anyone. You can see to all that – if we bother at all."

"But it was *your* idea." Now she did sound hurt.

"I can't think about parties today. I did mention it to – Well, I have mentioned it. I suppose Friday's all right."

She said, "I'll get cards printed then. Derek, try and be early tonight, will you?"

"Early! Not a hope today. I told you."

"I wish you would – there's something urgent." She dropped her voice.

"Eh? What's the matter? Speak up. Are you all right?"

"There's something urgent," she said again. What could be urgent since the start of their conversation? "We have to make a decision about something important."

"What in the world – ?" He swore under his breath.

"Derek, we *never* talk. Just getting through to you in the daytime –"

"Shirley, not *now*." Somebody ill? Her parents? Yet she was planning a party. One thing he couldn't stand was a mystery. "Well, tell me in one sentence. Quick."

"*No. You* come home for lunch." Was she crying now? An unheard of thing.

He felt like smashing the receiver. "Absolutely impossible."

"So leave at five. They don't pay you after that."

"If it was life and death you'd tell me now." He said it through gritted teeth. She had sounded so calm at first. To have cool, sophisticated Shirley infuriating him like everyone else today was the last straw! He snapped, "I'll be home when I can."

"I see. Goodbye then." And suddenly she wasn't there any more to argue with.

He slammed the phone down. What the hell was she on about?

He put his head in his hands, his jaw clenched. He thought, I'd have managed her better if *Paul* hadn't got me hot and bothered. He made me feel – no, there's no putting it into words. He's not Hugh Cole, on the outside laughing at us all. He cares about the job, efficiency and all that. Yet there's part of him held back. The swine believes he can do with one hand what ordinary mortals need two for. But Shirley! What in God's name – ?

There was the phone again of course. The wonder was he'd had a minute without it. "Lister here." It was a man he knew who might be persuaded to set up one of these new motels in the County if he was carefully handled. "Yes, certainly, Jack . . . get together on this . . . lunch? Tomorrow . . . delighted . . ."

"The c-cottages are substandard," Mason said, "but when I looked at the plans I thought they could be permitted development. In terms of cu- cu -"

"Cubic feet. Quite." Paul could feel Mason blushing. "I'm coming your way this afternoon. We can advise them on design and materials anyway. Seize the opportunity."

He could hear Mason chuckle at the comment. Then he said, "And oh, Mr Pembleton, you should have received an application from a farmer named Hodge."

"Hodge of Old Mill Farm – a bungalow above Blattingford?"

It was good that. He'd only glanced at the file but the name had stuck.

"He's anxious to get it b-built," Mason said.

"I hope to have time to see the site this afternoon."

Mason blurted out, "As a m-m-matter-of-fact m-my wife's a friend of his wife. It's a t-tough situation. They do need it rather urgently but it's not too well placed. I warned the C-Council but they'd got C-Cranston backing it as usual."

"We'll discuss it this afternoon. Right."

Paul put down the phone and smoothed his brow. Then he saw Miss Smeed gazing anxiously at him. She thinks I've got a headache. Damn it I *have* got a headache.

She rose and murmured, "I'll have the letters typed, Mr Pembleton, for when you ring through. Excuse me." She sidled out in a half-sitting position clutching her files

Paul thought, fancy Derek flaring up like that! No, it wasn't Derek but the Deputy County Planning Officer. Where does one draw the line? Is there a line?

In the main office Pennyman's giggle rose to a crescendo. "It tore right out of my grasp. There wasn't a thing I could do."

There was a general laugh. Then Hine said mockingly, "If he does take over from Cole he'll eat you alive. He never forgets a thing."

Roger Weston went over to the group and spoke to Pennyman, with a glance at Paul's cubicle. Pennyman threw up his head like a startled colt. At the same moment Hugh Cole looked round the door from Architecture calling, "Penny, Gordon's made the coffee." Earlier in the week Hugh had sent a memo round the office advertising for sale his share in their coffee tin. Pennyman took the chance to escape. Paul thought, if a miracle happens and Harry Wade goes to Morlton I'd like to see Roger in his job.

Now he became aware of brown corduroys and the frayed edge of a green jacket outside the glass partition. Leonard King put his flat deadpan face round the door.

"Paul, how about the Quarterly Report?"

"It'll be done in time."

King edged himself onto the corner of Paul's desk. "*I* don't care. It's Ron. Wants them sent off a week before the meeting. I'd better have yours tomorrow. I've got to knock them into one and have the copies run off by Tuesday."

There was another stir in the main office. A small boy had come in, apparently on his own, a boy with dry scruffy hair and a threadbare jacket. He had his back to Paul and was idly tearing the corner of a map. Neville jumped up and Paul heard his voice, sharp and surprised. "You mustn't do that."

Roger Weston rose too and put his large hand on the boy's shoulder. "Where've you come from, sonny? Aren't you with someone?"

The boy nodded towards the glass cubicle and Paul saw a replica of Leonard King. King slid off the desk and went over to the boy. When he was close he gave him a sudden blow on the head. Paul could hear it and winced but the boy made no reaction. Whatever would *Cathy* do if I hit her? he asked himself. Violence! It could *never* happen in our relationship. Pray God it couldn't.

Miss Smeed peeped round the door. "Oh Mr King, I tried to stop him."

King took the boy by his jacket collar and walked him to the door.

Paul called, "My report won't be ready by tomorrow, Len. I'll speak to Mr Foggart myself." Miss Smeed was following when Paul called her back. She scurried over. "What's the boy doing here?" he asked her.

Miss Smeed explained, with many apologies and earnest hopes that Paul and all his family had had chicken pox.

"As a matter of fact I think not." He passed his hand through his hair. Getting long, he thought. Bird will think I'm looking theatrical again. He smiled because she was watching him like an anxious mother. He handed her two more files. "Can you draft replies to these."

"At once." The phone rang and he saw she had observed the contraction of his brow at the noise. She knows I have a headache.

Wade's internal phone rang at the same time. The two instruments in the glass cubicles buzzed in frenzied competition until Paul languidly lifted his receiver. Roger Weston came over to answer Wade's. Paul saw his thick curls and strong neck through the glass while Miriam's voice purred huskily in his ear, "It's Mr Wallace wants you – from the County Surveyor's Department." She was free with her information for once.

Paul said to Miss Smeed, "If I can't see you again this morning, leave anything ready to sign on my desk. I might come in tonight."

She bobbed but hesitated at the door. "I wouldn't, Mr Pembleton, if I were you. You'll have had a long day." She caught her bottom lip with her teeth and hurried off.

Paul heard Roger say, "Yes, I can come through now."

He didn't add, 'sir', so it wasn't Bird, but his deferential tone suggested Lister or Foggart. Paul saw him go without collecting any files. Today everything was suspicious.

Sunlight streamed in, brighter and hotter now. Thank God, he would soon be out on the road. He said into the phone, "Pembleton here, Mr Wallace. Have you done the Fawley Corner access already?"

Wallace said, "I'm not touching Fawley Corner yet."

"All right," Paul said, "so what is it?" But before Wallace spoke he had a premonition that Neville's blunder at Lower Wooton was discovered. The ache across his brow tightened. He passed his hand over it to brush away the idea and the pain together. He thought, I'll be safe in London before that's ever uncovered . . .

The receiver gave Wallace's sad, reproachful tones to his right ear. "I wrote you a letter on April 29th this year." That could have been the date. It fitted.

"What's the matter? Haven't I answered it yet?"

"It concerned improvements to a house" −It was, damn it − "in Lower Wooton."

"Well?" It was like all bad news. You wanted to go back to before you heard it. There were a hundred things Wallace could have said. Why that? Why today, of all days?

Wallace said, "In my letter I asked for your observations. The house in question is affected by a road improvement line."

"I'll look out the file and let you know."

"Will you ring me back today?"

"I'm going out later."

Wallace's voice came smugly down the line. "The road improvement is scheduled to be carried out in the next twelve months." That was a blow. Wallace had more though. "The District Valuer's been onto me. The owner won't sell. The D.V. wants to know if we've got compulsory purchase in mind. *And* how all this came about."

"I'll look into the matter." Perhaps he could stave it off for a few days till Bird had decided about the office reshuffle. Lister had said, "Stay out of the limelight."

"This inquiry will be confirmed in writing," Wallace said and added, flatly but ominously, "this morning. You'll ring me back before you go out. All right?"

Paul put the phone down. That settled it. No stalling. Wallace would earmark the letter for Foggart, perhaps even Bird. And Foggart would leap on it with glee. By the time it landed on his own desk the words 'Please see me. RF' would ornament it. Wallace knew it and was enjoying it after his discomfiture at this morning's meeting.

Paul sat for ten seconds, his fingertips pressed against his eyes. He hadn't meant to antagonise Wallace but as usual *time had been short*. If this headache would go away his sense of the absurd might slip into gear again. Tonight he might laugh with Eleanor about it. And she would say, being so perceptive, "You're not laughing *inside*, are you?" For what he saw most plainly was Bird, shaking his owl's head. "Careless. Oh decidedly careless. Giving the Department a bad name." And Foggart, gleeful, hooked onto Bird's desk, "*There* is the evidence of the need for supervision." And Lister – damn and blast, why had he angered Lister? The Deputy was the man whose help he would need most.

He sprang into life, his chair squealing on the lino.

"Neville, I want you to look me out a file."

Hugh Cole said, "For God's sake don't let them give me a travelling clock."

Harris fondled his beard. "Why don't you want a travelling clock, Hugh?"

"Time doesn't exist in Africa. You say, 'I'll be there in five minutes and an hour later you're asleep and nobody's bothered you."

Pennyman giggled. "Don't African labourers work in shifts like anyone else?"

"Maybe, Penny. Maybe the cancer of Western civilisation has crept in so far. But does an architect sweat at a desk from nine to five? No, he lies naked under a mosquito net with glistening girls fanning him. When an idea strikes him he claps his hands. The girls hold up his drawing board. The great man draws his magic lines, only moving his hand. Penny, don't you dare laugh. If it's not like that I'll get the first boat home."

All this while he was turning over sheets of drawings scattered like huge fallen petals on every table and most of the floor. He wasn't looking for anything in particular.

Pennyman said, "You might be on the first boat back anyway. My Mum saw a thing on the telly last night which said they've stopped giving jobs to white men."

"I've a three-year contract, haven't I?" Cole threw some papers up in the air.

"That won't stop a knife in your back," giggled Pennyman.

Hugh went white. He shivered as he had when he recalled the drop to the river.

Harris muttered, "Shut up, Penny."

Hugh grabbed a binder full of heavy magazines to hurl at him when the door to the corridor opened and Leonard King slouched in.

He grinned. "Preparing a field day for the dustman?"

Cole clumped Pennyman on the head with the binder and then chucked it in the waste-paper basket. "That yes, but these!" He swept up an armful of papers from the floor. "How can I throw these away?" They slithered onto the table, except for a thin folder he clutched to his chest.. "My art! Child of my brain. Flesh of my flesh —"

Harris glanced over his shoulder, "That's a copy of the Written Statement to the original Development Plan."

"Oh my God!" Cole dropped it as if it were a firework about to go off. He wiped his fingers carefully on his shirt which he was now wearing outside his trousers. "That's Foggart's work! How did it sneak in here?"

King shrugged. "Useful for reference purposes?"

Hugh giggled, "Len, your remark borders — I repeat, borders — on the humorous."

King shuffled his feet. "Have you done your Quarterly Report?"

"That's another joke I hope. Didn't you know I'm leaving?"

"You've been here the last quarter."

"But all I ever say is 'I Hugh de Beaumont Cole, have, in the past quarter, executed several outstanding designs and layouts, notably' — then I pop in a few examples — and add, 'My assistants, G. Harris and J. Pennyman, have also been in the office.' Just, translate it into Trog language."

"Send me the examples then."

"I will if you take the hat round for my farewell present. You're falling down on your most important job."

"For *you*? You think they'll part with real money —"

A small being appeared behind him in the doorway.

Cole shouted out. "There are two of you, Leonard, and one of them's shrunk."

"You keep going away," said the boy. "I want some more paper to draw on."

"What have you there, child?" Hugh grabbed at the scribbles the boy was holding behind his back. "He's a genius. Where have you been hiding this boy? Why is he not selling these to American millionaires? Look at the beauty of those lines –"

King said, "He's had chicken pox. D'you want to get it?"

Hugh retreated. "Chicken pox! If it was typhoid, yellow fever, cholera . . . I'm safe from them but chicken pox –! Take him away and loose him everywhere else. Take your artistry, boy, and all your lovely germs. Scatter them up and down on desks and files and typewriters. Now I shall know how to picture you all. When my ship comes into port and natives swarm to meet me with garlands of flowers, I shall think of you, spotted, blotched and groaning and I'll shout 'A pox on County Hall! A pox on the lot of you!'"

"He's crazy," the boy said, "I want to go home."

King took him by the ear. "You'll catch it if you go wandering again. Come on."

When they'd gone, Harris said to Hugh. "You scared him out of his wits."

"Impossible. With Leonard King for a father how could he *have* any?"

"Well, Roger, would you apply for the job." The Chief Assistant was hooked on his desk in his vulture pose. He was on tenterhooks, not for Weston's answer – this interview was a mere stop-gap – but for a word from Wallace that he had phoned Pembleton.

Earlier when he had heard Wallace's voice in the passage he had peeped out and checked him as he turned to the stairs up to his Department.

Wallace had mumbled, "So? How's it going?"

"I think I've got Bird."

Wallace snorted with disgust. "Don't know why you want an Area. There could be a stink coming in the Planning Department. So just be glad it won't be your baby." He began to mount the stairs.

Foggart shot out a restraining hand. "Come on Arnold, what's this about?"

"Just something the District Valuer phoned me about this morning. Looks like somebody's bloomer."

"What about? Where?" Foggart's eyes and whole body were alive with curiosity.

"Oh some extension to a substandard house. We'd informed Planning about a road improvement line affecting it but it still got permission."

Foggart was dancing up and down. "You're carrying out the road improvement?"

Wallace drawled, "It would have waited till the year dot but there were a couple of accidents. Blind corner. Councillor Sands got on to Amberly and the thing was shoved onto next year's schedule."

"Next year's! And where *is* the house?" Foggart hung on his answer.

"Lower Wooton."

"Ah!" Foggart breathed a long sigh of satisfaction. "Pembleton's Area."

Wallace chuckled. "Vindictive brute, aren't you, Ron?"

"What are you doing about this?"

Wallace shrugged. His shoulders were like a skinny rabbit's. "The R.D. can't include that house in their clearance order because it's no longer unfit —"

"The owner's carried out his improvements then?"

"A few months ago I believe. He won't sell now of course. That's what the D.V. was beefing about."

"Have you told your Chief yet?"

Wallace sneered. "Nobody tells Dowland anything these days. We just get on with things and he signs them. He's not thinking about anything but retirement now."

"What action were you going to take?"

"I'll talk to Amberly. The D.V. will put his request for further instructions into writing —"

Foggart hooked himself onto Wallace's arm. "Phone Pembleton. Send him down a letter. Get something in black and white."

Wallace shook him off. "He can't put the house back the way it was. What's in this for you anyway?" Wallace gave a cackle. "Think you can persuade Bird it wouldn't have happened with you in charge?"

"Phone him," Foggart said again. "I'll do something for you next time."

"I've just been with the man. One of his snappy meetings. Talks fast so no one else can get a word in."

"Ay, you can't stick him either, can you? So phone him. Make it sound big. Maybe he'll go to Bird himself with it. But it's got to come out today — while things are in the balance. Phone him. *And* write. Put for my attention on it so no one else can get hold of it and keep it dark. I'll see it gets to

Bird's eyes."

Wallace shrugged. "I don't want to save his skin. He's too bloody sure of himself." He stumped up the stairs. Foggart watched him as far as the bend. Wallace's large hands flapped beside his skinny body like small sails.

For the next half hour the Chief Assistant had dashed up and down in the his office. Had Wallace rung yet? Had Pembleton wriggled out of it? He sat down at his desk and jumped up again. He remembered young Weston and rang for him, unaware that at the same moment Wallace had found an opportunity to ring Pembleton.

Weston looked up at Foggart. His question about Harry's job seemed to open a great many hidden traps. "Ahr – um –well." He knew his country drawl was infuriating to quick nervous talkers like Foggart.

"Don't think you've a chance eh?"

"What do *you* think, Mr Foggart?"

Foggart didn't relax from his vulture pose. "I can put in a good word for you."

Roger thought, I'm damned if I'll go for this as Foggart's nominee. I can get it on merit. I'd ask Dorothy Bird to marry me – except for that damned article about me. It's a slim chance Harry will get Morlton – but *if* – well, A.P.O. here would be grand. I want to be here for the rugby season. And I can see Dorothy again at the Christmas party.

He lifted his head and said boldly to Foggart, "I've had every intention of applying for the post from the moment I knew Mr Wade might be leaving."

Foggart sat down with a small sigh. "It's a fair jump of course to A.P.O status but I don't see why you shouldn't –"To Roger's alarm he gave a sudden grin. "When I first had an Area I hadn't even a planning qualification."

This was so appallingly out of character that Roger didn't know where to look. It was ancient office law that Foggart was extremely sensitive about his beginnings. He had failed more than once to get his planning diploma, while Harry Wade who had come in from the County Architect's Department had taken it the first year.

Now that Foggart was sitting Roger could see the sink in the corner with the kettle beginning to steam on the gas ring. Viewed as the goal of years of scheming, it was a depressing room in spite of the sunshine yellow and tan. The desk, slightly angled across the middle, almost cut it in two. Anyone entering and finding the Chief Assistant hooked onto his desk in his vulture pose had the impression he'd risen suddenly to conceal something diabolical in the other half of the room. In fact it was only a small sink.

Roger recalled the history of how Foggart had acquired the room. Hugh Cole, who had been present when Lister had sold the idea to Foggart, told the tale to all newcomers. "It was a beautiful bit of salesmanship. 'Ron,' says Derek, 'I've been suggesting to Bird we must find you your own office now you're going up in the world.' Foggart was hopping from one foot to the other, ears flapping, dying to see his own name on a door but determined to dislike anything Derek suggested. 'There's only one place of course, to be logical,' Derek says grandly. 'People come up in the lift and opposite them they've got the three top ranking officers, one, two three. Damn shame we can't do it like that. I think we'll have to partition a bit off Cole's room.' Ron scowled like the devil at that so I chipped in with my lines, 'Oh yes, we'd be delighted to have you,' and he nearly burst a blood vessel. 'Why can't we do like you said first?' he snaps. 'That room where they make the tea. There's a gas ring in Admin. They can do it there.' Derek stood shaking his head. 'It 'ud be too costly, Ron, taking out the sink and gas ring and having the room done up –' 'Leave them in,' barks Ron, 'put in a desk and I'll move in if the Council's so bloody hard up.' Ron's always walked into Derek's traps.'"

Roger thought, will it happen again – over the Areas? Foggart's after something, asking me in like this.

Foggart sprang back into his vulture pose. Roger immediately stood up too. "One other thing. Is the written evidence ready for the Botley Appeal? The Caravan Site."

Roger smiled. The Appeal was two months off. "Has something fresh cropped up about it, Mr Foggart?"

"No no. Get onto it though, will you?" The knuckles of his hands had become white as he gripped the desk. A thin white line appeared down the ridge of his nose. .

"Get onto it," Foggart said again, "that's all."

When he'd gone Foggart felt in his desk drawer for some indigestion tablets and took two. These young men were all too sure of themselves. He looked at his watch, then at his window with its tiny square of sky. He picked up the phone. He had no dignity to lose with Wallace. When he heard Wallace's voice he said simply, "Well?"

"He's cagey. Ringing me back. Leave me alone? I'm busy." And he rang off.

Foggart seethed. Of course Pembleton would say, "I'll ring you back". Things must move faster than that. But Wallace was a terrier. Once his teeth were in it he wouldn't let it rest. Then he grinned. Cagey eh? Pembleton knows it's a blunder. He's on a hook but he doesn't know who put him there. God, I'll make him squirm.

The kettle lid began jumping. Foggart rubbed his hands. After all it was going to be his lucky day. He got up and scooped some tea into the pot.

A bee buzzed up from a rose into Shirley Lister's face. She warded it off with her gloved hand. She had come out by the kitchen door so that Mrs Ball who was vigorously polishing the French windows wouldn't see she had been crying. She took the basket of dead flowers to the brick compost area Derek had built himself, on a large scale of course. It was hotter than ever in this corner. Shirley watched the petals drift onto the compost, yellow, peach, crimson, their edges faded, whitish grey. She thought, I pay my hairdresser to stop that happening to me. Why bother? She stepped back into the washed kitchen in no mood for gardening or anything else since phoning Derek. That clumsy, unplanned conversation had upset her day.

She recalled the annual cricket match. Hugh's assistant, the one with the beard, had planted a carrycot on the grass with a new baby in and there were two tiny girls in frilly white frocks. Hazel Wade had whispered to Shirley, "Three children under three. She's worn out." Hugh Cole had joked, "A baby a year for our Gordon – the bearded patriarch." There were the Pembleton children too, a gangling girl who rushed up shouting, "Daddy's taken another wicket," and a chubby shy boy. Paul was easy with them, affectionate. How would Derek be? They are a little alike, quick thinkers, efficient at their jobs, sportsmen. But there's a sensitivity and a flamboyance about Paul which Derek hasn't got. Derek said he wanted a son. He'd help him with homework, teach him cricket and golf, but would he, after a day like this? Could he be bothered to try?

It was at the cricket match that Eleanor Pembleton had told her and

Hazel that she was expecting again. She sounded rueful because John would be starting school and she could have been free to go back to teaching. Hazel Wade had laughed. "They can't help coming, poor little mites." And they'd all looked at the Harris children, howling and wetting themselves and getting grubbier every minute. Eleanor had been quick to say they were really thrilled. For heaven's sake, Shirley thought, she needn't have been ashamed. Who wants broken nights and sick and smells . . .?

She went to the telephone. It was a day for being impetuous.

Eleanor Pembleton said, "Shirley? . . . Next Friday? Yes, if we can get a baby-sitter . . . Thank you." And then "Coffee? Today? Now? I have to meet John at twelve."

Shirley said, "It's only ten-fifteen. I'll drive over and pick you up and take you back. Just ten minutes by the ring road. We'll have it in the garden. There must be more breeze here than in Newmont. We're so high up."

"It's certainly hot here," Eleanor said.

Shirley was on the road in her Mini two minutes later. She loved driving but somehow the pleasure she had hoped from the car had not matched her expectations.

Passing the wine shop on Westhill Road, where Derek stocked up their cocktail cabinet, she saw a big-boned woman in a flowery dress come out. Hazel Wade. She didn't have to stop but Hazel was a mother and grandmother – experience if not brains.

It took Hazel a few moments to realise that this cool, well-groomed lady was stopping for her. Then she couldn't believe it was only morning coffee time. So long a day. She explained how she'd been up all night and why.

Well, thought Shirley, an institution like Harry Wade going at last! I don't think Derek will be sorry, candidly. Hazel, hot and exhausted, got into the car. She seemed anxious to explain the wine shop.

"A bottle of sherry to celebrate. I'm going to do him a slap-up meal tonight."

Shirley found it hard to recall that when she had first met Eleanor Pembleton she had mentally classed her with Hazel Wade. That was because Eleanor had such a shy breathless way with strangers. But she had improved vastly on acquaintance. She had wit, even, and was certainly intelligent. Shirley believed a university degree showed through in the long run but

Derek pooh-poohed that. Nowadays he didn't demand much from his acquaintances, men or women. He only wanted them to listen and not argue. It amazed Shirley sometimes the level of conversation he was satisfied with at the golf club.

Eleanor was at her gate, ready. The garden was shabby, Shirley noticed, the grass worn under the swing, a broken scooter under a flopping peony. The hedge wanted trimming too. She wondered, is Paul, after a busy day, too happy playing with the children to bother?

Back at Westhill they sat on garden chairs with the sun umbrella up. Hazel, hot and damp, was happy to be in the shade and Shirley always protected her complexion. But Eleanor, to whom Shirley had given the reclining chair, lay huge and complacent with the full rays beating on her and her smooth skin not even pink on the cheekbones.

The way she was lying you could even see the baby move sometimes which made Shirley feel odd. Eleanor just murmured, "Keep still down there" in a detached easy manner which was very reminiscent of Paul. I don't remember her being as relaxed as this before, Shirley thought. Is it the age-old superiority of the fertile over the barren?

Eleanor half closed her eyes, her hands limp on the canvas chair. She floated above the wide valley. Today is a series of pictures, she thought. John's eyes huge and round as I left him. Hazel's face creasing with tears as we spoke on the phone, as plain as if I could see her. The milk bottles warm on the step. The house, like a stranger's without the children. Shirley phoning. The manicured hand holding the receiver. The tinted hair, the peach velvet profile. Jump, says the voice, and we lesser mortals jump.

Shirley started chatting in the most natural way about this friend of hers who might be adopting a baby. "She's older than I am. Must be early forties."

Liar, grinned Eleanor to herself. So that was the way of it.

"Of course Derek and I think they're mad. They've absolutely everything to lose."

"Well, I just live to see my babies," Hazel said. She meant her grandchildren. "When we're in Morlton I shall have them to stay. Let the parents go off."

Shirley laughed. "I think my friends will be wishing they'd thought twice – when it starts crawling and toddling. They've expensive furniture, beautiful carpets –"

"Perhaps they're tired of looking at them," Eleanor said to the sky. "It can cloy, things being immaculate all the time."

Shirley stood up and began offering second cups of coffee. Eleanor was contrite. She'd never imagined the Listers might want children but she shouldn't have pre-judged.

"Yes, I'll have another cup," Hazel was saying. "I never thought I wanted coffee in this heat but I don't know – however do you get it like this?"

Shirley handed round the cups. "We grind our own beans. I make it strong to get that tang and then it's fresh cream you know." She smiled sweetly at Eleanor as she put her cup on the garden table beside her. "So you think my friends should go ahead?"

"Well." Eleanor had to say it. "What have they got to live for if they don't?"

Lena Carr had been out to the market early. Her fingers were itching for the paintbrush but it was better to get the ham and some salad for Neville's lunch and then she wouldn't have to stop again. Bourgeois training, she giggled. Duty first. Besides it was better to be moving about, busy, while the painting was forming in her mind.

By the time she got back to Bosworth Crescent she was ready. An hour later the parcel of ham lay among the breakfast things but her canvas was covered. She had painted like one possessed. It was a moment pinpointed in her mind from the evening that the Pembletons were at the flat. Paul had been sitting in one of their two yellow and black armchairs. Neville had been talking of changing the world. Paul had been leaning back, smoking, saying nothing. Neville's monologue had dried up and Paul chose that moment to turn and stub out his cigarette. He was looking at her and she tried to share a sneer for Neville, but his eyes were remote. At the time she had thought, he's looking at himself, not me. And she had stared back, riveting his expression on her mind. Me? I don't think he ever knew I was in the room.

Painting him would be like lifting the lid of a smouldering furnace. It might die away or be fanned into white heat. Either way, she thought, it doesn't matter.

As she worked it wasn't only the face she strove at, but the violent black and yellow design which was how she had conceived the painting. The figure was held in the angle of the chair and his dark sleeve cut diagonally across the yellow chair arm. In the foreground his enlarged hand pointed a cigarette at the centre of the yellow ashtray, a small circle within the larger circle of the black-topped coffee table. The two circles leapt at you from the bottom of the painting. Above them sat the reversed L of the chair, and then in a nothingness of thick brown and grey brushstrokes the long oval of the head.

She stood back from the picture. The balance of tone was good. But the face? "I'm sure I've got the eyes." The straight stare which you couldn't avoid from any angle. But the rest of it went to pieces. The mouth and jaw were only roughed in but she knew how quickly one line could make or mar a likeness. If only she had a photograph . . .

She flung the lettuce into the sink and began to cut the cucumber, her head turned to the painting. Her art master used to say, "Jump in – both feet. There comes a moment when you must commit yourself."

She knew the expression she wanted to catch. The likeness must take its chance. She threw down the knife and snatched up her brush.

For a minute she stood still in front of the picture holding her breath. She wanted aloofness but so you couldn't tell whether it came from arrogance or indifference. It must be as enigmatic as the Mona Lisa but dynamic, not serene.

She approached the tip of the brush to the mouth. No, first she must strengthen the chin to give power. She deepened the shadow below the face and highlighted the point of the jaw. Good. She had confidence to try the mouth. She drew close again, seeing all the time how it must be. He was so devastating this man that as she put her brush to the lips again her hand trembled. She withdrew it angrily, flinging the brush on the floor. But when she looked at the canvas she was riveted. It was there, the look. And possibly the likeness. She laid down her palate. It wasn't finished but she dare not touch it again.

She went to the sink and shredded the lettuce. She was frightened rather than elated. Perhaps a bio-chemist would feel this way if he created life by accident.

When she did look round she was prepared to find the expression gone, but it was more overwhelming than she had thought. That there should be such a man crystallised her girlhood longings. Of course there hadn't been and she had married Neville soon after they met at University. Funny, she thought, turning from the picture to rip open the ham packet, I still live with him. I'm making him a meal. Bourgeois training again I suppose.

Neville had given her what she had needed then. "Your hair is beautiful," he would say. "That shirt is terrific on you. Your paintings are marvellous." At home everything she did was scrutinised and criticised. Early on too he had used what struck her as a most apt image for her parents. He hadn't met them then but she had railed against them. He said, "They've been over-zealous gardeners, turned the soil, added fertilizers, fenced you round, over-watered. And your father was the brutal amateur, tearing up weeds tangled with the plant, ripping off shoots if they didn't grow as he wanted." She thought him incredibly perceptive and a wonderful talker. For his own puritan reasons he wouldn't get into bed with her until they were married.

She shook dressing lavishly over the lettuce. Being happy with him had lasted about a year. They went to their different courses and met in the University Union for endless coffees and talk. They went on marches and demonstrations, he out of his idealism, she as a rebel, but they didn't bring their differences to the surface then, not enough to clash. Even over personal morality she didn't openly disagree. Generally he talked in abstract nouns like purity or the sin of compromise and his earnestness was fresh and convincing.

When the lunch was ready Lena looked wildly round the room, everywhere but at the painting. It unnerved her to know this man was in the room with her. The idea of him had come back after she got her first job. That was when Neville grew stale on her. He was still a student and she was independent for the first time in her life so all he said and did she stigmatised as undergraduate. His interest in her male colleagues took on the carping intensity of her mother's prying. She sought a man to admire from afar, cynical, sophisticated, self-assured, who would want no part in her or her life. All she found were older men desperate to tell the young designer that their wives didn't understand them.

Neville, taking diplomas in planning and landscape architecture, seemed set on staying a student but she was amazed when his tutor put him forward for a post-graduate Fellowship in the States. *Her husband* one of their best students! Was there more to him than she had thought? Then came the blow that a recent cut-back precluded wives going too. They had a great scene over this, with no reason on her side and when he applied for a job in this northern county she said baldly she wouldn't go. "Midcaster? Where the hell is that? I'll die of provincialism." The interview was on a Monday. Neville said he would go on the Friday and look for places to live. She was suddenly afraid he was more interested in the job than her threat to leave him. At the last minute she said, "I'll come." While he was in County Hall she discovered the Old Town.

She leant her elbows on the window-sill now and looked out at it. The Crescent had its late summer look. Hot and dusty. When she'd seen it that day it was cold and sodden. She'd stumbled upon it from the market, which had been as earthy and vigorous as a London market and the unfamiliar accents had given it an exotic flavour. She had seen down a canyon of warehouses a glimpse of mature trees. Bosworth Crescent's private garden. That day there was snow on the branches and there it was – a little Christmas card scene in a waste of blank walls. Close up it was grimy and shabby but she had told herself, this is where we're going to live. She had rushed back to fetch Neville to look at it. He was excited at getting the job and wanted to tell her about the interview.

"Of course you got it," she said. "They don't get American Fellowship winners dropping into their laps every day. Come on. It's the only street left standing in a desert of commerce. Pure Dickens."

"The County Planning Officer wondered why I wasn't looking for something on the design side." She was rushing him through the market. "I said I'd been in academia a long time. Wanted to be in the front line. He liked that. Then I was introduced to the chap who'll be my boss, Pembleton. Seems intelligent. Good heavens yes, early Victorian."

They had laughed then about this Pembleton being early Victorian and had walked through the Crescent and its garden hand in hand like the old days.

Pembleton, yes. It wasn't meeting him that spoilt things. It was *not* meeting him again after those two evenings, wondering if he was the man of her imagination, hating his dull wife and kids, bewildered by Neville's fluctuating reports. "He knows how to delegate. Keeps everyone lively." Later, "He thinks he's God Almighty." "I can't tell what he believes. Maybe he's like everyone more than a decade out of university – drop ideals and take some tired old compromise off the shelf." She didn't trust herself to probe too much about him and recently Neville's talk about the office had nearly dried up.

She didn't take a job because she knew she should paint. She wouldn't have a baby because she was afraid of the sentimentality that fatherhood would induce in Neville. Weeks went by. She had desultory friendships with people in the other flats, mostly students but they soon lapsed from intimacy. Then Neville took her the disastrous trip to Scotland. They missed Hugh Cole's party and a fresh chance of seeing Pembleton.

She spent a lot of time at this window. There was a gap in the trees through which the Cathedral spire was visible and to the right of it a square of sky which was just above County Hall. Today she could also see the top of a crane on the quayside but it was too heat-hazy to see the built-up skyline of Barton beyond the river.

Why don't I go down there – to the river? We may not have another day like this till next year. She yanked off her smock and stepped out of her slacks. She chose the coolest thing in her wardrobe, a Tricel dress in ice-blue. The shoulders had only straps. Her mother would call it a slip. It emphasised to absurdity her beanpole figure. She brushed her hair till it glowed like gold silk and spread it round her shoulders in a curtain.

She faced the man in the picture. "Notice me, damn you." Then she threw a not too clean tea-towel over the lunch plates and went out.

Paul had had a bad head the day he had found out Neville's mistake. It was just such a hot day as this, in July. Lower Wooton was one more in a line of scorched villages. He drove through it at speed. He thought of home and lying on the lawn and Eleanor bringing out tea. He was clear of the houses before he reversed into a field opening and drove back. New stonework on an old house had caught his eye down Dagwash Lane. Studying it he could see it drawn out on a sheet of tracing paper in Neville's dashing style, a rush job but good.

He turned to drive back. Something still worried him. At the junction to the main road a van swung round the corner, missing him by a foot. That was it. There must be a road-improvement line. The row of cottages abutting directly onto the lane made the corner absolutely blind. They were dilapidated, only two still inhabited. Scrap them and the line of Dagwash Lane could be altered to join the road at a safe right-angle and with adequate site lines. But the eighteenth century house back there would be affected too. Before the additions it was probably substandard. Could have been acquired with the cottages. Now – ? Hell, surely Neville hadn't forgotten to consult the County Surveyor?

The office was folded in a hot solemn silence. He had gone straight to the Files Room. It was no good going home without knowing the answer. It took him five minutes to find the file. Before he saw the words Lower Wooton he was far away, looking at this moment from his student days. The unimportance of such things was then so patent. He had seen his father, who was an accountant, frantically irritable for a whole weekend over some figures that 'hadn't come out.' He had told Eleanor – he was almost engaged to her then – how this had appalled him. She was teaching in the tough co-educational grammar school where his sister was Head of English. She laughed, throwing back her head the way he loved. "You'll learn."

When he had found the file he flipped over the pages till he saw the County Surveyor's letter-head. A.W. were the initials in the reference space. Arnold Wallace. That made him look at the end of the letter first. Wallace wrote like that – the sting in the tail. There it was. 'The house will be affected by a proposed widening and resiting of Dagwash Lane and it would not therefore be advisable etc. etc.' Damn. If they had not consulted the County Surveyor it would have been bad enough, but to ask him and then ignore his answer! And the proof of it staring at you from the file. He read the letter from the beginning. The first two paragraphs rambled about the house and the nature of the improvements. Then it stated that as a new access was not involved there could be no objection in principle to the alterations. That must be as far as Neville had read. He still had the intellectual's contempt for bureaucracy. Let him keep it if he would just learn to indulge its little ways. He hadn't even glanced at the attached plan where bold red lines ran slap through his precious house. And he had confidently told Paul when he brought the recommendation for his signature that the required consultations had been done. Well, there was only a line on a map. No action might be taken for five years, ten, perhaps never. It would have been tempting to show Neville how his high-handed attitude to routine had led him into a piece of carelessness that the office boy ought to blush for. But Neville *would* blush and would want to dash upstairs and lay the thing at Wallace's feet. So he had put the file back in its place, closed the cabinet and shut the File Room door.

Now he said to Neville, "Get me the file on a Mr Hubertson's house in Lower Wooton. You handled it in April."

He had not been gone long when the phone rang again. Miriam's voice breathed at Paul's ear, "From London. It's a field officer of the National Parks Commission."

"Well done, Miriam. Next time get his name too."

The man gave his name and Paul listened to his problem.

"Oh yes" – he recalled the circumstances and told him, "The Electricity Board is sending in an amended plan for the KV line. I'll let you have it as soon as I get it." The man began to talk about forestry.

When he could put the phone down he needed Neville to come at once with the Lower Wooton file. He must see Lister before Wallace's letter got into the wrong hands. He checked his watch and glanced round the office. Heads turned as if expecting the phone again. They knew he'd had a hell of a morning. In the heyday of the Pembleton Myth days like this could be light-hearted. Once he had clapped his hands and commanded, "Now the phone!" and instantly it had rung. There had been a general laugh.

Neville appeared with the file.

"Sit down and look at that, will you?" Paul wanted this over and done with.

Neville gave it the merest glance. "This is old stuff. He built his extension as soon as he got permission." He hesitated. "Have you seen the finished building? Looks good."

Paul drew in his breath. His right hand went for his cigarette but he kept it in his pocket, clutched over the packet top. Neville was looking at him, puzzled.

"Just read the County Surveyor's letter – if it's not too much trouble." Hell, why does he make me talk like a sarcastic schoolmaster?

Neville pursed his lips, shrugged and flipped through till he came to the County Surveyor's letter. He didn't read it, but looked at the attached plan first. He'd learnt that much by now, had he?

"Oh," he said. "Damn." His face flamed to the roots of his hair.

"Looks as if you didn't read the right bit of the letter when you got it."

Neville jerked up his head. The easy tone seemed to astound him.

"But this is serious. I can't think how —"

Paul thought, he's not going to let me play it down. Gerry Toms would have said, "Hang it, Paul, I'm sorry. What can we do?" Then the air would be cleared for action.

"'How' is unimportant now. They're doing the road improvement next year."

"Next year! Why?"

"Just take it they are."

Neville said, "So the Council will want to acquire the house by compulsory purchase and of course the cost will have rocketed since the improvements."

"As you say, rocketed. So the Council will *not* want to buy, even if the owner were willing to sell, which he isn't."

Neville was looking at the file. "This letter," he said. "It's a pity nobody ever taught Wallace to write." Paul made an exasperated noise. "I mean, if he'd put it clearly in the opening sentence —"

"And the plan? Its message is just as unfathomable?"

"No. The plan. I suppose I can't have looked at the plan. I don't know how —"

"No and nor will anybody else. If that's all you're pondering on —" He reached a roll of tracing paper from the shelf to his right, tore off a piece and placed it over the plan. "I want to find a way round this, literally and figuratively." He sketched in two lines. The rapid movements seemed to give an outlet to the tight ache in his head. "Look, if we swing the road over to here, and bring it out to the east of the present one, we can still straighten the bad bend, keep a right-angled junction to make the surveyors happy —"

"And miss Hubertson's house altogether!" Neville finished as if guessing the punchline to a story. "Well!" He sat back, put his hands up to his mat of hair and laughed. "Thank goodness for that."

Paul exploded. "Thank goodness for nothing." He slapped his hand on the plan. "You think that's just a line Wallace has drawn? Don't you see they must have surveyed it already? The District Valuer's started his negotiations. We can try to persuade the County Surveyor to alter it if possible and he might be able to convince the Roads and Bridges Committee that he wanted to allow Hubertson his extension as a praiseworthy bit of development —"

"Oh now wait a minute —"

"I beg your pardon?"

"I mean, you mustn't do that." Neville was blushing hotly again, flaunting his blushes, staring Paul in the eye. "I'm ready to go to Mr Bird now and admit my error."

My goodness, thought Paul, this is even worse than I imagined. Can I possibly laugh it away? "I hope you are, Neville, but we won't play martyrs for this. Mr Lister's friendly with his opposite number, Amberly. Between them they'll work something out."

Neville shook his head. "No, it's this hole and corner business. It's not right."

Paul felt a cold anger come over him like a wave. He kept quite still till it had subsided. Then he said softly, "Hole and corner? That's emotional language. In this game an incident is only as big as it's made out to be. If you take it to Bird it's got to be big."

"The big thing is not the incident. It's the ethics involved."

He's doing it deliberately, going in with both feet, wanting to be the only one with a moral sense. Paul answered quietly again. "Neville, don't come the boy-scout with me, please. I'm telling you how this will be handled. I know the people involved. You would create nothing but embarrassment, your way."

Unbelievably, Neville shook his head again. "The truth *is* embarrassing in a place like this. Honesty's somewhat at a premium."

"And you have a monopoly of it, have you?" Could he really be so obtuse as not to hear what he sounded like?

"I didn't say that." Perhaps he was a little shaken. "It's just — well, I can't help it." He straightened his back again and the gleam came into his eye. "I don't like intrigue."

It was the last straw. Paul's hand came down on the desk so hard that everyone in the main office looked up. He was aware of their faces like a galaxy of moons outside.

"And *I* don't like *inefficiency*."

They must have heard that, every one of them. Neville sat there, dumb.

If only the phone would ring, as it had for Derek Lister.

At last Paul murmured, "I don't want to discuss this any more at present. You'd better go back to the Agenda."

He kept his fingers pressed over his eyes until Neville was out of his office. He detested crude emotion. He had to meet Neville again as he would have to meet Derek.

The phone rang.

Miriam said, "It's a Mr Sim on the phone, from Pentham. He wants to know will you let him open a shop on the new housing estate. He says they have to get a bus –"

Paul couldn't help smiling. "All right. Hold your horses, Miriam –"

"What?"

"That's fine. You're doing very well. Only just leave the poor man something to say for himself, will you? It's his sixpence."

"Oh yes, well, do I put him through?" He'd probably confused the girl now.

When Mr Sim started talking Paul stole a glance into the main office. To his surprise Neville was speaking to Roger Weston. In his shoes most people would be glad to lie low. At least I can trust Roger's good sense but the draughtsmen have ears as long as – "Yes, Mr Sim, we can discuss possible sites –" He pushed the Lower Wooton file to one side in a hunt for his desk diary. The desk-top had become a shambles. "Can you come in on Monday, Mr Sim? Say eleven o'clock?" He made a note on the page.

Then quickly he picked up the internal phone and dialled the Deputy's number.

"Lister speaking."

"Paul here. Can I come in for a minute?"

"I'm up to the eyes. Is it important?"

"I think it will be."

"It'll have to be snappy."

"Thanks." That was all. Nothing detectable in Lister's voice but the normal frustration of a busy day. On the other hand meeting him face to face was a different matter.

Paul called Neville in again. "I'm going to Mr Lister now."

"About Lower Wooton? You want me to come?"

"Certainly not. Get on with the Agenda and don't discuss this with *anyone*."

This should have produced a murmured, "Oh no, Mr Pembleton," and a polite withdrawal but Neville stood his ground, his back to the glass door.

Paul stared at Neville and said nothing.

Neville said, "We're not in the army, are we?"

"What on earth –?"

"I mean, I don't have to accept orders. I happen to feel strongly about this."

Paul thought, Derek would tell Neville, "Get out and take your morals with you."

He said crisply, "Neville, this is my Section. There is a chain of responsibility. I take this to the Deputy because that is the level at which it can be handled. Wallace will ask Mr Amberly what to do. My *duty* is to inform Mr Lister. He's expecting me now."

"We get our story in before he hears it from anyone else." Neville hadn't moved from the door. This was indecent. It was too outrageous almost for anger. And then he added. "If I tell anyone it will be Mr Bird direct. I don't discuss things with *that* crowd."

"Right, Neville. Now get out of my way." The heat, the shortage of time, the two of them crowded in the little office, the absurd tension, had made Paul's head unbearable.

At last Neville seemed to register this. He tamely opened the door for him and said, "Well, I only wanted to take the blame for my own carelessness, Mr Pembleton."

Paul looked back at him. "That's the nearest you've come to an apology yet. A pity you didn't start with that. When I come back from Mr Lister when I Cottle electricity line and anything else in Wanwick area I can look at this afternoon. On my desk please."

Paul didn't look right or left as he left the room but he felt all their eyes following him. They'll make a new Pembleton Myth. A petty tyrant. The doors swung to behind him. Now for the Deputy and, please God, let's keep this encounter civilised.

"Mother won't do it again. She's better now."

Jane Hodge greeted Matthew with this at the field gate. He had grown from a tiny speck by the river to a little matchstick man climbing the stile from the bottom meadow into the sheep pasture. Now he stood before her, her own height, his face glistening.

He wiped his bare forearm across his brow. "I'm hungry for my dinner."

"It's not ready yet, I'm afraid."

"You've been stood here ten minutes watching me coming."

"Mother's been asking can they stop us building altogether."

He closed his eyes and the hand resting on the gate tightened.

She said, "No, please, I didn't want it to be like this when you came home."

"Why mention her then?"

"She's been downstairs for an hour talking. Peggy called. Then she came down."

"Is she still there?"

"I said I'd see if you were coming. I haven't been back in. It was good out here."

He looked into her face. "You feel like that too. Afraid to go into our own house."

She couldn't meet his eyes. She gazed down at the Old Mill and the chestnut trees shrouding the village. "Peggy said we ought to have more sense of humour."

"What did *she* come for?"

"Just out of friendship. I wish I could be more like Peggy."

"I wouldn't have married you if you had been."

She laughed then. "Yes, she might be a bit boisterous for you." He didn't need people around him at all. Yet he'd been drawn to her. It could only be because she was ill at ease with people too. She needed quiet, to contemplate changeless things about her, like the face of the moor, and a steady slow routine enfolding her life so that she could have rest from tension. In all this they were alike, except that she could get no satisfaction from animals, even felt jealous of Jess the sheepdog and Matthew's demonstrative love for her. Jess came bounding up now, having been nosing after rabbits in the sandy hillocks around the site for the new bungalow. She nuzzled against Matthew's leg.

"You wouldn't think she was a working dog," Jane said.

He fondled the silky ears. "She's entitled to her time off. If your mother pulled herself together she could help you with the cooking."

"The dinner!" she exclaimed, turning guiltily to the kitchen door.

They went inside. The basket chair in the corner was empty. Jane took potatoes from the pail and began to scrape them. "I shouldn't need help. I've done nothing yet."

"You used to have a routine." He kept looking at the basket chair. "Where d'you think she's gone?"

"I suppose up to her room."

"You said she was better. What did you mean?"

"I don't know. Livelier. Interested." The kitchen door was shut but she lowered her voice. "As if she wanted to have a say in things. I thought it was a healthier sign."

Matthew took a knife from the kitchen drawer and began to scrape potatoes too. "How can she have a say? In what? The bungalow?"

"Well yes. She listened on the stairs and heard Peggy talking. She asked me why *we* weren't going to Midcaster like Dr Andrews about his planning permission. She said my father always went to the top man. He was a proper businessman. Had contacts."

Matthew tossed a potato into the sink. "Odd your father left no money if he was such a good businessman."

"He was unlucky. The district was going down."

"He should have known when to clear out."

"Oh I know. She found fault with him then. Now she says he was so clever. Same with Dennis. He was thankful to get away from her into the army and she knew it. But after he was killed – oh he was the model son."

"Why *did* Dr Andrews go to Midcaster? Cranston said to wait and Pembleton or his assistant would come to us."

"Peggy said the doctor's case was different. He's buying land off the County Council or something. Mother didn't take that in. Said we ought to do something."

"Where is she? If she's up to one of her tricks!" He flung open the kitchen door. There was a click like the telephone receiver being replaced. "She's phoning!"

Jane followed him to the door and took the knife from his hand. "We've done enough potatoes."

Her mother came along the hall. "You had a wrong number. Is the phone sacred? Am I not supposed to be useful round here? Where's the dinner then?"

Matthew went to the back door. "Call me when it's ready. I'll be at the wall."

Again Jane followed him. "Don't. It's so pointed – the minute she comes in. Just stay and talk, kindly." She was drawn outside, pursuing him.

He said, "She was lying again. She'd been on the phone herself or we'd have heard it ring. When do we get wrong numbers here? It goes through Wanwick exchange. Would she dare phone the planning office?"

"In Midcaster?" They broke apart. Her mother had come to the kitchen door.

"What are you having with these potatoes, Jane? If you've meat to cook it'll be half way through the afternoon before we get fed."

"I'm opening a tin, Mother. It won't be ten minutes." She cast a pleading look at Matthew but he disappeared behind the barn.

Her mother said, "Tins! I didn't bring you up to live out of tins."

Jane took down two and opened them. "They're cheap. Mother, Matthew's sacrificing so much for you –" Her voice was a wire stretched to breaking point.

"Who asked him to sacrifice? I never asked for charity. Where can a widow go but to her only daughter? If Matthew's so hard up he'd better take my pension."

Jane put the chip pan on the stove and began to slice the potatoes. She was crying drily with choked sobs.

"Too much fat. It's not good for you. Chips on a hot day. Is that what you learnt from your mother-in-law at Beckbridge?"

"Mother, you must be living for the day when you have your own home. Do what you like. Eat what you like. No one'll wake you early."

"Oh ay, no one'll wake me at all. I could lie dying and no one'll come near me. You've your own friends. Your Peggy. You'd rather chat with her over a cup of tea than waste time on your mother. Don't cut them so small. They won't cook, they'll burn."

Jane said, "I hardly see Peggy once a fortnight." It had been the same with school friends. It was hard enough to make any but impossible to ask them home. Dennis did as he pleased and the more he went out the tighter grew her mother's grip on herself.

"What are you having for a vegetable?"

Jane took the pan off the stove and went to the door. "I'll cut a cabbage."

Her mother said, as she knew she would, "I'm sick of those cabbages. You've too much stuff ready at once. You should space the planting. Oh go and get it. And pick a bit of rhubarb. I don't mind that. I'll have a lie down till you call me." She got briskly out of the basket chair and went out shutting the door tightly behind her.

Jane listened for the slow plodding up the stairs. It didn't come. Then she heard a tinkle and her mother's voice, hurried and low. She made out the word Midcaster and thought, so we interrupted her before. That's it. Well, Matthew won't know. She'll just make herself a laughing stock. She won't move officialdom.

She cut a fat cabbage and walked back to the kitchen door, the heat pressing on her, slowing her steps.

Inside she ran the tap splashily over the cabbage. All the same she heard the click as the phone was replaced because her ears were straining for it. Could her mother have got through to Mr Pembleton himself? Somehow that would be too unbearably shaming.

The Deputy's square face hung in the gloom of the room like a lantern. These North-facing rooms always looked dim after the brightness of Control. Paul stood on the edge of the emerald rug wanting to clear the air after their last encounter. Their eyes met and both held the glance longer than normal. Simultaneously, they grinned. Nothing was said. They could start afresh. Paul began to speak but Lister cut quickly in, still smiling.

"Paul, if it's about Foggart's idea I've had enough. Bird called me in ten minutes ago to show me a diagram. Ron in the middle with the Central Area and the title Assistant County Planning Officer, Control. He's given him Harris. It's there in black and white."

"It's not to do with Foggart," Paul said. "Not directly anyway. But you're not going to like it."

"I'm not liking anything today."

Still standing Paul said, "We've dropped a real clanger in my Area, I'm afraid."

Lister looked up sharply. Then he let both hands flop onto the desk-top. He gave a long sigh. "Well, that's ruddy marvellous isn't it? I can see Ron Foggart rubbing his hands already. Honestly, that's all we needed. Well, sit down, man. What's the history?"

Paul opened the file but before he could say anything Lister banged his fist on the desk and exclaimed, "Damn it, Paul, you've run your Area for six years so that I knew it was the one Section in the office that went like clockwork. And now – when the whole set-up's in the balance – you have to slip up. I've been working on Bird but Foggart's got his claws in deep. Any sort of stink in Control could damn well clinch it."

His tone was angry but there was no venom in it. Paul thought, I suppose Derek began thinking in clichés about the same time he gave up reading and started golf.

He told him the story of Lower Wooton briefly and clearly.

Lister said, "Huh, I see why you wanted to get rid of young Carr. Weston would never have landed Harry in the cart like this. I always thought Carr was a clever chap."

"He is, in the sense that this is a very good design."

"Fat lot of use that's going to be now. He's only put more value on the house. Well, never mind. It might be worse. The thing is whether we can keep it from the old man." Lister leant forward and appeared to be mentally rolling up his sleeves. "We'll go straight over Wallace's head. If a letter comes in from him today I'll keep it out of circulation. Don't ring him back and if he rings you just stonewall like blazes. Whatever he suspects about how this happened doesn't matter a row of beans." He looked at his watch, a big one on a broad leather strap. "Getting on for twelve. I'll try and fix it to lunch with Amberly. Rule number one is we admit nothing." Unlikely as it had seemed at first, the Deputy was warming to the business. He'd always liked being asked a favour but occasionally he would demonstrate his power by withholding it. "In fact we can go further, carry the war into their camp."

Paul thought, it's funny, with Derek I'm the thinker. He's the man of action. But when I talk to a slow, stuttering man like Mason I'm in a different key altogether.

Lister said, "That's it. Begin with our own complaint and get them on the defensive." He was growing quite excited now.

"That would need some ingenuity."

"Not a bit of it. We were entitled to be told about this – suddenly bringing forward a trumpery little road improvement and putting it in next year's estimates when they're supposed to have enough work on trunk roads to last them till Kingdom Come. You know, if I word this right with Amberly it'll finish with Wallace getting the rap." He looked gleefully at Paul.

"Half a minute, Derek. They've got black and white on their side. We did ignore their letter. Amberly can't fail to see what happened." Perhaps it was unwise to undermine the Deputy's enthusiasm but luckily he caught at the word 'ignored' and positively clapped his hands.

"Ignored! That's it, Paul. Ignored. We're not obliged to follow their advice. We might make a mild apology for not informing them but here was a fine little house except it only had an earth closet and here was an obliging owner willing to accept our design as the best way to improve it. Why miss an opportunity like that for a potty little road line that might never happen? Especially when the line can be moved to miss the house –"

"I *think* it can be moved," Paul said, "and still be effective from the road safety point of view but it means cutting into the surrounding fields."

"We won't cross that bridge yet." No, Paul thought, but that may be where the trouble starts. He watched Lister squash out a cigarette with a brown thumb end as big as a spoon. "I'll get on the blower to Amberly and let you know how it goes. I hope they'll tell the D.V. they're abandoning the idea. In the end it's what's on paper that counts. You can't tell what Bird will look at. It's phrases like 'We apologise for the omission' that stand out a mile. Leave it to me, Paul. But take the file and draw up that alternative road line. Pop in after lunch."

"I'm sorry, I'm going out. Appointments at Wanwick and all places west. Will you still be here after five? I can call back but it may not be till half past."

Lister waved his hand at his full in-tray. "I'll be around. This morning's been nothing but talk, talk, talk."

Paul stood up. Looking down on Lister he saw how the Deputy's thick curly hair was thinning on the top.

He said, "Thanks for taking this on, Derek, especially today."

Lister grinned – his geniality seemed completely restored. "Have no illusions, old man. It's in my own interests to stop anything fouling up my other little plans."

Again the hint that he had a definite card up his sleeve. That he would allude to it now was reassuring but once out of the room Paul was disconcerted to find that the interview had left him with a bad taste in his mouth. Yet, as he'd told Neville, this was the way Lister would handle it if he handled it at all. Still there was no blinking the fact that Amberly was going to be told a lie – even if he didn't believe it for a moment, even if it was what he would have done himself. The Deputy County Surveyor was a tough little man and only admired toughness. All the same . . .

Paul remembered an argument he'd once had as a student – after the war, when he was no mere dreaming youth. His opponent had asserted that there was no such thing as truth, merely different interpretations of events. You made the one appropriate to the occasion. Paul had repudiated this with some heat. He'd gone on to declare that man's only raison d'etre lay in a continual effort to equate himself with the Absolute – truth, beauty, goodness. For Eleanor, from an Anglican Church background, that meant God. He had never been completely at one with her on that which was perhaps illogical.

Now he stood in the corridor shaking his head. He thought, I still believe what I said then but it doesn't belong here. This isn't a court of law. If it were I could tell a jury exactly what happened and why. The truth is there and always will be – even if I forget it. But just for the moment – in this context – it hasn't any relevance. Neville can't or won't face that. So which of us is being honest? And who cares anyway?

He went to the washroom and sluiced his face with cold water. His headache hadn't altogether gone but it had subsided. Just as Lister seemed restored after their talk so his own tension had eased. He felt sympathy towards Neville for all his clumsiness.

As he came out the office boy waylaid him with the mail. This made an excuse to avoid Neville's eye when he entered Control again. He dashed into his own office and began flipping through the letters. These had come in the day before and been through Admin. He made a few notes, intending to dump the lot on Neville when he left for Wanwick. But here was the lad himself – hesitating outside the glass partition. His choirboy's face was only tolerable when it was good-humoured. Anxiety made it ridiculous. What did his half-childish, half-cynical wife think of it? What was her name – Laura, Lorna? He nodded at Neville to come in and then the phone rang.

Miriam sounded worried but was half-laughing. "Oh Mr Pembleton, I don't know what this one's on about. She sounds awfully funny."

"I'm tickled to death."

"No, I really think she's mad."

"Aren't we all?"

"What –?"

"Oh put her through, girl, put her through."

There was a little click. "Hello?" Paul said. "Can I help you?"

"Are you the Town and Country Planning Man?" The words came in a husky intense whisper. "Double, double, toil and trouble" would have suited it better.

"I'm one of them. What can I do for you?"

"I heard them. They said a man called Pendington would come."

"My name is Pembleton."

"That's right. I can't talk long. She may be listening."

"Could you give me your name and address?"

"She's gone out to pick a cabbage. He came in for his dinner but it wasn't ready so he's gone out again. They don't talk much about the bungalow in front of me."

"Are you building a bungalow?" Neville had sat down to wait so Paul pushed the post over to him. It was unthinkable that anyone should be idle for a moment.

"It's a man called Cranston who's going to build it," the voice said.

"Ah Cranston." Paul shut his eyes and waited for the other name to leap to mind. It came, as it had when he'd been speaking to Wilfred Mason, the District Surveyor. "Are you by any chance Mrs Hodge of Old Mill Farm near Blattingford?"

The voice hissed in his ear, "Sh! She may be back in the kitchen. She's my daughter. Mrs Hodge is my daughter."

"The bungalow is for you to live in?" The situation was taking shape.

"You haven't to let them. Can you hear me? They're trying to put me out. He knows I'll not be able to climb that hill. It doesn't matter to you. You can say anything you like and they've got to do it, haven't they? Can you still hear me?"

Paul took a deep breath. "You must realise, Mrs —"

The voice snapped, "Never mind my name."

"You must realise, Madam, I have to view this as a planning matter, not a family matter. I've seen the application." It might be wise not to say he hoped to call later.

She broke in, "I don't want it down that hill. You can help if you choose."

There was a pause so Paul said, "Hello?"

"Sh! She *is* back in the kitchen but she's making enough noise — still, I'm supposed to be in bed. Just don't let them —!" There was a click and the phone went silent. Paul put down the receiver and raised his eyebrows at Neville with a smile. Neville had begun to ask something about Mr Lister but Paul wouldn't let him start on that.

"It looks as if I'll encounter this old lady this afternoon. I'll let you go if there has to be a follow up visit so you don't miss the fun."

"She sounded pretty desperate. The old are the worst, aren't they?"

This riled Paul when he wanted to keep things light. "What d'you mean by that?"

Neville opened his eyes wide. "Well, rigid ideas. Intense, eccentric. Easily upset."

Perhaps, Paul thought, he applies that to the office veterans, me included. He gave him one of his sweetest smiles — Eleanor called them his sweet-sinister smiles. "We still try." Neville remained unsmiling. "It's her life — this old lady. She's entitled to be *helped* to understand a decision affecting where she spends the rest of it. Don't you agree?"

Neville was now embarrassed by this persistence. "Of course, but as you said, it's a planning not a family matter. Luckily we're not personally involved." He laughed but his eyes were still dead. Paul thought, they only come alive when he's parading his own principles. I'm damned if he's interested in *people* at all.

Neville asked abruptly, as transparent as a child, "You saw Mr Lister?"

"He's contacting Amberly. That's all I can tell you."

"So you would say it's out of our hands?"

"*Action* is out of our hands. The error stays in this section whatever the outcome."

"That's what I wanted to be kept clear. I never asked for it to be hushed up."

Paul said, "You needn't worry, Neville. It's plain from the file whose mistake it was. It could end up very serious if it attracts press coverage, which it might, and then Mr Lister won't stay holding a hot potato. He'll throw it back where it belongs."

Paul was thinking of himself as Section Head but Neville said, "Oh I'm not one for false hopes. That was all I wanted to know." He got up, gathered the post together and added, "I take it you want me to go through these while you're out."

"Yes, I do. And I wanted Cottle Electricity Line and anything else pending in the Wanwick Area on my desk when I returned from Mr Lister."

"They're ready here." He suddenly sounded smooth and assured as if he'd made a decision. Paul felt uneasy. Does he plan to go to Bird the minute I'm out of the office?

The phone rang. Time was really pressing now. A farmer said he was putting up a hay barn and did he need planning permission? The country burr was so thick that the smell of heather and hay and animals wafted into the office. Paul took his briefcase off the floor by his chair. He indicated to Neville that he should hold up the files one by one as he put them in. At the same time he was trying to find out from the farmer where the farm was. When he'd grasped this he asked, "Will the barn be within eighty feet of the road or over five thousand square feet in area?"

Neville murmured, "Curry and Son. Gravel Extraction?"

Paul nodded and the file was slipped in. At this moment it was inconceivable that in about two hours' time he would be down by the River Wann looking at gravel banks.

The farmer said, "Nay, it's two fields off the road and only two thousand square feet. Does that make a difference?"

Paul made sure the Old Mill Farm file was already in his briefcase. When he'd dealt with this chap he would get up and go. "It means your barn is permitted development," he said into the phone.

Paul saw Hine and the other draughtsman, who followed him like a stumpy shadow, sidling out for their lunch. They weren't supposed to go together.

He might still manage a quick canteen lunch himself. He got up and tucked his briefcase under his arm. He glanced at his desk top to see all was in order. Lower Wooton was conspicuous on top. He put the file underneath and realised that Neville had seen this. He said, "I don't want that moved. I'll come for it tonight."

Neville said, "Very well," and opened the glass door for him.

Only Roger Weston was still in the office. Roger the dependable.

He was half way to the swing doors when the phone rang again.

"I'm damn well out."

Neville said, "It's the internal phone." Paul took two strides back to the glass cubicle. It was the sort of nightmare where you couldn't get away from one spot.

Lister's voice said, "Paul, I'm going up in a few minutes to lunch with Amberly. Have you spoken to young Carr since we talked?"

"I haven't mentioned what line —"

"No, good, well don't. I'll have to feel my way. Depends what Amberly knows and how far they've got with the D.V. Feel my way. That's all. See you this evening."

He rang off. Typical, Paul thought. He's leaving himself room to manoeuvre.

As he crossed the office again, Neville said, "Are you going to have lunch before you set off, Mr Pembleton?"

"I was hoping to. Why?"

"Your appointment at Nether Hopewood. The farmer says in his letter, 'Not later than one-thirty.' You have in your desk diary early afternoon which is not quite so precise."

Paul looked at his watch. "Damn. It's twenty to one now. Thanks Neville." He smiled at Roger Weston. "Perfect secretary eh?" As soon as he said it he knew Neville would take it as a piece of sarcasm.

When the swing doors squeaked and thumped behind him and he was alone in the corridor and no phone was ringing a tremendous weariness of people came over him.

He walked along to the washroom. I don't care what Neville thinks of me. I'm just tired of registering him at all. Thank God, I'm not meeting anyone else till I see the farmer at Nether Hopewood. Half an hour with the restful mechanics of driving.

He pushed open the washroom door and there were Cole and Foggart briskly washing in adjoining basins.

Ron Foggart had heard the Cathedral chimes clanging the quarter hour in the heavy heat as he pushed open the door to Admin. Quarter past twelve. He wanted Wallace's letter. If Pembleton had already got Lister's help on Lower Wooton the thing might escape him after all. He resented the camaraderie between those two.

. The first thing he saw was King's boy standing by Miss Smeed's desk and demanding, "Gi' us some more paper then."

"Miss Smeed!" Foggart almost shouted. The boy ducked back into his father's office, seizing some paper as he went.

Foggart stepped forward. "Miss Smeed, he must *not* hang about here."

Miss Smeed stood up, fingering her leaf brooch. "Oh I know, Mr Foggart." She looked upset. "*I* don't want to be ill. No one at home would look after *me.*"

He realised his irritation had startled the wrong person. He stepped to King's cubicle. "Take him away, man."

King fished in his pocket and handed the boy a threepenny piece. "Off you go then. That'll cover the bus fare."

The boy stood his ground. "I'll need something for grub. Mum's not expecting us. She said you'd take us out for fish an' chips."

Foggart understood that the 'us' was local dialect and didn't imply that there were more children secreted about County Hall. King found a florin. The boy grabbed it.

"That'll do, Dad."

Miss Smeed was still standing up. "Isn't Daddy taking you then?" Her colour was high. The boy hesitated, grinning.

Foggart felt impelled to back Miss Smeed.

"You can see him onto a bus at least." He knew King lived in one of Midcaster's pre-planning blots to the north of the city, tea-cosy shaped semis adjoining the trunk road.

King gave a sudden wink and the boy as suddenly vanished. He was out through the swing doors and round the corner to the lift which was there, gates carelessly left open. Foggart tut-tutted and went over to the window that looked onto the square. He saw the boy dash across and disappear down the steps to the quayside. Miss Smeed peeped beside him. Her face and neck were flaming with emotion.

"Oh Mr Foggart, he could be abducted. He wouldn't be missed for hours."

"It's not *your* fault, Miss Smeed." Foggart put a little warmth into his tone. "He seems spry enough." She still looked bothered so he pointed out jovially a young woman in a pale blue slip of a dress with long yellow hair who had come up the steps and was walking round the sailor on his plinth. He almost nudged Miss Smeed. "Look at her! Our parents would have said she'd gone out in her underwear."

This only made Miss Smeed blush more fiercely so he snapped back into his Chief Assistant role and demanded, "Anything come down from upstairs this morning?"

King, lounging in his chair behind his open glass door, was chuckling. "I told you, that kid's all there. Upstairs? County Surveyor? No, why? What's special?"

Foggart had to keep dark his prior knowledge about Lower Wooton. "There may be something urgent. See they're checked through at once, will you?"

King shrugged. "Trust old Jos for that. She doesn't think a letter's decently dressed without its distribution slip."

Foggart grunted, embarrassed that King might have overheard him at the window. He loathed King but he didn't want to leave Admin. till he'd got that letter. "What about the Quarterly Reports?" he snapped. "Get onto Wade for his when he gets back from Morlton. He should be here shortly."

"Ay, poor sod. He shouldn't claim expenses for a wild goose chase like that. But it's not worth mentioning QR's. Hasn't old Derek told you he's going to get them stopped? He said to forget about this month's too."

Foggart felt his throat tighten and his eyes blaze. "When was this?"

"Oh he rang through a few minutes ago. Said they're a waste of time. He thinks he can persuade Bird and the Chairman they should be quietly scrapped."

Foggart muttered to himself, "High-handed, overbearing –" and made for the door without another glance at Miss Smeed. He was heading for the Deputy's door but when he rounded the corner he saw Hugh Cole making for it too.

Cole waved some plans at him. "Plastics Factory. Not the postcard design of course. That was too good for this world. Sir said he wanted to see them."

Foggart could only growl. Cole grabbed his arm. "Do we have to show them to this top executive in the *Sinkhole*?" nodding at Foggart's room. "It doesn't seem decent."

"Unless your own room is fit to be seen."

"Oh well you can always make him a cup of tea, can't you?"

Foggart went into his room and slammed the door shut.

Hugh put his head round Lister's door and sang out, "Plastics Factory."

The Deputy, who was on the phone, glowered at him. "Did you say you *could* manage lunch? I had an interruption. Yes, a little matter we could clear up between us, Bob. If you *could* manage today . . ? Good. Give you a knock about ten to one? Right oh."

He put down the phone. Hugh put his hands together in a praying attitude. "Please sir, you wanted to see the Plastics Factory. The man's coming this afternoon."

"I didn't say you could come barging in here shouting at the top of your voice."

"Ah well, they always gave the Court Jester a lot of licence in the old days. Just think what this place'll be like after the end of next week." Lister reached across the desk and took the design. When he saw it he opened his eyes wide.

After a moment he said, "It beats me, Hugh, how you can do this sort of thing and yet enjoy fooling about with an ass like Pennyman."

Cole put his head on one side. "We geniuses need to play. Anyway, you like it?"

The Deputy pushed it back at him. "You don't need me to tell you it's good. What about the man who's supposed to be building it? How are you going to interest *him*?"

"Leave it to Ron. He grabbed the application when it came in. It's Harry's Area but Ron's arranged things with the firm. I haven't met the boss or whoever's coming."

Lister scratched his head. "You can't expect Ron to put this across. He may know it's better than what the firm submitted but he won't know *why*."

"I don't care. Honestly, Derek, as far as I'm concerned the thing's done with. Of course I'd like to say, 'Build that' and come back and see it up and working, but haggling over details – I've no use for it. Add anything to that or take anything away and it just isn't my work any more."

Lister shook his head. "You can't afford to be as high and mighty as all that – not in this job. Private practice, maybe, when you're famous." He nodded at the plans. "You could point out that a building like this will be a splendid advertisement for the firm."

"Oh yes, building of the year and all that. But Ron pretends I'm just his stooge. He'll say we've *slightly* amended their original design. It's his idea of good psychology."

Lister was musing. "Hugh, you really don't know *who* is coming from the firm?"

"Not a clue."

"Well, I think this needs the full VIP treatment. The old man might be peeved he wasn't involved. It's going to be the first big industrial development on the site. Bird had his teeth in that area first, you know, rebirth of industry in the County, and the motorway – when we get it – the life-giving artery. You were going to show it in the *Sinkhole*? To some executive used to six-inch pile carpets and potted plants!"

"That's what I said to Ron. But we're a poor county and the Sinkhole might touch the man's heart. If he's philanthropist enough to bring us all his lovely rateable value –"

"Oh shut up a minute. No, we must have this in the old man's sanctum. He'll have to wriggle out of any appointments he's got. What time is the meeting?"

"Three o'clock. Do we cut out friend Ron altogether then?"

"We can't. He's done the bread-and-butter stuff. He'll have to be at the party."

"If you're there too won't we be a bit over-weighted with top brass?"

"No, I'll get some of my own work done. I'll be glad to have the old man tied up for a bit. I'll just sow the seed and ring you back if Bird bites."

"You're really mixing them now, Derek. You must watch it. Will *you* tell Ron?"

"No, *you* can. I've *heard* enough about him today without having to *talk* to him."

"Is he still heading for Chief A.P.O?"

Lister growled, "Over my dead body."

"Oh," said Hugh, "well, he won't mind that, will he?"

At the door he said, "I wanted to show this design to Paul but I'm frightened to go near him today he's so busy."

"You weren't frightened to come to me."

Lister was already making notes on a file, his thick fingers clutching a ball-point pen and writing very fast.

The sight depressed Hugh. "You all do it, you front men. Two or three things at once. Thank goodness I'll soon be in the tropics – not even expected to do *one* thing at a time . . ." He talked himself out of the door as the Deputy went on writing.

Five minutes after Foggart had left Admin. the office girl from the Surveyor's Department came in with a tray of papers. She was a pretty girl, Miss Smeed thought, but her face peering through a curtain of hair was sallow. She looked towards Mr King's office. He was standing at his window which gave obliquely onto the square.

Miss Smeed said, "Just give those to me, dear. Is it nearly your lunch break? Why don't you have a walk in the sun? Get some roses in your cheeks."

The girl giggled. "I can't. I just don't tan. Ask any of the girls."

When she'd gone Mr King opened his door and called, "Jos, was that Beryl in here just now, the kid from upstairs?"

"I believe she's called Beryl."

"You'd better clear the stuff before lunch. Foggart was waiting for something."

"Very well, Mr King. I'll see to it."

"OK. I'll go to lunch then." He was staring out of the window again. "Funny, that blonde's walked round the sailor a dozen times. Keeps looking at this place."

Miss Smeed, attaching distribution slips, didn't glance up.

The typist nearest the window said, "Perhaps she's waiting for someone."

He grinned. "No one in *this* place could have a bird like that. She's got long legs on her, showing every scrap of thigh too. Damned skinny though, all bone."

The doors slid to behind him and Miss Smeed gave a snort of despair as several typists got up and went to the window.

"Cor, I see the one he means."

"Ee, me Dad would go raving if I went out like that."

Presently those who were going to lunch began powdering their noses.

Miss Smeed, hurrying through the routine replies to Consultations, came upon the letter about Lower Wooton. There was an attached slip: 'For the attention of Mr Foggart.' She thought she would please him by taking it straight to his room. And then a name in the first sentence caught her eye. Her pulse quickened a little and she began to read. 'With reference to the phone call this morning from my assistant, Mr Wallace, to your Area Planning Officer, Mr Pembleton' – the letter of course was ostensibly from Mr Dowland to Mr Bird. In practical terms it was from Mr Wallace to Mr Pembleton. Why then for the attention of Mr Foggart? Mr Wallace and Mr Foggart were old friends. The letter was obscure. Mr Wallace was good at obscurity, but if the facts were muffled the note of complaint wasn't. Mr Wallace was getting at Mr Pembleton and his attached slip suggested he wanted the thing to have maximum publicity. And if Mr Foggart knew the letter was coming it began to look like a conspiracy. Miss Smeed felt her colour heighten. This was excitement, an adventure. She set herself to read the letter calmly.

The most sinister reference was to the District Valuer. He was unable to pursue negotiations about a proposed road improvement line because a certain Mr Hubertson in Lower Wooton would not agree to sell his house and land. The last paragraph revealed that the County Surveyor had recommended on April 29th that planning permission be refused for extensions to Hubertson's house. The home thrust as usual with Wallace was in the last sentence. '*The observations of the County Planning Officer are requested as it appears that planning permission was granted and the work in question carried out.*'

Miss Smeed sat back with a quiver of glee. Mr Pembleton, the great, the infallible, her hero, had made — was it possible — a blunder? Of course he might have had a good reason for not accepting the County Surveyor's recommendation, but certainly something he had done or not done had produced this furore with the District Valuer. Miss Smeed had worked for the Council for too long not to know that where money was involved awkward questions would be asked and if private citizens were at odds with the Planners too the Press would leap in. The thought of Mr Pembleton in trouble, persecuted, vilified, captured her imagination. She would smooth the path, offer comfort, revile the revilers.

The Cathedral chimes at twelve-thirty clanged into her brain just as a score of memories from the past two months came jangling in and coalesced together to produce one clear note which said Mr Pembleton had been waiting for this to break. Then came another recollection. Hubertson. Lower Wooton. Names and places stayed in her mind. Lower Wooton was so tiny that it had figured only once in all Mr Pembleton's years as Area Planning Officer. And now it came to her quite positively that this was the first application he had given solely into the hands of young Mr Carr. This put a different face on the matter. To suffer for his own error was romantic, but to take the blame for a silly young man not fit to hold a candle to him —! Miss Smeed grew hot with indignation and her mind worked faster than ever. This would come out sooner or later, but not today, when he seemed hard pressed anyway. He knew the secret was out because Wallace had already phoned him. But other people needn't know. Could it be that Mr Foggart wanted to use this to further whatever little scheme he had in mind? She knew — who in the office didn't know now — that he was up to something. Mr Foggart had come in specially to inquire about this letter. He wanted something in black and white to show — Mr Bird?

She clasped her hands together. If that's his game, she thought, if discrediting Mr Pembleton is part of the plot, I shall put a spoke in it. I shall *scotch* it. She glanced round. Only three girls at the back of the room were left. They had to stay till the early diners were back.

Slips of paper, she said to herself, become detached. Pins come out. She pulled it out as she said it. Then she screwed up 'For the attention of Mr Foggart' as small as it would go and dropped the pellet of paper into the bottom of her tunic pocket. After she had attached an ordinary circulation slip and ticked the space opposite West Area Planning Officer she set off to see if she could catch Mr Pembleton before he went to lunch. It was the most thrilling thing she had ever done in the whole of her career.

3

THE LUNCH HOUR

Hugh Cole and Ron Foggart, unlikely pair, washing at adjoining basins. At once Paul's imagination was busy with them. They were gnomes in a pantomime. One merry, one glum. One fair, one dark. The good and evil genii of the place.

They both looked round. Hugh raised one arm in salute. Foggart turned quickly back and plunged his pinched face into his hands. He scrubbed it hard. Face and hands were so thin that Paul could imagine them grating together.

Strangely enough he had interrupted a conversation. Cole was saying, "Yes, Ron, old boy. It's all been moved up higher. Our mutual friend, Derek, has seen my gem, my masterpiece, and says it rates the red carpet no less. The Bird, he says, must, simply must be at home to welcome our gentleman into the Nest."

"How does he know Bird hasn't other appointments?" Foggart snapped. Paul heard all this while he was in the toilet.

Hugh answered in a muffled voice. Evidently his face was buried in the towel. "He does *not* know. If there are other appointments they shall be done away. You'd better go to the Nest and make sure there are enough vases of flowers and boxes of cigars."

Paul joined them and began to wash his hands.

Foggart said, "I'll see the Deputy first. He's very high and mighty with his arrangements today." This was unusually outspoken for Foggart, though referring to Lister by his title was typical enough. He was happier with the anonymity of rank. His notes came round '*The Chief Assistant Planning Officer wishes to draw attention to . . .*'

Hugh swivelling the roller towel round and round said, "Derek's lunching with Amberly upstairs. I heard him fixing it on the phone."

Paul thought, damn, never give gratuitous information to Foggart.

Hugh began imitating Lister's voice though he wasn't as good a mimic as Paul. "'Just a little matter you and I can clear up, Bob.' That's what he said."

Paul would have kicked Hugh but Foggart was between them, scrubbing at an ink mark on his hand. Hugh grinned over his head, saw Paul's frown and raised his eyebrows to the roots of his hair. He mouthed, "Non comprendo," his eyes dilated with mock fear.

Foggart straightened suddenly and reached for the towel. Hugh yielded it to him with a flourish and babbled on, "All the spicey business in Local Government happens amidst eating and drinking, don't you think? Especially among Deputies. When I grow up I'd like to be a Deputy. The Boss never hears the really interesting things."

Paul thought, Ron may not know about Lower Wooton yet but he'll damn soon get his nose to the ground if this goes on. He was about to say something, anything to stop Hugh when Foggart disengaged himself from the towel and faced him. Paul had never seen his eyes so alight with glee. The effect in the scraggy lined face was horrific.

He said, "That's right, isn't it, Paul?" The use of the Christian name was positively sinister. "The Boss is kept in the dark. Now I wonder whether Mr Bird has been informed of a certain little matter. What do you think, eh?"

He knows, damn it, he's known all along. Now he'll tell Bird. Why the hell can't Hugh keep his ruddy mouth shut? With an effort he produced the right note of bland detachment. "I'm not sure, Ron, what you're talking about. Isn't Bird too busy reorganising the office?"

For a second Foggart looked shaken. Then he grinned again. "Maybe the two matters might have a bearing on each other." He opened the door quickly and dashed out.

Hugh gave a shout of laughter. "Poor Ron! Can't exit a conversation gracefully."

"It's a pity you ever start most of yours."

Hugh's head jerked up but he went on laughing. "I knew you were sending stop signals," he spluttered. "I couldn't think why."

Paul could picture Foggart this very minute haranguing Bird on the need for supervision in Control. Hugh had even given him a legitimate excuse to go and see him about this afternoon's meeting. This wretched thing could just tip the scales.

"Well why the hell" – he found himself saying the very words he'd thought to himself – "why the hell couldn't you keep your ruddy mouth shut?"

Hugh's face went blank. Without a contortion of some sort his features were characterless. He had become a stranger. "Now just a minute, Paul —" His voice was stone-cold. Paul thought, I never knew he had a limit and *I* never talk like that to anyone.

"Damn it, I'm sorry, Hugh. It's Foggart. He knows something he wasn't meant to and you were shovelling him more ammunition. Hell, it's not important."

"*I* never thought it was. Is anything that goes on here as important as all that?" He was still angry. It was hard to say which of them was the more embarrassed by this.

Paul began to laugh. "As important as all what?"

Hugh said, "It happens to be the second time you've bawled at me this morning."

That was true and each time he'd been in earnest. He whirled the towel round to a clean place. He wanted Hugh to look him in the eye. He must laugh then.

"What d'you want me to do, Hugh? Crawl? Or send you a written apology?"

At last the ridiculous face crumpled. "Oh my God, I thought this place had finally done for you! Thank the Lord I'm clearing out while I've still got my insanity."

"Perhaps I'm too far gone."

"Stow it. In a couple of months you'll be starting a new life in London. Pembleton of the L.C.C. The swinging city."

Paul said, "There isn't anything new. You move to another place, another job. It's just a new wrapping for the same old article."

Hugh considered him, his head on one side. "I'll have a devil of a job putting you in my book."

Paul turned to the door. "What book?" Hugh could talk for hours in the washroom if anyone would listen. Perhaps it was the flowing of water that set him off.

"The book I'm going to write about this place as soon as I'm safely on the boat. All I've thought of so far is 'In the beginning was the Bird.'" Paul smiled. "Oh come on, Paul. It's good for a real laugh, that."

"Sorry, you'll have to find someone else. I'm so late now I'll not have time for lunch. I ought to see Derek and tell him the cat's out of the bag."

"But what did I *say*? I know neither a cat nor a bag to let it out of."

"Forget it. Don't worry about it."

Hugh grabbed his arm as he opened the door. "Did you hear what you said? Don't worry! To *me*!"

Paul patted his shoulder as if he were a pet dog. "Yes, yes, it's absurd. I just haven't time for the niceties of language today."

Cole bowed him out with much waving of arms. "Very well, Pembleton, if that's the way you want it. But don't come to me for a reference." He backed to his own room. He was laughing but looking at Paul all the time with raised eyebrows.

Paul knocked at Lister's door. There was no answer.

"Oh Mr Pembleton, Mr Lister just went upstairs." It was Miss Smeed hurrying along the corridor with a paper in her hand.

Paul said "Thanks" and turned to the stairs.

"Oh Mr Pembleton, this is for you." She was trying to press the paper into his hand.

"Just put it on my desk. I'm going straight out."

He had mounted two steps but she insisted, very red in the face, "Mr Pembleton, I think you ought to take *this* one with you."

He gave her his quick smile and took the paper and slipped it into his briefcase. She must think it concerned a site visit he might make. She was thorough that way.

"You'll still catch Mr Lister," she said. "He only *just* went up."

He said, "Thanks" again and galloped up the stairs two at a time.

Round the corner on the next landing Lister was just raising his hand to push open the glass door marked County Surveyor's Department. He held up his hand in a stop signal when he saw Paul.

"Don't tell me. You've dropped another brick."

"It's Foggart. He knows about the Lower Wooton thing."

"Hell! How d'you know? If it's because he's closeted with the old man this minute I know about that. It's about a meeting with Cole this afternoon. I fixed that up."

"He's telling him about Lower Wooton too, I'm certain." He explained briefly.

"You're only guessing."

"I'm quite sure."

"Well, for crying out loud! Who told him?"

"He must have known before Wallace phoned me."

"You think he's at the back of it all?"

"No, the District Valuer must have sparked it off but I think Wallace told Foggart and Foggart saw he could make capital out of it today."

Lister spread out his hands. "We don't *know* he's told Bird."

"I saw the gleam in his eye."

Lister raised his eyebrows. It was a look from a down-to-earth practical man to one who was over-dramatising a minor setback.

"Let him tell Bird. It could backfire on him. I'll go on as we planned. I may have a solution ready for the old man by the time I've seen Amberly. It's not your headache now. Get out in the country and enjoy yourself. *I* wouldn't mind a spot of Wanwick air on a day like this. See you this evening." He pushed open the door and went inside.

Paul thought, I'm damned if I can stand Derek *and* Hugh raising their eyebrows at me. He darted to the lift. It was imperative now to get out of the building.

At least going down from here, the fourth floor, he could escape any further encounters in the Planning Department. Footsteps and piercing voices checked him as he was shutting the gates. Two typists clattered in. They looked at him and their giggles grew self-conscious. Behind them, flapping his large hands, came Arnold Wallace.

Paul said quickly to the girls, "Feeding time, I suppose?" He pressed the basement button for them and the ground floor one for himself.

"It's sultana pudding day," he said to them. "Watch those spare tyres."

They were as skinny as sticks on their high heels. They shrieked with mirth.

Wallace lifted his drooping face. "You haven't rung me back yet, Mr Pembleton."

"I'm not Mr Pembleton. I'm just a large hungry animal." He said this to the girls. "Anyway, you haven't put it in writing yet."

Wallace said, "A letter went down over half an hour ago. Wouldn't go straight to you though."

The lift had stopped at the ground floor. If that remark was meant to be sinister it failed, Paul decided. He doesn't know I'm past caring.

He slid back the gate and gave Wallace his sweetest smile. "I'll answer your letter when I get it, shall I?"

One of the girls said with a high bold laugh, "I thought you were hungry."

"I am. I'm going to have a packet of cigarettes in the car."

Their faces slid from sight. A gale of titters rose from the lift shaft.

Across the foyer was a rectangle of sunshine framed in the neo-classical portico. He made for it thankfully.

Lena Carr watched a Norwegian cargo vessel unloading timber at the quayside. The pile of planks rose steadily on the lorry. She sat on a bollard ignoring the grins of the dockers. When the first lorry drove away the next one took its place, long, flat and empty and the crane lowered the first planks into it. It pleased her. She would have loved sturdy wooden toys like that as a child. She had had dolls and bead sets and a sewing kit.

The sun was burning her shoulders. She looked in her bag, a box-shaped thing in a mock basket weave. She hated it because she had now seen dozens of typists with the same kind. She found a tube of sun lotion and sat rubbing it into her shoulders and arms.

A boy, flat-faced and snub-nosed, who had come jumping down the steps from the Square, stood a few yards off and watched her.

"Do your legs too. You're showing plenty." He grinned, then ran off past the lorry and the warehouses to disappear among the stalls of the quayside market further up river.

Lena laughed. She walked up the steps to the Square. County Hall had been cleaned during the summer. The classical façade, black and grim she remembered, was now pale sandstone, glowing like a fairy building in the sunshine. She gazed at it, surprised and pleased.

He was in there unless he'd already left for Wanwick. She could walk boldly up to the third floor and say she was calling for Neville. But she wouldn't. She walked round the parapet above the quayside and then round the sailor's plinth, resting a hand on his stone thigh, looking up at the pointing arm, its sleeve spotted with seagull droppings.

She went to the corner of the Square where she could watch the portico of County Hall. A few girls came out with buns in paper bags and draped themselves along the parapet like flowers in their summer dresses. As if they'd been waiting for this moment seagulls from the roofs of warehouses and the tops of masts came wheeling over, crying and chuckling. The girls giggled and tossed up crumbs, exulting in the open air, the hour of freedom. Lena was astounded to feel tears rising. She thought, I've been an idiot. A job is what I must have, be someone in a group, enjoy the breaks.

She drew her eyes from the girls and looked at the portico again. Neville should be coming out soon. If I miss him he'll go home and think I've left him. The painting's against the living room wall. Will he recognise the likeness? How like in any event is it to the real Pembleton? How like is the real Pembleton to the man of my imagination?

She started. A man had appeared from under the portico, walking with long swift steps. He put up one hand to his eyes as he emerged into the sunshine from the dark interior. In the other hand he swung a briefcase. She walked without conscious thought down the side of the Square to intercept him before the steps to the car park. She could be almost upon him without him noticing. She studied him from top to toe. The blood quickened in her at the way his hair grew from his temples to the nape of his neck just as she'd remembered it. He was dressed elegantly for a day in the country. Light tweed jacket, mole-brown cavalry twill trousers, dark brown suede shoes.

Now he glanced round, hearing her quick step.

"Hello Paul."

He stood still, arrested in his hasty progress, his mind pulled back from far away. Now he was full face to her. Yes, that level, concentrated gaze. And the eyes were much more grey than blue. She'd got that wrong. The face was a long oval — that was right, the jaw strong but not square, the mouth firm, almost severe in the half-second when he was registering her voice and her sudden appearance in his working life. The lower lip was a little fuller and the smile at the corner of the eyes more humorous. In the fraction of time it took him to adjust to her presence, smile and say, "Well, hello," the man in her painting vanished. The sardonic man, aloof, challenging. Here was a friendly colleague of her husband saying what anyone might say, "I suppose you're waiting for Neville?"

"Yes, it was so sunny. I thought it might be nice by the river. Cooler."

He laughed. "It's not cooler, is it? It feels like an oven here."

"I sat right by the water watching the ships. You do feel a breeze there."

He said, "Well Neville shouldn't be long. You could go up."

"What I really came down for was to put an advert in the paper. I want a job. Aren't the newspaper offices somewhere round here?"

"Yes. The other side of the County Hotel. Down the steps into Rivergate."

"Thanks. I'll come back this afternoon. I've all the time in the world to kill." She put venom into this remark and was gratified to see him surprised.

"Sounds as if getting a job is a good idea."

"Well of course. I don't know a single soul in this God-forsaken place."

A plump man, bright red and perspiring, bobbed up the Rivergate steps. "Paul, Paul, hello there!" And as he reached the top, "Well, it's Lena! Hello to you too."

"Harry!" Paul said with warmth. And to Lena, "So here's someone you know."

"Oh yes." She gave Harry Wade a lop-sided smile.

"The train was late," he said, mopping his brow. "You're going out, Paul?"

"Yes and *I'm* late. Walk round to the car park with me."

Lena knew she had to let them go but to her chagrin she saw Paul look at her with pity. "Go and see Eleanor. She's not going far these days. She'd be glad to see you."

Harry said, "You and Neville must come to us again. Before we leave."

"Well, thanks." She turned away as they hurried off down the steps. She wandered back to a seat to wait. Neville at least was someone to whom she belonged.

Paul said, "Did I hear you right? Did you say, 'Before we leave'?"

Harry was bursting with glee at his surprise. "Yes, I got it. I got the job. What d'you think of that? There were six on the shortlist."

"Harry, that's splendid." So Lister had guessed right about Hazel's pantomime.

"Me a Deputy!" Harry was almost dancing, every now and then running to keep up with Paul. "Mind, number two in a County Borough. No big shot."

"Nonsense. It's Deputies who run things."

Wade's exuberance faded. "Not there, Paul. Just as well perhaps. The T.P.O is the active sort." They had turned onto the asphalt of the car park. The heat rose at them making them gasp for breath. The sweat was running off Harry's cheeks. "I'd guess he wanted a yes-man. The others were your type, your age. Full of ideas. T.P.O must have thought, that's a meek and mild little chap, what's his name, Wade? I'll have him. Won't be any trouble. And I won't. But will I like it there? In a strange place? At my age?"

"Come off it. You're tickled pink."

They had now reached Paul's new estate car. He had his keys out but was gazing in exasperation at the exit. "Just look where that blessed Hugh has parked his vehicle!"

"I'll tell him." Wade leapt into his helpful self. "I'll tell him when I go upstairs."

"He knew I was coming out. I was talking to him not five minutes ago."

Harry said again, "I'll tell him," but he made no move. He patted the bonnet of Paul's car as if they had all day. "I've been here since the office started. I've lived in Midcaster most of my life. Hazel doesn't want change either. I phoned her last night."

Paul shot him his most vivid smile. "Look, your kids have left home. You've been saying you need a smaller house. It's come at the best time for you." He unlocked the car and tossed his briefcase onto the back seat. He had to shut Harry up but he couldn't bear to hurt his feelings.

Luckily the unexpected happened. The slight, mop-headed figure of Hugh himself came leaping like a monkey down the steps from the Square, waving his arms at them.

"Here he is," Harry said. "So you think it's come at the best time for me?"

"Oh yes. You'll hear how Foggart's plans are ripening. And I'm in the doghouse over a gaffe of Neville's. If I get the London job I'll be damned pleased, I can tell you."

Wade's face creased in distress but Hugh thumped him suddenly on the back.

"Do I congratulate you, O Harry Boy, on leaving or staying?"

Harry told him. Hugh crossed himself reverently and bowed low. He saw Harry's overnight bag on the ground beside him. He seized it and put it on his head like a coolie.

"Let me conduct you, O Deputy-Elect of Morlton. Where is your chauffeur?"

"Stow it," Paul said, "and shift that thing of yours. I'm hopelessly late."

Hugh put down the bag and pointed solemnly to his car. "That *Thing* I am about to sell for a small fortune. I'm going to lunch with the future owner at his golf club. He's that rare bird, a wealthy student who comes slumming to Brynbank sometimes. I'll take him a mad run round the country and be back for a horrible Foggart meeting at three."

Harry listened in his intent way. "Oh dear, Hugh, you won't like bussing to the office next week."

"*Bussing*? What's that? No, if my student Croesus will buy the M.G. he must wait for it till I sail – if I don't put it in the river before then. Harry, I was as near drowning –"

Paul cut in, "Hugh, will you move your car at once and talk to Harry afterwards."

Hugh leapt to attention and saluted. "I've been in such trouble with this man today, Harry, you wouldn't believe –" He went to his car still talking.

Harry at once reverted to the unfinished conversation. "You *would* miss this place, Paul, wouldn't you? You and I and Derek, we believe in consistent policies –"

Paul said, "Now you can go and do the same for Morlton."

"But will it be different in a County Borough?"

Paul saw Hugh had turned his car and was waving him out as he drove off. He said heartily, "You'll stick to what you believe in, Harry. You always have."

He got into the driving seat. Wade leant on the bonnet lapping up reassurance. For Paul the morning was culminating in absurdity. Here he was in the baking car park, the rows of vehicles like sleeping animals and the streaming face of this sad, intense little man, pleading for faith in himself and his work. He started the engine.

Harry jumped back. "Sorry, old man. Yes, you're clear to go now." He brandished his arms like a clockwork policeman.

Paul saw him in his mirror, a spot of animation in the waste of dust and metal. He would go down like a pricked balloon till he could tell his news to someone else.

He crept slowly into the lunchtime traffic, a long way from Wanwick Moor.

Neville was tidying his desk top before going to lunch. Roger Weston glanced up.

"Pembleton was very sarcastic with you this morning. What's eating him lately?"

"He was no worse than usual."

"Come off it. He used to be a volatile character. Resilient. A morning like this one would be nothing. Throw it off with a laugh. Perhaps I'm thinking of before you came."

"What's that supposed to mean?"

"Maybe you two are incompatible. It happens. No reflection on anyone."

"Humph. He's too high-handed of course. Doesn't want to know other viewpoints. It's not civilised between educated adults."

Roger got up. "I'm starving. I was waiting to see Harry but his train must be late."

They walked through the swing doors together. Suddenly Roger laughed.

"Honestly, Neville, as a portrait of Pembleton that's pretty farcical."

"Oh? Well, *I've* had to work with him."

"I've known him longer. He's a most imaginative man – a great awareness of other people. Senses how they'll react. Likes to project an image too. Of course you haven't been here for an office party yet, have you?"

"Huh no. I've heard Pembleton's a good mimic. Sounds about office party level."

"Oh no, he's more than that. Used to go in for amateur dramatics. I know someone" – he hesitated – "who writes sketches for the local rag and does drama crits. Pembleton and his wife joined the Dramatic Society when they first came. He was Jack Tanner in *Man and Superman*. She said he made the rest of the cast look mediocre."

"Superman – he *would*." Then Neville said, "This journalist, does she know a big arty crowd? I wondered because my wife's a painter. She's a bit lonely in Midcaster."

"You should let her meet Hugh Cole's Brynbank set. You missed his party."

"Oh I don't mean those hippy types. I mean intelligent people genuinely interested in art. If I stay here I'd like her to make some friends."

"*If* you stay here —?"

"Yes, I won't — if I can get a better job."

"Hell, six months isn't long enough in your first post."

"I might not stay in Local Government," Neville threw out. "But this friend of yours. Could she introduce Lena around?"

Weston brushed it aside. "She's a freelance writer. Works on her own. Aren't creative people bound to be loners — a bit anti-social?"

They walked to the lift together. Voices were coming from Bird's office. Otherwise the Planning Department was stagnating in the lunchtime quiet.

Neville, sure that Roger had no understanding of art, persisted. "Creative artists must observe life and people. Their raw material. They need stimulus, activity."

When they reached the ground floor he expected Roger to stay in the lift, the canteen being in the basement. Instead he walked outside with him.

"I thought you were lunching here."

"I am. I want to make a phone call first."

"What's wrong with the switchboard?"

"Not for this one." Roger smiled mysteriously and turned right to Rivergate with giant strides.

Neville felt a small stirring of curiosity. Maybe this writer was Roger's girlfriend.

"Who's that great hulk?" Lena had appeared at his elbow.

"Oh! Where did you spring from?" He was quite trembling with surprise.

"Aren't I allowed to meet my husband?" Her voice had its usual edge but her presence and her words filled him with wonder. She tucked her arm into his. He had his jacket over one shoulder and he could feel her hot skin through his nylon shirt sleeve.

"You've caught the sun." Then he answered her query. "That's Roger Weston."

"Why does he wear his hair like that? It makes him even taller."

"To look intimidating on the rugby field perhaps. What made you come here?"

"Nice day. The quay, the river, the ships. I'll bring my easel tomorrow."

"Will you? That's good." He added, perversely to test her mood. "It would be ironical if you began to like Midcaster just when I'm sickening of it."

"Why? Don't you get on with Paul? He's friendly. I spoke to him just now."

"Friendly? You spoke to him?"

She just laughed and walked with her flowing stride to the car park steps. "Come on. I want to get on that bike." She loved riding pillion, but mostly fast, out in the country. He followed, frowning, and two minutes later they had left the car park with a roar of sound and a trail of fumes and were threading their way through the city to Bosworth Crescent.

On the way to the phone box Roger protested to himself that nothing Neville Carr had said could have influenced him. But he now saw Dorothy Bird's nightclub article in a new light. It was the *situation* she had used not *him*. Hell, she must have been sure of him to reckon he wouldn't feel hurt. A sense of humour was what they'd shared from the start of their acquaintance. He'd always been able to laugh with her, to enjoy her caustic articles . . . until that one . . .

He said into the phone, "Is that Mrs Bird? Is Dorothy in?" He had a premonition that if she wasn't he might not be able to do this again.

She said, "She's washing up the lunch things, Vicar. That *is* the Vicar, isn't it?"

His heart leapt. "Yes, it's the Vicar. Can I have a word with her?"

There was a pause, voices, a clatter of plates and Dorothy clearly saying, "Damn."

Then a heavy tread, a yard between the steps he remembered, and the receiver was picked up smartly. "Vicar, if it's the Christmas Fair, I'm not *thinking* about it yet."

Roger said, "Sorry to interrupt your washing up." He could hardly keep from laughing aloud at hearing her no-nonsense voice after the long weeks.

"What? That's not the Vicar. Mother's hopeless. I'm so sorry."

"I like the way you talk to him all the same. D'you know who it really is?"

There was a pause. "I do now." Another pause. "It's my clodhopping farmer."

A thrill ran through him. She couldn't have said anything better. How right it had been to phone! How wrong to waste so many weeks!

He said, "It's a hot day. Would you like to go to the sea for a swim this evening? I'll pick you up at five-thirty."

"It was hot yesterday and the day before. And all last week if I'm not mistaken."

"I know. I'm sorry. Can you not manage today?"

"I'll be ready at five-thirty."

"You will?" He thought, damn my idiotic pride. How many times this summer could we have done this! "Last time, I mean last time I phoned –"

"Forget it."

"I never gave you time to explain."

"I shouldn't have done it. Not to you. I didn't realise till afterwards how much – well" – she laughed – "it was *my* loss."

"Our loss." There was a silence while happiness became mutual.

"Are you ringing from the office?" she asked then.

"Heavens no."

"Good. Roger, has Harry Wade got back? Daddy said this morning he'd be on the train from Morlton." Like so many single women living at home she spoke easily of her father as Daddy. Roger found it charming, especially as Daddy was the County Planning Officer.

"He should be back but I haven't seen him yet."

"If he's got the job will you apply for his?"

Roger thought, that's the third time I've been asked today. The scene looked different now. "I ought to move for promotion."

"You've been made Captain of the County Rugby team. They'd miss you."

"I know. But all the same – we'll discuss it this evening, shall we?"

"We?"

"Of course. It's because of you I ought to get away."

"*From* me?"

"*With* you, Dorothy. *With* you. The C.P.O couldn't promote his son-in-law. Nepotism and all that. I wouldn't ask him to."

There was a longish pause. Roger realised what he'd said. He was as matter-of-fact as she and had spoken what he believed was in both their minds. He said, "Dorothy?"

"I'm here."

"Are you angry?"

"I'm just waiting." A laugh broke into her voice. "There are things a girl doesn't like taken for granted. Her acceptance of a proposal of marriage which has never been made, for instance." It was the sort of speech that made him yearn for her physical presence. She was all of a piece – body and mind, look and voice.

He said, "I love you, Dorothy."

"Well, that's a start."

"I've never met a girl who comes anywhere near you."

"In height," she said. "Of course."

"In everything."

"Better and better."

"I want to marry you."

"I'm glad."

"May I ask you again this evening? It doesn't seem right on the phone."

"Then it couldn't be right to answer, could it?" All the time he could hear the laughter in her voice, bubbling through. But not *at* him. This time he had no doubts. It was the exuberance of joy. It was a spring that had broken surface.

"Answer now and again tonight. As often as you like."

"I'll marry you."

There was another silence. Words seemed irrelevant now. Then she said, "Don't worry about Daddy. He's very fair. He'd appoint you on merit. And doesn't the Committee Chairman have a say too?"

"Yes. But I don't want to be in that position. We'll talk about it tonight. At least we'll know by then if Harry's going. You wouldn't mind leaving here, would you?"

"Timbuktu or the Arctic with *you*."

"Tell me, why didn't you come to Hugh Cole's party? I hoped I'd see you there."

"I wasn't invited. Hugh had enough with wives. He couldn't start on sons and daughters."

"Oh, I'm glad. I thought it might have been – but I couldn't ask Hugh."

"I'm writing a sketch about it though – from what I've gleaned. I'll bring my notebook tonight and you can help me. Mother only saw it through a gin-and-orange mist and Daddy just purses up his lips and looks sly."

"I suppose you're using the basic idea – Hugh's double life. The hippies and the Establishment. The essence of the thing. Is that right?"

"More or less. How d'you know?"

He hesitated. "That's how you work, isn't it?"

She sounded pleased as if there were now no shadow between them. "That is, my man, as you say, how I work."

When he returned to the cooler, panelled darkness of County Hall, with no recollection of walking from the phone box, he heard his name called.

"Roger, Roger! Slow up that seven league stride of yours, for pity's sake."

"Why Harry, you're back."

"I got it, Roger! I got it! How about that now?"

How about it indeed? At once he knew he wanted Harry's job. He could step into Harry's shoes tomorrow and feel easy as Section Head. And in Midcaster a rundown terraced house could be had cheaply. He'd do it up and make a profit on it. They needn't mention an engagement while he was applying for Harry's job. Three years as A.P.O here and enjoy his rugby and then number three in a small county or divisional planning officer in a large one. Bird might put up with a son-in-law in the office if he knew he'd move away soon. And surely colleagues here knew him well enough to be sure he wouldn't carry tales to the old man?

"Well, congratulations, Harry," he said. "That's splendid." He was turning to the stairs down to the canteen. "Are you coming? Did you lunch on the train?"

"I thought I'd just see if the old man's around. And you know, Roger, you'll have a good chance of my job. Better salary to marry on, eh?"

"I never said I was getting married."

"Oh well, no." Harry looked flustered. "Hazel had it fixed for you and Dorothy Bird. Splendid couple. Height and physique you know." Roger kept his face impassive.

Harry gave a worried grin and scurried into the lift. Roger ran down for his lunch laughing inside, planning his house, his future, and thinking of half past five.

Bird said, "Ah Ron." He was leaving his office as Foggart hurried up. "I was about to go to lunch. I know what you've come about. Mr Lister just phoned me. This Plastics Factory of Cole's."

"Ay," Foggart grunted. "The Deputy wants to butt in and reorganise it all."

Bird put his fingertips on Foggart's arm. "A very pejorative way of putting it."

Foggart said, "Did he tell you he's scrapping Quarterly Reports?"

"Quarterly Reports?" For a moment Bird looked taken aback. He recovered gracefully. "My dear Ron, you were mentioning this afternoon's meeting."

"I was talking about the Deputy's high-handed way of going on."

"You're a little excited, I'm afraid, Ron. Come into my room. I prefer in any event for Miss James to return from lunch. Phone calls you know. She won't be long."

As Bird shepherded him into the inner office and shut the door Foggart saw he could have made a damaging start and with an effort pulled himself together.

Bird didn't sit at his desk but occupied one of the charcoal grey armchairs and crossed his legs neatly, studying the polish on his shoes. Foggart took an upright chair.

"Shall we agree first" – Bird looked up brightly – "that the Deputy is in a position of seniority which justifies considerable initiative and freedom of action? And in the matter of the Plastics Factory I am in complete accord with him. A trifling rearrangement of my afternoon will enable me to put this room at your disposal to meet the gentleman you are expecting." Foggart opened his mouth to speak but Bird pressed on. "If I'm not mistaken the firm concerned is a subsidiary of a very large one which could put many other developments in our way, given the right encouragement. Though this is a single factory it seems wise to have the application handled at the highest level."

"I took it out of Harry Wade's hands," Foggart began quickly.

"Yes, well, we need not pursue the point. Fortunately it is not too late. I understand Cole has made a new design – which I have not yet been privileged to see – which bears little resemblance to that drawn up by the firm's own architect?"

"Huh, yes. He works like that. Can't improve someone else's stuff. Too big-headed." Foggart felt on safe ground as far as Cole was concerned.

Bird softly rebuked him. "He has been a trifle unlicensed in his behaviour lately but we mustn't underestimate his talent. Is the firm's architect coming along too?"

"They didn't say."

"One must be prepared. I will have a little chat with Cole before they come. He can show me what he has been *rustling up*."

They discussed for a little longer the tactics for the meeting. Then Bird, cocking his head and uncrossing his legs, exclaimed, "Miss James is here." He stood up at once.

Foggart, who had been struggling to manipulate the conversation, had to say bluntly, "I had another thing on my mind."

"Not now, my dear fellow, not now."

"It's pretty urgent. You like important matters brought to your notice."

"Well now." Bird stood and gazed at him, hands by his side, as if for just so long and no longer he would hold that pose and then, if Foggart had not spoken, would vanish.

Foggart jumped up too, flustered that the climax of his schemes had come too precipitately. "There's been a bad blunder by one of the A.P.O's. It'll cause a rumpus with the District Valuer, the County Surveyor and likely the press. And the Deputy's upstairs now plotting with the Deputy County Surveyor to stop it coming to your notice."

Bird's eyes which hadn't left Foggart's seemed to grow larger and brighter behind his spectacles. Foggart shifted his gaze, waiting for a reply. None came. Bird stepped to his desk and sitting down behind it, took off his spectacles and pointed them at Foggart. The gesture, far from being a prelude to speech, seemed to invite Foggart to continue.

Foggart was at a loss. Was the C.P.O so worried that words failed him? Or was he collecting his ideas? No of course, he wanted documents, files, letters. Bird's requirement always was "every relevant piece of paper." And he hadn't *one*. Lister or Pembleton had the file. And Wallace's letter had never come. Unless the Deputy had *intercepted* it.

He changed tack. The papers must wait. What couldn't wait was the inference Bird had to draw from the blunder itself. There wouldn't be another opportunity to drive home the lesson. He hooked himself onto Bird's desk, his eyes boring into Bird's face.

"You do see, Mr Bird, that with proper supervision this couldn't have happened." He was utterly convinced of this himself and put all the intensity he could into his words. "The A.P.O's are overworked. The application figures confirm it. They've got to be abreast of everything. Ready to talk to the public. Prepare Appeal Cases. Deal with the Local Authorities. So who watches *their* work? That's what must be settled, Mr Bird. You urgently need one senior person in overall charge of Development Control. At present as you know I relieve them of the knottier cases which are beyond them. The Deputy sometimes picks up a file because he calls the applicant by his Christian name" – he said this derisively – "but it's all haphazard. The scheme you have in mind would tidy this up. It should be implemented at once. If these duties had been defined earlier I could have saved Pembleton from landing the Department in this mess."

Bird took off his spectacles and wiped them as if to see Foggart more clearly, although in his vulture pose on the edge of the desk Foggart's face was only a yard from him. He said, "Pembleton – ah!" And this for the moment was his only comment.

Foggart, quite aware that this was the first mention of the culprit, took this as encouragement to expound on it. "Yes. Pembleton. I don't know what you think of him, Mr Bird, but he makes a great parade of doing everything very fast. He thinks fast, walks fast, writes fast, makes fast decisions. I have never seen how this can be consistent with real efficiency." He relaxed his grip on the desk to spread out his hands, practically grinning at Bird. "Now we know for a fact that it isn't. We've got our evidence."

Bird had been brandishing his spectacles almost wildly during this speech. Now he suddenly jumped to his feet. "Absolutely essential," he said, staring very brightly at Foggart, "that I go to lunch now. My afternoon schedule –"

"Of course, Mr Bird, of course." Foggart hurried to open the door for him.

As he passed him Bird said, "I'll ring for you afterwards."

In the outer office Miss James, a smart girl and hence assigned exclusively to Bird, looked up with interest. Bird told her he was going to lunch and then, as they walked through said in a neutral tone to Foggart as if he were about to comment on the weather, "Of course *evidence* is the one thing I haven't seen yet – in black and white."

As they emerged into the corridor the lift gates opened and Harry Wade came out, perspiring as if he'd been hauling up the lift himself. Bird turned to him all graciousness. Foggart hopped about within hearing to see what Harry's news was.

Bird overwhelmed Harry with congratulations, shaking him by the hand several times and ended by inviting him to lunch upstairs in the Senior Officers' dining-room.

Foggart went back to the Sinkhole. If only he'd been able to use this – a new man in Harry's place. The need for an older and wiser head to supervise. It could all have been put more logically, laid out tidily the way Bird liked things.

He filled the kettle, lit the gas-ring and with distaste took out the sandwiches Betty had made for him that morning. He wondered, was I too forceful? Bird likes clear opinions but distrusts emotion. Was I too excited, that's the question?

He selected the thinnest and moistest slices of bread and scraped all the fish paste onto them, then popped the pieces into his mouth one after the other as he chewed over the interview. From his case he grabbed a shrunken orange and tossed it into the wastepaper basket. With the action he made a decision. He had to have something in writing to show Bird. He got up with gritted teeth and tiptoed next door to Lister's room.

Lister's in-tray was full but there was nothing about Lower Wooton anywhere. It was unlikely he would have taken the file upstairs to Amberly. With that sort of manoeuvring the less written evidence the better. So Pembleton had got it!

There was no one in Development Control. That was slovenly. He would soon sort that out. He rifled Paul's desk. Ha! Hidden underneath. He drew out the Lower Wooton file and was out of the room in a moment. Now he could show Bird. He glanced through it and found nothing more recent than April. That was bad. Where was Wallace's letter?

The file still under his arm he scurried along to Admin. No Leonard King. No Miss Smeed. Three typists making up their faces. The office boy on the stool at the switchboard reading a comic, a cigarette drooping from his lips.

"No sir," said the girls, "Miss Smeed won't be back yet. She took her sandwiches to eat outside. She's only been gone ten minutes."

"Taken her lunch outside? Miss Smeed?" Foggart thought she disapproved of people chewing publicly in the Square. But surely she was incapable of scheming to avoid him. He glanced at her desk. There was the tray of letters from the County Surveyor. She'd had time to affix the distribution slips but not to send them round. With rising hope Foggart went painstakingly through them. Nothing on Lower Wooton. He thought, I'll kill Arnold Wallace if he's let me down over this. He glared at the typists, growled at Cyril on his stool and went back to his own room. There was nothing to do till the afternoon began but make himself a cup of tea.

The Senior Officers' dining room was on the top floor of the building. Lister had guided Amberly to a table by the wide window overlooking the river.

"The sun's damned hot through that glass," Amberly grumbled.

"I miss the view of the river from my room you know, but if –"

"No no, this'll do. So it's this Lower Wooton thing that's bothering you? Quite a history that. What's *your* interest?"

Amberly was as like Lister as a prune to a plum. Lister thought, he's not much older than me but his hair's already greying. He looks shrivelled and dehydrated. Well, I want to know his version before I say anything and he'll be as determined not to tell me. So over their soup, cold beef and salad they fenced good-humouredly. At last over the cheese and biscuits, Lister decided to attack.

"What we want to know is why we weren't informed that you'd *surveyed* this road improvement line *before* we consulted you about the house. You were proposing to carry it out imminently and you never bothered to tell us."

Amberly, pouring himself some coffee, put it to his lips and set it down. "Too hot." He grinned at Lister through the steam. "What you mean is you thought the road wouldn't be done till the year dot so you granted permission without telling *us*."

Lister was unshaken. "Quite. Fine old house. Owner agreed our design to extend it. Better than it falling to rack and ruin while you lot dithered over your precious line."

Amberly grinned again. "Derek, when we made our first move that house *was* a ruin. Well, little better. The chap who'd bought it was a lecturer at the University. He's retired now. Wanted a place in the country. Snapped it up for a song. Then one weekend he and his wife were clearing junk in the attic and found woodworm. Along comes our man a week later and says, 'Can we survey your land for a road improvement line and we might like to purchase the house?' Man, he jumped at the chance. The wife was upset because she had a fancy for the position. But I suppose he said, 'We'll cut our losses and start again somewhere else.' With a layman's innocence he thought he'd be selling it straightaway." Amberly stopped to take a sip of coffee. He was grinning at Lister. "Surprised how much I know about it?"

Lister shrugged. "Friends of yours?" It was no shrugging matter if that was true.

"No no, it's Jack Sands, the Councillor – he got to know them since they moved out there. I lunched with him the other day. He says Hubertson was quite bemused to get the District Valuer's recent letter about him selling, when he'd just spent two thousand pounds on the house and was well settled in it."

"But just a minute," Lister said. "How come he went ahead with his work when he was all set to sell to the County?"

Amberly cut himself a knob of cheese and spread another cracker. He was eating twice as much as Lister. Where does he put it? Lister thought. I'd be piling on the stones.

"Oh now, Derek," he said, "you know how these things drag on. Hubertson bought the house summer of last year I suppose. We did our survey in the autumn. When he didn't hear anything more about the Council purchasing he may have thought it was all off. Jack Sands said a lawyer friend told Hubertson it can takes years to get round to these things. So what with his wife still hankering after the place they got their own surveyor to look it over. The woodworm was very localised and the first estimates for renovating the house cheered them up a lot. During the winter they went up weekends and began to get more ambitious ideas. Hubertson sent in some homemade plans to you people and I gather one of your blokes got interested and did him a really decent job on a bathroom, bedroom and sun-parlour extension as well as making suggestions for the rest of the interior which weren't his business at all."

"Could be." Yes, Lister thought, Carr practising for a private architectural career.

"Hubertson carried it all out. Took his grant of permission to mean the Council wasn't interested in buying now. To the layman we're just the Council, all of us."

"Ay, didn't know your Department keeps its activities a dead secret."

Amberly shook his head. "You can't press that one. You don't believe it and I don't. Permission was granted in error. You might as well admit it."

Lister put his hand in a traffic warden gesture. "Oh no, hold that. Have you read Wallace's letter in reply to our consultation? Not one whisper that you'd done the survey. Hang it, by April you must have given the District Valuer the go-ahead to start negotiations. Your Committee must have passed the estimates –"

"Now *you* hold it. You interrupted the tale. Hubertson got his permission in April. In June he was retiring from the university. So from April to June he drove his builders hard and got the work done so they could move in July. Then he gets the D.V's first inquiry 'with reference to our preliminary chat the previous autumn' He's flabbergasted naturally. Writes back and says he's no longer interested in selling. Hopes that'll put a stop to it. Gets another letter, more pressing. His solicitor's on holiday, the D.V's on holiday but he writes to the D.V's office and says the house is now worth ten thousand, just for the hell of it."

"Good heavens, I bet it's not," Lister exclaimed.

"There we agree but the letter quietens the DV's office because it's now a knotty case which waits for the D.V. to get back. When he does he phones Hubertson and gets the message he's not selling. The D.V. knows the Council won't wear a Compulsory Purchase at that figure so he throws it back at us. How come we told him to go ahead and ran him into a mare's nest? Wallace will have *that* letter. Your A.P.O has had something from Wallace I suppose and got cold feet."

Lister gave a shrug and a laugh. "Nothing to get cold feet about. Why don't you people quietly drop the thing? It's only a potty little country road."

"Which joins the main road. We've got the Ministry of Transport's O.K. for a grant to improve the junction. We purchased the row of condemned cottages by the main road itself. It was going to be so easy to knock down Hubertson's house at the same time if he'd left it with its earth closet and woodworm."

Lister finished his coffee and sat back. "I still don't see why it was ever started at all. You've got plenty of big stuff waiting."

Amberly laughed. "That was Councillor Sands again. There were a couple of accidents at that corner. Local people were worried. Kids from farms higher up get the school bus from there. Of course he's a Parish Councillor and on the RDC, the County Council and the Highways Committee. He told them he personally would see it was done. Then he got involved in plans for a Clinic at Upper Wooton that kept him off our backs. But when he met Hubertson and found he was an ex-college bloke full of brains and nothing to use them on he roped him in for the Parish Council, heard about his house and remembered his pet road improvement scheme. He was mad to find it had run into trouble. Sooner or later he reckons there'll be a fatal accident there and he'll get it in the neck from local people."

"All right," Lister said. He could see strands of a web now, thicker and knottier than he had imagined. "All right. You feel obliged to do this improvement. What's wrong with a new line missing Hubertson's house? You can still get your right-angled junction a bit further along."

Amberly grinned. "Oh yes, says he, a new line. Easy as pie. Who owns the land west of Hubertson's house? Councillor Sands. He was approached originally. Loves his land, every inch of it. The other side brings in a good wheat crop for the farmer."

"Hell, you only want a few yards. Say a bit from Hubertson's garden and a bit from Sands – or the farmer, depending which side you can manage it."

"Oh I've no doubt we'll work something out but things will be said. Sands will demand a progress report at the next meeting. How can I avoid saying you people gave permission, ignoring our line? Then there's the cost of another survey. Ministry approval for change of route. That could set it back a couple of years. I might still slide it through unnoticed but with

Sands sitting there, knowing the history and happy to make a monkey out of the officials, I haven't a hope. And Hubertson is all worked up about it. Sands tipped me the word that he's dying to spill the story to the local press. Sands admits he said to lay off until after the next Committee Meeting in case it gets spicier."

Lister could now see barely a glimmer of hope. "What's this Sands really like? You seem to be on good terms with him. Won't he let it lie if you ask him?"

Amberly's face closed up, his mouth like a crack in the shell of a withered nut. He shook his head several times. "No go, Derek." Then he became more expansive. "Look, I know the man socially and his wife and kids. That's why we sometimes lunch together when he's in town. But in Committee he's the local representative, serving his people, making things awkward. He's a rich man, not specially intelligent, but all he wants in life is power, influence, to be talked about. If it was *my* gaffe, he wouldn't spare me."

Lister grunted. The picture fitted. He sensed Amberly wanting to go. The dining-room was emptying rapidly now. "I'll ask one thing, Bob. When you write your progress report the wording could make all the difference. An unfortunate set of circumstances rather than a specific error. Planning Department encourages a well-designed renovation of a derelict property – unaware of imminence of road improvement project etc etc."

"You'd like to write the report for me?"

"Well, that's what *we'll* say – only stronger – if we're asked."

"I get you." The cordiality died out of Amberly's voice. "You don't want a one-way rebuke from the Highways Committee to the Planning Committee, asking for more co-operation. You'd like *us* in it too. Would the *Surveyors* and Planners work together to prevent a recurrence etc. etc.? Well, Derek, just reflect what you'd do in my shoes."

Amberly went. Lister sat, heavy with depression. It had been a total failure and yet he'd begun by handling it pretty cleverly. Now I'll get the same rocket from the old man as Paul will – just because I was fool enough to get involved.

He pushed back his chair and found Bird right at his elbow. He and Harry Wade were passing from one of the far tables to the door just behind him.

"A good meeting?" the C.P.O. said, blinking like a little owl. "I like these things smoothed out at Senior Officer level. I have an inkling of the matter, just an inkling. I had Ron Foggart in before lunch. I'll see you down in my office presently. Just now you must congratulate Harry here. He's to be Deputy at Morlton. Quite splendid."

At twenty to twelve Eleanor told Shirley reluctantly that she would have to go to collect John. Hazel got up too, desperate with apologies for having talked all about her own affairs. "And you with your mind on that poor little boy —"

"I've hardly given him a thought. He'll be fine."

"But first day at school is a big step and he's shy, isn't he?"

"Far too shy. It'll do him good." Eleanor thought of her own first days, school, college, teaching. They were agonies she would never willingly experience again.

They walked through the house. The car was in the drive. Mrs Ball, who had been cleaning the front windows, was talking to someone in the road, wash leather in hand.

"Well," she said, looking round unabashed, "you don't often see me stop work, Mrs Lister, but just take a look at this. Just come here and take a look."

When she moved they could see a girl standing behind the low hedge, a solid girl with a coarse plait. Eleanor didn't know her but Hazel greeted her warmly.

Shirley said in her clear, commanding voice, "We haven't much time. Eleanor, this is Hilde. We met at Hugh's party."

Mrs Ball said again, "But look here. In the pram. Not six weeks old and he could be three months, the size of him."

Eleanor looked eagerly over into the pram. Shirley seemed to be hanging back but was drawn to look too by Hazel's and Eleanor's exclamations. "What a beautiful baby!"

Shirley said, almost angrily to Mrs Ball, "How is the baby here already?"

Hilde said, without animation, "My mother must go home soon, you see. So she come all night on the sleeping train. She brought him in a taxi at nine. Maurice and I were asleep." Suddenly she laughed. "That taxi. All ropes and hooks. Pram, cot. Cases of clothes, nappies, blankets, baby food. My mother had one little zip bag for herself. She go to bed now. I take him for walk to make the house quiet."

The baby was asleep, one hand curled in front of his face.

"Oh yes, she'll be tired, your mother," Hazel said.

"No it's for Maurice I must take him away. He is working."

"He's a sculptor," Shirley said to Eleanor. "He works at home."

Eleanor remembered Paul describing the couple but no baby had been mentioned. It excited her to look at him. All babies did these days. For so young he was plump and smooth, his dark hair soft. She wanted to pick him up, feel his shape, love him.

Hilde said, "I want to keep him now."

Hazel cried, "But you weren't going to part with him!"

The girl shrugged, "Maurice doesn't want him. He must have woman to feed him, pose for him. But baby – that is family. At once it is different – you see?"

Eleanor glanced at her watch.

Shirley said briskly, "Mrs Pembleton has to meet her boy from school. Your baby is lovely. You'll have to choose between him and Maurice." She moved towards the car.

Hilde said abruptly to Eleanor, "You are married to Paul, aren't you?"

"Yes!"

"He said at the party his wife couldn't come because you have baby soon?"

"That's right."

"You are lucky. He is man who live life deep or on the edge as he please. That is good. My Maurice has only one way – his work. He say it is not a time for babies. Too many dying. So? I say. *This* baby not dying." Her voice grew excited. The baby's eyes opened and his head turned towards her. "See, he needs food. He trusts." Quickly her animation was gone. She repeated in a listless tone, "Yes, you are lucky with your Paul."

Eleanor couldn't say a word, but Mrs Ball was voluble.

"You should finish with *your Maurice* and find a decent man who'd marry you and take the baby too. That's if nobody else can give the poor little mite a home." She looked round but Shirley was opening the car door for Hazel to get in.

"Sorry, we must get off. The coffee tray's in the garden, Mrs Ball."

In the car Eleanor was feeling too much to speak. She guessed this was the baby Shirley was talking about yet now Hilde was saying she wanted to keep him.

Fortunately Hazel couldn't help talking. "Eh, what a tragedy! Maurice must be one of today's men who won't take responsibilities."

They set her down with her shopping at the top of Lavender Terrace. She just remembered to say to Shirley, "Thank you, dear. It's been lovely. That *poor* girl!"

Eleanor made a few remarks about Hazel and the traffic. Then Shirley said in a neutral voice, "Perhaps you guessed. It's Derek and I who would like to adopt a baby."

So the façade was down. Eleanor felt warm towards her at once. "I did wonder."

Shirley kept her eyes on the road. "Derek broached it seven years ago." She gave a short laugh. "And we never seriously talked it out in all that time. One week he'd say, 'If we'd done it then we'd have a schoolchild now.' Another time it was, 'We wouldn't have made the team if we'd had a kid to look after.' Golf, you see. So it was a thing he wanted to do with half his mind. Next year would do. Do you and Paul talk *seriously*?"

Eleanor looked at Shirley's manicured hands on the steering wheel, the perfectly varnished nails. I'd like mine to be a pleasure to look at but I could never, ever make the effort. She said, "I think Paul and I settle big things as soon as they come up. Of course adoption's something you can't do in a hurry anyway."

"At our rate of progress we'll be in our graves. I'll have to make an appointment with Derek to tell him what *I* think." She said it lightly but to Eleanor it was very sad.

"Were you waiting to see if you had one of your own?"

The question seemed to relieve Shirley enormously. Though she had been open her tone had still been artificially flippant. Now she said quite naturally, "That's it in a nutshell of course. That and would I love another person's child? If I knew the answers to those –" She broke off to ask Eleanor where the school was.

"Round this corner but you can set me down here. If he saw me from the window coming by car he'd think I'd been gallivanting as soon as his back was turned."

Shirley looked her in the eye. "There you are. He's your own. You're in tune with him. I can't imagine being like that." She drew up at the kerb.

Eleanor, heaving herself out, said, "If he was yours from a tiny baby he would be utterly yours. Nothing that went before would live in his mind."

Shirley got out to help her, still cool and chic despite the midday heat. "Would it live in *my* mind, that's what I wonder. Might it make all the difference in the world?"

"I don't think so, but I can't know." Eleanor smoothed down her navy smock. "I know I'm sick of this pregnancy. If there was an easier way I'd opt for it right now."

Shirley shook her head and Eleanor wished she hadn't said it. It wasn't honest.

"You're in time," Shirley said, "Just two minutes to twelve."

Eleanor thanked her and as she went into the school she thought, Paul and I spoke of Shirley this morning and I said she frightened me but now I feel for her so much and it's taken only a few minutes. All our previous conversations didn't even scratch the surface.

"Mummy!" John pressed himself against her, holding tight, his cap pushed awry, his stiff new blazer creasing. When he was sure his world was back to normal he let go.

"We'll have these off," she said, taking the cap and blazer. "Too hot."

They joined hands and began to walk back home together, down the back lane.

When they came to the horse-chestnut tree in the wall, John stroked the bark.

"My elephant's still here."

"Of course it is. Does it seem a long time since we passed it this morning?"

He looked up with his large eyes. "It's millions of years," he said.

"You've been painting this morning," Neville said. "It's good."

Lena turned the face to the wall. "Sit down. Lunch is under the tea-towel."

They ate in silence till she said abruptly, "You can give me a ride back this afternoon and I'll put an advert in the paper for work."

He laid down his knife and fork. "I might not be staying in Midcaster. Well, I mean, I want you to have a job but I might chuck it in here. Have my own firm one day."

She stared as if he'd suddenly grown a physical defect. "What in heaven's name has brought that on – just since this morning?"

He told her about Lower Wooton. She probed him with questions. How had it been left? What had Paul said? She began to laugh.

He flared up. "It's no laughing matter. Might get into the press."

"But to talk about resigning!"

"If I was sure no one else was taking the blame I'd face it, live it down –"

"Oh the nobility of the man. Who's going to take the blame? I can't see Paul playing the martyr for you."

"According to their lights he's responsible – as Section Head."

Lena dismissed this with a sweep of her arms. "Everyone will know it was you and they'll be glad it wasn't them. Like when you see a man with a boil on his nose. They might be sorry for you for a while – if that's what you want."

"No I don't. But it's sickening the way things are done in Local Government."

She got up and dumped the plates in the sink. "D'you want coffee?"

"Yes. You see it *does* something to people after a while. Take Pembleton –"

"All right," she said, "gladly."

He scowled at her. "I wish you wouldn't be so flippant."

"I wish you wouldn't be so funny without laughing. Go on."

"Well, he's an intelligent man. I thought he had a kind of integrity. But his first thought was how to get round it – by asking his pal Lister to wangle it with *his* pal, Amberly. It's that sort of thing that makes me want to get out altogether."

Lena put her elbows on the table and gazed at him solemnly from between her cupped hands. "And what did *you* want to do?"

"Ring Wallace, the surveyor chap, and tell him the plain truth. I'd tell Bird if necessary. Nothing as honest as that seemed to occur to Pembleton."

"Which I suppose you told him."

"I let him know I didn't like his methods, certainly."

She put the kettle on for coffee and came back to the table. "Has it not occurred to your arrogant little mind that Paul was saving time? He's a grown man, he's not going to go crying to authority 'Oh dear, help, help.' He'll work out a solution. Good grief, the nerve of you, to belittle his integrity! You couldn't begin to think the way he does."

Neville gaped at her. "What are you talking about? You've only met him twice – oh and you saw him today." He broke off, suddenly suspicious. "Did you talk about *me*?"

"*You*? Why should we talk about *you*?" She got up to make the coffee.

He leapt up and gripped her arms from behind. "Come on, what happened?"

"You nearly made me scald myself." She put the kettle back on the stove and brought the cups to the table. He watched her movements under the wisp of a dress.

"Why did you put that on? You look undressed."

She grinned. "All I said to your Pembleton was 'Where are the newspaper offices?' and then Harry Wade came up. Oh and Paul said what you said this morning."

"What on earth was that?"

"He told me to make a friend of his wife. He said to call any time."

"*Did* he? So there was a lot more talk."

"No, he was just friendly. *You* don't like him but then who *do* you like?"

"Harry's all right. Did he say how he got on at Morlton?"

"He said we must go there before they leave."

"So he got the job. I'd apply but Roger will get it."

He put his cup in the sink. "You never washed up the breakfast things."

"I made your lunch."

He went over to the picture and turned it round again. "You were doing this."

"It's not finished," she snapped.

"Why are you so touchy about it?" He stood back from it. "That looks the sort of man one could admire."

She snorted. "That's marvellous!"

"Why, is it meant to be me?"

"Oh my God." She snatched up her bag. "Come on, if we're going."

He picked up his crash helmet. "I'm not staying to work with Pembleton longer than I can help. It's not worth you getting a job."

"So what do I do this afternoon? Go and ask Eleanor to plead with Paul for you?"

He stared, half believing she might. "You wouldn't? Every word you said she'd tell Paul. They're that sort of couple."

"And how do you – with your total lack of insight – know that?"

"Let's stop this. Everything I say – it's hopeless. Why not stay and tidy up here?"

"No, I'm coming. I may still take a job. If *you* leave it doesn't mean *I* have to."

That was so like her, to say something catastrophic in the most casual voice. "You don't mean that. You were waiting for me today. Why do you keep *saying* things?"

She was scrabbling among her art materials for a sketch book and B. pencils. "I'm going to draw at the quayside." As she passed the portrait she turned it to the wall again.

On an impulse he said, "Am I being a mug? Has someone sat for that? You've found someone else, here in Midcaster?"

She took his arm. "My dear man" – she timed the words jerkily down the steep stairs – "that man may not exist in the whole world." They reached the next landing. "I expect I'll be here when you come home but don't act the fool at the office. And laugh – *at* me, *with* me, at yourself, at Lower Wooton." She let go and jumped the last stair.

The bike was parked at the head of the area steps. Down there was a heap of newspapers and leaves. She looked down and then up at the heavy trees against the sky.

"Lovely hateful square. Why have I never painted you?"

He pulled the bike across the pavement. "Get on if you're coming."

He was sick of her mood changes. She slung her bag round her on its strap and clasped him round the waist. She has to, he thought, but it means nothing to her.

"Take it away, man," she sang. "Take it away."

Eleanor brought John in by the back door and started on their lunch straight away. John wandered along the hall looking for some toys and came back with a letter.

"Is this what Daddy's been waiting for? It's got printed writing on."

"Yes, this is it." She took a clean knife from the drawer. Her hands weren't trembling, her heart wasn't beating any faster. She wouldn't do histrionics like Hazel Wade. In a second she would know whether they were to be uprooted or left alone, but that second was a painful age while she slid the knife under the flap and unfolded it.

Her eyes flitted over the words. ". . .inform you that the post . . . has been offered to Mr William Grant . . . who has been pleased to accept . . "

Imbeciles! Who is William Grant to be preferred to Paul Pembleton?

"Are we going to London, Mummy?"

She bent down to hug him. "No darling. We can stay here."

"Daddy wanted to go to London. Will he be sad?"

"Oh darling." She sat on the leather armchair with him on her lap.

"Why d'you look so happy?" he asked.

"I love it here. So does Daddy. But people have to change jobs sometimes."

"Why?"

She tried to explain what he couldn't possibly understand. He knew she was trying and was satisfied. "Come on," she said then, joy and relief bubbling up, "lunch."

He patted her smock. "Have I been sitting on the baby? Will it be a funny shape?"

"No funnier than you. Come on, wash your hands."

"Why don't you ring up Daddy at the office and tell him?" he asked when they were eating sausage, beans and tomatoes, his favourite meal.

"He'll be in the canteen or out in the car by now. He'll have to wait till he gets home." She pictured him driving to Wanwick and felt an ache of longing to be at his side.

"Come on," she said, "let's take bananas into the garden for pudding, and if the ice cream van comes you can have one as well."

Dinner at Old Mill Farm had been a silent, dreadful meal. The old woman had eaten well, which disgusted Matthew after the fright she'd given them that morning. He himself always came in hungry but the sight of Mrs Pawson at the table, shrivelled up in her black wool dress with her eyes darting about like poisonous flies, made his stomach contract so that he could hardly eat. Jane, gaunt as a spectre, wordlessly served the meal.

Her mother wasn't talking either which was faintly sinister. Once he caught her smiling to herself and he thought, I'll swear she was on the phone to the Planning Office. He would have asked her outright but she would only lie. There was no truth in her.

After a few mouthfuls of rhubarb and custard she suddenly said, "Why don't you make the loft into a room for Martin? Any boy would love to go up a ladder to bed."

Jane began, "We store so much and it would need a window and a proper floor."

"Cost less than a bungalow."

Matthew got up from the table. "Don't discuss it, Jane. The boy's not going there. He was promised his own room at Christmas."

"It's a nice thing" Mrs Pawson said, "when the young are put before the old."

Matthew went to the door.

"Are you going out again?" Jane said.

"Of course I'm going out."

Mrs Pawson said, "What are all these things you store anyway? I haven't seen you make one pot of jam yet."

As Matthew went out he heard Jane defending herself. " . . .pounds of blackberry jelly last year. Martin and I had some lovely days blackberrying before his term started."

Yes, last year, when the joy in the new farm was still unspoilt. Jane worked twice as hard as she did now and was plumper, fuller in the face.

He went to the wall behind the barn. Having the old woman down the hill would be agony – but in the house! He broke up some stones with the heavy hammer, smashing them into smaller and smaller pieces until they were useless. When he realised what he'd done he stared at the chippings in alarm. He saw them as he'd seen the scratched face of the boy who had ripped up the baby bird. He had no memory of being the cause of it.

Jane said, "I'll wash up, Mother. You might wet that hand."

"I can wipe, can't I? I'm not going to be told next I'm useless."

Jane didn't reply to this and presently her mother said, "Where are these blackberries. Not in your vegetable patch?"

"No, in the hedgerow near your bungalow site but the village children get them first. The best ones are on the south-facing side of a gully up the hill."

"We'll take a basket then this afternoon."

Jane was pleased but she said, "It's a scramble."

"I'm not old. I could see you into the grave yet. You didn't know what Doctor Vine said when he packed you off to the country, 'If she doesn't go you'll lose her.'"

Jane smiled. It was one of her happiest memories. "Come on, then, Mother." She took down two baskets and lined them with greaseproof paper. "If *you* can manage it I can. But we must put hats on. The sun's hot on your head when you're stooping."

A few minutes later they started out. Jane led her mother by the side of the house under the shadow of the big barn. She could hear Matthew at the wall behind the barn but they were not in sight of him until they began climbing the flank of the moor. She paused and looked back then to wave but his head was bent over his work, his curly hair with the sun on it like ripe nuts. He'd draped his shirt over the wall. His bronzed back glistened.

"We're going blackberrying," Jane called.

He looked up then, not seeing them at once because the hills broke up the direction of her voice. Then he said, "There's plenty up by the burn. In the gully."

"Ay, that's where we're going."

He turned back to his work. Her mother watched him a moment.

"Ay, he's putting his heart into that. Loves his farm, doesn't he?"

"Of course he does." They walked on in silence.

Jane thought, I'd never have met him if I hadn't gone to Dr Vine and it was mother who badgered me to go. "Tired? At your age? See Dr Vine. He'll tell you to stop being a silly girl." But Dr Vine knew the set up at home. "You must get away. Go and live in the country. You're not a child. You're twenty-three. Live with some nice body who'll give you farm cooking – plenty of fresh eggs. You're anaemic, underweight, your nerves are bad. Don't worry. I'll frighten her into letting you go. You can take a quiet job but *walk* there.

Get yourself an appetite." So she had got the job in Beckbridge County Library and met the only farmer who was a regular reader, Matthew Hodge.

As the path grew steeper her mother's black leather-soled town shoes could no longer get a grip on the smooth dry earth. Jane took her hand. "Let's cut through the heather. We'll have to get you some stout shoes or boots."

They reached the foot of the gully where the burn sprang in a series of tiny falls. It was dried to a trickle. A few alders grew on the steep sides but all over, tangled among the rocks and over an ancient dry-stone wall, were brambles, laden with ripe fruit.

"How they've come on!" Jane exclaimed. "Now, mind you don't fall, Mother."

Her mother was ensconcing herself in a cleft between two crags where she could reach clusters dangling on all sides of her. She seemed oblivious of tears to her dress and stockings. Jane could have sung out loud with relief but she was afraid of breaking the spell. She stood in the bed of the stream, the hot afternoon humming overhead with the sound of insects, the baaing of sheep, the plopping of the burn. The brambles crackled drily as she bent down a bough. The sharp ring of Matthew's hammer came up to them.

She prayed, "Oh God, soothe him. Give him ease. Stop him tormenting himself."

She hardly knew what she prayed to, the heat on her back, the royal blaze of the heather rising to the skyline, the sky itself, shimmering at the edge, arching to intense blue, or the level of fat blackberries rising in her basket. It was all one – the soul in these things – and she yearned after it, ached for it to touch him too, to give him serenity.

Matthew looked up once or twice. At first they were hidden from view but later he spotted them higher up the gully. Jane's blue and white cotton dress and light straw hat were easy to pick out. Her mother in black he could see when she moved, the basket on her arm light against the shadow in the gully. At this distance they were like insects on a wall. There should have been nothing in the sight to hurt him but always the shape of her, talking to Jane, poisoning Jane against him, torturing her, made him shrink within himself, corroding the sane and reasonable man that he knew to be

Matthew Hodge.

The wall finished, he walked back to the farmhouse. He took a long drink of water in the kitchen. Then he walked through the house, opening every window and door wide, even the front door which he hardly ever used.

Satisfied, he went out again, across the farmyard, through the field gate, down the sloping pasture to his animals. The sheepdog, Jess, who had been out on her own affairs, saw him two fields away and raced to join him. He tickled her ears. She walked quietly down with him, at heel.

4

THE AFTERNOON

Paul drove north out of Midcaster but the city clung to him. He had to brake at a zebra crossing for a woman with a pram. His fingers danced on the wheel. As she passed she gave a quick vague wave. The gesture and the whole look of the woman, down to the angle of her body as she pushed the pram, were so like Eleanor that he laughed aloud. So much of Eleanor fitted the common denominator of woman. He found it enchanting and, if there had been nothing else, that would have kept him always in love with her.

He drove on. Soon Eleanor would be pushing a pram again. When Cathy was born neither of them had any experience of babies but they had laughed together over their awkwardness and their mistakes. Looking back now Paul thought that until Cathy reached the age of conscious naughtiness they regarded her as a game they played at together. With John there was less amazement over each phase. And Cathy took charge very often. "You go and sit down, Mummy. I'll amuse him. I'll give him his dinner." She startled them by her maturity and that brought home to them the seriousness of parenthood. More so to Eleanor of course who had so many more hours with them. Do I take them too lightly, he wondered. Find them still a bit of a joke? Will the new one shift the balance of the family? Will John, who is so solemn, be squeezed out?

The car was stationary again and the heat brought back his headache, overlaying the sensations of hunger. He had meant to buy sandwiches but with meeting Harry the time had flown. A police car went by escorting a lorry and trailer which bulged with a ship's boiler. The traffic eased. He accelerated through Rufton, the outermost suburb, well dotted with trees, where Bird lived.

He saw the sign with the County crest. He was leaving Midcaster and entering his own territory, all the county to the west of the trunk road. To the east was Wade's Area. Foggart was right for once that it wasn't ideal. The road, ruler-straight heading north, didn't so much cleave this part of the county as provide access to it. It should be one man's province as long as it wasn't Foggart's.

By now Bird would know about Lower Wooton. The office in a ferment was no place to do an exacting job. If he hadn't been so late he would have stopped at a phone box and rung Eleanor to see if the letter from London had come second post. But would the exhilaration of a new challenge be swallowed up in the problems of moving, a new baby, the children's schooling? There was surely so much more to being alive.

Five miles on he came to Old Pits. On a map the place looked ideal for expansion for Midcaster's overspill but Paul thought it would be kinder to let it die quietly. The shop where he could have bought a pie was closed. The straggling colliery houses ended in a hideous meeting house, converted before the Planning Act into a cinema and now a Bingo Hall. A lopsided signpost in a triangle of grass beside it pointed west – Nether Hopewood two miles and Ridd's Gap three. In Old Pits the hint of deep country close at hand always delighted him. His errand was at Hopewood Farm. Ridd's Gap was where the road passed between humpy hills, the first break in the coastal plain, an earnest of the high wild moors along the county's western border. In an hour he would be on the edge of them at Wanwick and in the heart of them at Old Mill Farm if he got as far as that.

Hopewood Farm was the first building in the village. There was an S. bend, then a downward sweep to the village with the Church spire in the centre of the picture and the tops of the hills of Ridd's Gap forming a backdrop in the distance.

The first thing he saw as he rounded the bend was that the farmer had begun building the cattle court and two silo towers. They were too near the road and the towers were light in colour, not dark. The church would still be visible as you came down the hill but two fifty-five foot high cylinders of grey metal would partly obscure it. Well, the farmer was the raison d'etre of the village. His labourers lived here, worshipped – if they did at all – at the church, drank at the pub. These days the farming community took silo towers for granted. But commuters who left the city for country views would detest them. So too would the weekend motorist. "Who's allowed *that* blot on the landscape?"

He drove the car onto the track which the builders' lorries would soon churn into a morass if this dry spell broke. Immediately a big man appeared from the back of the farmhouse. He was taller than Paul and broader, well packed into an old double-breasted blue worsted suit, boots and a tweed cap. As Paul got out he sensed the farmer sizing up the new estate car and the city man come to tell him his business.

And it was there again, the dread of encounter, as he and Eleanor called it. She could scarcely believe he still felt it. "You're so confident now." But leaving his safe tin box and invading another's privacy took him back to his over-sensitive boyhood. Like John he had a dominating elder sister. Vera shopped, got tickets, did the talking. Vera was ten years his senior and still thought of him as little Paul. Last time she'd stayed with them he had had an Appeal Case and challenged her to come and sit in the public gallery. "No," she said. "I'd suffer for you too much." He teased her. "I'm disguised in my public image. You know I can act. Today I'm 'the technical expert.' If I'm site visiting I'm 'the man from the Council.' I put on the disguise and I'm safe." It was true and not true. Some days the protective clothing was threadbare – like today.

He advanced towards the farmer across the hard-packed mud and got his greeting in first. "Good afternoon. I see you've started."

"Mr Pembleton? You're late."

"I'm sorry. Traffic hold-up." Paul pointed to the work. "*You* seem to be early."

The farmer had evidently expected this and began to talk, aggressively, about all the forms he'd filled in for the Ministry of Agriculture. It was obvious that he resented it although the outcome was likely to be a substantial grant.

"When I got *their* OK – and that took long enough God knows – why should I think I needed planning permission as well?"

"You'd begun before you found out?"

"Ay, some bloody nosey-parker in the village – city man – told the local surveyor. I wasted an afternoon going to the Council Office and filling in another blasted form."

"And on the form you wrote green for the silo towers. I took that to mean the dark green that is less obtrusive against a background of trees than yours will be from here."

The farmer waved his hands about. "Green, grey. They filled the form in at the office. I'm sure I said grey. It's their mistake. I'd had enough of forms."

"Shall we walk over to the site?"

It wasn't twenty yards away but Paul needed to see the other side, where he wanted it to go, much further back from the road. He could still insist it should be moved. His brain was laying out the pros and cons, and had given him the answer while the farmer uprooted himself and set his big body in motion.

Behind the site hay was stacked under tarpaulin covers. "You've had an old barn here that's been pulled down. You're going to need the towers as soon as they're ready."

"Of course. Late enough as it is what with the Ministry and materials held up."

Delays, Paul thought, could run into years if I take a stand on this. The Ministry's date for the grant to be taken up will expire. A new site will need a fresh application. This is the spot the Ministry agreed with the farmer for electricity supply and drainage. The towers must be at the end of the cattle court for automatic feeding. But if I'd been alerted at the beginning I'd have suggested angling the cattle court to bring the towers further from the road and so backgrounded against the trees. And the County Surveyor may want a straightening of that S bend. The towers could end up standing right above the road.

"Well sir," he said, "you realise this is unauthorised, starting without permission."

"Permission! That's all we ever hear about. My God, this is not a rented farm. My father, grandfather and great-grandfather had it. Not a penny of mortgage on it. I pay rates and taxes. You'd think a man could be free to do what he likes on his own land."

Sometimes it was a good idea for people to let off steam but Paul could see that the farmer was working himself into a rage. The only possible satisfaction from this business would be the gaining of goodwill.

"Well now, look, Mr Potter, I can recommend that the Committee grant you your permission and you'll be done before winter comes. But it isn't because you've started the work. I appreciate that the building is essential for your farm and we'll have to calm down your neighbours as best we can. I'm sorry you picked light grey for your towers. They'll be conspicuous for miles from the west, let alone the impact round here."

The farmer was grinning now. "I did look at the dark green things – different firm and fifty pound dearer. If city folks come for a run in the country and notice grey towers they'll have forgotten them two miles down the road. Is that worth fifty quid to me?"

Paul smiled at him. "I still think it's worth a little trouble to make one's surroundings as pleasant as possible. Take the roof of this cattle court."

Potter said suspiciously, "Well?"

"You're spending thousands on all this –"

"I'll say I am."

"So you want the minimum upkeep costs." He looked round at the concrete blocks, the sand and cement and gravel. "You haven't got your asbestos sheeting yet?"

"It's on order."

"I'd like you to have dark brown."

"You mean paint a huge ruddy roof? It'll take days."

"No, paint wears off and looks worse than ever, but sheets dyed right through weather perfectly. This will be a big building. You don't want it ever to look shoddy."

"They cost more, is that it?"

"Naturally – but in the long run –"

Potter questioned it. What was wrong with the whole building being whitish-grey? *He* didn't agree that a deep-toned roof could turn a vast porridge-coloured mass into a building of strength and harmony. Paul stood in the sun, the noise of the work going on over their talk, his head throbbing.

"Look, Mr Potter, the roof colour can be stipulated as a condition. *You* don't want delays. Nor do I. This can then pass at the next Committee Meeting without question."

"Oh all right. We'll have your ruddy dark brown roof."

It was at this moment that a youngish woman, plump and bonny, appeared at the back door of the farmhouse. "If you've finished come away in for a glass of beer."

Paul was telling Potter he'd want a letter from him accepting the condition. Potter was jeering, "You chaps have to have everything on paper. Beer eh?"

"Well," she said, "it's a mighty hot day." Her smile was broad, a little mocking as if she were thinking, men! They must have their beer.

Paul would have preferred water but he stepped readily to the door. "That's kind of you." Any less hearty response and he was sure she would have mocked still more.

She led him into the big kitchen. "That's the spirit. Sit you down."

The farmer followed. "While you're here you can tell me what to put in the letter and take it with you. If I don't do it now God knows when it 'ud get done."

"It wouldn't," she laughed. "I'd have to do it."

Paul looked round the room. All over the long table were trays of delicacies. The farmer picked up a sausage roll which wasn't as thick as his thumb and half as long.

"What are these potty little things for?"

The woman was bringing the beer. "Keep your great fingers out of those. They're for my miners' widows." She put a brimming glass in front of Paul. "*You* try one." She handed him two on a plate. "*You* didn't touch." She laughed as if they were both children.

At first Paul had thought she must be Potter's daughter, her face was so young, but she wore a wedding ring and talked like a wife.

When Potter said, "Get us some writing paper, Lil," she retorted, "Get it yourself," and he did, muttering.

"Well," Paul said, "these sausage rolls melt away. How do you do it?"

She stood over him, delighted. "Have some more."

"No, no. I couldn't deprive your widows. Is it an outing from Old Pits?"

"That's right. We bring them by coach. They have a wee service in the church, decorated for harvest and get the fruit and flowers at the end of the day. They love it."

Potter coming back into the kitchen said, "Ay, it costs enough. And all week they're playing bingo with their pensions, that's what gets me."

"So they're wicked old women," she laughed. "I might play Bingo if I'd lost you down the pit." She winked at Paul. "Wouldn't you if you lived at Old Pits?"

"I would," Paul said, "but some of them refused rehousing from the Council."

She laughed again, licking her fingers. "I know. Crazy old coots. One of them said, 'If I can't go outside to the toilet when am I going to get me fresh air? Helps me sleep.' She has a sister in an all-electric council flat, ten floors up. Never gets out and can't sleep a wink. Is that letter done, Joseph Potter?"

He was sitting, fountain pen poised in his great fingers. Paul dictated the letter and he wrote laboriously. "God, I hope that's the last bit of paper to do with this blasted job."

Mrs Potter saw Paul to the door. "Plenty paper'll fly out of his bank account before it's through eh?" She looked over at the site, the metal towers sprouting at the far end. "Blessed great things outside the door. But nothing's too good for the modern cow."

Paul thanked her for the refreshments as Potter came to the door behind her and demanded, "When'll I get the go-ahead then, Mr Pembleton?"

"As soon as the Committee's passed it. Within a fortnight." He didn't add "As long as none of your neighbours makes a formal objection." He hoped they wouldn't. He had spent forty minutes for what – a dark brown roof instead of an off-white one. But as he drove down into the village past the church he felt he had shown the human face of planning. If I'd sent Neville how would he have coped?

He drove ahead through Ridd's gap, the heat shimmering on the road, till he saw the lane cutting north-west to the valley of the Wann. His next call was at gravel banks on the Wann itself. A cock-pheasant ran across the road. "Bang! Bang!" he said out loud as he would have done if Eleanor had been with him. He wished she was. At her best she enjoyed life as Mrs Potter did. When they were camping she would unzip the tent flap and sniff the air. "Look," she'd say. "A day for living. Come out all of you. Let's live it."

After the office morning he hoped he could manage some of the afternoon for living. Neville and Foggart and Bird and office reorganisation were gloriously far away.

"Yes," Miss James said, "just go through, Mr Lister. Mr Bird's expecting you."

As Derek Lister walked through the outer office he wondered what to anticipate. When Bird had passed by with Harry after lunch his manner had been ominously bland.

Bird was walking about the room and didn't sit down when Lister entered. That was a bad sign for a start. His eyes also were very bright behind his spectacles.

"Sit down, Derek, sit down." He took another turn over the wine-red carpet. Then he stood still, feet together, hands clasped and looked hard at Lister who was trying to look at ease in one of the grey armchairs. "This is a bad business over Lower Wooton. Very bad. This has put a spoke in our little plans." He gave a genuine-sounding sigh.

For crying out loud, thought Lister, what has that old fox been telling him? *Our* little plans, if you please. It was better to say nothing and see who would catch it first.

"I am not exaggerating when I say I was shocked, deeply shocked."

Lister felt his face go red. If *I'm* in the dock it's outrageous. And if it's Paul the old man's making a hell of a mountain –

"Tale-bearing," Bird said. "Tale-bearing to discredit a colleague."

Oh my eye, thought Lister, beginning to laugh inwardly.

Bird went on standing solemnly before him. "A man in his responsible position – so petty, so small-minded –" He broke off as if he really couldn't find the words. Then he went to his desk, sat down, pulled off his spectacles and pointed them at Lister. "I shall want you there when I speak to him. I'm sorry if it'll be embarrassing but someone else must be present. Naturally it can't possibly be anyone junior to Foggart."

Lister had to put his hand in front of his face to hide his smile. He pretended to cough. "May I ask what Foggart *said* before lunch?"

Bird waved his spectacles about. "We were talking about the meeting with Cole – when he brought up this other business. Naturally I'll want to know the facts and how far you've gone with Amberly. I'm sure you would have brought it to me in due course."

"Naturally I would," Lister said.

"As I thought, my dear chap. But Foggart proceeded to give me a lecture – I can call it nothing else – on the need for supervision over Development Control. This slip-up couldn't have happened with a responsible person in charge, himself of course. He has been pressing me for a decision on our little scheme. That I could understand. He wasn't gaining in salary, only an extension of powers. I had some doubts about his judgment on Control matters but he handles Appeals well and can ignore unpopularity. Now, alas, he has left me no alternative. His attempt to make capital out of a colleague's error has put an end to any prospect he had of being entrusted with that

Section."

Good-oh! thought Lister. I told Paul that Foggart's plans might backfire on him. Good for the old man. "What d'you reckon you'll do then? Keep the status quo?"

Bird put on his spectacles again and looked at a piece of paper in front of him. "No no, there are elements of truth in some of the things Foggart said which I have been aware of and concerned about for some time. The increase in the number of applications, the burden on the A.P.O.'s. I was speaking with our friend Harry over lunch. As my original colleague, with Foggart, in the Department, I felt I would value his opinion. I didn't mention this Lower Wooton business. I asked him, if I were creating a post of A.C.P.O Control with a third area and the other A.P.O's definitely under one command, and supposing there were no suitable candidates from outside, to whom should I give the job. I was interested that he answered unhesitatingly – Pembleton."

"So he should," Lister said warmly. "And my answer would be the same."

Bird smiled at him soothingly. "My dear fellow, I intended to ask you, as next to myself. My own judgment I reserve to the end."

Lister couldn't help grinning. That was just what Paul had said that morning. "Bird will consult himself last of all." No doubt about it, he was a damn perceptive chap.

"You have no reservations – since this Lower Wooton business?" Bird asked, keeping his eyebrows up as cautioning arcs till Lister answered.

"None at all. Besides this was young Carr's gaffe. Foggart didn't let that out?"

Bird put his head on one side. "He didn't, no. But the Section Head is in charge. Carr must have been very new then. I take it this thing is some months old?"

"He'd been here two months. He knew the procedure."

"Oh tut tut. Two months! What's that? I admit I am not yet aware of all the facts. I would like the file – if it's available. But we should expect a Section Head to check a decision made by someone as inexperienced as that before he puts a signature to it."

"Well you'll find the decision wasn't in question – Carr did a very competent piece of work. He's a good architect. But he slipped up on a routine consultation."

Bird waved his spectacles. "We'll see about that. We'll see. When I have the file. Just now you've raised yet another interesting point. Unintentionally perhaps."

Lister sat up. For once in a dialogue with Bird he wasn't keeping pace with him.

"Yes," Bird said, putting on his spectacles again and consulting more papers on his desk. "I've been looking at some of our own young men the last few days. I believe it was you who discouraged anyone in the office from applying for Hugh Cole's job?"

"Cole's job? We're discussing that now, are we?" He hadn't liked the tone of Bird's last question. Bird obviously didn't like the tone of this answer either.

"I thought you realised, Derek, that the changes are all linked. We've had no suitable outside applicants for Head of Architecture and it was obvious that section needed tidying up so my thought was that Foggart, who does not court popularity, could do that job if the Section was split between the Areas and he had overall supervision. At the same time I had not dismissed as hastily as perhaps you did the talent we may have within the office. We are a County with a reputation in design. The models of Hugh's proposed village layouts and town centre plans have been much photographed and discussed. I have no objection to a young man of talent in that post. Hugh came to us straight from his fellowship in America. If we can I would prefer to keep that section."

Derek grunted. He felt Bird had accused him of something. "I only told Gordon Harris not to bother applying. As far as I knew no one else was interested."

Bird smiled. "My dear fellow, it gets round. The impression is formed that we have closed our minds to the young and inexperienced. Let them apply. At least one of the Plan Assistants might have wanted to try. But on paper, on the basis of qualifications and testimonials, Neville Carr is by far the most talented assistant we have." Bird let this sink in and then added, "Were you aware that he won the same travelling scholarship to America that Cole had but was unable to take it up because he was married?"

"Yes, I remember that at his interview."

"Do you get the impression that he has the self-confidence to handle a Section?"

"Ay, he seems confident enough. You might almost say cocky."

"That can be tempered perhaps by a few words from me on Lower Wooton. You agree it would be better to have a promising Section head there that none at all?"

"Of course."

Derek grinned to himself at the thought of relaying this to Paul who had wanted to be rid of Neville but hardly expected his promotion.

Bird took off his spectacles again and flourished them in the air. Now that he was eased of his anger with Foggart and had begun to cast out scraps of his plans for the reorganisation he seemed in a more relaxed and expansive mood. He picked up a sheet of typing from his desk-top and holding it in his hand, said, "This is as yet a confidential item for the Agenda. I dictated it to Miss James just before you came in. Please read it."

Lister bounced out of his chair and took the paper. One glance showed him that this was a recommendation for a new post of Assistant County Planning Officer in charge of Development Control. If Bird was putting this on the Agenda he must already have the agreement of the Chairman of the Committee and almost certainly of the Establishment and Finance Committees because he would never risk it being turned down.

"You've had this in mind some time then?"

Bird smiled faintly. "If our plan of this morning had gone through an ACPO post would have been intended for Foggart, a mere change of title, with relief from some of the other duties he undertakes at present. I explained to the Chairman that I couldn't define the exact function of the post till the question of Cole's replacement had been resolved. Now that Foggart has settled his own future so regrettably I have been able to put my recommendation into precise form as you see there."

Lister thought, when Foggart knows about this and that Bird has Pembleton in mind, he'll go up in smoke.

Bird said, "You are pretty friendly with Pembleton. Would you say, supposing of course he doesn't leave us for London, that he would be interested in applying for this?"

Lister grinned. "He'd be a fool if he didn't. With a baby coming and two other kids he's only moving to get up the grades, not because he's dying to leave the district."

Bird nodded. "But is he so completely right for the job as you and Harry believe? As our Department expands I'll want a team of first rate ACPO's in charge of each aspect of our work. The Control man is most in the public eye, dealing with tough, practical industrialists as well as with Ministry Inspectors and Q.C's in well-publicized Appeal Cases. Will Pembleton present an image of a long-haired intellectual? Will he wear his fancy waistcoats? I know it's absurd but that kind of thing could tilt the scales when some hard-headed tycoon is debating whether to develop in this County or the next."

Lister was bursting to reply but Bird held up his hand. "We'll call my question rhetorical for the moment." He checked his watch. "I must see Foggart next, then Cole about his meeting at three. After that I may ring through for Pembleton with the Lower Wooton file. I cleared today of engagements to settle the reorganisation."

Lister thought crossly, and I've not done one piece of real work all day. He said, "I'm afraid Paul's out site visiting this afternoon."

Bird said, "Then I shall see him first thing in the morning. I would still like to see the Lower Wooton file. See that it's sent in to me. Neville Carr can bring it."

Lister got up and gave him back the Agenda item. He wanted to escape now. Bird was ringing for Foggart but the bright eyes behind the spectacles were watching him.

"My dear fellow, you will oblige me by staying, distasteful as it may be." Bird was leaning back, polishing his spectacles on his handkerchief. "Ron Foggart is a colleague of too long standing for verbal castigation. I'm confident he will take my meaning from between the lines. Yes, I trust, between the lines."

"Well, damn it, yes. We've got to work with him afterwards." Unless, Lister added to himself, this finally uproots the bastard.

When Foggart came in the lines on his face tightened at the sight of the Deputy.

Bird began blandly, "We are having a short, necessarily short, conference to finalise our little plans." He handed him the Agenda item and smiled him into the other armchair. "Just glance at that and give me your comments, Ron."

Lister could tell by the gleam in Foggart's eye that here was the culmination of his hopes – ACPO Control and boss over Pembleton and the new APO. But gradually his brow furrowed. "You can't describe this as a *new* post, Mr Bird, the title and duties are new but" – he slapped his hand on the paper – "look what Miss James has put as the salary. Bottom of the scale. She must know that I'm –" He looked up because Bird had coughed. Uncertain he grinned from one to the other.

Lister thought, I wish to hell I could smoke but Bird dislikes it.

Bird coughed again and his voice went a tone higher. "I think you're under a slight misapprehension, Ron. Miss James has not made a mistake. This *is* a new post. I might say I have been *angling* for it for a good while." He stressed the colloquialism. "If my senior ACPO is to have further responsibilities" – he actually beamed at Foggart –"we must relieve him in other directions."

"Further responsibilities?" Foggart was perching nearer and nearer the edge of the armchair, the paper held out in front of him quivering in his hand. "But this *is* the Control post. This is what I – what you –" His lips were forming the word 'promised.'

Bird said quickly, "Things were at a tentative stage – even this morning. Many factors have combined together –" Lister felt him look to him for confirmation but he kept his head down, studying the fabric of the armchair. Bird started on a new tack. "You see, Ron, my aim in all this is tidiness. To have the Architectural Assistants working for the APO's involved an element of confusion. It obscured their true function. I think – and I believe I carry Derek here with me on this – that I have found a possible successor for Hugh Cole. That leaves the field clear to clarify the duties at a higher level."

"Clarify?" Foggart was staring at the paper as if a dastardly plot had appeared on it in magic ink.

"Yes," Bird said, more briskly than before, "the creation of that post addresses the problem caused by the increase in applications. It leaves me in a position to implement what has long been a *pet* scheme of mine." Derek intercepted a mischievous smile from him and was puzzled to know what was coming. Bird went on, waving his spectacles gently from side to side like a pendulum, "I have explored every possibility and taken into consideration your own very considerable abilities, Ron, as well as the substance of our little chat before lunch, and the inescapable conclusion is that *you*, as the senior ACPO, senior of two soon, later I hope, Chief of several," – he paused and pointed his spectacles at Foggart as if about to shoot him down, "*you* should have exclusive control over the administrative structure of the office."

Foggart leapt out of his chair like a cartoon character stung behind. "Admin!" He swung round on Lister, obviously sensing sinister counter-plots. "Admin!"

Lister shook his head vigorously and Bird said firmly, "*This* solution originated *solely* with me."

"*I'd* no idea what Mr Bird had in mind." Lister tried a chuckle to relieve the atmosphere but Foggart stood smouldering like a firework just lit.

Bird went on blandly as if his reaction had been quite normal. "Your first duty will be to report on the day to day running of the office with the aim of eliminating time-wasting procedures and achieving maximum efficiency. One hears of these Organisation and Method Studies but as the County Council has no plans to call in outside experts I would like to conduct our own. I know no one with a more thorough attention to detail or more skill in *winkling* out inefficiency than our own Chief Assistant. I would rather have his report than that of any outside body." He appeared now to be addressing Lister with the sideways smiles of one giving a testimonial in the presence of the recipient.

Lister knew that at any other time the prospect of a fault-finding mission would have been meat and drink to Foggart.

Foggart took a step forward and laid the Agenda item on the desk. "I'll do your report of course." He said it more like a refusal than an acquiescence. "I always supposed my job as Number Three in the Department gave me supervision over Admin. –"

Bird broke in, "My dear fellow, I want the borders defined."

But Foggart wouldn't be checked. "This, though," he put his forefinger on the paper, "this can't mean – I presume – those aspects of Development Control – Appeals, important cases – which the APO's have been glad to leave to me" – he was pressing closer over the desk and in a moment could be hooked on – "you're not proposing to remove *those* from me?" His voice suddenly cracked.

Lister looked out of the window, wishing he was Pembleton out on the moors.

Bird answered icily, "We could hardly advertise a post of ACPO Control and tell the applicant some of his work might be *poached* at any time by someone else." It was the first time his anger with Foggart had shown through. Lister thought, by God, in his way, the old man's tougher than I am.

Foggart found his voice, hooked his hands onto the desk and leant over Bird.

"Then give me this post and advertise for an ACPO for Admin."

The words fizzed with intensity. His eyes bored into Bird's face. Lister knew him so well and yet found it hard to realise how much this meant to him. But Bird had now concluded the business. He waved this away with a gesture of his spectacles and though Foggart remained hooked on, Bird spoke as if he were quietly sitting in the armchair.

"This morning we discussed a compromise. Compromises are not ideal. We *need* a Head of Architecture *and* a senior post in charge of Control with a new Area containing the key industrial developments and proposed motorway. The news of Wade leaving reinforced this and, as Pembleton too may be leaving, this Senior Post should be filled by a man with first class Control experience and" – he could sense Foggart bursting to shout that *he* was the man – "great restraint, tact, and *loyalty* in dealing with subordinates."

Bird sat back and looked at his watch.

Foggart sank away from the desk and back into the armchair. Lister remembered as a boy hurling a dud firework into the corner of the playground and seeing it lie there black and limp. Foggart looked like that, the life gone out of him.

Bird said, "Two-thirty. I asked Miss James to leave us undisturbed, but I wish to see Cole before his visitor comes since I am acting as host. Will you stay, Ron, or come back at three?"

It was asked courteously, casually, as if the day had never wavered from normality. Foggart said nothing and then, just as if Lister's dud firework had flared for an instant, he sat up in the chair and exclaimed, "You wouldn't give this job to *Pembleton!*"

"My dear fellow!" Bird dropped his palms down on his desk, then spoke in the former matter-of-fact tone. "If Pembleton was the best applicant, the

Chairman and I –"

Foggart cried, "What! Even after –?" He stopped. The flash was over. The black limpness returned.

Lister had got up to go. "You'll see Carr after your meeting?" he asked Bird.

"Yes, unfortunately I can't fit him in before."

Foggart had got to his feet now. The volition had gone out of him. He seemed to get up only in imitation of the Deputy. He repeated, "Carr?"

Bird was watching him in some concern. "I shall ring for Cole now with his plans. Are you staying, Ron?" He spoke rather loudly as if Foggart were deaf.

Foggart said, "Cole? I thought you said Carr just now." He seemed to be muddled by the names. But now Lister had opened the door to the outer office and Foggart's feet trended in that direction. He looked back at Bird with an effort. "I'll come back at three."

Bird, with raised eyebrows, arrested Lister's progress for a second, but the Deputy had had enough. He returned the look with a shrug and as he closed the door heard Bird pick up his phone and tell Miss James to call Mr Cole. He escaped to his own room.

Roger Weston, when he came back from his canteen lunch, flung open every window in Control that could be opened.

Hine, the beanpole draughtsman said, "Ay, the heat seems to get worse."

There was always a slow start after lunch. They were like children staying in the playground till the last minute. Roger stood at the window watching the river. The river went to the sea and soon he would be there with Dorothy Bird. He could see her lying on the sand, long, strong and powerful. It was her power he loved. She was not graceful. He had never been attracted to the petite or dainty as some big men were. He was so absorbed that he hardly noticed Harry Wade come in, pink and well-fed from the Senior Officers' dining room, till he walked up and whispered, "Have you told them?" His first thought was of Dorothy. Then Harry's face, all aglow, brought him back to earth.

"Oh no. I thought you'd want to tell them yourself."

"Yes, I would," he said and told them.

The draughtsmen made a poor audience. They seemed most successful in showing their astonishment. To make up for it Roger followed Harry into his glass cubicle, ostensibly to show him the recommendations to sign for the Agenda. Once inside he asked him all about Morlton. They were still talking when Neville came back.

"Does he know you got the job?" he asked Harry, nodding at Neville.

"I saw his wife. So he may know now."

The external phone rang so Roger left him to it and went back to his desk.

Neville looked up. "Is Harry very busy? I wanted a word with him."

Roger shrugged. "Should be. Make it quick. Pop in when he's off the phone."

Neville was telling himself he was mad to think Harry's advice worth having, but he must talk to someone. As soon as Wade was free he went in and bombarded him with a battery of questions: "Did you never fancy private practice, Mr Wade?" "How easy is it to be a pure architect after Local Government?" "How soon can one get a partnership?"

"I don't know, Neville. I always fancied a steady salary. Surely Local Government hasn't turned sour on you in six months?"

"It's personalities." Neville looked at Harry, sitting there, round, puzzled, perennially naïve. "I can't work with Pembleton. We're not compatible."

Harry raised his eyebrows. "You mustn't take his jokes to heart you know."

"Oh he was dead serious this morning. I've made a damn silly mistake and I want to admit it openly. But oh no, it's got to be wrapped up and the issue obscured —"

Harry held up his hand. "I don't want to hear this, Neville. Paul knows very well the proper way to handle these things."

Neville felt himself flush with anger. "But that's what I mean. Proper for whom? I believe in honesty but in Local Government it's the old boy network, scratching backs."

Harry shook his head. His face was moist as if Neville were generating even more heat in the little office. "It wouldn't be all purity and light in an architect's office. There's a professional approach and a non-professional."

"And who's made it like that? It doesn't have to be. We settle for relative solutions because it's easy. Like Pembleton over this business —"

"I said I don't want to hear that. Paul would never be unscrupulous. And don't forget, as your Section Head he's responsible for your actions."

Neville spread out his hands. "There you are again. This hierarchy business. I want to be responsible for my *own* actions."

"In private practice the *firm* would be responsible for your errors. That's life."

"That's not life. That's our paper civilization. There's nothing inherent in life or in human nature that means we have to obscure our values in this farcical way."

"Oh now, Neville, if you've made a slip-up, forget it. Paul will live it down. And don't go telling Mr Bird about this. It never does to make a mountain out of a molehill."

Neville returned to his desk. He thought, what a waste of time! If Harry was drowning and an idea floated by like a lifebelt he'd never catch it.

Roger said, "You shouldn't consult the other A.P.O when your own's away."

Neville didn't bother to answer. After a few minutes he took his work and went and sat in Pembleton's office. He couldn't concentrate. Lena had been in such high spirits when they parted that she was almost hysterical. "I shall fill this sketchbook – from here to the sea. Then I'll need a gable end. The flat's no good. Some things are bigger than us. Bigger than Lower Wooton. Bigger even than Paul Pembleton. I may be here at five o'clock – if I'm still alive." Then she had run down the steps to the quay.

The internal phone rang. Bird's voice said, "Carr? I have a few minutes in hand before three. Please bring in the file on Lower Wooton."

Neville jumped up, delighted. Bird knew. So it *was* serious. And Lena had tried to belittle it all. He knew where Pembleton had slid the file saying it mustn't be moved. It had to be now if the CPO wanted it. But it wasn't there. Somebody had taken it.

He rang through to Mr Lister who sounded cross. "No, I haven't got the blessed file. Mr Bird wants to see it *later*. He's got a meeting at three. ... Oh he wants it now *and* you. Well, there's only one other – try Mr Foggart." And he put the phone down.

Neville scurried out and along the corridor. He'd told Bird he'd be there at once. Foggart's door was firmly closed. Well, I don't give a damn for him.

He knocked a tough, treble knock.

Foggart's voice rasped, "Come in."

"Sorry to bother you but I believe you have the file on a Mr Hubertson's house at Lower Wooton?"

Foggart looked different, smaller, hunched. He gave one glance to see who had knocked so imperiously and then just mumbled, "What do *you* want with it?"

"Mr Bird wants to see me to explain it to him."

"He can't want you now. He has a meeting at three."

"He's rung for it now." Neville was sure he could see the file on the desk. Foggart practically threw it at him.

"Thank you. Do you want it back, Mr Foggart?"

"Want it? No. The thing's nothing to do with me."

Neville tucked it under his arm and was at Bird's door in three seconds.

He began apologetically. "I'm so sorry for the delay, sir. I had to find the file."

Bird told him to pull the upright chair up to the desk but instead of opening the file he put his head on one side, his eyes as bright as beads, and looked at Neville.

"Do you not know where Mr Pembleton keeps the files he's dealing with?"

"Yes, sir. I knew where he put this one, but somebody borrowed it at lunchtime."

"Ah, I see." Bird seemed pleased with the promptitude of this answer and its discretion. Now he took the house plan out of the file and studied the design of the extension. "Was this close to what the applicant originally submitted?"

"No, sir. That was a homemade plan. He was a history lecturer at the University."

Bird permitted himself a twinkle. But he said, "You do realise, Carr, we're not paid to save him the cost of an architect?"

"Yes, sir."

"So why did you go to so much trouble in this case?"

"I liked the potential of the house and its situation. The applicant was willing to co-operate. It was a chance to get a decent piece of development done."

Bird nodded. He took off his spectacles and sucked one end for a few moments.

"Would you say you get a lot of satisfaction from that sort of thing, Neville?" He was looking at him very brightly as if this was a key question.

Neville was bemused by the way the interview was going, not a squeak about the road improvement line, and this sudden use of his Christian name was disconcerting. But he could only answer a straight question in the same spirit.

"Yes sir. That is the aspect of the job from which I get most satisfaction."

Bird put on his spectacles again, put his fingertips together and shot suddenly at him, "So you never thought of going in for private practice?"

Neville felt the blood rush into his face. That was it, was it? Get rid of him but as courteously as possible.

"I have sir. Especially since I realised my error in this application. It was most careless of me and I'd like to apologise for any trouble it brings on the Department."

Bird's eyes opened wide and then he positively beamed. "Thank you, Neville." He whisked off his spectacles again and went on briskly, tapping the plan with them. "What I was really questioning was whether you hadn't thought of it during your training. You were recommended for a Fellowship in America. Is there something you enjoy about the day to day Development Control duties that would preclude your settling to this sort of work all the time behind a desk?"

"Well no, sir." Neville was now sure he'd been right about making a clean breast of it to Bird, even if these questions concealed hints that he would do better elsewhere. "But I've always deplored the view of some architects that planners are a nuisance or at best a convenience when wanted. That's quite erroneous and also unfortunate from the point of view of our total environment. Co-operation –"

"Yes, very interesting. Well, you haven't been with us long and have your career to develop. But would you say that at the present time your goal – if we can put it like that – is a job where you can mainly exercise your talent for design in a planning setting where the powers of a Local Authority give your work greater scope and influence?"

"Well yes sir —"

"Of course you wouldn't gain individual recognition. Hugh Cole for example is more likely to become known in the architectural world when he is on his own —"

"Oh I'm not troubled about *fame,* sir."

"No?" Bird sat back, closed up the Lower Wooton file and pointed his spectacles at Neville. "Then why, my dear fellow, have you not applied for his job?"

"His?" Neville was staggered. He felt blushes rising again. "Cole's job? I didn't know — I was under the impression — Gordon Harris has had longer experience than I —"

"He hasn't your paper qualifications. In any event I intend to invite him to apply. It mustn't be thought we had a fixed intention to go outside the office. I like to see the younger men applying for any senior post that falls vacant if they honestly think they can handle it. Diffidence is an excellent quality but I think the Committee and I may safely be allowed to distinguish the suitable from the impossible in cases like this."

"Of course sir." Neville was now feeling a warm glow inside like a child who has won a totally unexpected prize.

"You would have a lot to learn about the management of a Section."

Neville thought of Hugh Cole. "I think I could do it sir. I don't mind hard work." He noticed Bird had glanced at his watch. It was five to three.

"I like extreme conscientiousness in Section Heads, close attention to detail, punctuality, precision, as an example to those under them."

"Of course sir."

"And now may I know briefly what error you made over this application."

"Oh yes. I'm sorry sir. I thought you'd been told. The County Surveyor's letter explained there was a road improvement line affecting the house."

"And you were so pleased with your nice design that you ignored it?"

"No sir. I failed to read it all. It stated there was no objection on access grounds. The road improvement line was mentioned in the last sentence. I told Mr Pembleton the consultations were done and he signed the recommendation. It wasn't his fault at all."

"Had you been pressed to deal with the application as quickly as possible?"

"Mr Pembleton likes speed but I fear I was impatient with the verbosity of the letter. I thought I had the gist of it. That was why I never looked at the attached plan."

Bird nodded. "That's very clear — and honest. I too abhor verbosity. But one must beware of an impatient response which impairs our own efficiency — as in this case."

"Oh I know, sir. I now read everything. It won't happen again."

"Good. I'll keep this file for the time being as I have an appointment now." The phone on his desk rang as he spoke. He picked it up as Neville rose to leave. "Very well, Miss James, please ask Mr Foggart and the gentleman to come in and will you find out if Mr Cole is back yet. He is due at this meeting. Thank you." He put down the phone and pointed his spectacles at Neville who had retreated to the door. "Pick up an application form in Admin. for the Architectural post. We'll name a new date for interviews."

"Yes sir, thank you very much, sir."

The door now opened behind him and he jumped aside for Foggart and a pale, heavy man in a charcoal grey suit with matching hair and eyebrows. Foggart frowned at him as if puzzled by his parting words to Bird and his jaunty step. Neville grinned back.

As he passed through the outer office he heard Miss James say sternly into the phone, "Tell him, Gordon, the minute he comes in. Mr Bird is *waiting* for him." Neville thought, her status as the boss's secretary lets her to talk down to the younger assistants. She won't do that to me if I'm a Section Head. Then his mind began to grasp all the delightful aspects of what he had just heard. Not having to work with Pembleton, talking coolly as one Section Head to another. "Yes, Paul, my Section can have that for you next week." And Lena? She *must* be impressed! And the salary! They could buy a house! And then he recalled, like a sharp pain returning, the weird mood she had been in earlier.

In the Control room he looked out but the quayside was below the square. Knowing she might be there, so close, harassed him. He wanted to tell her his news.

He went into Pembleton's office and sat at the desk again. Her mad gaiety today gnawed at him. That painting this morning. Why had she been so odd about it? Gazing through the glass he saw Roger Weston's eye on him and set himself to work. The notes in front of him were some Pembleton had written after a site visit and he had to translate them into a letter to the applicant for more information. He had several letters to dictate to show Pembleton tomorrow but if he sent for a typist he wouldn't be able to think. He looked at the notes. Why did the wretched man run his words together? Why had Lena kept dragging Paul into the conversation? She had spoken with him briefly in the Square but claimed to know him better than he did. Her words and tone of voice came back to him suddenly. "What do you know about him, what he thinks or feels?" He had ignored that because she said so many extravagant things. She was a bright deadly insect among flamboyant flowers. But maybe he had spotted her now!

He pressed his clenched fist to his head and told himself, she's in love with Pembleton! It fits. She was meeting *him* today, not me. Was her mad talk because he agreed to go off with her? The portrait was Paul and I said that was a man I could admire and how she laughed! I've been a brainless fool! He told her to go and see his wife – to break it to her! And I said they were a close couple and she found that funny too.

He realised he had his hands clasped tight round his head. If Weston's looking again he'll think Bird's given me a rocket. But if this comes out he'll laugh! I told him my wife's a lonely artist. He took his hands out of his hair and picked up his pen again. What did she say about my hair this morning? Like a mat. And she compared it with Paul's. She must have seen Paul often to notice that – not a mere two evenings months ago. God, she's probably stroked it often enough to know the way it grows.

Now the reality came home to him. The physical reality. Pembleton was tall. Lena would like that. And Lena looked beautiful undressed. Long-bodied, small-breasted, narrow-hipped with her light hair flowing over her shoulders. She'd soon make an opportunity to let Pembleton see her like that, once they'd agreed to meet clandestinely. Pembleton could call at Bosworth Crescent on his way out to site visits, with Neville safe in the office. And his wife was pregnant. Maybe she was happy to let him have fun as long as he stayed with her. He knew other people's lives were like bad novels, sordid, seamy. You peeped and gave a nauseated gulp and prayed it couldn't happen to you.

The phone rang. He snatched off the receiver, angry at how it had startled him. It was a lady who wanted to know why she hadn't heard from them about her guest-house.

Neville found the file and tried to imagine the Pembleton she had seen, suavely explaining what the Council would require, and the same man going to bed with Lena. He fended her off for a few minutes till she said, "I don't like your tone, young man."

"I'm only telling you the facts. Our job is to get the appropriate use of land and buildings. It's the law that says you need permission to change the use of your home."

"Humph. There are a lot of very silly laws. Mr Pembleton didn't say I *couldn't* have my guest-house. He had morning coffee with me and saw all over the house."

Ay, and where had he been before that? "Look, madam, I didn't say you *couldn't* have it. He's put a note on the file that you'll let us have in writing that you agree about the garage and parking. Then we can recommend the Committee to grant permission."

"I think I'll ring up and speak to him about it. Will he be in tomorrow?"

"Yes, Madam." He rang off. Tomorrow? She would tell Paul he'd been rude to her and he would say, "Neville, you must try not to cause offence."

Offence! What about Pembleton's offence? Neville wondered where the blind anger was that he should be feeling. Just now all he felt for Pembleton was contempt. The great man had been reduced to pinching his assistant's wife. He was furious with Lena for letting him but strangely flattered that Paul Pembleton should desire something of his.

He hadn't forgotten Pembleton's look when he said, "And now, Neville, will you get out of my way." That, he thought, is just what I won't do. But suppose Lena has ended it today. Did the portrait get him out of her system? There was a kind of relief about her, perhaps an intention, in her odd oblique way, to start afresh. But I will let her know I know, and him too. I'm not going to be the mug they fooled and got away with it.

He looked at his watch. Three-fifteen. An hour and three quarters before he saw her – if she was still around. But – if she *had* finished the affair – what might she not do? He half started from his chair. The scraping of it on the lino made the faces in the outer office turn to look at him. He stretched his arms behind his head and settled again.

It was impossible to sneak out. Anyone might ask for him. Today was crucial. He was sure Bird meant him to have this job. But Bird could change his mind. Gordon Harris was to apply, plodding and uninteresting as he was and disfigured by his beard which Bird almost certainly disliked. Still he was always around when wanted. He wouldn't vanish after a recalcitrant wife in the middle of the afternoon. No, he must stick it out.

He pressed down his wiry hair as best he could, made a neat pile of the files that required draft letters and rang through to Admin. for a typist.

At three-fifteen Gordon Harris looked up as High Cole burst into the Architectural Section, rosy and damp with haste, and began talking almost before he was in the room.

"I've been on a thing with six wheels and steep stairs so you fall down when it jerks and people sweat germs over you and you *pay* for the experience. Still I've got a real cheque for an unmentionable sum." He waved it about. "Has anyone missed me?"

"Of course. Bird asked for you long before three to see him about your meeting."

Cole pushed his hands up through his hair. "Mine? I don't feel particularly drawn to it. I'm sure Bird can deputise for me very nicely. I suppose the Vulture's there too."

Pennyman said, "You had to come back by bus? Wouldn't this student chap let you keep the car another week?" Gordon noticed how Pennyman drooped with boredom when Cole was out. Now his presence had restored him to life as moisture to a flower.

"Alas, my favourite assistant, you speak truth. He has to impress a girl tonight. I stood in front of the scratch till he'd signed the cheque."

Gordon said, "I promised you'd go through the minute you came in. I had to take the designs in myself at five past. What could they do without them?"

"And why need they me, my hairy friend, if they have the fruit of my brain?"

But he went, tucking in his shirt, straightening his tie and putting on his jacket which he had slung over Pennyman's desk. He even whipped a comb out of his pocket and pushed it through his straw mop which only made it stand on end more than ever.

Harris shook his head with a smile like a rueful mother as the door closed on him and Pennyman wilted visibly at his desk.

Bird had sensed at once that the charcoal grey man, whose name was Baynes, had a workaday personality as drab as his appearance and that he had come expecting a workaday meeting. So Bird went out of his way to build up a sense of occasion.

"My dear Mr Baynes, I found the arrangements were to preclude my greeting you in person. I soon put that right. And how is –?" He named a top man in the company who had once given a talk he had attended and to whom he had been briefly introduced.

When Harris brought in the designs Bird made great play of the fact that he had never set eyes on them before. "You must show me round," he said to Baynes. "Having just brought myself in on this it's all quite new to me – what you've been hatching with Mr Foggart here and our designer who'll join us in a moment, De Beaumont Cole."

After a few minutes' scrutiny he looked hard at Baynes and said, "Well, I'm impressed. I must say, impressed." The tone suggested he was a difficult man to impress.

Baynes perhaps wondered if he had got into the wrong meeting but he began to explain that their architect should have come along but he was on holiday abroad and the chairman hadn't wanted the decision held up. "Still," he said, "our requirements don't vary. We have other factories. The internal layout will be much the same you know."

"Quite," Bird said, "but externally you want this one to be special. I appreciate that. There's tremendous publicity value in your move north. And as yours will be the first building on our new industrial site there'll be great press interest here." He laughed gaily. "Even the most powerful firms don't mind a little free advertising – eh?"

It was a few minutes more before Baynes could insert a word about the original plans his firm had submitted and by this time he was sounding apologetic about them.

Now Hugh arrived. Bird glared at him but when Baynes turned to see who it was Bird introduced him with a flourish. "De Beaumont Cole, our Head of Architecture."

The meeting didn't progress quite so smoothly after that. Bird could see that Foggart hadn't minded *him* monopolising things but he wouldn't stay in the background to Hugh Cole. Baynes too, who had only met Foggart so far, began making digs about things being changed without consultation and why had he been led to suppose their usual design would go through without trouble.

Bird felt the situation moving out of his control when Hugh grasped the sleeve of Baynes' jacket and exclaimed, "Your factory will be a beautiful gleaming thing lying on a desolate sea of mud and concrete. It could be months or years before there's another one within half a mile of it. Everyone driving by will see your logo and remember it."

Baynes said he'd have to talk to their architect and muttered darkly about cost. Foggart said that with the unemployment here he could be sure of a docile labour force.

"That'll keep your costs down and let you stick to your completion date."

Bird asked if the Chairman of the firm was coming up. "I'd be so pleased to meet him and entertain him."

"Not that I know of," Baynes said dourly. "He approved the site selection from the map and from the report of my discussions with Mr Foggart."

But Bird felt that the mention of the Chairman had subdued him a little. Perhaps the Chairman would like to see his factory on the front pages of architectural reviews. At all events, after a little more hedging, Baynes agreed to take away Hugh's designs and have them considered. He had smoked two of the cigars Bird had offered him and drunk tea from the stainless steel and glass tea-set which Bird kept for special guests.

Foggart showed him out. Bird put a hand on Cole's arm and restrained him as he was following. "What was so important that your lunch hour lasted until after three?"

"Yes," Hugh grinned. "Sorry about that. Still it seemed to go all right without me. Pretty dreary chap, wasn't he?"

"You haven't answered my question."

"If I said I was saying a long goodbye to my widowed mother it wouldn't be true. Actually I was selling my car. I'll have to use public transport for the rest of my days here, so I'm afraid that may play havoc with my time of arrival."

It was hard to credit the irrepressibility of the man, Bird thought. "In view of the time of your arrival this morning, to say nothing of the *state,* may we be allowed to hope for an improvement?"

Hugh bowed. "Hope, sir, is free. I too will hope. In fact I'm rather hoping Derek Lister will drive round by Brynbank for the next week. He quite likes that route."

Bird blinked his eyes once or twice. "If that brings you here on time, good. You draw your salary I understand for another week. I have an old-fashioned view that we should give value for money in this life."

They were standing a yard apart, the same height, but Bird, aware of his own trim plumpness saw Hugh like a wild sandy-haired troll, and then in a moment the mischief faded out of his face. Alone with his boss he must be finding it hard to play the fool.

He said, "Well you know, sir, with me you have to weigh the fact that most of my best work – like the plastics factory – is done between midnight and four in the morning."

Bird couldn't help a twinkle. Cole was rarely seen working but splendid designs somehow appeared. To be fair, he thought, the County's had its money's worth from him.

"You may have a point there." He went to his desk and sat down behind it and said, as though on impulse, "I want to ask you what you think of young Harris?"

"*Think* of him. Harris?" Hugh, jaunty again, pranced back to the desk too. "For *my* job? Are we not to be honoured with Ron Foggart?"

"There are changes afoot. Please drop no hints, but you can take it that they will not involve Mr Foggart in your Section."

Bird put on his most solemn look and saw Hugh open his mouth for a snap comment, think better of it, cock his head on one side, and repeat, "Harris?"

"Yes. Tut, tut, Harris has worked for you for nearly two years. What is he like?"

"He wears a beard."

"I know what he *looks* like."

"I'm sorry, sir, but his beard is the first thing that springs to mind. It's rather large. However, he is not without other qualities. For example, he works – all the time. It's noticeable in our room. And he's phenomenally patient. If I don't like something he's done he agrees quietly and starts again. I would tear things up or throw things."

"I can see that he's a contrast to you." Hugh bowed. "But he sounds like a follower rather than a leader, a copier rather than an originator. Is that fair?"

Hugh hesitated. Does he ever seriously assess people? Bird wondered.

"He's very competent. He'd organise the Section much better than I ever did."

"But you were appointed for your creative ability. How does he score on that?"

"Maybe five out of ten, but he could use others' creativity. He knows what's good and he always checks what's due when and he's a *genius* at finding things I've lost."

Bird nodded. "Like a good secretary. I'd rather see the lead man with the creative talent – if we can't find a man with both. But I wouldn't want to lose Harris. Would he work under a less experienced man with more qualifications? Or up and off in a huff?"

"Never, you couldn't have a more modest man. *And* he's rather rooted here by his family. It branches rapidly, at least a new twig every year. They're Catholics."

Bird, like any good Church of England man, had a strong admiration for Catholics as bulwarks against the new theology. He was sorry he couldn't reward Harris. He must keep an open mind till the interviews but it looked as if Neville Carr was the man. It was like a jigsaw. The last piece must fit. Carr was not absolutely right but he was the nearest to the right shape for the hole.

"Very well, Hugh," – he pointed his spectacles at him – "tell Harris he is invited to apply but that others are being asked too. Your second assistant, Pennyman –"

"Good Lord, he's not even qualified."

"Quite. I'm aware of that. So nothing need be said to him. That's all."

When Hugh had bowed himself out with a small flourish, Bird sat back with some relief. He was seeing the shape of the office for the foreseeable future and with Cole gone and Foggart absorbed in the minutiae of Admin. he felt he had achieved a commendable stability and tidiness. He lifted the phone and asked Miss James to remove the tea tray.

As soon as Cole was back in his room he called to Harris, "Gordon, get an application form from Admin. and apply for my job."

Harris laughed, "Got the sack? They don't even want you another day?"

"Wrong. Utterly wrong. Bird still loves me. More and more when he thinks of the wretched material from which he's got to fill my place."

Pennyman and the draughtsmen were agog. It wasn't in Hugh to do things quietly.

Harris said, "You don't mean *Bird* said I had to apply? Seriously?"

"*Had* to? Far be it from Bird to compel anyone —"

"Ah now look, Hugh. Did he mention me? Because you know what Lister said."

"On my oath the Great White Chief named you. But infer no foregone conclusion that you may disport your fungus in the inner sanctum the week after next. All kinds of riff-raff are to apply. Some maybe better riff-raff than you. At least in Bird's eyes."

"I see. It's like that. They'll have someone in mind – perhaps from outside – and they want a few more to make a show of a short list." Harris turned back to his work.

"Don't be down-hearted. I gave you a good testimonial."

Harris glanced up and grinned briefly. "Did you?"

Hugh looked uncomfortable and seemed glad when Pennyman said, "Who else would they ask? D'you think it's someone *inside*?"

"It's not *you*. Bird said he would strike a medal if you passed your exams."

"I'll send you a postcard. But who else is there? Ken Myers in Plan? Or Roger Weston or Neville Carr next door?" Office gossip was meat and drink to Pennyman.

Hugh struggled to clothe the names with personalities. They were mere faces ready to laugh or not at his jokes. "Roger will go for Wade's job. Ken Myers? The super-clean one? No use here. Neville Carr? A baby in a crash helmet. I wouldn't like to give up my throne to *him*. It's really scraping the barrel – just *thinking* of such people. And the idea of them fighting to get into my desk before I've even left it —" He stopped talking suddenly and went into his own office and shut the door.

Pennyman giggled and half got up as if to follow.

Harris said, "Sit still and get on with your work."

Pennyman said, "Well, what's he up to now?" as if expecting some new foolery.

"Nothing. We're all talking blithely about his successor and he doesn't like it."

"What? Hugh wouldn't be bothered by that. He *started* the subject."

"Much you know about anything."

"Will you apply?"

"Of course I will."

One of the draughtsmen called across, "We'd like to see you get it, Gordon."

Harris laughed. "The devil you know."

In his office Hugh heard them and stirred up clouds of papers like a smoke screen. But nothing checked the sickening feeling that he was in a condemned cell listening to his gaolers discussing the day after his execution. He threw everything into a heap and came out again. Talking was the only panacea. He began to tell them about his meeting.

"This Plastics Factory man. Charcoal grey all over. Hair, eyebrows, even his face was pale grey. Suit, socks, shoes and a very dark grey personality. Can you imagine selling my beautiful factory to such a man? I did it though. The Bird stood there blinking his beady eyes and twittering that he knew the company chairman and the Foggart uttered a few vulture screams but no one took any notice of him."

"We'll send you a photo of it," Pennyman said, "when it's built."

A voice said to Lena Carr, "Hey, you can draw, can't you!"

It was the same boy who had spoken to her in the morning.

Lena turned a page of her sketchbook. "Here, you try that crane."

"Na, that's dead hard."

"It's not. It's a simple basic shape."

He took the pencil from her and very tentatively put in the upward line of the crane and the downward line of the cable.

Lena said, "Good. You've gone for the essentials."

"Uh?" He looked at the real crane. "I could never do all that stuff at the bottom."

"Maybe not but what's a crane for?"

"Lifting things o' course. Heavy things. I'm not daft."

"So it's got to be strong and stable, steady and firm." She took the book back and added the cabin, the hook and the planks it was lifting, the quayside and a few figures.

He was just starting to make admiring grunts when he stopped and scratched his head. "Yeah but them planks would pull it over." He took the pencil from her and added a bold line completing the supporting framework. Then he gazed at it in astonishment. "Ee, that makes it right doesn't it? I done that." He looked at her for approbation.

"Well, you know what you'll make – an engineer."

"Hey, that's better than an artist, isn't it?"

"Better paid, but you could be both, only you'd have to work at school."

"Huh!" He pulled a face. "I'd work if *you* was our teacher."

"What school are you at?"

"Cranwell Road Junior. It's a crummy joint. Why don't you get a job there?"

"I'm not trained as a teacher."

"You'd be a flaming sight better than the lot we've got there."

"Why are you not there today?"

"Had chicken pox. I've spent what me Dad gave me for the bus home. I bought a pie an' crisps an' a bottle of pop an' an ice-cream. So I'll hang around till he comes out. He works in there."

"County Hall? So does my husband. Stay and draw then."

"Oh I don't know." He looked about him and spotted an older boy heading for the stalls on the quayside market. "*He's* skiving. He'll be in the money. He does drugs." He dashed off and caught the lad up

Lena sighed, put her sketch book into her bag and climbed the steps to the Square. Here the heat was fierce. She ran over and went down the steps where Paul had directed her to the Newspaper Offices. She found them in Rivergate but as she approached she saw an entrance leading up some stairs. A brass plate on the door announced, amid a medley of shipping firms, that on the fourth floor was a scholastic agency.

On an impulse she climbed the stairs. In the small office at the top a girl was filing her nails behind a plastic topped table. She smiled at Lena and lifted her eyebrows.

"I want a job as an art teacher but I haven't a teaching diploma."

The words sounded in her ears both thrilling and astonishing and she was sure the girl would say, "Sorry, that's no good then."

Instead she got up and went to a filing cabinet saying merely, "What age group?"

"I don't mind."

"Well, we get the private school vacancies mainly. There's a Head of Art at St Hughes for next term." She pursed her lips at Lena. "Are you straight from College?"

"No, I trained in London and have been working in Commercial Art." The thought of St Hughes was like a douche of cold water on the project. She had seen its girls in grey blazers and panama hats. Should she turn tail and run now?

But at that moment a gentleman came from an inner office, round-shouldered and flabby but rubbing his hands eagerly as he walked. He beamed at Lena and came round the table to shake her hand. "We have the pleasure of the company of –?"

"Mrs Lena Carr."

"Delighted, Mrs Carr. Always take particulars first," he said to the girl. "Now how can we help you?" He motioned her to a chair by the window and took one himself. "Even though term has begun you'd be surprised how many schools start under strength."

Lena sketched in her background and in less than ten minutes he was dialling to make an appointment at The Grosvenor School.

"Mrs Kellett says can you come today?"

Now she was shivering with excitement. "Yes, where is it? I'd have to go home first for my portfolios and references, and I haven't a car."

"It's in Newmont. Plenty of buses."

"Say three quarters of an hour then."

He spoke into the phone, his eyes on Lena's skimpy dress and long bare legs.

"Should I change first?" she asked, her face burning.

"Change! Mrs Carr, I think you're just what The Grosvenor wants."

Twenty minutes later she left Bosworth Crescent with a fat portfolio and caught a bus to Sutton Avenue. The Pembletons live in Sutton *Terrace*, she recalled. I could pop in on Eleanor. All the time she was thinking, this can't be happening but if Neville wants to go away, let him. If I love this job I'll stay. Only I wish it was young boys not awkward pubescent girls. That was all she knew so far about The Grosvenor School.

It proved to be a big Victorian house with a garden concreted for a playground. A few girls were playing tennis with neither skill nor vigour. A signboard announced 'The Grosvenor School for Young Ladies. Secondary and Commercial. Principal Miss Mary Grosvenor M.A.' Over this had been inadequately pasted Mrs Z.S.Kellett BSc.

Lena thought, Good grief, what am I doing here? She rang the bell.

A flamboyant female with blue hair and heavy eye make-up opened the door.

"Mrs Carr? Come in. I'm Mrs Kellett. The secretary's busy. Term only started on Tuesday and we're still in a muddle."

She led her into a Victorian parlour unchanged except for a large desk and shelves with pigeon holes. They sat down in chintz armchairs by the green marble fireplace.

Mrs Kellett rushed on, "Miss Grosvenor died last year and I'm hauling the school into the twentieth century by its boot straps. You'll see the basement I've turned into a club run by the Senior Girls. Much of our work focuses on it – a café with food made in cookery class, hairdressing, fashion shows, music, drama. It's run on business lines and those weak at maths *plead* for extra lessons." She drew breath. "Tell me about yourself."

Lena, feeling breathless too, gave her as snappy an outline as she could.

"So you've had nothing to do with teenagers – ever?"

"I was one myself – for seven years."

"Good answer, but they're changing all the time. What struck me about these ones was how little they were involved with life out there. They've heard of the cold war and atomic bombs, but what they want are easy jobs, money for clothes and a husband and kids. I stirred them up a bit at Assembly one day last term and the most *thinking* girl in the school came to me afterwards and said, 'You've made me realise this world is hell. Suicide's the only answer.' Now what would you have said to that, Mrs Carr?"

"Me? Oh dear. Sometimes I'd agree with her. I couldn't say that, could I?"

"It's honest. I like you, Mrs Carr, though I'm not sure yet that you want to be a teacher or that you ought to be. What about the times you *wouldn't* agree with her?"

"Oh! Well, being alive has lots to offer too, like the chunkiness of a block of wood, the smell of oil, the colour of it on the surface of water, the sound of dry leaves."

"Of course, you have the heightened senses of an artist. May I see your work?"

Lena showed her. "I've been unsettled since we came to Midcaster. I gave up work to paint full time but I need outside stimulus. There's some of my work in these magazines. I was design consultant for a company – graphics, showroom layouts etc."

"It's good. You have a flair. Come, let me show you the club." She jumped up and led the way to the basement stairs from which rose the chatter of girls. "Just observe the lettering on notices, the colour scheme, the general layout. There's no one on the staff with any training in that line. The girls experiment but it's hit and missy."

Lena, trying to avoid the stares of many eyes as she was whisked round the rooms, saw nothing that she wouldn't want to change. Her excitement mounted.

When they were back in Mrs Kellett's room she said, "So it's not going to be like art lessons I had at school. Paint a day at the seaside with six colours and a thin brush."

Mrs Kellett chuckled. "We still have a dear soul who's been here twenty years who does just that with the lower forms but I've eased the older girls out. Their timetable is quite flexible. Yours would be a new post. Design Specialist. How about that?"

"Are you offering me the job?" Lena found she was hanging on her answer.

"I'm giving you my idea to see what you think. But wait! I must tell you the other project I have in hand. The suicide child is head girl this year and she and I had a long talk ranging from God to treading on beetles by mistake. I told her the house next door was for sale, very neglected, badly converted into tatty flats and I wanted to buy it for the school to run for destitute families. Would she enthuse the girls to help? She said yes."

"But that's brilliant. Will they work on it in school time?"

"Anything we can justify to the parents as educational, yes. But I hope the girls will eat in the school café and work in the evenings when we get going. It's very long term. We really need an architect first to look at it professionally."

Lena leapt to her feet. "But my husband's an architect. Honestly, I'd really love this job and he would help as well." She couldn't believe what she was saying.

Mrs Kellett rose too clapping her hands. Then she made a gesture of reining herself in. "Ah no. You see, I can take money out of fees for school refurbishment but not for this other house. I'm hoping some of the staff will work for love, but experts –"

"No, you don't know him. Wild horses wouldn't keep him away. He was a ban-the-bomb-marcher. He's one of life's natural martyrs. He'll want to come and *scrub*."

Mrs Kellett ran her hands through her blue hair. "What a lovely man! Well, have I got two for the price of one? I call that doing business. Can you start next Monday?"

"*I* can. *He* works full time for the County but there's evenings and weekends."

"Well, this is just a miracle. So, Lena – it *is* Lena isn't it? And I'm Zoe. Now sit down again, my dear, and we'll do the thing properly. Your starting salary . . ."

Lena walked out half an hour later onto the hot pavement and wondered if she had been in a mad dream. But there was the house next door, shabby, up an overgrown drive. So whatever had she done? She had wanted to show Neville she had her own life apart from his. But now she had involved him and she feared his enthusiasm might smother hers to bits. She stood, arrested by an urge to rush back and obliterate him from the scene.

Her eyes, flickering wildly about, focused on the street name of a turning at right angles to this one. Sutton Terrace. Where *Paul* lived. So close! After school I could call. I could *baby-sit*. I could become immersed in his life. Find out if he is really anything like the man I drew. She crossed over and looked at the first house number – 62. Theirs was 11 on the side with the bigger terraced houses and the long front gardens. Neville had vanished from her mind. There'd be nothing odd in calling since Paul had suggested it and she'd told him she wanted a job. What more natural than to tell that dull frump of a wife of his that she'd got one already.

She tossed back her hair, tucked her portfolio firmly under her sticky armpit, and, despite the heat, walked briskly down Sutton Terrace.

A few miles below Wanwick the Wann entered a lazy meandering stretch among shoals and gravel banks, transformed from the clamorous torrent above the town where it leapt down from the high moors in the series of steps known as the Falls of Wann. Paul, cutting across country from Hopewood, stopped the car when he reached the Wann valley trunk road. Here he examined a twenty-five inch map. Mrs Potter's sausage rolls and beer had made a small impression on his emptiness but it was half past two now. Perhaps the mad woman of Old Mill Farm would give him a cup of tea – if he had time to go there.

As he sat in the car studying the map the sun's warmth was like high summer. There was a lushness and dreaminess over the river levels that a south-countryman would never associate with the north. But he had been born in the county though he was only eight when the family moved to London. He had come back with an instant recognition. If he went to London now he would miss the variety and the spaciousness.

He folded the map and drove on. He would approach from this, the south side. A path for anglers was marked on the map but it might be overgrown now. The shoals would have shifted too and they were what he had come to see. He ambled along looking for a break in the tangle of vegetation that covered the slope to the river. He caught a glimpse of the long brown back of a gravel bank like a huge crocodile lying in the water. This was the spot he wanted. He parked the car on the grass verge and, finding a natural gap between two clumps of broom, he plunged down towards the river. The slope fell in two big terraces. He scrambled down to the first easily enough but on the next was a broad boggy patch with moss of an electric green and clumps of marsh grass. It looked impassable. He was enjoying the exercise and the utter cleavage between this and the office morning. But he didn't want to appear in Wanwick scratched and muddy. And time – as usual – was against him. He should have driven straight on to Cottle, crossed the river there and driven back on the B road the other side. A lane ran down to the water there. That was the way Curry and Son would take their lorries out.

He sat down on a smooth grass slope. The sun beat on the back of his neck and he felt drained of energy. He wanted a rucksack bulging with ham sandwiches and water bottles, and Eleanor lying beside him with her arms stretched behind her head. There had been many hot afternoons like this when they cycled out from London to explore the Home Counties and each discovered they wanted no one else in the whole world. He was invited to Windsor and Mrs Harvey, who hadn't a son, loved him for Eleanor's sake.

He closed his eyes. There was no sound but the lazy sucking of the river in its summer channels. The present was irrelevant. He was thinking of the first time he had met Eleanor. His sister Vera was Head of English in a big London high school and she told him about her newest assistant who was helping with the production of *Hamlet*. "Her fourth form crucifies her because she's too nice but she's sticking it. She'll be useful in the play as she had drama experience at College, make-up and lighting and things. Says she can't act though I bet she could if she tried. She's shy but look what *you* were like!"

He only met her because Vera came home on the Sunday a week before the play and moaned, "Hamlet's got measles. Mr Marsh is his named understudy but he's twice as old as his mother and he's put on weight and can't get into the costume." She looked across the dinner table at Paul. "We need a slim, handsome young man, who knows the part and has free time for the next week to rehearse with our bunch. Like a university student whose vacation has already started." "I suppose it might be amusing," Paul said.

"I hope not," said Vera. "It's meant to be a tragedy."

So his first meeting with Eleanor was in the boy's cloakroom. He had struggled into the costume and Vera had brought in a lanky girl with short brown hair and no make-up and said, "Miss Harvey'll put you right in a jiffy, Paul" and left them to it. Assorted soldiers and courtiers milled in and out yelling, "Miss, where's the safety-pin box?" "Me tights have split, Miss." "Hey Miss, Osric pulled me beard off and I can't find the glue."

Miss Harvey looked him up and down and took refuge from shyness in being very professional. "You're longer in the body than Peter Watson but at least you're not as fat as Mr Marsh. Thank goodness Hamlet wears black. It won't show if I insert an extra length of material at the waist. I'll pin it now for the rehearsal but give it me afterwards and I'll stitch it tonight." As she worked round him head bent and pins in her mouth Paul could not have imagined anyone less attractive. Her features were rather large, her skin an even pale brown, her hands big and capable. When she stood up he gave her one of his dazzling smiles and said, "Thanks. That's less draughty round the middle." She smiled back, then exclaimed, "Goodness it's just struck me how weird it is that boys who are so horrible grow into men who —" She stopped, embarrassed and said quickly, "I'll put an extra ruffle on the sleeves to lengthen them, otherwise it'll look as if Hamlet outgrew his shirt at College." They both laughed and the moment passed.

Years later she told him, "It was terrific after all those swarming boys to have someone who stood still without fuss and then thanked me with a wonderful smile. If anyone had said, 'That's your future husband' I would have said, 'Oh yes please.' And you were devastating as Hamlet. I sat in the wings and quite forgot to turn the pages of the prompt copy. When you died at that first rehearsal I thought how dead you looked and I nearly cried."

Paul lay back now on the grass, as limply as he had lain then. The 'four captains' had come to lift him and hadn't been able to get him off the ground. They had dissolved into giggles and Vera had slain them with the edge of her tongue. "The man's *dead*. He can't *help* you." After that a stretcher draped in purple was devised. He was edged onto this and borne successfully off.

Vera was saying, "Paul. You're on next. No, it's not *Hamlet*. The pantomime's called 'The Witch of Blattingford.' Get him ready Miss Harvey." Eleanor put a dunce's cap on him which Cathy had made from rolled up newspaper. "It'll do very well," they said. "You're the wizard." He didn't want to admit he didn't know the part. It was so hot. It must be the central heating. But it was in the school grounds. This was grass.

He sat up. There was a swimming in his head and an ache behind his eyes. He looked at his watch. He had only dozed for a few minutes. The heat lay on everything with the weariness of late summer. Through the overgrown vegetation the gleam of the river had a sultriness that depressed him. He had to get down there, bog or no bog. Thirty yards to his right a young larch tree grew out obliquely over the marshy ground from between two rocks. He took off his jacket and laid it on the dry sward, taking from the breast pocket a notebook and pencil which he stuffed into his trouser pocket.

He walked over to the larch, grasped its leaning trunk with both hands and tested it with his weight. It was springy but strong. Swinging his legs off the ground he heaved himself along the bending sapling and dropped onto firm ground beyond the bog. He was on the edge of the final slope to the water and grabbed at a bush as he slithered down to the stony shore. Bird would say, "It's for this kind of thing that you have an assistant. Senior Officers are not expected to scramble about the country like schoolboys."

The biggest gravel bank was immediately in front of him. He jumped a stagnant cut-off channel and climbed to the crest of the long shoal to stamp the whole scene on his mind. He was on the inside bend of a long meander. The river had pushed up this bank of gravel and formed smaller ones. They had thickened since the map was drawn and now the current bit more deeply into the soft mud of the opposite bank. Rich cattle pastures over there were being steadily eroded. If Curry and Sons extracted gravel it would be an excellent thing.

He took several deep breaths. It was fresher here and the aftermath of daytime sleep had left him. Curry and Sons must not remove so much gravel that the increased flow caused flooding lower down and they must touch only the existing shoals not the grass grown banks. Then there was access. The lane to the B road was the only feasible route but that passed under a railway bridge. Paul could see the ruler straight line of the embankment crossing the far meadows. He'd already sent off the letter of consultation to British Railways. They would want to make Curry liable for any damage to the bridge. He made rapid notes and sketches. Neville hadn't had a gravel extraction before and wouldn't realise that one must acknowledge the River Board as the experts on flow and erosion. Neville was not very good at deferring to superior knowledge.

Anyway, he was enjoying this. His headache had gone. The pages of his notebook flapped as a westerly breeze stirred over the open reaches of the river. He looked at his watch. Only three-fifteen. Barely forty minutes since he'd left the car. He strode along the gravel bank his shoes scrunching the river-smooth pebbles and leapt the stagnant channel again. Seeing a gap he climbed up using a whitened root as a handhold and found that the bog was narrower here and he could jump over. "I've come up a different way," he told himself. He had walked upstream on the gravel bank so the larch tree where he had left his jacket should be to his left. Irritated at the slight delay he scrambled along the edge of the marshy ground, slipping once or twice so that the mud came over his shoes.

Just then to his right up the bank he saw the gleam of red metal. A car must be parked by the roadside, probably not far from his own. At the same moment the head and shoulders of a man in a tweed jacket emerged from the bushes up there and moved towards the car. He disappeared from sight but Paul heard the car door slam and the engine start up. The red gleam moved away and daylight appeared where it had been.

A second later Paul spotted the larch tree ahead. He quickened his pace, reached it and stooped to pick up his jacket from the grassy bank. It wasn't there. He looked further round, pulling aside bushes and plantain, but that was ridiculous. There wasn't cover for a jacket anywhere. With rising panic he knew it had gone. The man in the red car! He thought, he was wearing *my* jacket and in the pocket are *my* wallet and car keys. God, I'm stranded.

He went hot and cold. He had thought the man had stopped to relieve himself. Perhaps he had and had seen the jacket and been tempted. Or had he thought it was lost and was taking it to the police station at Wanwick? He began leaping up the bank, forcing his way through broom and gorse so that he was scratched and one shirt sleeve torn when he emerged onto the road. If he could get a lift! He looked along the road and there was his car. How could the other man fail to connect the jacket and the car? Hadn't he seen him on the gravel bank? So it *had* been stolen. This was a hell of a mess. If he had to walk six miles to Wanwick he'd be in a right state. Too many people there knew him. Councillor Cranston would have a good laugh. Even a decent chap like Mason waiting for him now in the District Surveyor's office would be tempted to spread the story round.

He walked back to the car and looked inside. His briefcase lay on the passenger seat, files bulging out of it. Knowing he had locked it he tried all the door handles. He thought, I ought to be briskly on my way, at least to Cottle for a phone box. That's only three miles and I might be able to hitch a lift. He looked longingly down the empty road. Not a vehicle was in sight.

It was the dead time of mid-afternoon.

Then he heard a shout from the opposite direction. He spun round hoping irrationally that the thief had come back. A short bearded man in fisherman's boots was approaching from the direction of Cottle. Improbably the words he called out were, "Excuse me, can you give me a lift to Cottle."

Paul studied the man as he came close. He was dressed shabbily but his voice was cultured. It was an odd combination so he demanded, "Where have you sprung from?"

"As a matter of fact I've been watching you by the river. I hope you'll forgive me for being curious. When I saw you coming away I hurried up to see if you'd give me a lift home. There are few drivers who stop these days. I find it better to ask a stationary one. It's perhaps a little sooner than I wished but the light's altering already. Is there anything wrong? You've hurt your hand I see."

Paul looked down at a scratch which was bleeding. "It's nothing."

"There's a path about a hundred yards back. That's the way I came up. You're in no hurry to go, I see. I can collect my gear then. I left it at the top of the path."

He turned back to head the way he had come.

"Just a minute." Paul said, "I *am* going to Cottle, but I can't give you a lift. I've lost my car keys." The little man's bland self-assurance made him put an edge to his tone that he never normally used with strangers.

The man turned round with an eager smile. "Have you really now? I thought something was wrong."

"They were in my jacket pocket. It's the jacket I've lost."

"Well now, that's a big thing to lose, a jacket. Intriguing though. I thought to myself down by the river, that man's an official who's not normally in his shirtsleeves. I hope you don't think it impertinent of me. I just happen to be interested in people."

Paul said, "I'll have to walk to Cottle and ring the police."

"That might be premature," the little man said, his beard wagging up and down.

"For goodness' sake," Paul burst out. "I saw the thief drive off with it."

The man put his head on one side. His pale eyes smiled in a kindly way at Paul.

"Now don't be angry. What's a jacket? You're a whole man standing there. You mustn't be so hidebound you can't be complete without a jacket. But let's sit down on the grass and you tell me step by step what happened. It's not a life and death matter but it would be helpful to find it. Otherwise your car is no use to you – or to me for that matter. Now I have to be good at finding things because I'm always losing them. So I've evolved my own simple little method. Now tell me what you did from the beginning."

Paul hesitated but there was something compelling about the little man who had sat down on the bank by the roadside and patted the ground beside him. Shaking his head at the absurdity of it Paul joined him and outlined his movements. Immediately the man got up rubbing his hands with glee.

"By your own admission you've not tried the one essential first step. Show me where you entered the bushes the first time."

Paul shrugged his shoulders. They crossed the road together and soon came to the gap in the bushes. There were marks on the grass where tyres had recently crushed it. The red car must have stopped just there.

"All right," said the little man. "Here we go. He led the way in and cautiously negotiated the slope. "There you are," he said at the bottom. "It always works."

Paul stared over the man's shoulder. On the bank lay his jacket. He snatched it up and felt in the pockets. His wallet was there and his car keys.

"In heaven's name –!" Then he understood. He'd flung his jacket off *before* he walked to the larch tree. *This* was the bank he'd dozed on. He went along to the larch and looked back. You couldn't see it from there for the thick vegetation and humpy ground.

He walked back. "You must think me a damn fool."

"Not at all. Only it's unwise to *assume* things, better to retrace your steps *exactly*. Besides by your own account you had just risen, muzzy with sleep. But I do hope you're mentally apologising to the man in the red car."

While the little man chatted Paul drew on the jacket, finding unbelievable comfort in the feel of it on his back, and they climbed up to the road.

Here Paul faced him with one of his best smiles. "I'm most grateful. You've more than earned your lift. Where's this fishing gear of yours? Let's be on our way."

"My –? Oh it isn't fishing tackle. If you'll drive along we'll see it by the stile."

If he's a magician I won't be at all surprised. Paul unlocked the car, moved the briefcase to the back and wound down the windows. It was stiflingly hot.

The little man settled in as Paul checked his watch before driving off.

"Ah, I see time matters to you. Would it be impertinent to ask if you *are* an official of some kind?" Before Paul could answer he pointed to the stile. "Here we are." Beside the stile was an easel with a couple of canvasses and a small haversack. "No, no, sit still." The little man was out and piling them all into the estate car as if he owned it. When he had jumped back in he said, "I noticed the briefcase and a glimpse of files."

"Yes, I work for the County Council. And you are a painter, I see."

"I dabble. But now you interest me. I thought you would have an outer self for routine matters. I do very well if I keep my mind on one thing at a time."

Paul, trying to drive as fast as the road would let him, still felt shaken by the very thing the little man had put his finger on. His outer self had let him down badly. He must concentrate hard for the rest of the day or reality would slip away from him. "Officials," he said, "are still mere humans."

The little man chuckled. "I have a theory about this – the de-humanising process. I thought I'd write a book but I am only a butterfly. That's why I'm so interested in *educated* nine to five workers. I believe some of you people are University trained?"

"I was at Oxford after the war."

"Now you'll be – let me see – turned thirty. I wonder what officialdom has done to you over the years. The man behind the forms, who says yes or no to the general public." His manner was really too disingenuous to be called impertinent.

Paul answered lightly, "I'm nearer forty than thirty and I *think* I'm surviving."

"Good and I'm nearer seventy than sixty. It's time we introduced ourselves. My name is Thomas."

"Happy to know you, Mr Thomas. My name is Pembleton. But I don't think I want to be a case history in your book."

The little man exploded with glee. "Ah, the reserve, the barriers. We

English! When I said Thomas I *meant* Thomas. Surnames are labels but the first name is the man. I always give mine at once as a short cut. I fancy that when you were a student you would have responded readily to an honest attempt at a give and take of ideas."

Paul laughed. "If it's any help my name is Paul."

"Well Paul. It makes you feel a little naked doesn't it, telling a stranger? And you were a little naked without your jacket. Still it's a good thing, isn't it? I don't believe in embarrassment. We should rid ourselves of it."

Paul saw with relief the chunky tower of Cottle Church ahead among the trees.

He said, "You think because I represent officialdom I can't be myself." He was thinking of Hugh Cole saying, 'We are THEY.' "Why assume incompatibility?"

"Ah but I don't assume it. I'm sure that you set out with high ideals but are they not constantly eroded – like your river – by people who see your forms merely as troublesome pieces of paper which restrict their freedom?"

Paul said, "Here's Cottle. Which end of the village do you live?"

"I hoped you would come and have tea with me. Or a glass of beer."

"Thank you but I really haven't time."

"Of course. The domination of the clock. Set me down here so that you need not leave the main road."

"I have to go into the village. With all this gear I must drop you at your door."

Paul began driving slowly down the leafy road which was Cottle's main street.

The little man gestured to The Sheaf of Corn. "I live in a caravan at the back."

Paul drew in, took a map from his brief case and got out to help Thomas with his gear. "I have to consider electricity lines here but I'd better look at your caravan too."

The little man's guileless face dissolved in laughter. "I've told the wrong man, haven't I? Joe said to keep quiet about it as it wasn't official. I'm afraid I was thinking of you as Paul, a friend, not in any other capacity. You see the pity of it. I am just Thomas."

"If you ever earned a living you must have had another capacity as you call it."

"No no." The small beard wagged up and down. "I was myself. This way. There's a path to the back of the inn." They emerged into a desert of weeds, tipped ash and sad cabbages. "Joe's allotment. The landlord of The Sheaf. I hope you won't prosecute *him* for letting me put my caravan here. So you are rivers, electricity *and* caravans."

Paul propped the easel against the caravan steps. "I work for the County Planning Department. What I'll do is ask the Rural District Council to send you a form on which you can apply for planning permission. Incidentally, how long have you been here?"

Thomas pinched his beard between his thumb and forefinger. "Three months, Paul, I should say. So I get a form – the answer to everything."

Paul was now looking at the map in his hand. His mind was on the electricity transformer. He located the spot where Neville had marked a T on the map.

Thomas sat down on the step to pull off his boots. Paul said, "Just fill it in, send it back to the R.D.C. who will add their comments and send it on to us. We may have to recommend permission be refused."

He strolled across to the boundary wall which separated the allotment from the field where the remains of Cottle Castle stood. Yes, if the transformer were concealed on this waste ground beyond the caravan the line could go underground past the castle.

"You mean, to put it brutally, I should look for somewhere else to live." Thomas had followed and was peering up at his face. He had changed into rope sandals. "No, brutal is not the word. It's done with a piece of paper. You Paul can decide to put me Thomas out of my home not because we are enemies or you covet my dwelling –"

"It's County policy." Paul laughed. "I've nothing against you personally."

"But that's just it. I wish you had. If you armed your clerks with billhooks and staves and led them against my caravan I'd barricade myself in for a siege – *that* I could enjoy." The little man returned to his caravan and mounted the steps. "We could have had a pleasant conversation if you'd stayed to tea. I have an open mind."

"One moment," Paul called to him. "It would help if you'd tell me your surname."

"Ah you see why I dislike surnames. A Christian name can't be used against one. My name is Smith." Paul laughed. The little man looked offended. "Professor Smith if you like. I held the Chair of Classics in Midcaster. You'll find me in the records there."

"I'm sorry. I wasn't doubting you. It's just that Smith still leaves you fairly anonymous. I often regret that people remember Pembleton only too well."

"Now you sound friendly. Now that you can place me. Curious how our minds work in opposite ways. You must know I am a Mr T. Smith, owner of a caravan on land rented from The Sheaf of Corn Inn, Cottle, near Wanwick. Do I get a file number now?"

"That's right." Paul flashed his sweetest smile. "I wish you good afternoon and thank you for your valuable assistance."

"In fact I'm just a man called Thomas." The professor, perched in his doorway, tapped his breast and wagged his beard up and down. Paul was reminded of those little wooden figures that pop out of clocks. "Just a man called Thomas. Farewell, Paul."

In another five minutes Paul was in Wanwick market Square and the clock tower showed precisely four o'clock. In spite of everything he was still up to schedule. He should even have time to get to Old Mill Farm though whether he fancied the Mad Woman of Blattingford at the end of a day like this was debateable.

This time, when he had parked and put his hand in his briefcase for the files he wanted, the paper Miss Smeed had pressed on him as he left the office came out too. I've probably passed this one already, he thought. Should have checked it sooner.

He unfolded it. It was the letter from Wallace about Lower Wooton. He had put that wretched business from his mind but now he thought, how extraordinary! Miss Smeed insisted on me taking it. She knew I wouldn't want it lying on my desk for anyone to see. How truly involved she is in office life!

He pushed the letter to the bottom of the briefcase. By now Bird would have acted on what Foggart told him – perhaps scrapped any deal Lister made with Amberly. On the strength of that absurd blunder the reorganisation could now be settled. Hard to credit it, here on the hot pavements of Wanwick, but the office had only an hour more of today to run. An item could already be typed on the Agenda that Foggart would be A.C.P.O in charge of Control – and then wouldn't life be fun! Paul slammed his car door.

As he locked up he noticed the back bumper was very close to the car behind – a big red Vauxhall, perhaps the car of the man who didn't steal his jacket. He made some notes on the file about an illuminated sign at The White Horse Inn opposite him and then turned and dived into the obscure entry which said 'Rural District Council Offices' in yellow letters on a brown board fastened to the tiled wall. The passage led round the back of a baker's shop up stairs covered with strips of brown lino and onto a landing lined with labelled doors. Paul made for the second on the left, marked 'District Surveyor.'

As he approached he heard a loud voice proclaiming, "I don't give a damn what Pembleton says –" And he knew whose the voice was and also the red Vauxhall outside. He had no wish to meet Councillor George Cranston but there was no help for it. As he lifted his hand to tap at the door he reflected wryly how impossible it would be to cope with this if he obeyed the little professor's urging to be just a man called Paul.

The sky was still blue above County Hall but across the river the sun hung in a red haze over the warehouses of Barton.

Around four o'clock Harry Wade had a phone call from his wife.

"I was trying a special recipe but it's a mess. I'll have to open a tin. I wanted to know if Roger's coming." Harry glanced across the room at Roger's curly head bent over his desk. His huge shoulders made his office chair look small and cramped. Hazel went on, "I thought we might celebrate on our own." Her voice didn't sound like a celebration.

"Are you *feeling* all right," Harry asked.

"I didn't sleep much. Empty house. But I wouldn't want to offend him."

"Offend Roger? Nonsense. I'll tell him you're a bit off colour. And beans on toast will do."

"I ought to *try*. There'll be cocktail parties and goodness knows what."

Harry chuckled. "In Morlton? I only saw industry and a few housing estates." She gave a little grunt at the end of the phone. "What?" he said. "What?"

"I was afraid it would be like that. Well, I mustn't keep you."

He said, "We'll have a good talk tonight. All that's wrong is we haven't *talked* yet." He knew that when he'd reassured her he'd have reassured himself.

Roger brought some recommendations over for him to sign. "By the way, Harry," he said in his quiet emphatic way, "I have a date tonight. Hazel won't have laid on anything special will she? I try to let you know in advance but this only came up today."

"Of course it's all right, old man. To be honest she's a bit het up about the move. Takes women like that. I'm a bit het up myself, tell you the truth. Too long in one place."

"You'll be fine." Roger recalled what Dorothy had said. "Timbuktu or the Arctic with you." In an hour he'd be on his way to her. Surely the weather could hold out. "Do you think the day's closing in a bit?" he asked Harry.

"Ay, it's got a funny look that sky. Got some sporting event on?"

"Sort of," Roger said and went back to work.

Bird sent for Leonard King and while he was there Miss Smeed saw a procession of young men begin to come through for application forms for Head of Architecture.

Neville Carr was the first. "Mr King gone home already," he asked her.

"Oh no, Mr Carr. He's with Mr Bird. Can I help you?"

"I just want an application form for Mr Cole's job. Are they in Mr King's office?"

Miss Smeed took him into the glass cubicle. She thought, our Neville's hoping to escape Lower Wooton and leave my Paul to take the blame. She found a form.

"I have to make a note, Mr Carr, for the record." She wrote down his name and the date. "Are they holding more interviews?" She didn't feel shy with young Carr.

"They'll have to" – he grinned at her – "if I apply, won't they?"

Humph, she thought when he'd gone, he seemed a bashful lad when he started, a bit clumsy with people but well meaning. Funny the way people come out of their shells.

Ten minutes later the bearded Gordon Harris came along and then Ken

Myers from Plan while Harris was still there. They eyed each other and chuckled while Miss Smeed wrote down their names in her round careful hand.

Harris said, "They want to make up an identity parade for the look of the thing."

"Very likely," said Myers. "Anyway I'll get up the grades by keeping on the move. Time abroad looks good on an application form."

They went out chatting. Miss Smeed shook her head. Young Myers – unmarried, only himself to consider! It quite upset her, the thought of all that freedom.

When Mr King returned he beckoned her into his office. "Stuff for the Agenda."

"I'll pass it on to the typing staff," she said coolly.

"Oh you can look. We're getting Foggart over us. Chief Assistant County Planning Officer with special responsibility for administration. That's jolly isn't it? He'll never be out of here."

"Mr Foggart is very particular," Miss Smeed said. Was this what he'd been after?

"They're making another A.C.P.O over Control. Wade's going so I suppose they'll give that one to Pembleton. He'd be a fool to leave if he can have it."

Ah, now that *was* something. For once merit would have its reward in this life.

"It'll be advertised," she said. "We mustn't talk about it as a foregone conclusion. It would do him no good." But it was plain that Mr Foggart had wanted Mr Wallace's letter to prejudice Mr Bird against her Paul. She was glad she'd risked taking out that pin.

Mr King was grinning. "Jos the Clam eh? You can't stop people talking in a place like this." He wiped his forehead with the back of his hand. "Is it getting hotter? It's damned stuffy in here after the old man's room."

"All the windows are open but there just isn't any air."

"Ay." He looked at his watch, pulling back the shabby sleeve of his green jacket. "Get away sharpish tonight." It was an order to himself not her.

Miss Smeed went back to her desk. Did he ever get that jacket cleaned? His poor boy was as bad. Well, Mr Foggart would soon see who kept the wheels turning in Admin. That was good. Better still, Mr Pembleton might stay for years if he got this promotion. She clasped her hands together under her desk-top. That was something to pray for.

As Lister tried to reduce his in-tray he knew he should be phoning Shirley to find out what the hell was so urgent earlier. It irked him like a shadow he wanted to brush away. But she'd been secretive and she knew he couldn't stand trying to pump someone. When he got home he wouldn't mention it. She could start – if she wanted to.

He was also bothered that when Bird had seen everyone else – and he could hear them coming and going next door – he would want to know what had been planned with Amberly. Pembleton was by no means out of the wood. Heaven knew the top councillors cared little about their technical officers but if one dropped a clanger it would come to mind whenever the name was mentioned. If he didn't watch it he'd get caught in it too.

When the summons came from Bird it was twenty to five. Lister found him sitting in one of his grey armchairs. Not lounging – he was too small and round for that but as far back as the shortness of his legs would permit. He waved Lister to the other armchair as if for a fireside chat but Lister at once laid the picture before him in a few sentences. Bird asked questions, edging further forward and finally jumping up and pacing about.

"It smells bad, Derek. This will be fresh in the Chairman's mind if he comes to interview Paul for the A.C.P.O job. Worse, some critical memo may come down from Highways in time for the very meeting when we hope to set up the new post. We could be in bad odour with our own Committee. Costing the Council money for a foolish error and at the same time seeking extra for internal expansion. It could be touch and go."

Lister said, "Dare we admit that the error occurred because we're short staffed?"

Bird stopped and faced him. "But would it be true, Derek? I've looked into it and I must say I was impressed with young Carr's honesty and clarity over how it happened."

"You admit it was *his* mistake, not Pembleton's."

"Technically, Derek, yes. In practice we know Pembleton's responsible. When it gets to Committee level *I* am. I rather wish you'd brought it to me first before speaking to Amberly. Pembleton of course brought it to you – as a friend."

Lister got up. He couldn't sit any longer if Bird would walk about the room.

"If I'd known all the history I would. If Paul had known before Wallace phoned him – but hang it all the Surveyors have been damned cagey about this."

Bird pursed his lips, twirled his spectacles and sat down again behind his desk.

"That may be true but do we have a grievance if there's no official form on which they're obliged to detail their proposals for our benefit?"

Derek exclaimed, "They *never* hand us info on a plate but this was a *glaring* omission. They *said* there was a road improvement line but they're always drawing *them*. They'd surveyed this and were negotiating to purchase the very house we consulted them about. I bet Wallace glanced at the plan, drew in the line and wrote his letter in his usual wrapped up way, never thinking it was the house Councillors were going bald over –"

Bird tut-tutted at the extravagant expression. "Would he *know*, at his level? But if he did it won't help us to press that point. It was our job to read his letter, note the line and, if we thought it insufficient reason to refuse Hubertson his permission, Pembleton could have consulted Wallace about it and all would have come to light."

"Ay, *we* can see what might have happened but the Committee won't. If we get our grumble in first it'll create a smoke screen. The thing'll be thoroughly muddied up."

"I see." Bird's eyes were piercing as he looked at the Deputy. "That's how you'd handle it. Pull the wool over their eyes. Hope we escape unscathed in the confusion."

Lister reddened. "Why not? The surveyors *are* at fault – in their whole damned unco-operative attitude. Why should they get off scot-free and laugh at us?"

Bird stood up. "Almost five o'clock. We must not be emotionally involved, Derek. I shall certainly use this as a lever to set up official machinery for co-operation in future but I am not going to take advantage of the muddle-headedness of other people. This is the fault with modern politics. Public relations are no longer an instrument for enlightening the public mind but a tool for manipulating mass reactions. We may think little of people's intelligence but we still have a duty to lay matters clearly before them." Bird obviously did not expect the point to be disputed.

Lister was seething. "Not one politician in a hundred would agree with you."

Bird beamed. "As I said, that's what's wrong. I have an old-fashioned *faith*" – he used the word with curious emphasis – "that people recognise truth and respect the man who speaks it." Lister had rarely seen him smile so affably. He now opened the door of his coat cupboard and took down his grey trilby and rolled umbrella. He was surely the only man in County Hall still carrying an umbrella after two weeks of a heatwave.

Lister said, "But people get hold of any damn fact they hear and pile up their emotions around that one." He was standing stubbornly, feet apart on the wine-red carpet. Bird would have to walk round him to get out of the door.

"Of course they do, Derek. True facts are scarce. A starving man will make a meal of a crust of bread."

Lister thought, it's impossible for a man with as neat a mind as his to know how the majority react. He said, "Look, Quentin, they get information poured at them from press and telly and they believe the ones they want to believe and reject the others. I hear it all the time on the golf course. They quote a journalist one minute and then say 'You can't believe a thing you read in the papers.' Closed minds. Educated people too."

Bird was re-tidying his desk-top. He looked up with a flicker of an eyebrow at Lister's use of his Christian name. But it was turned five o'clock – outside office hours. Lister didn't expect him to comment, and he didn't.

"Then education is falling short," he said. "Citizenship lessons are too vague. Children should be taught the utmost precision of thought and speech and how to seek it with discernment in all forms of media. The Consumer Associations are making a start in the world of advertising but it behoves all of us in public positions to set an example."

Derek was going to blurt out that Shirley had just become secretary of Redhill's Consumer Group but he wouldn't bring *her* into the conversation. Nor would Bird want to be reminded of his own wife, famous for embarrassing him at office parties by the waywardness of her remarks. It hadn't struck him before but Bird's choice of wife was the one flaw in his tidy life. The thought tickled him and his irritation vanished.

He noticed Bird slipping the Lower Wooton file into his briefcase.

"Oh I think Paul will need that tonight. He wants to sketch an alternative road line to offer the Surveyors tomorrow."

Bird drew out the file and handed it over. "You'll see Paul on his return?"

"I said I'd hang on here for a bit. I've had no chance to clear my in-tray."

Bird twinkled perceptibly. "But the reorganisation is tidied up — a good day's work. Will you tell Paul to see me at 9.15 tomorrow *with the file*? I shall then contact Dowland and the Chairman myself. No doubt a new line will have snags."

Lister moved to open the door for him. "Ay, there are always snags."

Bird nodded, lips compressed over the tangle that lay ahead. The late holiday his wife wanted would be feasible only if this were sorted out first. It could be pleasantly mellow in mid-October in the Lake District. The autumn colours . . . quieter roads . .

He said brightly, "Good night, Miss James. The sky looks a little threatening. I wouldn't hang about, my dear, if you have no coat."

And so finally he was gone. Pompous so and so, Lister thought. I'd have managed it better my way. I can handle people.

He shut himself in his room as soon as the lift gates clicked and pulled his in-tray towards him. Shirley would be hoping he had left by now. She could jolly well go on hoping.

"Hello, she's back again." Mrs Ball had the front door open and was tucking away her money in her handbag.

"Who's back?" Shirley asked and glanced round Mrs Ball to the front gate.

The German girl was just wheeling in the pram. Oh no, Shirley thought, she mustn't bring it in the house. Not that baby.

Hilde came straight up the path from the sunshine on the pavement into the indigo shadow cast by the house. Her pale puffy face was damp from hurrying up the hill from Brynbank. Like porridge with the steam rising, Shirley thought. Hilde took no notice of Mrs Ball but looked direct at Shirley, just long enough to show that her opaque dark eyes were glistening with distress. Then she looked away and said in a toneless voice, "You can have him – if you want him."

As she said it she swung the pram round so that Shirley could see him. Incredibly he looked exactly the same as he had when she had first set eyes on him. Immaculate, sleeping, hand before his face, little cheek just denting the pillow.

"Has he never moved?" she murmured, more to herself than the girl.

Hilde said scornfully, "Of course he is fed and changed. He was wet and soiled through to his shawl. My mother take everything off and bath him. How he scream. Now of course he is tired. He sleeps."

"Your precious Maurice wouldn't like that eh?" Mrs Ball said.

She had got herself off the doorstep but looked prepared to stay the rest of the afternoon to see the outcome.

Shirley put on her bright, employer's voice. "We mustn't keep you, Mrs Ball."

Mrs Ball pulled her hat down on her head and went. She never came without a hat and coat. The girl too was in a leather jacket and jeans as she had been that morning. Beside them Shirley knew she looked as cool and fresh as a model on a magazine cover.

She said to Hilde in her best hostess voice, "I'll open the garage door and you can wheel the pram through to the garden."

The girl stared as she passed the new Mini in the double garage and came out into the basking garden. She gazed up at the house, the hot red brick, the roses, the open French windows, the wide view over the valley.

"You have everything, yes?" she said. "And a big man. I remember him at the party." She gestured across her shoulders. "Big here. And curly hair. If you had not been there he would have flirted with me. He is sexy, no?"

Shirley gulped. I'm damned if I have to be subjected to this. She said, "Please sit down. Is the baby too hot there? Move him into the shade if you like."

"You want him, yes?" Hilde said. "But you not admit it."

Shirley sat herself in one of the deckchairs under the sun umbrella.

"Well now, Hilde. You don't mind if I call you Hilde? I'm Shirley you know. Has something come up since this morning?"

The girl walked the baby into the shade. "It is Maurice," she said, talking over her shoulder in the same toneless voice. "When he saw the baby naked –" she put the brake on the pram and came back and stood in front of Shirley – "Of course then he want to draw him. Me too undress and feed baby so he make drawing for sculpture. But of course I have no milk." The girl sat suddenly on the grass and clasped her arms round her knees. "I had much. The doctor gave me tablets."

"I thought Maurice wanted to go to India."

"Oh he will I suppose. But he is artist. When idea comes he must do it. At once. He shock my mother. She call him names – in German you know. She has little bit English. So now you see I must go back to Germany. You will take the baby. It is healthy here." She looked round the garden again, then laid her head on her knees turning her face from Shirley. In a thickened voice she mumbled, "I suppose you send him to English public school. How he will be lucky, my baby."

Shirley swallowed the hard knot in her throat. "But Maurice wants the baby now and yet you say you must leave him. This morning it was a distraction to his work."

Hilde looked up. "*Wants* him? Maurice want him only to make piece of stone. Art before people – that is Maurice. Who wants *me* now? Hugh go to Africa but he not want me. It is all joke, joke with him. There is young man at home in Germany. My mother say he has good job now. When I knew him he was still student. Now he will marry me."

"He knows about the baby?"

"Ach no! No one know there. He and his family think I still au pair to nice English family and my mother here on holiday. She is tough, my mother. She not tell."

Shirley got up. "I'll make some tea."

"Oh sit down, sit down. You people can never talk without tea, tea."

"Well, won't you take off your jacket? You look so hot."

Hilde unzipped it and flung it off. Underneath she was wearing only a brassiere.

Shirley thought, I won't even notice. In her clearest voice she asked, "Could you marry someone without sharing the most important thing that has happened to you?"

The girl sat there, heavy-bodied, her eyes assessing Shirley. "What is important? You are half way in life. What has happened to you that you call important?"

"I asked you the question first."

"*Me*, I still looking. You just wait for death." She laughed and rolled onto her back, her arms behind her head. Her underarm hair showed thick and coarse like her plait.

Shirley walked over to the pram. The baby hadn't moved. Dirty and wet through to his shawl? She thought, do I want more than his head and those absurd little hands? She was shaking with fear. Could I forget that he came out of her body?

"Why not say it?" Hilde stepped up behind her. "You not had child and *this* is your important thing. Not empty years. For you baby more important than clothes and house. So, he is yours. I bring you his things."

Shirley walked away across the dry lawn. "One can't make arrangements just like that." She spoke loudly as if Hilde were deaf or stupid. "Adoption takes time. It has to be legal. I haven't even talked to my husband yet."

"Oh he want him." Hilde followed her again. "That man — he must have son. You are lucky he kept you so long when you had no baby."

At last Shirley flashed at her, "There is nothing wrong with me. I could have had babies as easily as you."

The girl clapped her hands. "See, you are there — inside." She seized Shirley by the arm. There was an animal power about her that revolted Shirley.

"What do you mean?"

Hilde laughed. "Nothing. It's O.K." She released her. "I'm thirsty. Water with ice in? Maurice and me we have no fridge."

Shirley looked at her arm. The girl's grip had made a mark on the smooth flesh. She led the way into the kitchen. There, while she made two long drinks of lime-juice, Hilde alluded to her appearance for the first time.

"My mother take all my clothes." She laughed, placing her hands on her fleshy midriff. "She say nothing clean. Maurice's too. She fill every tub and sink and pail. All the baby's dirty things. Disinfectant everywhere. Maurice think her very funny. When she strip our bed he say she take away sin with bleach." She took a gulp from the glass Shirley gave her. "Of course Kurt is religious a little bit. He do boys' club at the Lutheran Church. Maurice's father is vicar too. It's odd. Many people still believe in God."

Shirley leant against the formica-topped bench sipping her lime-juice, the ice cubes bobbing against her lips. She was determined not to betray herself again. "I wonder how you can bring yourself to marry this Kurt. Marriage will mean so much to him."

"But he is sexy, Kurt. We good together. It will be O.K. Maurice is sexy too but different. When he has me it is finished. Kurt loves me. I not want that then. I was bored. Now perhaps –? Anyway, what else I do? I have no money. What you pay for baby?"

Shirley set down her glass. "*Pay* for him?"

At that moment they heard him crying. They looked at each other.

"So," said Hilde, "get him."

Shirley went into the garden. He was turning his head on the pillow, his face very red. She felt every nerve in her as tight as a hawser as she inserted her hands under the covers feeling for his little body. She picked him up, shedding the irrelevances of shawl and blanket. His legs dangled bare against her dress, his arms clutched at her. She saw he was wearing one of those nylon romper suits buttoned under the nappy. Below his chin was a very white bib. He was all there in her arms, every bit of him. His face worked. She remembered about patting babies' backs. She patted him very gently. He made a burp and his eyes opened wide and stared at her and his mouth twisted into a smile.

"Oh my God," she exclaimed and clutched him to her shoulder.

Hilde stood by the kitchen door. "My mother say they smile with wind."

Shirley walked past her into the kitchen.

"Yes," laughed Hilde, "he dribble down your dress." She took the dishcloth off the sink and rubbed the back of Shirley's dress.

"It doesn't matter," Shirley said. "It'll wash." She cradled him in her arms. He turned his mouth to her and nuzzled her dress.

"Anyone is O.K. for mother. He is small. Good you have him now." Hilde watched Shirley as she perched on a kitchen stool with him. "Your husband, why he not go to doctor? It is big waste of your lives."

Shirley wouldn't reply. She had already said too much. It could become Brynbank gossip. Hugh Cole might tell the office! And next week they were giving him a farewell party! Till now their lives, hers and Derek's, had been an expensively bound book of which the world saw only the cover.

She thought, I gave Eleanor a peep today – but Paul is too sensitive a man to gossip. Only now this wretched girl has goaded me.

Hilde said, thoughtfully, "You pay for the baby things? There is my fare home." She was playing with her plait, running it down under her brassiere between her breasts. Her flesh was pale and puffy as if it seldom saw the light.

"I imagine we could come to an arrangement," Shirley said. She stood up and handed over the baby. "If we did decide, that is."

When she took him Hilde looked no more at ease, Shirley thought, than she had felt herself. Mrs Ball and her like would handle a baby comfortably, playfully, aware that it was only a small human being.

Hilde took him out to the pram. He was going to cry but she wheeled him about and he quietened, gazing up at the roses, screwing up his face if the sunlight fell on it.

"If we talk about it," Shirley said, "Derek and I, you won't change your mind, will you? This morning you said –"

"I not seen him since four weeks. My mother and I had not talked. Oh I want him but Kurt and I will have babies. Maurice just use him and put him aside. He uses me, hits me if he is angry. Oh when I am old I shall say, my first-born son and I shall cry."

Shirley, peeping at her sideways, saw that the brown eyes, opaque before, were covered with a film of moisture. Shirley began shepherding her out with the pram. "But you won't change your mind? And you must give us time." She felt a sick tightening of her stomach. "He doesn't know yet," she persisted. "You understand?"

As Hilde wheeled him down the front path the phone rang in the hall.

"You cautious English," Hilde cried. "Go answer your phone. Then do what you *want*." She disappeared round the hedge.

Shirley ran back into the house. If only it could be Derek . . It was the golf club secretary. They had a pleasant casual chat and afterwards Shirley couldn't credit what had happened. But a smell that had irked her while on the phone made her go upstairs and take off her dress. Down the back was a trickle of a stain.

She washed the dress and herself. Freshly powdered, in a cool lemon two-piece she went down to the garden and hung the dress to drip-dry. A thick sullen look had come into the sky from the south-east. The garden seemed airless. She looked at her watch. There were still two hours before the earliest time Derek was likely to be home.

Lena paused at the gate of Eleven Sutton Terrace. She could see down the long front garden Eleanor on her knees on the lawn, her bulge nearly touching the ground. A small boy was pedalling his tricycle along the path. Seeing Lena he tumbled off and ran to his mother. She looked round, shading her eyes. Lena, with a bright smile, marched in.

"Oh hello. It's you, Lena! I was digging up a dandelion." Eleanor laughed and held up the root and a worn knife. Then she struggled up and added, "Cathy'll be home soon but she comes the back way. How nice to see you! Sorry, I'm a bit grubby."

What you mean, Lena decided, is 'go away'. But I don't care. I'm here now. She plunged into her tale about being nearby after an interview at the Grosvenor School.

"I got the job. Should be fun."

Eleanor said, "That's terrific. Do sit down and talk to John. I'll make some tea."

She indicated the garden seat. John stood two yards away, sucking his thumb.

"Nice tricycle," Lena said. What the hell did one say to shy infants? "I think I'll help your Mummy." She put her portfolio on the seat and walked boldly in.

She could see Eleanor laying a tray in the breakfast room at the end of the hall.

She looked up and called, "Oh Lena, if you're too hot, do go into the sitting-room. I won't be long."

This was just what Lena wanted. She studied the room. In a corner were a music stand, a tatty violin case, a paint-box and a tray of farm animals. Her previous visit had been a formal evening occasion, no clutter, no visible children. Now she had intruded on a home, where no one was ever bored. She struggled to see Paul here. There were no family photos but as she looked along the bookshelves she spotted a pile of photograph albums below the bottom shelf. She took one out and sat cross-legged on the floor to study it. It was labelled 'Camping Holidays'.

She became so engrossed that she didn't notice Eleanor at the room door till she said, "Would you like it here or in the garden?"

She jumped up and replaced the album. "Oh the garden's fine. You're good at taking photos, aren't you?"

Eleanor laughed. "Am I?"

As she crossed the room Lena noticed a radiogram, tape-recorder, cine-camera and projector, paid for, she guessed, through economising on holidays. She followed Eleanor into the garden, fighting a sense of depression.

The tray contained banana sandwiches, some biscuits and apples and the tea.

"Just a drink for me," Lena said. "Let John have the sandwiches." John took one and walked over to the hedge with it which was a relief. "Your daughter is very like Paul – judging from the photos," she went on. "She's not home yet?"

"Any minute now," Eleanor said. "Yes, she's like Paul, in many ways."

"Paul comes out well in photos – or it's your genius for getting the right shot. He has that 'Here I am, take me or leave me' look which is hard to achieve in family snaps." She wondered, am I dragging him into the conversation too obviously? No, she's delighted with the compliment about her photography. But he's not the man in my painting. He's relaxed, urbane. How could he have been angry with my idiot husband?

They heard a door slam in the back of the house. Cathy began talking as she came through to the garden. "I'm going to put my bathing suit on. Has John got his on? We're going to hose each other down. I'm sweating."

She came into the garden, trailing her blazer, her frock crumpled and grubby. What a scruffy waif, Lena thought, as Cathy stopped and stared at her, glowering.

"I'm still going to get hosed down." She dropped her blazer and retreated.

Eleanor said, "Cathy, this is Mrs Carr. Will you say how do you do and pick up your blazer. *Then* you can put on your bathing suit."

"Can I really? Hello, Mrs Carr. Thanks, Mum." She swept up her blazer and ran in. John followed her. They could hear Cathy saying, "Hey, you've been at school today. I bet you didn't learn anything. Well, what did you learn?"

Lena said, "It'll be upsetting for you if you have to move to London."

"Oh we're not. The letter came today second post." Then Eleanor looked guilty. She's told *me*, Lena thought, and Paul doesn't know yet.

"Oh well, I expect you're relieved with the baby coming. Neville was talking about moving but now I've got this job —" She took a drink of tea.

"Neville? He's only been here — what? Six months. Where does he want to go?"

"Private practice maybe. He told me at lunch that he's made some gaff. Of course he has to do something melodramatic. He hasn't Paul's balance." She forced a laugh.

The children came rushing out dragging a hose-pipe.

Eleanor said, "Aim it away from us, please."

"They look good," Lena said, "with next to nothing on. I ought to draw children."

Eleanor said anxiously, "Neville mustn't resign just on account of some slip-up."

"He said Paul was pretty mad about it. Aren't the children enjoying that?"

"*Paul* was?"

Now, Lena thought, she's really interested. "Yes. Doesn't he get mad sometimes? If he was *always* detached he'd just be floating around in space. I gather he can be quite *involved* at the office, odd as it may seem."

Eleanor called to Cathy, "Don't churn the flower bed into mud." Then she looked oddly at Lena and said, "Of *course* he's *involved*. *You* want to be involved with those teenagers or you wouldn't take this job, but they'll probably infuriate you sometimes."

"Neville *is* infuriating. He's very moral." Eleanor looked surprised. "Yes, moral. Neville spreads a moral paste over everything. It sets in a hard, brittle surface. What does Paul make moral judgments about?"

There was an obvious movement under Eleanor's rounded smock. She laid a hand there and smiled. Pity, Lena reflected. That's let her out of an embarrassing moment.

Eleanor waited till the baby subsided but made no allusion to it. Then she gave her breathy laugh. "I'd say the difference between Paul and Neville is just experience in Local Government. Paul can see the nagging consequences of whatever this is. But if he lost his temper I'd say it was more to do with tired nerves than moral judgment. At home *I* get cross – with the children because I see more of them. He keeps discipline on a much lighter note. But the office is *his* day-to-day world. When he talks about it he can laugh but I know which things bothered him at the time. It doesn't go very deep though."

Cathy came to the table and took some sandwiches. "It's not much of a tea. Can I have supper with Daddy?"

"Of course, but it's fish pie. We've had so many salads lately."

"I don't mind fish pie." She stood by them dripping water, her scarlet bathing suit darkened and clinging to her lank body, her hair in wet wisps over her sallow face.

Lena saw Eleanor smiling at her, this being to whom she and Paul had given life. She herself felt the child's presence acutely. John was hardly out of babyhood but this girl was packed with skills, emotions, needs, responses. For the first time ever she saw that 'having a baby', which Neville said was their next logical step, meant the start of a fearful act of creation from which there would be no escape. But to have *Neville's* –?

Cathy said, "Ugh, my hair's dripped on the sandwich and made it soggy. John, I'm going to change. Come on."

Lena stood up. She wouldn't get anywhere with Eleanor. She thought, if I could talk to Paul on his own I could find out what he cares about. She doesn't know. To the children he's just Daddy – off in the morning and back at night. To her he's a steady husband with a good job. Maybe overtired lately. Give him a nice fish pie. My God!

"I must go," she said. "Neville will be leaving the office in ten minutes. He might think I've jumped in the river. Will you and Paul come to dinner one night next week?"

"Oh!" Eleanor heaved herself up. "Well it's really our turn to –"

"Wouldn't you like an evening out before the baby comes. Say Monday?"

Cathy had come and stood in the doorway, a towel round her head and her vest hanging over her rolled down bathing suit.

"Monday?" Eleanor said. "I think we'll be going to the Listers' later in the week. There'll be a baby-sitter to get. I'm a bit low on points in our rota."

Cathy came right out, pushing her bathing-suit into a red sausage clinging round her hips. "Mummy, you're so *vague*. You know you're not doing anything on Monday. And Mrs Thing next door said she'd always stand by if you wanted to go out. I can knock on the wall if John falls downstairs. Just say yes and stop flapping."

Lena laughed. She was quite taken with Cathy.

Eleanor said, "Here, don't be so rude." Then she put her arm round her in a sudden gesture that was inexplicable to Lena. She squeezed Cathy hard, then lightly spanked her skinny bottom. "All right, funny face, we'll go out. You go and get dressed."

She turned back to Lena. "Well, it's very nice of you. What time would you say?"

"Seven-thirty? Would the little boy be in bed by then?"

"Oh yes. He needs hours more sleep than Cathy did at his age. I will get someone in of course. Can Paul let Neville know tomorrow? He may have a meeting."

Lena thought. I won't tell her I saw him today. Then if he tells her she can think it odd. I could make her jealous if I tried. But there was something about Eleanor that frightened her. The shy anxiety to be pleasant was nothing. Underneath there was an ease and confidence about her family – like that spontaneous hug for Cathy – that was outside Lena's experience. How did one get so close to another being? She tucked her portfolio under her arm and walked to the gate.

Eleanor followed spluttering, "Oh Lena, had you forgotten you'll be working on Monday. Your first day? Lessons to prepare?"

"Nothing so vulgar as *lessons* in that place – *if* I go. Neville may want to move on. He needn't stay for me." She looked at the garden with the hose coiled over the lawn, John's tricycle on its side, the tea-tray still on the table. "Well, *you're* staying. That's nice, isn't it?" She waved and set off with the long stride which she knew looked incongruous under her sheath of a dress.

A glance back showed Eleanor scurrying up to the house. She imagined her peeling potatoes and Paul heading home from the country. A bus passed the top of the road. Damn, she said aloud. I'll buy a bike to get to the school. But can I really see myself going there every day, day after day?

In Wanwick District Surveyor's office Mason and Cranston were sitting in their shirtsleeves. The tiny room faced south west across the square and had been sucking up the heat all afternoon. Both men looked up and Cranston gave a grunt, as if Pembleton's sudden appearance at the mention of his name was only to be expected.

"I've been waiting for you," he said belligerently.

Paul slung his briefcase onto Mason's desk and smiled at him. "You've got the oven full on."

Mason jumped up and perched on his desk as Cranston was occupying the only chair for visitors. He tried to convey a look of apology for the Councillor's presence as he stammered, "T-take a seat, Mr Pembleton."

Paul had never seen him in his shirtsleeves. He had the physique of a weedy boy while Cranston bulged hugely over his trousers like an old bruiser. Not accepting the seat Paul stood over Cranston and remarked pleasantly, "Did we have an appointment?"

"I knew you were on the way. I've been at Dunford. Passed your car on the road. Saw you on the gravel bank."

So *Cranston* was the man in the red car. He glanced round the office. There on the door hung his light tweed jacket.

Cranston gave a hoarse belly laugh. "Ay, we're twins today."

Mason tittered, turning his head from one to the other like a startled rabbit.

"Was there something you wanted to see me about?" Paul asked Cranston.

"It 'ud be poor old Curry you're after, eh? Frightened he'll spoil the pretty river."

Mason, balancing on the desk, made a little clicking noise with his tongue. "Mr Pembleton's a busy man, C-Councillor."

Cranston heaved himself up. Spreading his great hands on the desk he leant his weight on them and looked at Paul. Mason fluttered like a bird on an insecure perch.

"It's the cottages at Dunford," Cranston said. "We'll be up to eaves level by the end of the week. Need the tiles week after."

"Well?" said Paul knowing what was coming.

"Those fancy things you wanted. They're quoting me two months' delivery."

"When did you order the tiles?"

Cranston flapped his hands about. "Week ago. Ten days."

"But it's many months since the Housing Committee accepted your tender. What do you want to use instead?"

"Dark brown interlocking are a good tile."

"Cheapest thing you can buy you mean. Look, Councillor, we're serious about this. Dunford is a stone village. Every single house has a stone or slate roof."

Cranston settled back in his chair and lit himself a cigar. "Labourers I'm building for won't give a damn."

Paul took Mason's chair at last and said to Cranston, "Dunford is the gem of the County. These cottages must fit in."

"And how am I to roof the cottages if I can't get the damn things?"

Paul's head was aching again in the stifling room. "Look at the permitted list. You'll find immediate delivery for one of them – even if they come out a bit dearer."

"Dearer!" Cranston exploded out of his chair, blocking out the light like a mountainside. "I've got to cut down not –" He stopped, seeing the gleam in Paul's eye.

Paul pushed back his chair and stood up. He was taller by two inches than Cranston. He said, "You knew the design specifications when you put in your tender."

Mason gave a little sigh. Cranston had compromised himself.

Cranston stumped to the window puffing like a small engine. Something out there made him grin. "It'll look good in the Wanwick Gazette. Housing held up by County Planners." Paul thought, he can see the Gazette Offices from the window and he's a pal of Frame, the editor. "I'll see Joe Frame today," Cranston said.

"It won't be the first time." Paul looked him in the eye. "Well, Councillor, if you put the wrong tiles on they'll have to come off." He said it in a tone of dismissal of the subject and Cranston. In this case he felt that any adverse publicity would be Cranston's. Too much was known in business circles about how he obtained Council tenders.

Cranston grabbed his jacket and said something like, "We'll see about that."

Paul, thinking of Professor Smith, said, "I'm going on to Old Mill Farm after this. You're building a bungalow there. Do you want to come?" This would be a test.

Cranston jerked round. "Oh ay. I damn well ought to be there. Hodge is a babe in arms. Is he expecting you?"

"No, his application only reached my desk this morning. But while I'm here –"

"Well, are you coming now?"

"Give me half an hour with Mason. We'll go in my car. I'll come back this way."

"Huh. I'll go and see Joe Frame then."

Paul sat down in the visitor's chair as soon as Cranston was out of the room. It looked more comfortable and he stretched out his legs.

Mason shuffled his papers. "So sorry about all that."

"Let's forget him." Paul reached across the desk and pulled a sheet of paper towards him. "Is this the plan for those washhouses? We can't have brick and a tin roof. Roughcast and a felt roof at least." They talked for five minutes about other applications.

Then Mason said, "Before you go to Old Mill Farm I ought to tell you about Matthew Hodge. He and his wife have worked so hard on this farm but now just when they're enjoying it Mrs Hodge's father dies and her mother comes to live with them. The bungalow's for her. She's in the boy's room now. He's at b-boarding school."

Paul held up his hand. "That's interesting" – he was thinking of the old woman's phone call – "but we can't let bungalows pop up in the countryside. The accommodation should be integral with the farm buildings. When Mrs Pawson dies Hodge can rent it to a labourer. The site should use the same access road." He took the file from his briefcase. "Look where they want it. Right on a bend in the B road. It's very steep there too."

Mason sighed. "I told the Plans Committee. I said the County Surveyor would never allow it there. C -Cranston had promised Hodge he'd push it through."

"What's the set-up between Hodge and Cranston – purely business?"

"No, they were at school together, but the Hodges are a reclusive couple. They don't say much but my wife, Peggy, says they're under great strain. She called today."

"I suppose Mrs Pawson is grieving for her husband and unhappy at moving."

"Maybe. To outsiders she might seem just a poor old thing but she c-could be the d-devil to live with."

Paul looked at his watch. He must go or he'd be hopelessly late back. As it was he'd never catch Lister at the office now. He jumped up, stuffing his files into his briefcase. Mason stood up and opened the door for him.

Paul clapped him on the shoulder. "So long, lad. Keep fighting." He had taken two steps down the corridor when he swung round again. "I nearly forgot." Mason popped his head out like a mouse from its hole. "There's a retired professor called Smith living in a caravan at Cottle. Did you know?"

Mason hesitated. Of course he would know. District Surveyors found out everything. "I did hear something."

"Just get him to make an application. We can't have that sort of thing."

He dashed down the stairs and found Cranston puffing over from the Gazette Office with a grin on his face. In a few minutes they were on their way to Old Mill Farm.

The view from Development Control was fuzzed with red mist. The chunks of warehouses and the skeletons of cranes floated in it like ghost ships.

"It's uncanny," the draughtsman Hine said. "Ruddy windows are still wide open and it's as hot as hell. I reckon we'll have a storm. Heatwave couldn't last much longer."

He was perched on his desk, newspaper folded under his arm, ready for instant departure.

Harry Wade bobbed up in his glass office and waved to Weston. "Roger! Nothing more for the Agenda? I've signed them all? It's a miracle! I should go away more often."

Hine muttered, "Doesn't know how true that is, does he?"

The stubby draughtsman said, "What's been going on today? No one tells us anything but everyone's been seeing everyone else like mad all day."

Hine said, "Gordon Harris was in the queue beside me at lunch – seemed to think Foggart was getting Architecture when Cole leaves. No one told you anything, Roger?"

Weston was the only qualified officer near enough to be drawn into the talk. He glanced up. "My advice is wait and see." In two minutes he would be on the road to fetch Dorothy Bird. Just now that was the only thing in his life.

"He hasn't a clue. He only knows where *he's* heading." Hine slid off the desk. "There it goes."

He strode out of the room. Over the river a factory hooter was wailing. Five o'clock. The office emptied.

Harry saw Neville Carr was still in Paul's cubicle and rapped on the glass. "Come on out of that goldfish bowl, man. They've all gone. I wouldn't wait for Paul. He'll be late back if he doesn't go straight home anyway."

"There was a file he wanted when he came back. Unfortunately Mr Bird has it. I'm just writing a note to that effect." He left the note in the centre of the desk. They went down in the lift together and out into the oven heat and the lurid haze.

The Square was criss-crossed with lines of office workers streaming home. Neville looked up and down for Lena. She'd never had any sense of time. If she was drawing she would sit and sit as long as she was absorbed. *If* she was drawing . . .

"Your wife meeting you again?" Harry asked.

"She may be down on the quay. She was going to do some sketching." If she'd left him would it be possible to hide it from the office? If she'd gone off with Pembleton!

"Have a look. I'm not going to the car-park. Got to get a bus today you know."

Neville stared at him vaguely. "Yes, I'll just —" He ran off across the Square.

Harry looked after him, eyebrows raised, thinking, that lad — private practice! Not compatible with Paul! And Bird had him in about something — this gaffe presumably. Well, what's a slip-up? I've made dozens. But he makes heavy weather of everything. I suppose we'll have to have him round, him and his wife. I did invite her.

He trotted off to the stop by the cathedral and scampered for a bus marked Infirmary. He longed to be with Hazel even if she was still upset. He hadn't seen her since Tuesday afternoon. That was too long. Wedged in with the perspiring crowd he was borne off to Lavender Terrace.

At quarter to five in the Architectural room Hugh Cole said to Pennyman,

"Ring up my new taxi service, please. Tell the man I'll be ready to leave in fifteen minutes."

"Eh?" Pennyman appealed to the others. "What's he on about now?"

"Ring our friend the Deputy. Do you expect me to *swim* up river to Brynbank?"

"D'you mean seriously?" Pennyman put his hand gingerly on the internal phone in Hugh's cubicle. He goggled through his huge spectacles at Hugh who was wandering about the office, shirt hanging out again, collecting papers and dropping them in the wastepaper basket. "You don't mean seriously?" he said again.

Hugh glared at him. "Roll on the day when I shall clap my hands and minions will do my bidding instantly. Ring the man up."

"He won't like it."

"If he's ousted the Vulture from its nest-expansion plans he'll be in high spirits."

"You ought to do it yourself, Hugh," Gordon Harris said, stroking his beard.

"Penny's got to learn the civilised arts sometime. And stop fingering that thing. You might disturb something."

"Mr Lister's not answering." Pennyman put down the phone with relief.

"He could be with Mr Bird," said Harris. "Then he'll likely do an hour's overtime. Will six o'clock suit you?"

Hugh shook his head. "Try him again at five, Penny. How sordid it is to be without a car!"

"Talking of Carr," said Harris, "I mean Neville Carr –"

"A joke," cried Hugh, tearing his hair. "Our bearded friend has made a joke. Shall I give you – when I leave – a double portion of my spirit, O hairy one?"

"I was going to say Carr's name was on Miss Smeed's list. He took a form to apply for your job. Wasn't he offered that U.S fellowship you had, but didn't take it up?"

Hugh wrinkled his nose. "There is a smell of truth in that, Prophetic One, and also a smell of the ways of Bird. Pattern, symmetry, logic."

Pennyman broke in, "They couldn't put Neville over us. Gordon's been qualified longer than he has."

"Ay ," Harris said, "but he's got more letters after his name than Myers or me."

"He might be better than Foggart," one of the draughtsmen grumbled, "but I'd rather they gave it you, Gordon."

"Try the Deputy's taxi service again," Hugh demanded of Pennyman but Lister could not be raised by five o'clock. At ten past, when the others had left, Hugh, not enduring to be alone, went and knocked at his door.

Lister had just settled back to work after Bird's departure. When Hugh put his head round the door and sang out, "*There* you are! Aren't you going home yet?" he snarled, "This *is* home. And what the hell's it to do with you anyway?"

"I've sold my car. Didn't a little Bird tell you?"

"We've had more important things to settle."

Hugh closed the door carefully and tiptoed with exaggerated high steps to Lister's desk. "Such as," he mouthed, "Neville Carr for my job eh?"

Lister put his large hands on the desk with an exasperated sigh.

"My God, this ruddy place. An idea can hardly come into one's head before someone's talking about it at the other end of the corridor. Has Carr been blabbing?"

"Draw rein, old son," Hugh said soothingly. "There are only a certain number of possibilities. If everyone talks long enough and fast enough they'll cover them all. Carr may have been the only clam in the office. Or the air around him is full of think-balloons saying 'I've got it' and he's the only one who can't see them. I take it it's true then?"

Lister looked at him threateningly, like the square of sky outside the window that was deepening from dirty yellow to umber. "If *you* start saying anything that scuppers my plans – God knows it's dicey enough with this Lower Wooton business –"

"What Lower Wooton business?"

"Lord! Is there actually something you haven't heard about?"

"Ah, the thing Paul was mad about this morning – what Foggart shouldn't know. I wonder if you all realise how ridiculous it sounds to one about to shake off the dust –"

"Oh yes? Try telling the press it's ridiculous if *they* get hold of it and see whether that saves our reputation. Now I'm clearing my in-tray and hanging on to see Paul when he gets back. You'll get home quicker by bus. And don't look for me in the morning if you've fog down there." Hugh was bowing himself out when Lister added, "Oh and we want you to come to a little do at our place. Friday next week I think Shirley said."

"I will come to your party with pleasure. Can I bring Hilde, the German girl, who lives next door with the hairy sculptor?"

"Isn't she *his* girl?"

"More or less. They had a baby I think but I don't know what happened to it. I borrow her occasionally. She's like a German sausage, heavy and solid but hot under the skin. Only she was a bit bowled over by Paul. I suppose he'll be there."

"Yes, but with his wife. He won't mind bringing Eleanor to our place even in her condition. It'll be a respectable party. Your Hilde had better wear a dress or something,"

"She generally wears *something*. But I'll warn her."

"Right." Lister looked towards the door.

"O.K. I take the hint." He opened the door. "I say, Derek, I think I'll hire a motor boat for next week. It would be great to commute by water and if it's foggy I'd be in no danger of running off the river into the road . . ." He went out of the door still talking.

At five o'clock Miss Smeed stood by the window while the Admin. room cleared, waiting to begin her hour of overtime. The scurrying crowd was slowed by the oppressive heat but one figure caught her eye staring with upturned face at the Planning Office floor.

"Isn't that your boy?" she exclaimed. "Isn't that Christopher, Mr King?"

Leonard King was just slouching out of his glass cubicle, hands in the pockets of his green jacket. He drifted over and gaped down. The boy waved.

"Little monkey. Knew his Mum 'ud think he was still here."

Miss Smeed clutched her leaf brooch. "Where can he have been all this time?"

King shrugged. "By, you'd have been a right worrier, Jos, if you'd had kids. He got back here at five to cadge a lift home. That's pretty smart isn't it?" He turned to go.

Miss Smeed watched him meet his son, cuff him on the side of the head and walk off to the car-park, the boy trailing behind. She went back to her desk, flushed and upset.

"He's breeding a young criminal!" She spoke it aloud in her distress. "Be a good thing if Mr Foggart takes charge. There's a right way to do things."

The last two typists looked at each other with round eyes. "It'll be murder!"

Miss Smeed called "Goodnight" to them when they were at the door.

"Oh cheerio, Miss Smeed." They glanced at her as if she were part of the furniture. Then Sandra said, "No one else is doing overtime. Look at that sky!"

"Well," Miss Smeed said, "we need a storm. It'll clear the air. Don't worry about me, pet, I don't mind a bit of rain." They were already at the lift gates when she said it.

Foggart hoped to make his exit with no one else about although only Bird and Lister knew of his humiliation. The lesser fry might believe Admin. was what he had always wanted and he could work out his bitterness by making life irksome for everyone.

About ten minutes past five there was a tap on his door, a slight treble knock which he knew well. Arnold Wallace looked in. Even he, from whom he had no need to hide anything, was unwelcome.

"Well, how's it gone? D'you get your precious Area?" Wallace's voice sounded as drained of energy as his skinny body.

Foggart said sharply, "You never sent me that letter."

"Come off it. I sent the ruddy letter – before lunch. Marked for your attention. Pembleton didn't get it. I went down with him in the lift just before one. He *said* he hadn't had it."

"You sent it with the rest of the stuff – from your department?"

"'Course I did. Did you expect it on a silver tray by itself with red roses?"

Foggart got to his feet. "If that bastard Deputy –"

Wallace flapped his large sad hands about. "Forget it, Ron. The thing'll turn pretty sour on all of us. Amberly says *I'm* the culprit. Never told the bloody planners we were doing the improvement line next year. I said, since when have we started telling them our programme? But he was in a cussed mood – like yourself. So what's happened down here? Bird know about it yet?"

"Of course he does. I made sure he did. But without the right bits of paper it went bad on me. Bird's slippery. You can't trust him an inch. D'you know how it's going to finish up? Pembleton's going to get ACPO Control – a new post. When I think of it –"

"You mean Bird's going to give Pembleton what he was going to give you?"

"Unless –" Foggart hooked himself onto his desk as if about to harangue Wallace. "Unless Lower Wooton makes such a stink the Chairman won't *let* him be promoted." He relaxed a little. "Bird's aiming for a team of ACPO's over the different sections. I'll be *Chief* ACPO with responsibility for Admin. He'll have to upgrade the post." He rubbed his hands together to try how a little satisfaction sounded. "I'll virtually run the office."

Wallace said, "Hang it, you're as pleased as a cat with two tails. This is much more up your street. If you're off colour one day you can do damn all. When you're on top form you'll be in everyone's hair. That's a sight better than Control where there's always stuff waiting for you. Will you even get out of the Appeal work you do now?"

Put like that Foggart saw he'd been a clever devil to lose it. It was a chore. You might get publicity but who – in *his* world – cared about that. Besides – this Lower Wooton thing – it just showed what might come of being in the limelight.

"Ay," he said, "I wangled out of that when I saw Bird poised to give me Admin."

Wallace had tired of the subject now. "I bet you were after this all the time. The other was a smokescreen. I know you. Well, I'm off, if you're staying here all night."

Foggart picked up his attaché case. "I'm coming. Mind, don't let this make you slacken up on Pembleton. I'm damned if I want to see *him* crowing."

"Huh, if I can make more mud stick to him the less I'll get. But Amberly'll see to that for his own sake. If it gets to the Press it'll be Pembleton's rap all right."

"You've an idea it'll get that big?"

Wallace wearily filled him in with the background. They came out of the Sinkhole and drifted along to the lift. No one else was about.

Foggart was lapping it up like a sponge but he cut Wallace short at the lift gates.

"I'll slip into Admin. Miss Smeed often stays late. She'll remember the letter."

Wallace trailed after him. "Why should she among all those bits of paper?"

Miss Smeed looked up as they came softly in. Mr Wallace and Mr Foggart – together. She thought, this is it – retribution! Never deviate from the straight and narrow. But it was for Mr Pembleton and I'd do it again if I had to.

Foggart began, "There was a letter earmarked for me this morning in the batch from the Surveyor's Department –"

"I really don't remember." She looked red-faced out of the window. "There's so much comes every day, and from other Departments you know."

"That's what I said," Wallace muttered. "Come on. It's of no importance now."

"It's odd," muttered Foggart. "Miss Smeed, did any of the Surveyor's stuff go to the Deputy – before lunch. Did he come in and look for anything?"

"Oh no. He sends for things." She hesitated. "I did take my sandwiches outside. I thought it might be the last sunny day. Looks as if I was right." She laughed, still flushed and glancing towards the thickening sky outside.

"Ay, we'll get caught if we're not careful," Wallace said.

"It's a mystery." Foggart stood staring at Miss Smeed's desk as if his eyes could draw out the letter from among the neat piles. "D'you know if the Deputy's gone yet?"

"No but I really don't think it went to him. One of the girls might have taken it to Control when I was outside. I mean, if it was earmarked for Mr Foggart," she addressed Mr Wallace, "the slip of paper might have become detached. It's possible, isn't it?" In the pocket of her tunic the tiny screwed up pellet of paper felt as big as a football.

Wallace took Foggart away. In the lift Foggart said, "I'll swear she knew more than she was saying. I've never seen her as flustered as that."

"Go on. You put the wind up people when they're as innocent as the day. What's one piece of paper to her among thousands? I can hear thunder in the distance."

They hurried across the darkening car-park.

"You see, there's the Deputy's car," Foggart said. "He hadn't gone after all."

"Well, why should *she* know?" Wallace stopped by his own grubby car and glared at Foggart's Consul gleaming from the showroom.

They parted without formality, Arnold Wallace weary of the day but expecting nothing more of any other, Foggart already planning the Report on Administration, artistic touches leaping to his mind that might make life unbearable for others and give him the flashes of amusement, the little colour that made it bearable for him.

Just before six the Deputy strolled along to Admin. Miss Smeed was at her desk. He looked at the sky which sagged heavily now over the warehouses and the river. It had more substance than the water, a thick blanket quality, mud brown.

Miss Smeed jumped to her feet. "Can I do anything for you, Mr Lister?"

"Well, Miss Smeed, I was expecting Paul Pembleton back before this. If he comes in you might tell him I'll be over at the County Hotel till about six-thirty if he cares to join me for a drink. And could you give him this? He may want to go straight home but he had something to do on this. Of course if he doesn't come just leave it on his desk. He'll want it first thing tomorrow. Don't hang about waiting, will you?"

It was the Lower Wooton file. Miss Smeed took it carefully. When he'd gone, she thought, well, *I've* nothing to hurry home for. If this is so important I reckon he'll come back for it. She waited, fluttering with hope, to hear his footsteps.

"My goodness, have we been burgled?" Mrs Pawson said, when she and Jane came back, laden with blackberries, to the farmhouse.

"Burgled? You don't get burgled in the country," Jane said.

"Every blessed door in the house is open." She went about shutting them.

"To let some air in." Jane set down her basket. "I'm dizzy with the heat."

"Told you I'd outlast you, didn't I?" Her mother came back into the kitchen. "I suppose Matthew came in and did that."

"And why shouldn't he? It's his house."

"Well, I think he's crazy your Matthew. Sometimes I think he's really crazy."

Their bickering was half-hearted, the tension drained away by the heat.

"We'll have a cup of tea," Jane said.

"When will you make the jelly? There's about six pounds of blackberries here."

"Tomorrow, if it's cool enough to set it."

"If you keep it it'll go mouldy this weather."

"Shall we not argue about it?" Jane put the kettle on. "You've enjoyed yourself this afternoon, first time since Father died." She had to speak as if his dying had been a grief, not just a shock to her mother.

"My shoes are a nice mess. Scratched to bits."

Jane put out a loaf and a hunk of cheese. Matthew would be up soon from the bottom meadow. He must have gone down to the bullocks when he finished the wall.

Her mother said, "What if you're refused permission for the bungalow?"

"We'll see Mr Pembleton. Peggy likes him. He helped her over Westways."

"Oh yes, the great Mr Pembleton. That's his name is it? I thought it was Pendington but I'm an ignorant old woman who must be kept in the dark."

"Mother, give it a rest. Tell Matthew about the blackberrying. Just be friendly."

"Like he's friendly with me? You never expect *him* to make an effort, do you?"

"Sh! He's coming." Jane heard the clang of the iron catch on the field gate. The kettle boiled at the same moment and she made the tea just as he walked in the door.

He stood there, perspiring from the climb and looked round the room. The lines in his face, burnt in by the sun today, looked harder and deeper.

He said, "It's stuffy in here." He left the back door open and walked through and opened the door to the hall. "I only came back for a cup of tea," he said.

He went to the sink to wash his hands. She stood beside him and mouthed, "Be nice to her." When he made no response she whispered, "She was better this afternoon."

She could tell that the desperation in her voice clawed his nerves.

He said, "I just want a cup of tea."

"Sit down and eat something too."

"I'm not hungry." But he sat down and cut himself some bread and cheese.

Her mother reared up out of her corner and came to the table too.

Jane looked from one to the other. "We got all those." She pointed to the baskets which she'd pushed under the bench. "You enjoyed yourself, didn't you, Mother?"

Her voice trailed away. She knew he felt like the outsider, that she wasn't on his side any more, that they were finally driven apart.

While they were sitting, with the atmosphere in the room tightening like a bowstring despite the open doors, Pembleton's estate car was humming over the purple moor towards them. They passed the spot where Eleanor loved to have picnics. There was a gorge to the left with the tops of young larches level with the road and occasionally the thin gleam of a waterfall. Paul thought, I'd like to stop and listen to the larks. Eleanor would say when they were camping, "Will you watch the children? I just want to walk up that hill and *be*." She would do the same for him too.

There was no haze up here and they were driving right into the sun. Paul adjusted the visor. Cranston was watching the speedometer. The needle flickered on sixty. He probably does eighty here, Paul thought, and waited for him to say so. It wasn't possible for him to be content to be borne along in silence through the blue and golden afternoon.

"You shouldn't go scrambling about. You scratched your hand," Cranston said.

Paul glanced at it. The blood had dried on it in tiny clots.

Cranston bellowed, "Look out!"

A young sheep leapt from the ditch and hurled itself at the car. The next second it plunged round and frantically scrabbled up the bank on its sticks of legs.

Cranston said, "God, that was a narrow squeak. Nice start to your meeting with Hodge if you'd killed one of his lambs. You were doing seventy on an unfenced road."

Paul didn't argue. The end of the day was in sight. This meeting was his last duty. Then a fast drive back to Midcaster. It was just possible Lister would still be in the office or he might have left a note. The Lower Wooton thing seemed piffling out here but it would nag at him till tomorrow if he didn't know what developments there had been.

Cranston said, "What are you going to say to Hodge about this bungalow?"

They were approaching the sharp left turn down to Blattingford.

Paul said, "You did him no favours letting him pick a site like that."

"What d'you mean?" Cranston would know very well but he would play the exasperated layman now. "Level ground above the road. Lovely view."

Paul pulled the wheel over and swung the car onto the B road. They could see Old Mill Farm at once below them in the scoop of the hillside. The bungalow site was further down round the bend but it was the farm track he was looking out for. Here it was.

"Will you open the gate?" He wasn't going to explain his reasons to Cranston which he would have to repeat to Hodge.

Cranston grumbled his way out. When he'd clanged the gate behind them and was back in his seat Paul just said, "You know new buildings should be beside the farm."

Cranston snorted, "Matthew won't like that."

Paul thought, then I hope to God he's not the argumentative type. He drove up the farm track, feeling empty, drained of patience and energy, unready for this encounter. It had been reckless to come, even more to bring Cranston.

Ahead of them the square, snug little farmhouse was ablaze in every window with the late afternoon light.

"Pretty place," Cranston said. "Isn't it?"

Mrs Pawson sat with her teacup in her hand, her eyes darting from one open door to the other. Jane nearly said, "Are you in a draught, Mother?" But she held the words back. To Matthew they would be one more sign of betrayal.

Suddenly her mother began to talk. "People told me I'd gain a son when Jane married. They didn't know Matthew Hodge, did they? You've got enough love" – she suddenly addressed him direct – "for some sheep and cows and the dog and then you're finished. I've never seen one sign that you love Jane. As for the boy, sending him off to boarding school! I never see *him*. Now I'm here he'll spend his holidays at Beckwood. That's all the grandparents he knows. Born and brought up there of course. Jane, your poor father used to say, 'We don't know we've got a grandson. Never allowed near us.'"

"Martin's home is here," Jane choked out.

Matthew looked at her. She had stuffed some bread into her mouth but her throat was so contracted with suppressed weeping that she couldn't swallow. He dug his nails into the palms of his hands. He began to say, "We're trying to eat." His clenched fists beat against his knees under the table but he was unaware of it.

The old woman shot up her eyebrows. "*I'm* not stopping you."

"You are," he cried and Jane looked at him in alarm. "If we put food into our mouths we can hardly swallow it. Look at Jane. She's never been so thin. You talk about me not loving her —" His voice broke.

Jane couldn't bear to look at his face. Never in their life together had he come near to mentioning his love for her in front of a third person.

Her mother said, "Jane's been thin since you came here. Running a farm with no help. You'll lose her and you'll have no one but yourself to blame."

Jane pushed back her chair and ran from the room. Oh God, stop her, she was crying soundlessly. She fled up to their bedroom. Let him kill her now was the thought that came into her mind. Let him kill her.

The room was aglow with sunlight which took her by surprise and checked her. In the kitchen at the back it had seemed already dusk. I didn't mean that, she thought. Tears were bursting inside her head but she took two deep breaths of the warm air and felt calmer. She went over to the window and looked way down to the left, the steep lush view down to Blattingford. She could see, just glinting brown through the trees, the sandy knoll where the bungalow would stand above the dark plunging curve of the road.

When her mother was there they would have meals by themselves. Matthew would come in without that shadow in their home. There had never been this terrible tension at Beckwood, though they were seldom alone, but even there she had hardly known the man he could be, rarely heard him laugh. When they had moved here he had chuckled at the black hen as it hopped into the kitchen, "You greedy old thing, you." She thought, I shouldn't have worried about anything in those two years on our own. We could have been even happier. If I could be like Peggy Mason could we still be happy?

Then she thought, Mother will struggle up the hill. We'll never know when she may walk in. And if she's ill I'll have to nurse her here, killing his joy in the farm, even in his animals. Can she ever change? She spent her life killing love, my father's, my brother's, mine. Could we change her, even now, Matthew and I, if we had enough love?

She pressed her forehead to the window. The glass was warm. An estate car, smart and new-looking, was coming down the road from the moor. It was no good. How could she expect Matthew to love her mother now?

Then the car turned into the farm track and stopped for the gate. Oh no! Who –?

"Matthew!" She ran to the head of the stairs. "There's someone coming. A car."

He was half way up. He must have been coming to see if she was all right. What had happened down there in the kitchen?

"Strangers?" he asked.

"I don't know the car. Oh Matthew, what did Mother – what did you –?"

"I told her *she* was killing *you*. That's all."

"That's all! Oh –"

"Stick up for her if you like but it's true. I can hear that car. Who is it?"

She ran back to the window. She could look down on the roof of the car. Both its doors opened together. Two men in light tweed jackets emerged, one ponderously, the other as quick as a knife. The heavy one was George Cranston. The other looked up at once at the farmhouse. She had to jump back behind the curtain. His face, tilted towards her, was a long, pale oval. She was excited. She hadn't met a stranger for months.

"It's Cranston and another man," she called softly to Matthew. "I'm going to change my dress."

"Why? They must have come to see the site down the road. Could be Pembleton." The bell rang. He sounded excited that things were moving at last.

"It's all torn and stained from the blackberrying. Aren't you answering the door?"

Matthew went as Mrs Pawson stuck her head round the kitchen door. "What's happening? Who is it?"

"Nothing. Someone for me." He looked at the blank back of the heavy oak front door. If this is Pembleton, he thought, I'd rather have met him alone. Not Cranston, not the old woman, not even Jane nearby. Just talk to him, man to man, civilised, quiet. "Go and finish your tea," he said to Mrs Pawson. Then he lifted up his hand to the latch.

As soon as he opened the door, Cranston, filling the doorway, started gabbling at him. "Said we should have gone round the back and walked in on you. Never use the front door in the country, I told him." He gave a bellow of laughter.

The tall man standing behind was all this time studying Matthew's face. Matthew thought, this is Pembleton. He's got level brows, a straight look. The high forehead suggests brains. His hair is a little long like an actor's. I don't mind. I'll accept any conditions he suggests to get the old woman out of the house. Jane will know if he's a good man. I wish she'd come down. She always says, "I can tell by the eyes."

"Well," Cranston said, "this is Pembleton. I told you he'd be along sometime."

Paul, sizing him up, said, "How do you do, Mr Hodge?" The farmer looked younger than Cranston because his body was lean and hard, his hair crisp and curly like Derek Lister's. His face though was tense and lined. I don't think he'll waste my time, Paul thought, if I can just get him on his own for half an hour. . .

Hodge seemed determined they shouldn't come in. "You'll want to come down to the site." He began elbowing his way out, coaxing them in front of him.

"I don't think that'll be necessary," Paul said.

Hodge exclaimed, "It's all right then?" He was trying to close the door behind him. Paul thought, someone else is there. Is it his wife or the mad woman?

Cranston was drifting towards the car. He seemed not only determined they should go down to the site but also that they shouldn't go on foot.

"I know where the site is," Paul said to Hodge. "I'm afraid it really isn't suitable for a cottage connected with the farm. It's isolated from here and from the village."

The farmer looked at him in disbelief. "But this is not a cottage connected with the farm. It's not for a farm worker." He still had his hand on the door handle.

Paul smiled a reassuring smile. "I know. It's for your mother-in-law. But Planning takes a long view. She may live five, ten, maybe fifteen years. After that it'll become available for its natural and obvious use, for someone living and working in farming. That's the only basis on which we can grant permission for new housing in the country, apart from existing towns and villages. You see the point?"

Cranston was dancing with impatience but Hodge nodded slowly. "You don't want town people retiring to the open country. Keep the land for those who work it?"

"That's the general policy."

"All right. Call it a farm worker's cottage. Give it permission as a farm worker's cottage. It won't make any difference to us as long as that keeps your policy right."

Cranston bawled out, "Are we ever going to get down to the site?"

Paul turned on him with a flash of anger. "I told you, Councillor, I told you in the car and Mason must have told you at your Council Meeting, the proper site for more building is beside the farm." Easy now, he warned himself. Talk to Hodge. If you asked Cranston here to test your patience it's no good letting him rattle you.

Hodge had come down off the step. "I beg your pardon. You said —"

"The logical place is a site beside the farm." The farmer stood speechless.

And then the old woman appeared in the doorway. The Witch of Blattingford, Paul thought at once, the face sharp, the grey hair in a wild cloud, the black dress torn at the hem, the shoes scraped and dirty. She peered out, dazzled by the low rays of the sun.

"What's going on? Is that you there, George Cranston? Who's the other man?"

Hodge seemed unable to introduce him. Cranston said, "This is Mr Pembleton, the Area Planning Officer" and aside to Paul in a whisper, "The mother-in-law, Mrs Pawson, the old girl they're building for. Crazy as a coot."

"Ah ha! Is it? Mr Pendington?" She came down the step like a bundle of rags blown by the wind, made straight for Paul and seized his hand. "How d'you do, Mr Pendington?" Under her breath she hissed, "I knew you'd come. Remember what I said."

Cranston pushed his big red face at the farmer. "You're a fool, Matt, if you let him get out of looking at the site. He's scored a point. I said you were a babe in arms."

Paul said to Mrs Pawson, "Excuse me." He turned to include Hodge. "Would you accompany me round the farm and we can discuss a possible site as you show me round."

Mrs Pawson still clung to his arm. "That's better, Matthew, isn't it? I won't have to climb up a hill to see my daughter. Mr Pendington doesn't want it down the hill." She lowered her voice. "I knew I did right to ring you. My late husband used to say 'Go to the man at the top.'" She edged forward along the front of the house, tugging at his arm.

Paul stood still, waiting for Hodge, who came up with an expression of anguish.

"Not the farm. Not this land –"

"One moment," Paul said, "there's something I'd like to get straight." Cranston drew alongside too, shuffling his bulk from one foot to the other and still muttering about the site down the hill. "Mr Hodge," Paul said, "your mother-in-law phoned this morning and asked me to refuse permission for the proposed site. I want to assure you that had no bearing either on my coming here today or on my view of your application. I was in the area anyway and, as I said, it's a matter of principle on which national policy is based."

The farmer looked away, up at the crest of the moor. The brightness had gone out of the sun. It was going down in a yellowy haze, an unhealthy sign.

"I believe you," he muttered. "I'm sorry you were troubled by her on the phone."

Mrs Pawson lifted her hands. "So I'm not allowed the phone. They spy on me."

Cranston began to be playful with her and pretended to poke her in the ribs. "Go on, you're very naughty, Mrs Pawson. Trying to get in with the Planners eh?"

Paul took the chance to walk ahead with the farmer. They were at the northwest corner of the house. "What's wrong with here?" he said. "Design it as an extension of the house. Connecting door if you like. Now just a minute before you dismiss the idea" – he had seen the look on Hodge's face – "Think of the future. It's a small farmhouse – two bedrooms and a loft? You may well find yourselves cramped –"

"Why? We've only one child. Not likely to have more at our age."

"But a single-storey extension with a modern kitchen and bathroom and two other rooms would eventually leave you with room for guests and your present kitchen for dairy work, animal feed and so on. I'm sure your wife would like a modern kitchen. And if she has to nurse her mother as she ages, it would be better to have her close by –"

Hodge broke in with a frantic wave of his hand before his face as if he were brushing away an encroaching web. "You don't understand. *Here – this* spot – I'll need to expand the *farm*. *Not* the house. A bigger barn would come to here. There's little enough level ground. I can't sacrifice it to a bungalow."

Paul said patiently, "An extension such as I'm envisaging wouldn't cover a lot of ground." He was prepared to pace it out.

Hodge cried, "You can't *make* me put it here?" The grooves on his face deepened.

"My dear sir, no. All I've said is that we couldn't consider the other site." Paul gave the farmer his most dazzling smile. "I'm not obliged to suggest alternatives."

Hodge looked at him and looked away again. "Oh I see you want to help."

"It's not just that. Planning's constructive, not negative. We only refuse permission if the proposed development cuts across a wise policy or a positive plan for the area."

"What's he doing, preaching you a sermon?" Cranston came up, perspiring.

Mrs Pawson stood in the middle of the newly suggested site, which was rough moor grass. "Yes, this'll do. Jane was going to make a garden of it but she never did."

Hodge strode over to her. "It's needed. This land is needed. It'll come right to here, my new barn. The old one yonder is rotten. I need more space. I must have space."

Mrs Pawson sucked in her lips till her mouth was a slit across her face. "First I've heard of any new barn."

Paul said, "You wouldn't want the new barn right alongside the house,

Mr Hodge. Can we just walk round the back?" He led the way himself into the farmyard. There was a canyon between the old barn and the byre with a smell of dung and silage and damp moss underfoot. "Why not make the new barn L-shaped, further from the house than this, and fit it in that corner under the bank, carrying it up to this side of the byre. You would eliminate the wasted passage between and you could move the hen houses to that side."

Cranston blustered, "What the hell are we here for? To settle the plans for Mrs Pawson's bungalow or some ruddy barns Matthew may never put up."

Paul compressed his lips. "I'm showing Mr Hodge that planning sees it as one problem – making the best use of the available space for extra living quarters and any new outbuildings needed, all related, functionally and aesthetically to the existing farm."

"Another sermon! Pity these long-haired chaps can't talk like ordinary mortals."

Paul said to Hodge, "You could build an annexe to the farm at a half or a third of the cost of a separate bungalow."

It was at this moment that Jane came to the kitchen door. "Oh you're all out here."

Paul saw Hodge stare at her in astonishment. She was wearing a green silk dress and lipstick. She was smiling vividly.

"Good afternoon, George." Then she looked at Paul.

Hodge said in a tight voice, "Jane, this is Mr Pembleton."

She came forward and held out her hand. "I thought you were down at the site till I heard you talking. Will you have some tea, Mr Pembleton?"

Paul could see through the doorway the uncleared table. "I'm afraid we disturbed yours, Mrs Hodge." The sight of the loaf and cheese reminded him how ravenous he was.

"We'd finished." Jane laughed. "Please come in if you don't mind the kitchen."

"We always eat in ours at home," Paul said. He was aware that her husband was hating this. She was fussing round him, settling him into a chair, pouring out tea.

Mrs Pawson pushed her way in too, crying, "I don't know what you've dolled yourself up for, Jane." Cranston followed and sat down opposite Paul.

Hodge stayed outside looking in, agony on his face.

"You'll come in, dear, and talk about it over a cup of tea. I made a fresh pot," his wife said. She too, Paul felt, was taut with anxiety for him.

He turned away and began walking about the farmyard.

She looked after him in distress while he was in sight of the door. When he disappeared she murmured something about him "not being quite himself today."

Mrs Pawson said, "He's crazy, our Matthew."

Cranston guffawed. "You've got him all worked up, Pembleton. He's a quiet lad – as he was at school. But by the Lord I've seen him really stirred up – so he didn't know where he was or what he was doing."

The colour rose in Mrs Hodge's cheeks. She said quickly, "Have some cake, George."

He took a piece of fruitcake and while he was silenced with it Paul began to put Mrs Hodge in the picture. She was easy to talk to though she looked older and more strained, now that he was close to her, than she had appeared at the kitchen door.

Mrs Pawson broke in once or twice to exclaim, "That's the answer, isn't it, Jane?"

Jane looked at her helplessly and then back at Paul. "I didn't quite follow –"

Paul realised that her eager listening had been only an expression of face. Her mind was concerned with her husband. He began again but Cranston, who had gobbled up his cake, interrupted.

"It's all bluff, Jane lass. *He* hasn't got the last word. He needs the Committee's O.K. He'd like you to withdraw this application and send in a fresh one for the site *he* chooses and then he thinks he can push it straight through. Get it? He's bluffing."

Paul saw Mrs Hodge looked more bewildered than ever.

"Councillor, you're not helping," he said. "The Committee would have to back a refusal on road safety grounds anyway. The access on that bend is impossible."

"Ah but Jane," Cranston said. "Jane, I know a few fellows on the Committee."

"Matthew wouldn't like anything like that," she cried. "Not favours."

Mrs Pawson said, "What's the matter, George Cranston? You want the bungalow down there because it'll cost more to build than an extension to the house, eh?"

Jane put her hands up to her face. "An extension to the house? Is that – you mean that's what you'd allow? And you've told Matthew that?"

Paul said as gently as he could, "Isn't it your best solution – *apart* from planning policy? You could lead separate lives just the same as if the bungalow was down the hill, only it might help if you were closer. Think of the hill in winter with ice and snow."

"They were," Mrs Pawson said. "That's why they wanted it down there."

Paul sensed that there was truth in that at least with the farmer.

"D'you really mean," Mrs Hodge asked, "if we want it at all it's got to be attached to the house? Really part of it?"

"Not necessarily attached but using the same access road as the farm. An annexe to the present building would be cheaper of course, but that's up to you."

"Cheaper!" Mrs Pawson cried. "Matthew would sell the coat off his back to get me out of the way. And d'you hear what *she's* saying now? *If* we want it at all! You expect me to go back to Midcaster now, Jane? Is that it? Put me away somewhere?"

"Please Mother –" Her hand shook as she pushed Paul's cup closer to him. "Do drink your tea, Mr Pembleton."

Paul lifted it to his lips and then saw, over the brim, the figure of Hodge darkening the doorway.

Matthew had walked about the farmyard, wild plans forming in his mind. He saw a whole crop of new buildings like a model farm. Of course even to make a start next year was laughable but every stick and stone of the farm, every trampled square of mud was sacred. To set some aside for that woman . . . He had leant over the field gate gripping the top rail till his hands ached. If she had to have any of his land that knoll down there would have done. Out of sight for most of the year and he'd plant evergreens to hide it in winter. Why should there be any power on earth to stop him? "My land, my money," he cried aloud. Who was this elegant man come down from his city office to plan their lives for them?. . I must keep calm . . . and if Jane will stand by me . . .

Then he had come back to the kitchen door and seen like a tableau, Jane, with bright colour in her cheeks, urging Pembleton to drink, looking up into his face, and he, flashing his smile at her, noticing no doubt the painted lips and the low cut silk dress.

A shutter came down over Matthew's mind. He muttered, "Come outside, will you? Talk better outside – show you what I mean –"

He saw Pembleton put down his cup and leave the table. He saw Jane's face, a moon of doubt and alarm. Cranston had lit a cigar. He would be too lazy to join them.

Pembleton walked out with him, speaking lightly. "Have you been looking ahead, Mr Hodge? Do you want more time to consider a lay-out for your future farm buildings?"

Matthew didn't speak. He led the way to the milking-shed which was out of sight of the kitchen door. Pembleton was glancing up at the sky. The breathless day was dying in little gasps. A flurry of air came down from the moor and swung the top leaf of the door out from the wall. Almost at once another breath, warm from the valley, swung it back. It should have been hinged back but it wasn't. There had been stillness all day.

"Well," Pembleton said pleasantly, "as a countryman you'll know what that portends. Will we have a storm do you think?"

Matthew said softly, "Shall we go in? You can see the size of this? How do I expand my herd unless I have a big modern shed with milking-machines?"

The city man was adjusting his eyes to the dimness. "It is smallish. But surely you're more of a sheep farm up here. Were you planning on dairying on a big scale?"

Matthew saw the dark back of the head, the white collar, framed in the square of the doorway. No thought passed through his mind as his hands seized the top leaf of the door and swung it.

At the same second the man half-turned as if deciding there was nothing more to see in there. The corner of the door struck him hard above the left ear.

Jane was now calling in a frightened voice, "Matthew, Matthew." It was the same voice as that day when he had begun to thrash Martin for kicking the puppy.

Matthew stepped round the corner of the shed. "It's all right. We're over here."

As she ran across he turned to speak to Pembleton. The man was leaning against the wall, white-faced, fingers pressed to his head. Aghast, Matthew put out a hand to him.

"What's up? What happened?"

Jane was staring, as ashen-faced as Pembleton. "Oh Matthew," she murmured. Then she ran to grab Pembleton's other arm as if she feared he would fall to the ground.

To Paul it was like the only other time in his life when he had suffered momentary concussion. As a boy he had stood up smartly under an open cupboard door. For a second the world had spun and he'd called to his mother to stop whirling him about. In fact he'd made no sound and his vision had cleared at once as it did now and the man and woman clinging on to him became Mr and Mrs Hodge, both looking at him with faces like death.

"I'm all right." He tried to smile. "I'm terribly sorry. Did I walk into the door?"

She said, "I suppose you must have. I was just coming to look for you both." She still stared at her husband's face as if she were dazed with shock.

Hodge looked all about and up at the sky. A quick breath of wind smote them.

He said, "Of course. A gust caught the top flap of the door. Swung it just as he came out. I should have pinned the thing back. It's supposed to be fastened to the wall. Jane, don't you remember it banging – the very first night we slept in the house?"

"I remember," she said quietly. "Can you walk now, Mr Pembleton? You must sit down. I keep brandy in the house for Mother." She held his arm as they crossed the yard.

Hodge walked behind muttering, "The wind, it could only have been the wind."

As they entered the kitchen Cranston shouted, "Hello, were they scrapping out there, Jane lass? Ay, Matt, at school you *would* take on lads taller than yourself. By God, you've drawn blood though." His tone changed. "I *am* joking, aren't I?"

Paul took out his handkerchief and wiped his hair and the top of his ear where a trickle of blood had moistened it.

Mrs Hodge said quickly, "The wind caught a door. It just got him on the side of the head. Now sit down, Mr Pembleton. I'll get the brandy."

"Wind, what wind?" cried her mother. "There hasn't been a breath all day." Her eyes darted over Hodge's face, challenging him.

"It's getting up," he said. "There'll be a storm."

Cranston said, "Good grief, Pembleton, it's not your day at all, is it? Scrambling about, scratching yourself, nearly running over Hodge's lambs. Now walking into his doors. I should have come in my own car. Maybe we won't get back to Wanwick in one piece. Struck by lightning on the top of the moor, I shouldn't wonder."

Paul sat, sipping his tea and pressing his handkerchief over the bruise, feeling too sick of the whole situation to answer. Cranston's cigar fumes floated round him.

Mrs Hodge came back into the room with the brandy, cotton wool and a bottle of disinfectant.

"I don't know if it needs a plaster," she began, taking Paul's cup to add a spoonful of brandy to it.

"No, no." Paul smiled at her. "I don't think a plaster would stick there anyway."

Cranston said, "Just as well you don't patronise the barber often or it might have been worse. If the wind starts throwing doors at me, Matt, I haven't any protection."

Jane said, "I'll clean it up anyway. I'm afraid the door would be dirty."

Mrs Pawson got up. "Here, let me, Jane. You're all of a shake." She sat down beside Paul as if delighted to have a man under her hands again. Briskly she rubbed the cotton wool, soaked in disinfectant, over the bruise, laughing when he winced. "Ay, you'll have a ripe lump there. Your wife'll be telling you to apply for danger money." She commanded him to drink up his tea and hold the cotton wool over the place till the bleeding stopped. "It's properly put my bungalow out of everyone's head, hasn't it? Well, they ought to do what you want after getting you knocked about with doors."

Paul drank off the tea. He wanted them all to have time to calm down. The brandy revived him. He got to his feet, despite Mrs Hodge's protests. "I'm sorry to have caused you so much trouble. Shall we arrange another time to discuss this when you've had a chance to think out your other building plans, Mr Hodge. Meanwhile you could withdraw the bungalow application –"

"Hey now," Cranston said, "Don't you agree to that, Matthew. That's the dodge these planners like best. They'll always shirk Appeal cases if they can."

Hodge came and sat down with the first spark of interest he'd shown since the incident outside. He looked from Cranston to Paul. "Appeal? Who does one appeal to?"

Paul sat down again. If they could avoid another meeting it would be better all round. His head throbbed damnably but he began to explain.

Mrs Hodge was murmuring, "You shouldn't trouble him, Matthew, not now." But her husband brushed her words aside.

"So ultimately I can appeal to the Minister?"

Paul said, "You'd incur a lot of trouble and delay for nothing." He felt Cranston about to interrupt so he hurried on. "No Ministry Inspector would uphold an Appeal on this one. It's national policy to discourage sporadic building in the countryside so why should he reverse it for a site with so many other disadvantages?"

Cranston got his word in. "Look Matt, it doesn't have to go to Appeal. Pembleton doesn't *know* his Council will back him. I can work on Willie Landor – that's our local representative on the Area Committee and get a few others – no, it's not favours, it's common sense. They can't be rigid in their policy when farmers' relatives are involved. Poor old widow, must live near her daughter. I'd soon soften them up on this one."

Mrs Pawson snorted, "Your sympathy's for your own pocket., George. Mr Pembleton" – she was surprised into getting his name right at last – "wants me *nearer* my daughter."

Hodge cried, "I need all the land up here so he's stopping me doing it at all."

His wife began, "But you don't, do you – ?" Then she checked herself.

Paul saw she was torn between fear of her husband and anxiety for himself. She filled up his tea again as the only thing she could do.

Paul said, "Thank you," and to the farmer, "You could draw up some plans – we would help you – to show what expansion you have in mind. By merely extending the house, say twenty feet on the north west side, you would solve your problem and barely encroach on the rest of the level ground you have up here."

Hodge burst out, "Why do *you* want to solve our problem? Yes, you're paid to tell us national policy but why *here*? Except on Bank Holidays barely a dozen cars go by to Blattingford. Who will care if there's a bungalow there? It seems that if you say yes, this Committee will say yes. Why then don't you do this? For us, for all of us?"

His voice shook with emotion. Paul thought of Professor Smith who would say, 'This is a man called Matthew and you are a man called Paul. Help him.' But a phrase of Derek Lister's also came into his head. "Let's get out and tell them what we're after. What the hell if we sound like crusaders? Why shouldn't we be?"

He took a deep breath. "If it helps, Mr Hodge, let me tell you I believe profoundly in the policy that affects your application. It's sound on road safety grounds as well as in sociological, cultural and aesthetic terms. The only reasonable solution is for you and your dependants to live here with good access to the road at a safe junction."

Hodge said nothing. He sat with his shoulders hunched up and his young-looking curly head bowed over the table.

His wife looked at him and when he didn't reply answered for him. "I'm sure we're both very grateful to you for taking the trouble to explain —" Her voice faltered.

Paul gave her his sincerest smile. "You have the right to the fullest possible explanation. Many people won't try to understand. Many more won't even listen."

Cranston cried, "Matt, are you going to take all this lying down?"

Hodge lifted his head and looked Paul in the eye. "All right, since you're so reasonable, tell me what *you* would do in *my* position."

Paul was sure now that he was speaking as one man to another, Matthew to Paul. Cranston had lit up another of his disgusting cigars. Paul stood up. "We'll take a turn outside, Mr Hodge. Give your wife a chance to clear away. I'm all right. I'd like the air."

She watched her husband as he followed Paul to the door. The lines in his face were sunken as if with defeat. His hands hung by his sides, the fingers slack.

"Don't be long," she said. "I'm sure Mr Pembleton will be late home as it is."

Paul checked his watch. It was half past five. The office would be empty except for Miss Smeed and maybe Derek Lister still waiting in the hope of seeing him.

Cranston shouted after them, "Watch out for doors, Pembleton."

They walked to the field gate in silence and stood looking over.

The pasture that sloped away at their feet was still mottled by the evening glow but the rich light and the intense shadow that should have picked out every tuft had faded. Only the tops of Blattingford's chestnut trees were reflecting a bronze sky.

"I suppose you're thinking it's pretty," the farmer said.

"The beauty's there whether we notice it or not."

Hodge jerked his head towards the farmhouse. "Does *she* not blight it?"

"Your mother-in-law? With all this aren't you able to accept her?"

Hodge gazed over the burnished landscape. "People like her have all the power."

Paul thought, no, the power is in the tongue. That's where the venom lies. He said, "Her power's gone the minute you stop minding what she says."

"Let her say what she likes to me. It's her power to hurt Jane that wounds me."

"But I see her worried about *you* being hurt. Are you sure you're not creating a situation that needn't exist? Each worked up on behalf of the other?" Hodge's face tightened. Paul thought, he believes *I* created the situation with my cursed planning principles. "I'm sorry, Mr Hodge. I would never have presumed to speak if you hadn't seemed to be asking me as a neutral outsider."

Matthew turned his head away. "There's the boy too. He's at boarding school."

"How old?"

"Thirteen."

"Life is full at that age. Just plug the line 'Poor old Grandma, she's eccentric. We must be kind to her.' He won't be hurt unless he sees both of you upset by her. So leave him out of this cycle of worry. If you yourself are immune then break the cycle by going back now and telling Cranston you're getting plans drawn up for an annexe. Don't let *him* do it. Get an architect. You'll find that's the best arrangement for you all." He turned away inviting Matthew to follow him back to the house.

Hodge groaned aloud. "You don't know what it's like to have land. I love every stick and stone of it. I created this place for us. But since she came –"

Paul turned and faced him. "So don't pretend you're worried about your wife."

He knew suddenly that the farmer wanted to hit him. He took a step back and said gently, "Come on into the house." Hodge's hands were clenching and unclenching at his sides, the grooves in his cheeks like scars. That door, was it possible it had not been an accident? Paul repeated softly, "Come inside. There's no point in discussing it just now. Come along."

Hodge's hands relaxed. He stood a moment more, animation draining out of him. At last he said in a tone of bitter weariness, "I suppose you're the sort of man who's always in the right." And he followed him to the kitchen door.

Mrs Hodge was standing there, vivid against the dark side of the house in her emerald dress. "Have you settled anything?" She searched their faces.

Hodge said with an effort, "Mr Pembleton has given me advice – unofficially."

She smiled. "Thank you." She seemed to be trying to hide what was going on in the kitchen. "My husband's really very reasonable. But we'd set our minds on that site. I had a picture of the garden I would make with a little rockery by the steps to the road."

Paul smiled at her. "But would your mother have gone there, Mrs Hodge? I told your husband she phoned me at the office this morning and was very emphatic that she didn't want to be down that steep hill. Only I assure you it wasn't because of that that I'm here now. I had many other matters to attend to out this way."

She opened her eyes wide at her husband. "Of course, Matthew, I was forgetting. To Mr Pembleton we're only one case in hundreds."

"Oh I didn't mean to imply –" Paul began.

From inside the kitchen Mrs Pawson called out, "If those men are there, Jane, for goodness' sake bring them in. I want Mr Pembleton to see what we've been doing."

Mrs Hodge with a piteous look at her husband let them in. Her mother and Cranston had their heads together over some scraps of paper.

"Hang it, you couldn't put your bath there," Cranston was saying. "You'd muck up the plumbing for the whole house."

"Look at this, Mr Pembleton." Mrs Pawson made him take a paper, covered with squares and scrawled writing. "George here is very stupid. But that's *my* idea. And Matthew, I've marked in my own front door and if you put a connecting door inside I'll keep it locked. I don't want dirt trampled on my carpets. I have different standards from what Jane's come down to." She pointed to the pails of chicken feed on the flagged floor. "I've my own life to live. I won't bother you and Jane."

Jane looked pleadingly at Matthew, murmuring, "You see how it could be."

Paul was thinking the same thing. Planning was not the problem here. It was human nature. But he must put an end to the talk. He said, "Mr Cranston, I've advised Mr Hodge to employ an architect. He'll save money by building an annexe."

"You've not agreed to that, Matthew?" Cranston was back to his belligerence. Behind his hand he added, "I've just been amusing the old lady – not because I went along with Pembleton's idea. You can still fight it, Matt. Blow me, I said you were a babe in arms. Architect indeed! Think I can't build a ruddy annexe?"

The farmer still stood as if in a stupor.

Cranston blustered on, "You're an architect, Pembleton. Why don't you give us your ideas now? I can wait. I'm not a nine to five man."

Paul said quietly, "Neither am I or I wouldn't be here now. I've thirty miles to drive home after this. I shall be glad to make any suggestions if a new plan is submitted and the old one withdrawn. Meanwhile I don't think Mr Hodge wishes to be stampeded into anything." He glanced at Hodge who seemed to be striving to reply.

Mrs Hodge said quickly, "I cut you a piece of cake, Mr Pembleton. Please have it – with that long drive before you."

Paul leant across the table and took it. "Thank you. It looks homemade."

"I'm afraid it's not. It's delivered from Wanwick, but they're a good baker."

While he ate it, Mrs Pawson said, "*I* shall do my own cooking. And what about my plan?" She saw him lay it down among the tea things.

"It's a little early for details, Mrs Pawson, but if you want a through living-room, you would need light at the back as well as the front. You've shown no window there."

"Bless your heart, I don't want to look at his precious farmyard. I shall have a divan bed at that end. I don't want his great cows looking in on me in a morning, do I?"

Paul smiled, but his head was throbbing. The talk was whirling round in the room like Cranston's cigar smoke. "Please settle it among you and let me know." He held out his hand to Hodge. "I'll be happy to come back if we have a new application to discuss. I'll confirm in writing what I've said this afternoon. If you don't reply, this application will go to the Committee in the ordinary way, but to avoid delay I advise you to withdraw it and start afresh as soon as possible." He glanced at Cranston. "Are you coming?"

"Have to if I want a lift in that van of yours." He got heavily to his feet.

"Well, Mr Hodge, I'll hope to hear from you." Paul was digging for a response.

His wife said, "I think we'll settle for the annexe." He turned his eyes on her and she fumbled on, "That is, we'll have to talk about it. And are you sure you're all right, Mr Pembleton? So very sorry – about that door!"

"It's nothing," he said. "My own carelessness. We'll just go out this way."

Hodge had shaken his hand but had not spoken. Now, as Paul thanked Mrs Hodge again for the tea, the brandy, the cake, he said suddenly, "I'll walk round to your car with you, Mr Pembleton," and they stepped outside together.

Paul looked back and saw Mrs Hodge sit down beside her mother and begin to examine her sketch. Hodge looked back and saw it too. They walked round the other side of the house, past the vegetable patch. The light was fading rapidly, the sky thickening.

Cranston said, "Just let it go through, Matt, as it stands. I'll make a stir with the Committee, get the press onto it. 'Planners kill widow's dream cottage.' That would look nasty." He lurched ahead to the car and Paul saw Hodge look after him as if he were so much dung.

"I'm finished with him," Hodge said. "Believe me, I wouldn't let him touch it now. I would never use the press. I don't think the way he does. You and I – we try to be reasonable." He seemed to be hanging back, urging Paul to agree with him. Cranston stumped impatiently beside the car. "I've tried to understand your planning principles. They make sense. The country for the workers on the land. Keep it from getting cluttered up with buildings. I apologise if I allowed my personal feelings —" He stopped and looked desperately about for words.

Paul said lightly, "Most people agree with a policy till it conflicts with their own plans. But" — he sensed the farmer needed reassurance, "you've tried harder than most to grasp what we're after." They were at the car. "Would you agree to an extension now?"

Hodge looked like a hounded stag.

"By God," Cranston said, "don't let him bully you, Matt. Leave it all to me."

"I'll write to you, George," Hodge said.

"Write? Give me a ring if you like but I'll get things moving."

"I'll write to you. You'll do nothing."

Cranston shrugged. "You're a funny blighter. O.K. I'll do nothing till I hear from you. God knows I don't need to go looking for work." But Paul saw he was put out. His face was red as he heaved himself into the car.

Paul stood one moment more, his hand on the car door handle, to see if Hodge would bring himself to say anything further. Over the farmhouse the sky now hung like a yellowing blanket. The last glow of sunlight drained out of the scene.

Hodge muttered, "I can't say what I'll do yet. I don't know."

"You think about it," Paul said, getting in, "you and your wife."

Hodge looked round at the house and the hump of moor rising behind it. "It's still my house," he said, "my land." A chill wind suddenly flapped about the car. "We'll have a storm," he called to them. "I said there was a wind."

Paul made a farewell salute. Hodge returned the gesture but in his face and the rigid line of his body Paul could read, 'I wish to God I'd never set eyes on you.'

As they went down the track, Cranston said, "By gum you get a kick out of mucking up people's lives, don't you?"

They drew up at the gate. "Oh certainly," Paul said, "I really enjoyed that."

When Cranston had closed the gate behind them and was back in the car and they had swung round onto the B road he looked curiously at the side of Paul's head.

"Can't think how you got in the way of that door. Damned if I didn't think for a minute he'd had a go at you." When Paul made no answer he added, "Right stirred up you had him. Right stirred up."

Far beyond on the south-eastern horizon beyond Wanwick the first flicker of lightning played across the sky.

5

THE EVENING

The sea was a leaden grey mass sweeping up the beach like a great oil slick. The sky was darker still. A few local residents home from work in the city were hastily walking their dogs along the sand with anxious glances overhead and urgent whistles.

Dorothy Bird rolled over onto her front and cocked her head to look at Roger.

"All right, so you've seen me reclining on the beach. What next?" Where they were lying was above the tide line and the sand was grey and dry here. It clung to the backs of her thighs. He brushed it off. Her legs were tanned right up to the edge of her bikini. Her whole back was the same chestnut colour except for the turquoise strap of her bikini top stretched across it. He lifted the strap. The skin was white beneath it.

"This is what you sunbathe in, in the garden."

"Of course. Rufton wouldn't harbour a nudist colony."

"That tan and that turquoise blue – you're the only bit of solid colour anywhere."

"Solid yes. Thanks very much. You're pretty solid too. Sit up. There, just look how much sand your shoulders have pressed down. More than a yard across."

He laughed, rolled her over and dragged her to her feet. "Come for a bathe."

"Bathe? I should think we'll get all the bathe we want just by staying here."

As she spoke more lightning played over the sea to the south east beyond Brynmouth pier. Thunder growled and the dogs on the beach howled in answer. A huge raindrop splashed on the ground at their feet. Roger seized her hand and they raced over the fast speckling sand to the sea.

The dog walkers rushed for the cliff steps and the shelters on the promenade.

Dorothy hesitated. "Our clothes?"

"Under the concrete projection. Come on."

They tore into the water. There were no waves. The surface was grey silk, pock-marked all over with little holes as the rain came on in earnest. Roger left go of her hand and hurled himself under the water making a great plume of spray. "It's warm," he shouted. He began swimming out to sea.

Dorothy watched him for a few seconds. His great powerful body that looked so hulking in his office clothes streaked through the water with grace and beauty.

"My man," she said out loud, hugging herself. "My own man." Then she plunged in after him, thrashing to catch him up, laughing at the rain.

When they came out their clothes were still dry under the shelf but the rain was now streaming down.

Dorothy giggled. "How do we get dry without getting wet?"

Roger seized the bundles in their towels. "Come on. Up to the car."

They pattered up the cliff steps and crossed the road to the car park.

"You get in the back," he said. "Never mind your muddy feet. Get in." He slid into the front seat, slammed the door and turned round to clasp her slippery body.

"Steady on," she said as his hands found the button on her bikini strap and tried to undo it. "A prosecution of indecency in a public car park would be a bad start in Daddy's eyes." She enveloped herself in her towel.

He laughed, rubbed his back and chest with his towel and pulled his crumpled shirt over his head.

"You look so funny," she said, "with your hair hanging down all lank. Your face looks quite different, not having all those curls standing up." Under the towel she slipped out of the bikini top and struggled damply into her brassiere. "How does it feel to be you? Here I am. Me. And there you are. You. But you're inside your body just as I'm inside mine. And we can't get out. Isn't it weird?"

Roger laughed. He had the towel round his middle and was somewhat pointlessly squeezing his wet trunks out of the window. She wondered if he had anything else on yet. He said, "Will your mother tell your father who you are with tonight – if she guessed? She saw the car."

Dorothy had been looking out for him and he hadn't had to get out. But they had seen her mother peeping from the front bedroom window as they drove off.

"She wouldn't know the car." Dorothy pulled on her cotton dress and let the towel slip down. "She's the most unobservant person I know. But, Roger, do you mind if they know we're seeing each other again?" They had talked about this a little on the way. He had told her Harry Wade was leaving. "You see, I'm not much good at secrecy."

He said, "Nor am I, but I like the alternative even less." He was stooping down, working his legs into his trousers. His voice sounded muffled.

"How d'you mean?"

He buttoned himself up and began rubbing his feet. Then he said, "Some people would presume on a past acquaintance with the boss's daughter if they were angling for promotion. You know, win a sympathetic ear at court."

"But Daddy knows you're not like that."

"No he doesn't. Why should he?"

"He saw you – outside the office – when we were going out together before."

"Yes, he had two or three polite words with me. I was never asked to a meal."

"I'm sorry. I hope you weren't offended."

He twisted round to look at her face, saw her eyes twinkle and said, "Hang it, no. He was being wary, and quite right too."

"You were pretty wary yourself."

"There was a lot at stake."

"If that's an allusion to my size again –"Then she became suddenly serious. She paused in rubbing her hair with her towel and let it hang round her neck. "I wasn't wary, Roger, was I? I blundered on with my damned writing –" He shook his head but she went on. "No, I've got to say this. I showed as much delicacy as an elephant. I'm impatient I suppose. You hadn't said a squeak about the future so I just carried on with my life, my habits. And one of my habits was to use situations I came across as a basis for my sketches. I had terrible qualms though when I sent that one off." She bent down to slip her cold feet into her sandy beach shoes.

"Did you?" he asked. "Of course I had my own ideas for the future. It just seemed a bit early to put them into words."

"I know. But this is only one more meeting and look where we've got to."

He was sitting round now with one knee up, trying to pull on a sock which kept twisting round on his still damp foot. "We won't forget *this* meeting, will we?"

She laughed, shivered a little and drew round her shoulders a scarlet cardigan with a big collar. She put her arms into it and buttoned it up to the neck.

"You're cold," he said.

"No, I'm fine. I brought my raincoat as well – when I saw how the sky was changing. You've only got your jacket. What I really am is hungry."

"So am I. Let's see if this benighted place has anywhere open after six p.m."

"There's a snack bar on Marine Parade selling hot pies and crisps all evening."

She scrambled over into the seat beside him, leaving the wet bathing things and towels spread out on the back seat.

They were in a little world closed in by the streaming wet but when he had switched on and got the windscreen wipers going they could see the deserted car park, sodden grass, and out there the grey sea and sky merging together. He turned the car and headed into the town of Brynmouth.

She pointed with her comb. "That neon sign. It's the snack bar. It looks awful but it's clean and the food's in plastic bags."

When they were inside at a table, unwrapping their pies and packets of crisps and sipping the hot coffee she said, "Why did you pick on today?"

"I didn't. I just wanted you, on the spur of the moment."

"But you had your bathing things with you."

"No, I stopped in town and bought the trunks. I always have a towel in the car for showers after rugby. It wasn't planned."

"Ah I wondered. And I thought about you this morning. I tried to picture you at Hugh Cole's party. I thought if we'd been engaged I could have gone."

"It was dreary. Waste of an evening. What have you written about it so far?"

"I've got my notebook in my bag but I don't think I'll write it. I wanted to say that despite their disguises the hippies and the professionals were all members of the human race. Under the long hair and leather jackets *they* were hiding how sadly ordinary they were as individuals while the establishment types were being brightly intellectual to show that their collars and ties and cocktail dresses were just cloaks for their terrifically independent minds. The editor would have called it too philosophical, not funny enough."

"It was like that, though, the party. Forced atmosphere. Old Hugh wandering about pretending it was such a scream. Your father put in an appearance just long enough not to seem rude before he took your mother home."

"He was afraid she'd get tipsy. She thinks she can take alcohol like tea. We don't have it at home. Daddy's very health-conscious *and* he thinks it's a waste of money. He'll approve of you, physique-wise, for a son-in-law." She shook out her crisps onto her plate. "You know, I'm sure if we came straight out with this he'd accept that Harry Wade's leaving was pure coincidence."

"Maybe he would." Roger ruffled up his hair which was drying into curls again in the hot little café. "But when the interviews are held the Chairman and Committee will know I've just become engaged to his daughter. He'd feel obliged to have someone else for the look of the thing."

"Then we needn't announce our engagement, officially, till you're appointed."

"And how would it look then? Bird recommends me in the face of possibly strong outside opposition and then it turns out I'm to be his son-in-law."

"You're very sure he'll want you for the job. Maybe he'll fancy an outsider?"

"It's not likely. Pembleton may leave and I think your father's planning on three Areas. Neville Carr's too raw to get an Area of his own so your father will want me for continuity. It fits his tidy mind. I know the county well." Roger ate up his pie and wiped his mouth. "We could keep things quiet for a few weeks till after the interviews. Then I'll get cracking in the job – I'd be starting in two months when Harry goes – and we'll meet again publicly at the Christmas party and pick up from there. Get engaged about March and married in May or June when the weather's decent for a honeymoon."

"Oh darling, the way you say it – so cool and well-thought out!"

"You wanted it matter-of-fact."

"I know. And we'll do what you say and the weeks will fly, Daddy will be happy to give me a perfect wedding and I'll be Mrs Weston next summer – but oh dear, you've got to let me flutter a little just thinking about it even if I *am* nearer thirty than twenty."

"You go ahead and flutter. I'm fluttering quite a bit myself. Let's have another coffee. That was good."

Quentin Bird drove his car into the garage at ten minutes to six. His wife was struggling to hang a deckchair on a nail. He got out and helped her.

"Dorothy could perfectly well do that for you."

"She's not here. She was watching for him from the sitting-room window. I thought it was over between them. She ran out and he had the window down so I got a glimpse. I was so hot in the garden I went up for some eau de cologne. I was at the dressing-table or I'd never have seen him. It *was* a greeny-blue car he had, wasn't it?"

Bird fastened the doors, collected his briefcase and rolled umbrella from the car and ushered his wife into the house. A glance at the sky told him he had been wise to take the umbrella. Very soon the storm rumbling in the distance would be upon them.

Not until he had hung up his umbrella and grey trilby in the cloakroom, given his wife a small kiss on her forehead and washed his hands, did he say, choosing his words carefully, "So it's Roger Weston you believe Dorothy has gone out with tonight, is it?"

They walked through to the dining-room where Dorothy had set the table. There was nothing to do but lift the lids off the dishes.

Mrs Bird said, "No one else has all that high curly hair like Roger."

"All the same," Bird replied, examining the salad, "you could be mistaken." He approved to the last detail the way his daughter had set it out. She had remembered the squeeze of lemon, the beetroot separate with the minimum of vinegar, a dish of grated carrot by *his* plate because her mother detested it, and she had put the Health Store salad dressing in a tiny sauce boat, knowing how he disliked a bottle on the table.

"But they'd look so splendid walking down the aisle. I know we'd miss her terribly. I really don't know how we'd manage, unless they'd live here of course."

Bird looked round the table, sat down and shook out his napkin. "I would certainly miss her." He helped himself to grated carrot. "But it would be most inappropriate to have them living here. You could have paid help in the house I imagine, should the eventuality arise." He took a slice of ham and cut off the fat. "Was this meeting arranged by phone? She wasn't anticipating going out, I believe."

"Well, the vicar phoned when we'd just finished lunch."

"The vicar?"

"Perhaps it was Roger. A deep sort of voice. That's why I thought of the vicar."

"What I'm wondering," Bird said, "is whether young Weston feels in a position to resume the acquaintance. His Area Planning Officer, Harry Wade, has surprised us by obtaining the post of Deputy at Morlton. Weston may feel in line for promotion now."

"Oh and they could buy a house somewhere near and she could still pop in. Now wouldn't that work out nicely? I thought they'd quarrelled. I was only talking about him this morning but I never know what she's thinking. She'd be very silly if she turned him down now just when you're going to promote him."

Bird considered explaining procedure to her and decided against it. In fact it was not obligatory to advertise the job but it was customary and under the circumstances most desirable. If outside applicants were below Weston in qualifications and experience he could be appointed without any other interviews. That would be the best outcome. He had already decided, driving home, that he wanted Weston in the job. Though young the man had an air of authority and confidence that was impressive. But a son-in-law in the office – that would need careful handling. No son-in-law was a pleasant prospect. Dorothy said extravagant things but it was stimulating to have her about. Her intellect was sharp, her temperament buoyant. A tete-a-tete existence with his wife would be a poor exchange.

As he noted how all his little foibles had been catered for, even the electric coffee percolator filled up, waiting only to be switched on, he found something touching in the sight, like a farewell feast. He wasn't given to premonitions but he couldn't help feeling she knew he would be hurt and this extra care tonight was an offering to soften the blow.

He switched on the percolator. Perhaps, he thought, if they settle in

Midcaster they'll invite us on Sundays for lunch and maybe afternoon tea. She would never forget to have home-made scones, from wheaten flour of course.

There was a brighter flash of lightning and thunder followed close behind it.

"Oh I do wonder," his wife exclaimed, "where he's taken her. She just called out, 'I'm off out. Don't wait up.' That was all. Just 'Don't wait up.'"

Bird felt a sickening twinge in his stomach. The cheek of the man – an Assistant Area Planning Officer. No by your leave, nothing. *His* daughter. 'Don't wait up' indeed.

He said, "I see no reason to worry, my dear. He'll take good care of her." He cut a slice of organic cheese to eat with a wheatmeal cracker while the coffee percolated.

Her eyes flitted nervously to the window as another lightning flash lit up Rufton.

"I wish they were safely married. Courtships are unsettling."

He recalled how cleverly he had managed Foggart. "A light touch on the tiller is all it takes. A quiet word to Dorothy when she comes in. She is very open."

"You'll wait up for her? *I* couldn't. I've had too much sun today. If I don't get to sleep early I'll lie and think and I always wake hours before the alarm goes off."

Bird poured the coffee. "That's all right, I shall wait up for her," he said.

Outside the first drops of rain came drumming down. He got up and carefully closed the windows.

Neville Carr found the flat as they had left it, the lunch plates on the draining board, no tea ready. No Lena. He flung his crash helmet on the bed and pulled open the wardrobe door. Her clothes were still there. But she would up and off if she had a mind to, just as she was. And then he noticed that the box in the corner, where her old drawings and magazines were piled, had been disturbed. So she *had* been in. Had *he* been there with her? Had she shown him the portrait? Its face was to the wall.

He turned it round. It *was* Pembleton. She'd got the forehead and hair but surely he hadn't sat for it? The mouth and chin were wrong. Or was it her idea of him — a super-ruthless Pembleton. Ruthless enough to leave a pregnant wife and children? Neville ground his teeth. That look when he had said, 'Neville, will you get out of my way?' Did the man think he could have her and he would do nothing about it?

He picked a knife off the bench and approached the portrait.

"Have you guessed who it's meant to be then?"

He spun round as if he'd received an electric shock. She was standing in the open doorway, alone, wearing the same dress, her hair hanging about her face, a little lankly from the heat, a bundle of folders and magazines under her arm.

"I've just been having tea with his wife." She flung the bundle onto the bed, knocking the crash helmet to the floor where it rolled noisily into a corner. "What were you going to do with that?" she asked.

He looked down at the knife in his hand. "I was just — I was drying up. Going to get the tea. I just thought I'd take a look at the picture. See if you'd done any more."

"I've been out all afternoon." She went to the sink and began to splash cold water over her face and arms. "Anyway," she said, looking round, "if you want to destroy a painting a blunt table knife's no good. Canvas is tough. Throw a pot of paint over it, then it can be used again. What's the matter? Still mad with Paul? His wife says you won't need to resign over a bit of a slip up. Well, I told you so, didn't I?"

"His wife? You've really been to see his wife?"

"I told you he suggested it when I saw him at lunchtime. Why are you looking at me like that? I even left in time to be home first like a dutiful wife only I missed a bus."

"I walked about the quayside looking for you." It was all he could think of to say.

"Well, well, like a loving husband." She rubbed her face dry. "So are you going to resign? Did you see the great Bird?"

He wanted to go up to her and shake the truth out of her but he kept his distance.

"I don't believe for a minute you went to see Eleanor Pembleton."

"Why ever not?"

"You said you were going to sketch by the river."

"And I did. I also said I'd advertise for a job. I did even better. I *got* a job. Starts Monday. And I said I would see Eleanor. I did that too. Asked them to dinner on Monday evening. He'll tell you tomorrow if it's OK. So you see, a productive afternoon."

"You did *what.*" It was too fantastic not to be true. "You don't think I could entertain him here!" Perhaps she was planning a civilised foursome at which they could discuss their future dispassionately. It seemed nothing was beyond her.

She flung herself down on the bed, pushing her papers to one side. She lay on her back, legs outspread, hands cupped behind her head.

"I shall give them something really exotic. D'you know what she was giving him tonight for his supper? Fish pie. His daughter's like him by the way. Live wire. Bags of personality. The little boy's just a shy sort of pudding."

"His daughter? His little boy?"

"Well, stop gawping, man. You believe I've been now?"

"You didn't see *him?*"

"Of course not. She wasn't expecting him home till late."

"And you dared to talk about Lower Wooton? You knew I wouldn't want you —"

She flapped a hand. "It came up casually. I said I'd got this job but you weren't settled. Had had a brush with Paul and talked about private practice. It was chat between office wives. Won't make a scrap of difference to meeting them socially. Should *ease* the tension. You've got such a *thing* about this man. I can't think why. They're an ordinary family. Go camping. What's so special about Paul that you get so worked up about him?"

Neville came over to the bed and sat down near her feet. Her words might have convinced him that he'd built up an utterly false notion in his mind, except that her tone of voice was bitter, even wretched. She had loved Pembleton and he had thrown her over. She'd found out today that he wouldn't leave Eleanor. Why then would she torment herself by having them to dinner? Did she want a dramatic scene when she would expose their liaison to Eleanor and himself? He felt, at last, that he was sorry for her.

"Look," he said, "I don't give a damn for Pembleton. I'd meet him socially if I had to and carry it off easily. This silly business at the office — about Lower Wooton — it seems he'll have to take the brunt of it whatever I do.

I saw Bird. I told him just what happened and why. I made it quite clear it was my error not Pembleton's –"

"Noble you," she said automatically, but looking at him with crinkled brows as if puzzled where this was leading.

"Well," he said, pleased at her interest, "Bird took it the way I hoped. He likes honesty. I knew it would be the right thing to tell him straight out."

"Oh cut the self-congratulations. What are you trying to say?"

"He's going to promote me. He's going to make me Head of Architecture. A Section Head. Hugh Cole's job."

"Well, lucky you. So you get out from under Paul's feet and get paid for it too."

It was the best she could say, he supposed, for the moment. "Well, so now I can meet him as an equal. He can't come the arrogant boss any more. So now it's up to you."

"Up to me," she cried, sitting bolt upright. "What's that supposed to mean?"

"Look," he said, "I'm not blind. That blasted portrait. I know he's hurt you. I'd like to wring his damned neck for thinking he can chuck you over. But show him you don't care. And he needn't think he can hoodwink me. But leave his wife out of it. Let him stew in his own guilt. See if he can live with his conscience if he's got one."

He stopped talking and reached out a hand to her. She had tossed herself back on the bedcover and turned her face into it. Her shoulders were shaking.

"Come now," he said. "He's not worth it. And you've not told me about this job. That's a good thing. Take your mind off him. That was why you came in for those folders and things? Well, tell me. This is a fresh start for both of us. What? What have I said?"

She sat up violently and thrust him off the bed. There were no tears on her face.

She cried, "Oh God, Neville, don't be so *corny*." She swung her legs to the floor and laughed in his face. "I've seen you in some ridiculous roles but that of the forgiving husband is just too funny. For God's sake let's have something to eat. I'm starving."

"I was going to suggest taking you out to a meal to celebrate my promotion. If I'm so ludicrous perhaps you'd rather go alone."

"Now it's the hurt dignity game." She went to the window. "There's going to be one hell of a thunderstorm or hadn't you noticed. We'll open a tin."

"I really thought you were crying before." He followed her into the kitchen alcove. "D'you know you really are the most damnable bitch."

"Oh I say." She swung round. "That's good. I like that." She took a tin from the cupboard and opened it. "Tomato soup. I'm chilly. Well, go on, call me more names."

"What good does it do? Living with you is impossible. If I want to be cheerful you're depressed and if I'm serious you laugh."

She dipped her finger in the soup and dabbed some on his nose. "Darling Neville, you just are funny when you're serious. You always have been."

He wiped his face on his handkerchief. "I know why your father used to hit you. You goad and goad and goad until what else can one do?"

"Well go on. Hit me." She banged the tin down on the bench so that some soup slopped out. She faced him, hands by her side. "Go on, hit me."

He couldn't lift his hand, any more than he could have slashed the painting. He said. "But you hated your father."

"I know. Maybe that's the only sort of relationship I can manage. Assault and battery on one side. Rebellion on the other. *You* don't give me anything to rebel against."

"Did Paul?"

"Paul?" She began to break out again, trying to hide her mirth. She turned away, poured the soup into a pan and put it on the stove.

"What's funny?" He gripped her arms from behind. "What the hell's funny?"

"Let go. I can't light the gas." He dropped his hands and she lit it. "I wish I could carry it off," she exclaimed suddenly. "I wish I could save it up for secret laughs."

"What the hell d'you mean?" He took hold of her again, crushing her tightly. It was better than striking her because it was akin to love. He even pulled her across to the bed and thrust her back onto it.

She gasped, still laughing, "You think I've had an affair with Paul Pembleton?"

He released his hold a little. "You haven't?" Dare he believe her?

She said, "I never set eyes on the man from the day they came to dinner till this lunchtime. What a waste of your speck of imagination! What sparked it? The portrait?"

"That and so many things you've said today." He still didn't know for sure that she wasn't brazening it out. "You've been obsessed with him anyway?"

"Oh yes." She laughed. "Him or an idea of him. I wonder if anyone does exist like that." She pointed over his shoulder at the painting, then dropped back against the bedcover as if she'd lost interest in him, the man she had created.

"And Pembleton? Truthfully, you haven't seen him." He looked her in the eye.

She giggled. "It was a great story — your wife having an affair with your boss."

"Then you were waiting for *me* today — at lunchtime."

"Of course. I wanted a lift home."

He thought, she'd still like to hurt me. It's the only fun she gets. He took another look at the painting. The eyes followed one everywhere. Such sardonic aloofness was unbearable. He had an impulse to turn the picture to the wall again or do as she said and throw a pot of paint over it. But he was afraid if he moved she would escape him again.

"All right," he said. "Let him watch."

"What are you doing?" she cried but he didn't give her a moment to doubt.

She fought him with a surprised and furious joy. Then she took command herself and they struggled into a kind of ecstasy together.

When they lay quiet, she murmured, "You've got to be rough with me. You're all I've got." Then she sniffed and sat up suddenly. "Christmas! The soup!"

She opened another tin while he cleaned up the stove. Then she told him about the Grosvenor School and Mrs Kellett. So while they ate and the storm broke outside, she rushed on and told him about the old house next door to the school and how she had said her husband was an architect and would love to help.

"You said that? You really knew what I could put my heart into? There's never been anything we've done together." He thought, it may not last but we can try.

She laughed. "I came on marches with you."

"Ay, for all the wrong reasons."

"For no reason at all. And nor would this be. I don't believe in reasons. I'll do it while I want to. Same as I'll do the teaching. I'm no glutton for work."

"But it might get hold of you – like your painting does, sometimes."

"It might but it's not a reason for living." She got up to find something else to eat. "Life's something we're stuck with. It has flashes." One lit the room. "It has flashes like lightning and damn great rumbles like thunder but mostly it's nothing, nothing at all."

"Nothing without a bit of help – from the people living it."

She didn't notice the remark. She went to the window, a loaf of bread in her hand.

"The rain," she said. "It's trying to wipe everything out."

He came to the window. He had almost said, "Yes, it's cleared the air" but he stopped himself in time and just stood looking at it beside her.

It streaked down over the Crescent's private garden, slashing at the beech leaves, shimmering the stems a glossy black, churning the grass into mud, flattening newspapers.

"Wonderful," she cried. "Wonderful, wonderful."

He said, "I could buy a house now, you know, in the suburbs, but you like this, don't you? I like it too. Shall we stay here?"

"Oh wonderful," she said, pressing her face to the window. "Wonderful!"

Paul dropped Cranston by his Vauxhall in Wanwick market place. On the way Cranston had told him he was standing for County Councillor next year and wouldn't it be interesting if he got onto the planning committee. Paul had made no comment.

Cranston swung his thick legs to the ground, about to walk off without a word.

Paul thought, hang it all, let's be civilised. "Goodnight, Councillor."

Cranston swung round and peered in at him. "Oh and goodnight to you, *Mr* Pembleton." He slammed the car door and stumped across the square.

Paul let in the clutch. What did I expect? He knows I loathe him. No one so small-minded, so grasping, should be in a position of influence. He drove out of the town.

The bowl in which Wanwick lay was muted green but the brassiness of the sky was reflected in the Wann, winding away down the valley ahead, with a glint of brown in it like a peat stream. Paul stopped thinking. His brain was bruised as well as his head. The road was a river pouring towards him. The chunky tower of Cottle Church came up on his left unnoticed among its trees.

Then the nose of a van popped out of the turning to the village and startled him. It waited but he was alert again. If it hadn't been for that he'd never have noticed the two short men thumbing for a lift beyond the turning. He drew up. It might be good to have company. His outside self was letting him down again, this time from sheer weariness.

The smaller of the two men grinned and waved. It was Professor Smith, wearing the same shabby clothes and rope sandals as before. As a concession to the cooler evening air he wore a blue beret. With that and his pointed beard he looked like a Frenchman. The other man was the archetypal English colonel, stocky, red-faced, flaxen moustache, balding head, tweeds and a stout stick. He seemed embarrassed by the situation.

Smith was perfectly at ease. "How delightful! I thought you might come back this way but not as late as this. Excuse me. This is Douglas. Douglas, Paul, a friend of mine."

The military man said, "How d'you do?" and bowed.

Smith climbed into the back, easing Paul's briefcase along. "Douglas is here for a long weekend. First time for ten years. Hop in, Douglas. Paul is sure to be in a hurry."

The colonel struggled in. "Sorry, gammy leg. Damn it, I've never done this kind of thing in my life. Hitch-hiking I think it's called." He spoke the word with distaste.

Paul smiled at him. "Hardly that, I think, if I'm a friend of your friend."

The colonel cheered up. "That's true. Lucky you happened to come by."

"Where are you making for anyway?"

The professor answered, "Anywhere at all. We're on a pub crawl."

The colonel winced. "We just met," he explained. "I'm staying at The Sheaf of Corn in Cottle. Went out for a walk and ran into old Tom. We used to come walking tours in the area years ago. I'd no idea he was living here now. He's been telling me about his caravan. Scandalous business. Did you know he's to be turned out?"

Paul could see in the driving mirror the professor chuckling and his little beard wagging. I will not get into this, he thought. "I heard something of it."

The colonel shook his head. "I don't know what this country's coming to. Might as well be in a police state when a man can't live where he likes."

Paul sighed. If he made no reply the colonel would soon dry up but Smith's eyes were challenging him. So with his sweetest smile he said, "You were in the army, sir? You'll appreciate the need for order."

Smith squeaked out at once, "Well, Douglas, what do you say to that?"

The colonel became a little pinker. "Of course, the army. That's the place for it. Order and discipline. But we fought for freedom. We can't regiment civilians like that."

Paul drew in close to the bank to let a hay-cart pass. When it had gone he tried another line. "Planning isn't new. In earlier times some public-spirited land owners did the job pretty well – till the industrial revolution when things got out of hand. Cities spread, slums happened. Now we've become aware of the need for statutory planning."

The colonel looked round at Smith. "I didn't know your friend was one of these socialist chaps." He was trying to laugh it off as if he'd found himself in the wrong club.

"I don't know," the professor said earnestly. "Are you a socialist, Paul?"

"I don't hold a brief for any political party at present. Maybe my sympathies are with the Liberals for having been underdogs for so long."

The colonel seemed to warm to him a little but was still puzzled. "You're not saying you approve of Tom here being turned out of his caravan."

Paul was flogging himself to reply, to defend his raison d'être at the end of this impossibly long day. He said, "The landlord of the Sheaf of Corn should have applied for permission."

"You seem to know a mighty lot about it," the colonel said as if the knowledge was somehow disgraceful.

"No more than any citizen should know."

Smith was nodding his head. "This is so beautifully in character. Perhaps you can tell Douglas what harm my caravan was doing there. That seemed to bother him."

Paul saw he'd have to come out in the open. He kept his eyes on the road.

"Perhaps you've realised, sir, that I am connected with the Planning Authority. In fact it was I who advised Mr Smith this afternoon about his caravan."

The professor clapped his hands. "Splendid, splendid. We've got to it at last."

But the colonel exclaimed, "You were keeping this dark, sir! And you, Tom, you led me on." His face was very red. "Kindly put me down, sir."

"It's all right, Douglas," cried the little professor, leaping up and down with sheer exuberance. "I forced Paul into this position and he's behaved just as I expected, with more restraint than you, I may say. We can't get down yet. There's a public house about five miles on which you and I know very well. The Fisherman's Rest at Beckbridge."

"Ah, the Fisherman's Rest at Beckbridge." The colonel's voice mellowed.

"So while we're getting there Paul can tell us exactly why it's so necessary to remove my caravan. Please go ahead Paul. We're listening."

The colonel muttered, "It's your childish habit of calling everyone by their first names. Made me think he was an old friend."

"Children are good at human relations. Besides Paul *is* my friend. Anyone is my friend who accepts my friendship. Paul has an official capacity but underneath the man himself is, I'm sure, ready to be my friend. Isn't that so, Paul?"

Paul met his eyes again in the driving mirror and gave him his warmest smile. Smith nodded happily. The colonel, sensing this interchange, shifted about uneasily.

Smith said, "But do give us the policy on caravans, Paul, to satisfy Douglas here. There must be something you can recite, like a child's catechism."

They were entering a magnificent avenue of beeches. In the deteriorating light it had the evocative atmosphere of a stage backdrop. A rabbit ran across the road, its white blob of tail concentrating what little light there was. Paul wanted to laugh. An Alice in Wonderland aura lay over everything. He thought, if I recite the policy on caravans will the words come wrong, like 'How doth the little crocodile –?'

He began to intone, "The policy on caravans is twofold. Firstly the Council is opposed to their use for permanent residence except in very special circumstances, on the grounds of their being a substandard form of housing and a potential nuisance to adjoining property. Secondly, caravans for recreational purposes should be grouped on suitable sites, that is, not in built-up areas or areas of exceptional scenic value, and should be screened from view as far as possible. Finally all sites the Council approves must be supplied with adequate sanitary facilities." He grinned at Smith and added, "Amen."

They had emerged from the avenue of beeches and Smith gave a little sigh of pleasure. "Thank you, Paul. That was beautiful."

"Very fine trees, beeches," said the colonel.

Paul, still smiling, noticed a ramshackle boathouse by the Wann, the first outpost of Beckbridge. He was negotiating with the owner to have it rebuilt or demolished. He said, "We're coming into Beckbridge. Have I satisfied you, gentlemen?"

"Douglas and Thomas, please. Just one thing, Paul. If *I* don't mind living in substandard housing why should the Council worry?"

"It's out of keeping with the stone dwellings round it." Paul drew up at the inn.

"Come on, Tom," said the colonel. "Whole thing's just as I said. They decide what's best for you. Might as well be in Russia."

"But I'm interested. Won't you come in and join us, Paul? You see, Douglas, these people are idealists. They want to raise us to better things despite ourselves."

"Surely you're not attending to his arguments. I'm sorry sir," he said distantly to Paul, "I'm obliged to you for the lift but I cannot stomach college boy bureaucrats who set themselves up as dictators."

He got out and stepped up to the inn door. There he waited, not looking round, one hand resting on his stick, the other clasped in a tight fist in the small of his back.

The little professor poked his head forwards. "Oh if only we talked to each other as human beings! Douglas is a great sorrow to me. He was going to like you very much till he knew your professional capacity. Do come in for a drink. Perhaps we could persuade him you'd left the planning officer out here."

"It's kind of you but I'm really not two separate people. Anyway, neither of us wants more delay. We have a wife and family to get home to."

Smith nodded. "But you will come and have tea in my caravan while it's still there? You must meet so many hostile Douglases. I wonder what it does to you."

Paul ignored this. "If you state in your application that the caravan is a base while you look for a house in the area you may get temporary permission for a limited period."

"Ah, the rules are flexible!"

"You'd have more space for your art in a cottage. And if you need to phone County Hall ask for Mr Pembleton not Paul. Look, the colonel's getting impatient."

Smith jumped out, chuckling. "Funny you called him a colonel. You needed a label. Lucky you didn't say it to him. He rose to Major General. Well, goodnight, Paul."

As he drove away Paul saw the two figures disappear into the saloon bar, Thomas hopping at Douglas's side, pointing his remarks with the tip of his beard.

He looked at his watch. It was quarter past six and he still had fifteen miles to go. He headed towards the storm clouds that filled the sky in the direction of Midcaster.

Hugh Cole on the top deck of a bus could see the slopes of Barton across the Bryn, the cooling towers of the power station and the tops of Brynbank's encircling trees.

Above Brynbank he could see the high treeless roads of Westhilll. It was even possible to pick out Lister's house, big and square staring across the valley.

At the Brynbank stop he got off and walked over to his cottage. The row butted onto the pavement and the other side was the river, twenty feet below the road. He looked up at the sagging yellow sky and shivered. Floods had been known at this spot.

Between his cottage and the next was a cinder track going round the backs. Here he normally parked his car. With a pang he realised he would never see it there again. Now he noticed a pram parked there, next to the side door to Maurice's cottage. Hilde came out with a baby.

"Hello," Hugh said, "I thought you had one of those. I was just telling old Derek you had one of those. Where have you been hiding it?"

"Derek?" She screwed up her face. "Derek Lister? You tell him about the baby?"

"I tell everyone everything. It's my nature."

She grunted. With the baby on one arm she was trying to turn back the pram blanket. "Here, you hold him," she said.

"Eh? What? This way up?"

"You and babies. That's funny."

"Why?" He took a look at it. "This is a nice one. It looks very clean."

"Mother's changed his clothes four times today."

"Your mother's here?"

She explained grudgingly what had happened. She took the baby and bedded him down. At once he screwed his head round and started to cry.

"Oh dear," said Hugh, "is he hungry?"

"No, this is the time my mother say he will be cross. Then he have more milk and go to sleep. But he not cry if I take him a walk. I go up to Westhill. You come too?"

"Why Westhill? It's steep all the way up."

"I show baby to your Derek Lister."

"Lister? Why? Is he a connoisseur of babies?"

She wheeled the pram up and down without answering. Hugh looked at her, running his hands through his hair. "Anyway," he said, "there's a thunderstorm coming."

"They will adopt the baby." She too glanced at the sky.

"They what? The Listers?"

"She has seen the baby. His wife. Now *he* must see him. Then they adopt him."

Hugh looked at the baby as if there must be something phenomenal about him.

"It's not big enough yet to carry golf clubs. What else could they use it for?"

She swore at him in German. "You! You know nothing about people. People are a joke to you. You are nothing but a joke yourself. So goodbye."

She put up the hood and prepared to set off.

"Hey Hilde, I left Derek at the office. He was waiting for Paul. He may be ages." She hesitated. "Come on back, Hilde. Have some tea. Bring the baby in."

She came in, pulling the pram behind her over the step. Hugh had already begun to discard his office uniform.

"See what there is in the pantry while I have a shower."

She said, "I'm wheeling the baby. I don't like hearing him cry."

When he came out of the shower she was still pushing the pram up and down.

"But he's asleep," Hugh said, peering under the hood.

"So, I am soothing myself."

Hugh had dressed in old corduroys with his long flame-coloured shirt dangling over the top. He took the pram handle. "*I'll* soothe myself and you look in the pantry."

She gazed at him. "You are such a boy. I have years and years more than you." She went to the kitchen and pulled down the blind over the small side window. "Maurice can see. He is very jealous, even of you. Let him think I have gone for a walk."

"Is he working?"

"No, he's asking my mother about the war. You have nothing here to eat!"

"I'm running down my stocks. Aren't there any eggs?"

"Two."

"And there's some flour in the bag. We'll make pancakes. Is there a lemon?"

"No."

"*You* must have one. Slip over and get one."

"No, you go. Tell Maurice you saw me go up the village when your bus came in."

Hugh walked across the cinder track and put his head round the sculptor's door.

"Got a lemon, Maurice?"

The mother called out in German, "Where is Hilde and the baby?" Hugh got the sense of that plain enough. So when Maurice appeared from the kitchen he asked him, "Does it matter very much if she's having tea with me?"

Maurice shook his shaggy head, and fetched two lemons.

"If he ask thy cloak give him thy coat also."

"Oh it's like that is it? Mind, I don't want to keep Hilde – or the baby."

"Hilde," said Maurice, "is not important. You asked for a lemon so I gave you two. Hilde's had a meal just now. She exists only on the animal plane. She is not interested in human suffering. Suffering is the only reality."

"Oh fine. Well, thanks for the lemons." Hugh dodged back into his own cottage as a lightning flash cut the sky beyond the power station. He handed Hilde the lemons.

"Has Maurice gone religious or something?" he asked her.

"I don't care." She whipped up the batter with a fork. "I am sick of hearing about the war. That storm is getting nearer."

A few minutes later when a pancake was sizzling in the pan a great explosion of thunder right overhead made Hugh shudder and produced a wild squeal from the baby.

"Pick him up," Hilde said, "and hold him tight. He may comfort you."

Hugh laughed uneasily and took up the baby. "There, come and tell your Uncle Hugh not to mind the silly storm." He walked about the living room, keeping his eyes from the windows which were lit up almost incessantly now.

Hilde brought two pancakes to the table. When she saw Hugh clutching the baby to his shirt, murmuring to him, she laughed and laughed, pressing her hands to her sides.

"You could be my man," she cried, "if you not go to Africa. You are so funny." She fetched the lemons and a jug of coffee. "Put him down. I can rock him while I eat."

"You've had your tea," Hugh said, sitting down to the table. "Maurice said so."

"Ach, that is nothing. I like pancake." They ate and talked till Hilde pushed back her chair. "I go up to Westhill now. Your Derek Lister will be home. Are you coming?"

Hugh took her to the front window. Cars with their lights on flashed through a curtain of rain. The top of the bank across the road was being pounded into mud.

Hugh grinned at her. "Sorry I haven't the car, luv." He put an arm round her flabby waist. "We'll have a cosy evening. Give the Listers time to think about the baby."

She pulled away. "I not want them to have time. They have years of thinking. Now they must see a baby. Want it. Want that one."

"Come now. Even our Derek must have seen one before. They're all the same."

"You think so?" She picked the baby out of the pram though his eyes were almost closing. "There. Look at him. He is himself, this little scrap of life, only himself."

The baby blinked and then made a pet lip, his face crinkling up.

"Look what you've done," Hugh said, "just when we could have some peace."

"You like him, don't you? You want him?"

"Me?"

"Yes, if you didn't go to Africa I could marry you. Otherwise I must go back to Germany and marry Kurt. I think you will be more fun than Kurt. Kurt is not very funny. You see they will not let me stay in England, but if I married you —"

"Hang on, Hilde, I can't break my contract."

"Why not?"

"It might be very expensive or illegal or something —"

"You could discover an incurable illness."

"I've had my medical and my inoculations. I've sold the cottage and the car."

"You still like better to stay at home. Wouldn't you like to marry me, Hugh?"

He looked at her. He didn't think he would, even if his plans had not been made. If he ever married it would be to combat the demon loneliness and pander to his laziness. She must be good fun but not too unpredictable. And Hilde was unattractive too. His wife would have to be more fastidious about her appearance. Derek had it pretty good with Shirley — maybe too much so, never a hair out of place. It was hard to believe they wanted a baby but Hilde would have to manage her own affairs. He'd reached the point of no return.

"I'm not the marrying kind," he said lamely, trying to laugh it off.

"Don't be ridiculous. All Englishmen are marrying kinds. You like babies too."

"No I don't. They terrify me. Put it away."

She put the baby in the pram. "So, I'll go back to Maurice and my mother. You want so much and no more. I shall go to Kurt when it is settled about the baby. There is something you not understand. Kurt loves me."

"Don't leave me on my own, please, Hilde."

"It's your choice."

"Can I come over then?"

"No, stay there. If the rain stops you can walk up to Westhill with me." She opened the door and raced across the cinder track and into the sculptor's house.

"It's set in for the night," he called after her.

She looked back, round the door, her face just visible as a white disc through the streaming rain. "I've left you the baby," she laughed. "Didn't you notice?"

He turned and nearly fell over the pram. The baby squirmed and began howling.

"My God, some mate you are," he reproached it. "Come on then." He put him on his shoulder. "Hang on while I do the washing-up. What! You need holding? Where's your muscles, lad? How can I wash up with only one hand?" He went on talking to the baby, his voice as incessant as the rain drumming on the slates.

Just before six-thirty Miss Smeed set off along the corridor to see if Mr Pembleton had returned. She passed The Nest, the Deputy's office and The Sinkhole. One of the cleaners had left the door open. The glimpse of the chipped sink and naked gas ring was indecent as if County Hall was showing its underwear. Miss Smeed closed it, restoring the dignity of the panelled corridor. She turned the corner and went through into Control, though she could see from the glass panel that there was no light on.

The room was unnaturally large and mysterious in the dim reddish light that lingered over the river. Papers lying about were patches of intense whiteness. She opened the glass door of Mr Pembleton's office and sat down at his desk. Neatly in the centre of it was a note which read, "Mr Bird has the Lower Wooton file. He asked to see it. N.C."

"Oh no, Neville, he hasn't." Miss Smeed tested her voice in the emptiness. "I have it." She added to the note: '6.25 p.m.. Mr Lister asked me to leave this file and say he would be at the County Hotel till about 6.30 p.m. if you wished to join him. J. Smeed.'

It was disappointing. He wouldn't come now. She had hung about for nothing. Her aunt would say, "You're later than ever tonight, Jocelyn." They didn't like her fussing with her meal while they were watching television.

She placed the note on top of the Lower Wooton file, a small white square on the larger beige one. The symmetry pleased her. Then she heard thunder. She was going to be caught all right. She went over to the big windows and looked down. The river flowed, dun-coloured, past the sharp slabs of warehouses and under the bellies of ships.

"He's probably been at home with his wife and family for a whole hour by this time," she said aloud. "Get yourself home, Jocelyn Smeed, and stop acting the goose."

She hurried at last, letting the doors to Control swing to behind her. She ran with little steps, her body poked forward like a hen, back to Admin., collected her raincoat and bag and descended the stairs. She never used the lift if she was alone in case it got stuck. She was three steps from the ground floor when somebody clanged the lift gates.

"No oh no!" She leapt down in time to see two feet disappearing from sight. Mr Pembleton had been wearing dark brown suede shoes like that but anyone in County Hall could have returned for something. For her to go back upstairs would be immoderate, even immodest behaviour. She would not even take a detour down to the car park to see if his car was there. She walked out heavily, shoulders drooping.

Paul stood and read the little note on the Lower Wooton file. His whole brow was aching. The last miles from Beckbridge, driving fast in the declining light, had used up the dregs of his energy. He put the file in his briefcase. He could draw out the alternative line tonight but the whole thing might have been scrapped in the course of the day. He imagined going over to the County and being politely told by a white-coated barman that Mr Lister had left word to phone him at home after seven.

He went to the washroom for a drink of water and to wash away the dried blood over his left ear. Then he walked along to reception and stood at the switchboard, a little daunted. He pressed something, dialled a number and heard the phone ring at home.

"Mrs Pembleton speaking," Eleanor said in her telephone voice. It was a little thrilling to hear her after the long day. He wanted her very much.

"It's the man from the Town and Country Planning."

"Darling, where are you?"

"At the office but I'll be a few minutes yet. I want to dash over to the County. I might just catch Lister there. He's left a message."

"Won't it wait till morning? Your supper's been ready half an hour."

"I won't be long."

He heard Eleanor say, "Yes, it's Daddy. D'you want to speak to him?"

He said, "I'll have to ring off or I won't catch Derek."

"Cathy says there's some news – what, Cathy? Oh the letter! Of course! Darling, the letter came. You haven't got the job. I'm really sorry if *you* are."

He could hear Cathy saying, "Honestly, Mummy! You'd forgotten."

He said lightly, "It doesn't matter. It's all for the best – with the baby coming. I'll see you soon. Bye, darling."

He picked up his briefcase and hurried to the lift.

The County Hotel was a modern slab of a building which had shot up on a bombed site overlooking the docks. The bar was in an unfriendly room with a blue and silver wallpaper, so that coming from the oppressive atmosphere in the streets was like entering a vast ice cave. Then he saw, like a familiar landmark, the broad square back and large head of Derek Lister. He was hunched over the bar, drinking alone.

Paul walked softly up and rested his elbows on the bar beside him.

"Were you waiting all night for me till they turned you out? I'm touched."

Lister jumped. "It's you, you old so-and-so. Ay, you *are* touched. Coming here expecting to find me still around at this time."

Paul smiled. "But you *are* around." He knew Derek was glad to see him. A sturdy vitality had come back into his posture.

"Ay, but I'd given you up half an hour ago. Bob was here just now or I'd have been home long since."

"Bob?" Paul reflected that Lister, like Professor Smith, though not for the same reasons, was on Christian name terms with everyone.

"Amberly of course. What'll you have?"

"Whisky and soda please. I thought you were lunching with him."

"I did and no joy I can tell you. I ran into him here by accident. I thought we might have got further over a few drinks but the so-and-so wanted to get home."

"Don't *you* want to get home?"

"I could just as well ask *you* that." Lister's mood was hovering between the jovial and the surly. He beckoned the barman and ordered the drinks, large ones.

"Let's take them over there and sit down," Paul said.

Lister took a look at him then. "By Jove, you're all in."

Paul laughed. "Does it show?" He knew that when he was at the end of his reserves he went very pale. "Confusion to our enemies," he said and took a longish drink. Instantly he revived. It would be a fleeting sensation but it was certainly potent.

"What's up?" Lister asked. "Been running round in this heat? Man, I can give you the best part of ten years and I wouldn't wish anyone to have had my day."

Paul took another drink and leant back in his chair. "Come on then, Derek, are you preparing me for bad news?"

"Fifty-fifty I should say." He put on a dead-pan face and said, "To start with Foggart's getting Admin and Neville Carr's going to be the new Head of Architecture."

"O.K. O.K." said Paul, "I'll laugh but I want the news not the comic strip."

"I'm not joking," Lister said heavily.

"But this can't have happened in an afternoon even in our lunatic department."

Lister offered him a cigarette and took one himself. "Right, I'll put you in the picture." Paul thought, he's not the tough, independent character he likes to appear. He needs an audience. Putting people in the picture is what he enjoys most, next to golf.

The story unfolded, first with the Foggart saga. Lister said, "I've never seen the old man so excited. I didn't know if he was angry with you, me or young Carr. When I realised it was with old Ron for telling tales out of school I nearly laughed aloud."

"How did Foggart take it?"

"Badly. It was hellishly embarrassing really. When Bird threw him Admin. – like a bone to a dog – he practically snarled at it."

"I thought that was what *you* had up your sleeve this morning."

"You were damn right." Lister paused uneasily. They were both recalling his burst of anger. "You were just a bit premature with your guess."

"Well, we could have done with three Areas if they hadn't involved Ron. I expect I can stagger along for another year or two. I'll have to. I haven't got the London job.

I rang Eleanor from the office just now. The letter came second post."

"Oh." Derek took a sip of his whisky. "Well, don't be disappointed. Bird's going ahead with three Areas. Creating a new post of ACPO Control with special responsibility for the central one. I told him you were the man for the job, so did Harry. But don't assume you've got it yet. He wants to see you in the morning about Lower Wooton. Mind, Foggart looked pretty sick when he saw his plum falling into *your* lap. You will apply?" He raised his eyebrows.

Paul laughed. Lister looked like a Santa Claus whose present has fallen flat. "Of course I will and thanks for the testimonial." Everyone wanted that – promotion without the trouble of moving. Eleanor would be delighted. But just for the moment it left him cold. The daily job was like walking a sunken pathway through the fascinating landscape of life. This would be a new turn but still too circumscribed to see over the top. He thought of sharing the picture with Derek. No, *Eleanor* would understand. Lister's eyebrows were still raised.

Paul lifted his glass. "Here's to Lower Wooton. There's some magic in it when Neville and I are both to have a chance of promotion."

Lister shook his head. "It's a bad egg. Have another drink. Bob told me just now he's had to take it to his chief because he had a hunch Councillor Sands would be ringing him up and if there's one thing Dowland hates it's Councillors nattering on at him about things he hasn't heard of. I told him Bird knows." As the story of Sands' interest in Lower Wooton became clear Paul saw it could grow very troublesome indeed.

He said as lightly as he could, "So do I draw the alternative line through Hubertson's garden and the farmer's meadow or Councillor Sands' estate?"

"Either way we could find the whole story in the press. If Sands could be deflected onto some other local project he might let this slide."

Paul shook his head. "What if there's another accident? It's a poor junction. I'd like to see it done myself. Perhaps we could get by with an island and 'Keep Left' signs."

"Well, have something to show the old man tomorrow but don't expect him to fall on your neck. He'll want to bawl you out first before he listens to anything."

Paul sat up. He said softly, "Is that what Bird wants me for?"

"Well you know the facts of life. A piece of carelessness by a new boy to which a senior officer signs his name – looks bad."

Paul suddenly thought of the road by the Wann and the little Professor telling him, "You're yourself standing there," without his jacket or his money or his car. He was himself whatever Bird thought of him. But Bird would never forget – if the day came for him to write a reference it would be part of the data he had stored up and ticketed to Pembleton in the intricate file-room of his brain. Stop it, Paul told himself, there'll be other bends in the channel. We've got a good home and enough to live on. What does it matter?

"All the same," he said to Derek, "why would Bird promote Neville after this?"

"Carr fitted, roughly. Clever young architect. Bird wants the County to be known as the breeding ground for top men when De Beaumont Cole is a household name."

Paul set down his glass. "If he can see Neville Carr in that light he's getting to be an incurable romantic in his old age."

Lister held up his hand. "You underestimate the old man *and* young Carr. He let you down, so you reckon he's not an efficient machine –"

Suddenly Paul was angry. "Efficienct! D'you think that's all I care about? No, Neville Carr's not in the same street as Hugh Cole. Hugh has vision, genius if you like. Neville's all right in two dimensions. He's a two dimensional character. And he'll be horribly swelled-headed if he's promoted. He'll feel guilty towards Gordon Harris which will make him a bad boss. Only Harris is too decent to mind."

"Oh Harris is invited to apply and Ken Myers from Plan. But Bird liked the way Neville up and admitted his mistake like a good schoolboy."

That brought back Professor Smith again. 'Children are good at human relations.' Paul thought, a man called Neville stood before me and I was the Area Planning Officer.

He drained his glass. "I met a comical professor today, Derek, who was curious about the effect of professionalism on our characters."

"Oh?" said the Deputy guardedly.

"He wants us to talk as one human being to another, no barriers of professional etiquette. My most honest thought just now would have pleased him."

"And what was that?" Lister was looking at him with raised eyebrows again.

"When I asked myself why it matters – what Bird thinks of me, for example."

Derek grinned. "He's the boss after all."

Paul smiled back. That was the pleasant thing about Derek. He preferred to be on good terms. Even with Foggart he made an effort. It was just that other things often got in the way. "O.K." Paul said, "so Bird's the boss and his opinion of me can affect my career up to a point. But does it matter as long as I don't let it affect *me*?"

"It did a minute ago."

"Touché." He could feel a torrent of words ready to flow from him. The pent-up half-thoughts of the day were crystallising into language. "We're hidebound in a free society by a sense of our rights. To be truly free we should be free even from the need for freedom."

"Come again?" Derek was amused but wary.

"One needs to be very mature to live a full life in a free affluent society. We circumscribe ourselves with our jobs, our homes, our mortgages. We dig down into our appointed channels and are happy to stay in them."

"What on earth has that to do with you and Bird?" Lister had probably not been involved in a conversation like this for a long time, Paul reflected, and he looked like someone on the edge of a bog, wondering if he ought to risk stepping into it.

Paul threw back his head and laughed. "It's all the same idea." He rushed on, "You see, we're used to justice in this country so we feel we have a right not to be misunderstood. When we are our blood boils. But that's what corrodes us – not the injustice that caused it. Our minds aren't free when we're angry."

"But hang on," cried Derek. "You're as good as saying why have rights at all? Why improve society? Why fight Communism or any police state? If someone innocent is chucked in jug he's got to be mature enough to put up with it."

"No, of course we must give people freedom first. You feed a starving man before you play Beethoven to him. I mean we limit ourselves *despite* our freedom. Worse, we channel our attitudes. To the public we are a solicitor, doctor, accountant, planner. We'd like a uniform but if there isn't one we wear a professional manner which saves us from the need to think. I bawled out Neville today as a Section Head to an assistant."

"Quite right. You're good at playing the part."

"But I wasn't acting."

Lister laughed. "I never am."

Paul said quite seriously, "But I am one being, not Paul the man and Pembleton the Planning Officer. I told the professor that. He has an unauthorised caravan at Cottle."

"Well, don't forget that your job is to get rid of it."

"It isn't the job I'll forget, it's the humanity. There was this family. A farmer and his wife and mother-in-law – oh and a son away at school. Their planning application's tangled up with their family problem. The wife, poor soul, was embarrassed at inflicting it on me, a professional man. The husband resented me as an outside power –"

"Of course. They always do," Derek said.

"But this was more intense." Paul found uncomfortably that he didn't want to think about that encounter. "I wonder, really, what I ought to have done."

"Well, that *is* unusual for you. Spun them the tale, right use of land or whatever."

"I did but I could see that the muddle they were in over the human problem was the core of it. I'd have liked to shake them by the ears and make them each face what they wanted. At one point the farmer seemed to be begging me to and I began to answer him, but there wasn't time, it wasn't my job."

"Just as well. He'd probably have knocked you down."

Paul looked up startled and his hand went to his bruise. He had instinctively been keeping his left side turned away and Derek didn't notice the gesture even now.

He was saying, "People don't like home truths even if they ask for them, which is why we should stay professional. In the end they have to accept because we're 'from the Council.' Do you remember Hugh babbling about that this morning. 'We are THEY.' It's civilized."

"Is it? When there's never time for anything beyond 'Let me have this in writing. Good morning.' It's a hell of a way to conduct human relations."

Lister snorted. "Perhaps you'd rather be a vicar?" He seemed determined to wrap up the subject so it could be put away and forgotten. "Come on, man. Who wants frank human relations with every Tom, Dick and Harry?" He pushed back his chair. "D'you realise it's seven fifteen? Let's get home." He looked, Paul thought, uneasy as he said it.

Paul got up. "Sure." Then he added, "The wise Professor's name was Tom."

They began to walk out together. The whisky had given Paul a spurt of energy like a flame and he had burnt it out with talking. "I'm sorry you got landed with all that, Derek. But thanks for listening."

Lister laughed suddenly. "I like a bit of meaty talk. Wouldn't do at the golf club. Mind, don't think I approve of all that rigmarole you spouted." He looked down at his large feet stepping on the soft pile carpet and muttered, "Too much introspection."

Paul made a noise between a sigh and a laugh. "Had you noticed the storm's broken?" Through the outer door they could see the rain.

"By Jove, so it has. Funny, cooped up in that mausoleum of a bar we never heard a thing." Lister was so patently glad to be back with a nice safe subject like the weather that Paul's buoyancy came back with a rush and he laughed aloud.

"I've no raincoat. Have you? Look at it. I know what it reminds me of. I took the kids to a pantomime last year and one scene was shown through a curtain of shimmering lines – quite magical. Kids loved it. So did I. My car's in the office car park. Is yours?"

Lister looked at him curiously. "Ay and no umbrella. It might ease off."

"Oh I don't think so. Come on. We'll run for it." Paul plunged into the rain.

In the two hundred yard sprint to the car park it was each for himself. Paul ran like a hind, his head clear, his limbs invigorated. With the storm it was now quite dark but the air was fresh, full of noise and cascading wet.

When he switched on the headlamps the rain appeared as gleaming rods meeting the fuzz of spray from the surface of the road. He drove forward slowly and crept through the black, streaming city towards home.

At seven-thirty the storm had not yet broken over Wanwick Moor though the sky had thickened and darkened till it looked more solid than the moor itself. The wind was wilder but still coming in fitful gusts from all points of the compass.

After the milking Matthew went round every building to make all safe. When Jane saw him by the milking shed she came out to him. They walked in silence to the door and he examined the upper flap to see it was shut fast. She looked away over to the field gate and the lightning playing above the valley.

Then she spoke what was in her mind. "It wasn't the wind, Matthew, was it?"

If she didn't ask now she'd never do it. Since Mr Pembleton had left she had thrashed at it in her mind, while her mother sat in the basket chair talking of carpets and colour schemes. If he's ill, she thought, if Mother's life's in danger . . .? She could ask Peggy if she could do it without betraying Matthew. But not tonight, not till she'd given him a chance to answer her himself.

"Matthew, it couldn't have been the wind," she said.

His hand fingered the catch on the door as if he could find an answer there. Then he grasped her arm and walked her over to the field gate. They leant on it and looked down on the chestnut trees. The tops were restless as the storm centre moved nearer.

"The man," he said at last, "Pembleton. He said it was the wind."

Then she was sure he had been thinking about it too. "No, *you* said it was the wind." But she didn't know whether it was wise to seem to be arguing. After all, there was still a doubt . . .and if Matthew himself didn't know − if that were possible . . .?

She said in a brighter voice, "Mr Pembleton was just like we hoped, a good man."

"Oh yes," he said, "he was doing his job. He's good at his job. Yes."

"More than that. He's a good man, I'm sure."

"Good?" Matthew looked all round the moor and up at the sky. "We'd all like to be good – if we were given the chance."

"Well why not," she said quickly. "Does anything have to stop us?"

"D'you know what he said to me, at the gate here?" Matthew waved his arm in an encompassing gesture. "With all this, he told me, I ought to be able to accept her."

"Her? You mean Mother? That's true. He's a wise man. I knew it."

Matthew looked at her hard. She felt self-conscious in the lime silk dress and the red on her lips but they didn't seem to anger him any more. "Yes, well, I thanked him when he left. I was polite, reasonable."

Her eyes watched his hands clutching fiercely at the top rail of the gate. He became aware of it and cried, "But what could he know, a stranger, about what it's really like for us? What right had he – it was so easy for him to say accept –"

She shook her head and answered gently, "More than accepting. You said yourself just now, Matthew, 'if we have a chance to be good.' Being good is more than accepting. Couldn't she be our chance, Matthew?"

"*You* ran away from the tea table. You couldn't bear it, Jane."

"I know, but I thought, upstairs, before the car came, if we had enough love –"

He ground his teeth. "How does one love her? How is one good to her? She's possessed. Isn't she possessed by a devil? How is one good to a devil?"

"Matthew, it's the life she's had – with my father. She was always churned up, watching the foolish things he did. If he could have given her a little ease and security –"

"She didn't help him. If she had a head for business why didn't she help him?"

Jane shifted her feet about wretchedly on the baked, cracked earth. It always came back to this: that her mother had given so little to anybody throughout her life. But then what had her mother's childhood been like?

Jane had seen her grandmother in old photographs, a tight, crabbed face with a mouth turned down at the corners.

"You know my grandmother pinched and scraped all her life. It was what she left that set my father up in business. Mother couldn't forgive that. It was *her* money."

"She let him lose it so she had a stick to beat him with. And you say, love her."

"Well, wouldn't my grandmother have done better to love her children in her lifetime instead of leaving them her money when she died?"

Matthew began to speak but a clap of thunder, the nearest yet, broke in on his words. The semi-circle of moor took it and echoed it round and round. When it had died to a low grumbling he said, "We don't have to be bound by our childhood. Who hasn't had a hard life, one way or the other?"

"No we don't have to be, but we are. We let it happen." She looked at his face and then at his hands again. She picked up his right hand and turned it over, studying it. He let her do it then drew it back, harshly, as if he'd only just realised what she was doing.

"What are you after?" He looked at it. "My right hand."

"Oh Matthew." She was distressed that she couldn't hold back the words. "I have to know what happened."

More thunder overhead. The south-eastern sky was cut by lightning from end to end. He held out both hands, palm upwards. "There's the first raindrop. It's been long breaking but it's coming. We'll go in."

She stopped him. "I have to know what happened, Matthew, for all our sakes."

"D'you want to get soaked?"

"Tell me."

"Why did you put on that dress?" He knew the dress had something to do with it. He said in a rush, "Out here, by the gate, when he was so smug – we should do this and that and it would be all right – I could have knocked him down then, for all he was taller than me. But I did nothing. I could see he meant no harm. Can't you feel the rain now?"

She said, "But that was afterwards. What happened by the milking-shed?" She thought, if he's ill this may be the worst thing to do, probing him with questions.

He turned his face from her. "I saw him gasping, leaning against the wall." He whispered it so low she could hardly hear with the wind rising suddenly and bringing a great rush of rain from across the valley.

"All right," she said, "Forget it." She thought, if he's ill *I* can help him myself. I won't ask Peggy. "Forget it, my love. Come in." He still stood, hanging on to the gate. "Matthew, he went away all right. He didn't say anything. He won't *do* anything. Come in now."

"He said he walked into the door. He said it was a silly thing to do."

"Well of course it was and it's a silly thing to get wet." She was half-laughing, coaxing him like a child.

Then her mother called from the kitchen door, "What are you two playing at out there? Can't you see it's raining?"

They turned and came across the farmyard hand in hand. Jane was murmuring all the time, "Don't worry about it, darling. It doesn't matter. Just don't worry about it."

Her mother said, "I've been trying to get my television going in the sitting-room but there's no picture. Is it the storm?"

"I told you to sell the set," Jane said brightly. "We can't get it here. We'd need a mast on top of the moor or something – for the reception."

"What'll I do in the winter without telly?" She grinned at Matthew. "I was going to put it next my bay window in the annexe. I like a window facing south west. You never sit in your room that side. And I shall plant nasturtiums and have them climb round the window. You won't know the front of the house when I'm finished with it. Well, come in, man. Don't stand at the door. Get it shut. The rain's blowing in."

Matthew sat on a chair and began to pull off his boots.

"You've made yourself a cup of tea, Mother," Jane said, noticing the brown teapot on the table with steam rising from the spout.

"Ay, no harm I suppose. It's allowed is it? I thought he might be thirsty after he'd tramped all round the blessed farm."

"You made it for Matthew?"

Her mother set down three cups. She said, "I suppose he'll let us share it."

Jane looked at the back of his head as he bent over his boots. Her eyes were imploring him to say something kind, as if he could *feel* the look.

He got up and stood the boots in the corner by the pails of chicken feed.

"When I'm next in Wanwick," he said slowly, "I'll consult Barnstaple, the electrician. Maybe if we had a very tall aerial — we never asked about it, Jane, did we?"

She gazed at him as his meaning dawned on her. "No," she cried, "we never asked. Wouldn't it be nice, Mother, if you had your television?"

"Ay, he wants me glued to it so I'll not bother you of an evening."

Jane began, "Oh Mother —"

"Nay, I'm not blaming him. If you have to stand out in a thunderstorm to get a minute alone —" She poured a cup. "Here's your tea, Matthew."

He took it and looked at her and Jane thought, he's truly going to speak to her. She waited, keyed up. "What'll you do this evening," he asked. "Listen to the radio?"

"Ay, I can only hear that decently in my bedroom, isn't that it?"

"No," he said, and Jane thought, he didn't give up. "No, I wondered if you might help Jane make the blackberry jelly. She's tired."

"Oh she'll be tired, working in the heat. I can make the jelly by myself."

Jane said, "No, you couldn't lift the big pan, Mother, with that sore wrist. I'm not tired now. We'll all be fresher now the rain's come."

"Fight it out between you," he said. "I'll make a bite of supper. We didn't get much tea" — he hesitated — "with company coming."

Mrs Pawson rolled up her sleeves for the jelly making. "Ay, we could do with company more often, seeing nothing but cows and sheep and hens day in, day out. We all took to Mr Pendington, didn't we, Jane? I hope he got home all right, don't you?"

"What d'you mean?" Matthew cried suddenly, turning from the pantry where he was fetching down some eggs from the shelf. Jane looked at him in alarm.

Her mother said, "Why, before the storm broke. George Cranston was talking about getting struck by lightning."

"Huh." Matthew snorted. "That was his joke. You're quite safe in a car."

"Yes," Jane cried. "He'd be fine. A car's safe. A car has rubber wheels." She began to laugh. "Rubber wheels." The day's strain broke out of her in helpless giggles.

Her mother said, "The heat's gone to your head. She was like this after exams, Matthew. Hysterical. Well, when he comes back we'll know he was safe in the storm – with rubber wheels."

Matthew looked round again, this time with the egg pan in his hand and six brown eggs in it. "Who'll be coming back?"

"Mr Pendington, about my annexe."

"He won't need to come," Jane said quickly. "Not if we do what he wants."

"Let him come," said Matthew. "I can talk to him."

"He was right about an extension being cheaper." Mrs Pawson lifted the baskets of blackberries on to the bench. "And quicker. Like jelly, we don't need pick out stalks."

Matthew lit the gas under the eggs. "Ay, an extension could be built before Martin's home." He filled the dog's dish with scraps and her bowl with milk and set it down by her. "There you are, old girl. There's your supper."

Jane saw her mother start at the caress in his voice. She hadn't known the dog was in the room.

Then Matthew said, "I'll ask him to come back on his own this time. I want nothing more to do with George Cranston."

"Oh," Jane said. "I'm glad. If I asked Peggy she'd get Wilf to help us."

"Is that Wilfred Mason, the surveyor," her mother asked, "your Peggy's husband? He might do it for free. I never asked you to spend much on me, Matthew."

"I know," he said. "You never asked me to."

They were silent then. The only sounds in the room were the hiss of the calor gas as Matthew made some toast to eat with their eggs, the running of the tap as Jane and her mother washed the glossy fruit and the lapping of Jess at her bowl.

Outside, drowning the soft indoor sounds of living, the rain streamed across the windows, drummed on the corrugated roof of the milking-shed and filled the gullies on the moor till they roared like waterfalls.

A bus had skidded on the road out to Westhill and was slewed across both traffic lanes. Derek Lister pulled up. Here was an excuse to tell Shirley. He refused to feel guilty about the time he'd spent in the bar. She had provoked him with her mysterious phone call and that was her punishment.

He was not a man to sit waiting, however. He was alongside a side road which would take him down onto the Brynbank road. He squeezed the car out and headed down towards the river to come back up to Westhill by the road beyond Hugh Cole's cottage. Water flowing out from the steep hillside across the road made him slow down.

When he reached Hugh's cottage his eyes turned to it automatically and there was Hugh at the window with a baby in his arms. My God, he thought, it's his and he said it was the sculptor's! He grinned and waved. Hugh saw him and flung open the window.

"Thank the Lord, you've come. Back onto the cinder track. The road's too narrow to park there."

"I'm not calling," Derek shouted over the noise of the rain. "I'm going home."

"I thought you'd come for the baby."

"You *what?*" He couldn't have heard right. He was just going to wave and drive on when there was more shouting and doors banging.

Hugh turned and spoke to someone in the room. He called to Derek, "Hilde's just come in. She wants to see you. Come in and have a quick one."

"What the hell —?"

The German girl came to the window and beckoned urgently. It was like her nerve. But why had Hugh said, "Thank the Lord you've come"? A quaking fear leapt into his mind that something had happened to Shirley.

He looked up and down the road and reversed the Zephyr onto the cinder track.

They came to the door like a family group, the baby still in Hugh's arms. As soon as he was inside, Hilde put up her hands to his hair and shoulders.

"Oh you are wet! I'll see if there's anything to drink." She went into the kitchen.

"God," said Hugh, "she's pawing you already."

"What the hell is all this about? I haven't come on a social call. What was all that yelling at the window?"

Hugh said, "Easy, old boy. Sit you down." He sat himself down as he said it. "I've been walking about with this yowling brat for hours. I only went to the window to see if the rain had stopped so I could dump him back on his mother — if you can dignify her with a name like that — and there you were, arriving to rescue me. The little villain stopped as soon as he heard you, which is a good sign."

"Will you stop talking in riddles?" Lister, thumping angrily about the room, was brought to a halt behind Hugh's chair by catching sight of the baby draped like a small sack over his shoulder. Its head lolled against his flame shirt, a dark pool of dampness where its mouth rested, lips pushed into a pout, eyes tight shut.

Lister felt his own mouth twisting into a smile. "It's asleep. Put it in the pram."

"Get him off me then," Hugh cried as if a snake had coiled round his neck.

"It's *your* baby." The incongruity of Hugh and a baby was tickling Lister's fancy.

"*My* baby! This!" Hugh leapt to his feet. The baby blinked, its head bouncing on his shoulder.

"Here," said Lister, "you'll hurt him." He unhooked the baby – it was gripping a fold of shirt in one small fist – and cradled it in his arms. "D'you want it in the pram?"

Hilde came in from the kitchen, a bottle of beer in each hand. "Oh that is so good. Your so big arms and he so little. Yes, put him in the pram. I see you put him in the pram." Derek laid him in, bunched up as he was in his shawl. There was a little movement, a snort and then stillness. Hugh clapped his hands.

"Done like a true Daddy! That'll take a load off Shirley's mind."

"Shirley –!"

Hilde clouted Hugh on the head with a bottle. "Imbecile!"

Hugh howled and Derek looked from one to the other in bewilderment. Could Shirley have been to the doctor, whose surgery was further on this road, and learnt she was pregnant? Had felt ill and couldn't get home? Was she in the next door cottage?

"I am sorry no whisky," Hilde said, opening the beer bottle. "You are so wet. You have not been home yet?" She wheeled the pram to one side and drew out a chair for him at the little table. She herself sat on the bed alongside. "You have not seen your wife?"

Derek sat down then as if she'd pushed him. It *was* to do with Shirley.

"What's up?" he cried. "What's wrong?"

"Have your drink," Hilde said. She was winding her plait round the forefinger of her left hand. "It's not to worry about. Your Shirley would like to adopt my baby."

Derek stared. "Shirley would – ?" He looked round the room. "Where *is* Shirley?"

Hugh laughed. "At home I suppose, cheesed off waiting for you."

Derek got to his feet. "What are you keeping me for then? She's all right?"

"Mentally?" Hugh asked. "I did wonder but Hilde thinks it was on the level."

"You are a fool." Hilde threatened him with the other bottle. "I wanted you to see the baby, Derek. I would walk up to Westhill to show you but Hugh say you are still at office. And then storm came. Mother sent me to fetch baby. So lucky that was, because you were outside. Your Shirley has seen baby, two times."

She went to the pram as if to lift him out again. Lister held up his hand to stop her. "Don't wake him." He had to say what must be said to people with babies and then get out of here. "He's a nice little chap. How old is he?"

She smiled and touched his shoulder. "You are English gentleman. I like your curly hair, your rosy face and big shoulders. He will be big, like you. I am big. His father is big. No, *you* will be his father. I like that. He looks little now but he is only six weeks. That is right age for you to have him. They said that in the Nursing Home."

Derek said, "So Maurice is his father? I thought at first –" He looked at Hugh.

Hilde scoffed. "Him!" Hugh only giggled.

It was insufferable to Derek to talk any more in front of Hugh. He must get home and see Shirley. This was all wrong. Shirley must have met the girl shopping and they'd talked about babies as women would. Shirley had let slip that they'd once thought of adoption and this wretched girl had assumed they'd take her unwanted baby. But what about that phone call and the urgency in Shirley's voice, even of tears.

"Look here, when did you see my wife?"

Hilde said, "About twelve o'clock and again this afternoon. She had time. She thought about it." It didn't make sense. She'd phoned him at half past ten.

Hilde held out his glass of beer. "You haven't touched your drink." He tossed it off. "I must get home. There's been a misunderstanding."

"Oh Shirley say to me, 'You won't change your mind, will you?' Tell her I won't. In Germany I cannot keep baby. So you will say she can have him and all his things."

Hugh said, "Special offer. One male infant. Complete with pram, cot, bath, nappies – all inclusive. Late season bargain. As new."

Derek edged to the door. He felt his face flaming with anger and vexation. This had gone too far.

Hilde put a hand on his arm. He wanted to move the pram so he could open the door. She said, "I must have money of course. Just for his things – and expenses. I won't be any trouble. I not ask what he is doing, how he is." She caressed his arm feeling his muscles. "You play golf, don't you?"

And then the door was flung open from the outside, crashing into the pram. The baby wailed. Maurice appeared, huge and hairy, in the doorway.

"What's this?" he cried. "What are you doing to the baby? Who is this man?"

"It is you that wake baby. You –" And Hilde slung at him in German what Derek recalled from his army days as pretty coarse swear words. Then she stopped with a laugh. "Surely, Maurice, you remember Mr Lister, the Deputy County Planning Officer?"

Hugh guffawed. Lister knew he would store it up to tell the office.

"Excuse me," he said to the sculptor between clenched teeth. "I'm leaving."

Maurice didn't move. "This is the husband of that woman you saw today?" Hilde nodded. "Well let me tell you –" he turned to Lister – "I haven't given consent for him to be adopted. Hilde may not want the baby but *I* might."

"You!" she cried again. "They wouldn't give you – how you say? – custody. I tell them what you do when you are angry. You just like *idea* of baby – for a moment "

Lister said, "Sort it out between you." Miraculously the baby had gone to sleep again. "Hugh, I want a word with you before I go."

Hilde pulled the pram out of the way and Maurice followed it, threateningly.

Hugh came across the room. "The voice of the Deputy, I heard him declare."

Lister opened the outer door so that the noise of the rain would drown their voices. They were sheltered by the cottage eaves. He gripped Hugh by his nylon shirt and glared at him. Hugh's body, slight as an elf, trembled under his hand, whether with fear or cold, Lister thought, didn't matter a damn.

"If you so much as breathe one word at the office about this so help me I'll come down here and thrash you black and blue."

"All right, all right, old man. So I'm frightened. Now will you let go of my shirt? It cost me five guineas and you're crumpling it."

"By God, I mean it though." Derek left go of him. "And don't forget it by tomorrow morning. Not a breath outside these four walls."

"But you'll tell folk when he's adopted. You can't hide a growing boy for ever."

Lister stared at him. "You've got the cheek of seven devils, haven't you? There won't *be* any adoption. D'you think I'd have the child of two maniacs like that?"

"They're very good pedigree. Hilde's sire's a lawyer and Maurice's a clergyman. With you and Shirley the baby would revert to type. Best upper middle class stock."

"I've had enough of this." He looked into the room. Maurice had sat down to drink the rest of the beer. Hilde had an arm twined round him. "Tell them I've gone."

He dashed out to his car. In a minute he was roaring up the hill for home.

Shirley didn't stir when she heard the car. She was eating a sandwich, curled up in the deepest armchair – Derek's chair – and reading a biography of Catherine of Aragon. She had not quite equated Derek with Henry the Eighth but she was seeing all men as cruel, gross and utterly selfish. She thought, I won't lift my eyes when he walks in.

"Shirley!" he bawled, when he was barely in the house. "Where are some dry clothes? I'm soaked." She could hear him throw off his shoes on Mrs Ball's clean kitchen floor. He came into the sitting-room in his socks. His face was red and his thick hair flattened by the rain so that he looked older. He saw where she was sitting.

"Like that, is it?" He flung his wet jacket onto the chair she always used. He strode up close and stood over her. "Nothing to say, have you?"

She put her hand over her nose. "Oh! You've been drinking beer."

"My God!" He backed away. "Attack the best weapon of defence. Is that it?"

"Defence?" She sat up. "*I'm* not on the defensive." She had resolved not to mention the time first. "You know it's eight-fifteen."

He came close and loomed over her. "I had to see Paul and he didn't get back till after six-thirty. And then there was a hold-up and I had to go round by Brynbank *and* –"

She put her hands over her mouth. He had called on Hugh – and the girl was there! – Oh it was cruel if he'd found out like that. "What –?" She couldn't meet his eyes.

He turned away. "When I come down I want my supper and a hot drink."

She went for the prepared tray, her hands quivering. This thing was too big to speak of in anger. When he came back he sat down, saying nothing, tucking into the food, not looking at her.

She thought, what am I shaking for? He's behaving like a bear. She asked in a level voice, "And who did you see in Brynbank?"

He laid down his knife and fork. "I saw the whole lunatic lot."

"And the baby?"

He banged down his coffee cup. "And the baby." He looked at his watch. "Come on then. Let's hear what it's all about. That spy serial starts soon."

She clenched her hands. "Oh no. Not a deadline for anything as important as this. Didn't I say on the phone – when do we *talk*? Is a spy serial more important than –" After the long hours of waiting for him she didn't know how to say it.

"Oh come on Shirley!" He let out a blustery laugh. It wasn't in him to sustain a silent sulk. "The girl put the idea in your head. You'll be tickled to death tomorrow that you ever gave it a thought."

She asked quietly. "You saw the baby? How? They wouldn't be out this weather."

He told her. "What I want to know is what were you phoning about at half past ten, when you didn't see him till noon?"

She related what Mrs Ball had said and then coolly outlined the rest of her day.

"You didn't discuss the baby with Eleanor and Hazel?" She shook her head. "But the sight of Eleanor made you broody. Huh! Women!" He looked at his watch again and poured himself more coffee from the flask. "I told the girl it was all a misunderstanding."

She kept her voice very calm. "I phoned you *before* I saw Eleanor. Derek, why are you talking as if this is a passing whim of mine? Adoption was *your* idea originally."

"Yes, years ago. You didn't fancy the idea so it got shelved."

"I wanted our own. I still do. There may be a perfectly simple explanation –"

"We needn't go into all that again. We didn't adopt then and it's too late now."

"Why? It's not even too late to have children of our own. I'm fit and well and hundreds of women start families at my age or even older."

He was flushing angrily again. "*You'd* never put up with nine months of looking a frump. And what about the discomfort, the pain? You're not the type."

"I'm –" She jumped up and, to hide the tears in her voice, began packing up the things on the tray. "What do you know about my type? *You* couldn't even stand the thought of going to a doctor." She hurried into the kitchen. She could hear him get up out of his chair. If he put on the television – ! She turned back and bumped into him coming out to her. "Oh Derek!" Her hands were planted on his chest. He looked bewildered.

"Come on then, old girl, we'd better talk this out."

She thought, he's humouring the little woman, but she let him lead her to the sofa where he caressed her hand in his great brown hairy ones.

"You couldn't spoil this with dirty nappies."

She killed the emotion in her voice. "Derek, I can garden without spoiling my hands. I'd prove how easy it is to keep well-groomed even with a baby."

He was grinning at her. "I know you've got determination. You go out for a game of golf every time, as cool as a cucumber, determined to win. But in the four walls at home when the brat howls and there's no audience to play to?" He shook his head. "You know we've been on our own too long. We're too used to pleasing ourselves."

"I don't know when I've pleased myself since I married you." She said it so casually that he took time to take in the words.

"In heaven's name what does that mean?"

"You've never looked at it like that, have you? I was a private secretary, remember? It was interesting work. I was a key figure in that firm. They didn't want to lose me. But you never liked working wives, you said –"

"Come off it. You loved being a lady of leisure. You worked all hours there."

"I *had* to love being a lady of leisure. *And* I'd never played golf till I met you."

"That's a nice one. You're keener than I. You play when I'm working."

"Yes, since I was picked for the County Ladies. It's something to do."

"And what about if *I* hadn't been married. I'd have moved more often, gone abroad. By now I'd have had my own county."

"Have I ever said I didn't want to go abroad?"

"No, but I'd only think of these things if I was a free agent. And I wouldn't have had you on my mind all day. I could have enjoyed a chat with Paul or Hugh after work without being made to feel guilty."

"So it was a chat with Paul, was it, not office business?"

"Of course it was office business but we can mention other subjects, can't we?"

She saw this was getting nowhere. "All right, Derek, we can leave the saga of our wasted lives. I believe Adoption Societies dislike the notion of acquiring a child to save a marriage. D'you think that applies in our case?"

Now he did look hard at her. She kept her composure in her cool lemon two-piece beside the scruffy old clothes he'd put on.

"God damn it," he said, "can you honestly see yourself with a family?" She didn't answer and he took hold of her chin and turned her face to the light. "You look different tonight. Were you crying because I was late?"

"I was not." She pulled away from his grip, stood up and looked at herself in the mirror over the fireplace. "I haven't put my evening make-up on, that's all."

"You change your make-up for the evening when we're just staying in?"

"Of course. After I've washed I make up differently."

"And what happened today? Hadn't you time with all these comings and goings?"

"I had aeons of time between Hilde going and you coming." She looked at herself again, touching the skin under her eyes with the tips of her fingers. "I didn't think of it."

He got up and stood beside her. "I know what it is. You look older - that's it."

"That's what I thought about you when you came in tonight."

He guffawed suddenly. "My giddy aunt, we're a nice pair. Paul was talking about a farmer's family he met today. He wanted to shake them by the ears to make them each face what they wanted. Shirley, I'm forty-six and you're forty-one. Of course we'll stick together but maybe you're right we should have kids before we're any older."

She stared at him. "What! Are you serious?" He squeezed her waist. He was chuckling, delighted to have surprised her.

"You mean it! You said kids – in the plural?"

"Well, start with one."

"You'd have to come home early to see him. Otherwise he'd always be in bed."

"Oh sure. I'm not having you teach him how to swing a golf club."

"At six weeks? Will you learn to change his nappy first?"

"Ah but I'm wondering whether we shouldn't have one older. Or twins?"

She swallowed and turned and walked about the room. She stopped by the window and looked out at the wet garden. A sodden rose drooped against the window in the light from the room. "Derek, it's *this* baby we're having. Hilde's and Maurice's."

"What!" he shouted across the room at her. "I wouldn't have theirs in a million years. They're both off their rockers."

She turned round fiercely. "What would we know about the parents if we adopted from a society?"

"So you like that couple, do you? She's a sex maniac to start with."

"The baby won't be tainted with their morals at six weeks. Mrs Ball said her father is a lawyer and his is a clergyman."

"Oh I had that from Hugh Cole too. And isn't that marvellous – all the people who'd know where the baby came from! Mrs Ball and the whole blessed village down there. I put the fear of God into Hugh but it'd be a miracle if he kept his mouth shut."

She thought, Eleanor would tell Paul. "Derek, what would it matter who knew?"

"What would it matter? If I adopt a child no one must know who the parents are."

His word "If *I* adopt" was hurtful but it was true that their friends at the golf club would think of the story whenever they saw the child.

Derek pressed on, "And whatever agreement those two signed we'd never feel safe from them. And the child? If we tell him he's adopted he's bound to ask who his real parents are sometime. Do we say we don't know? No, the whole idea's preposterous."

Shirley hid her face from him. The case he put was overwhelming. But she could see the little cheek denting the pillow, feel the tiny fists waving as she lifted him. She clutched the edge of the curtain and bowed her head against the glass. She sobbed.

Derek took three strides across the room. "Hey now, steady on, old girl. We'll have one as a baby if you want, have the fun of seeing it grow up"

She leant her head against his jacket. He'd worn it when he touched up the fence and she could smell a whiff of creosote. "It was *that* baby," she managed to say. "He was beautiful and he smiled at me – if you'd had him in your arms – if men can feel that –"

"As a matter of fact I did have him in my arms. Yes, I felt *something*. He was so small. But he was theirs. If he'd been mine now –"

She noticed "mine" again, not "ours." "D'you mean *really* yours?" Her voice was still choked with sobs.

"You never cry." He was truly distressed now.

"I did when the doctor told me there was no reason why I couldn't have a baby. And you did nothing."

He held her head against his shoulder and spoke muffled into her hair. "We'll have a last check-up ourselves. Phone the doc tomorrow and make an appointment." He lifted his head. "Because I'm not having that baby. They're probably drug addicts."

"Yes, Derek, all right." She tormented herself. What would they do with that helpless mite? The thought came to her, if Hilde puts him in a home we might still get him. Mrs Ball would know but Derek wouldn't.

He said suddenly, "It's a damn nuisance we fixed this send-off party next week. Hugh asked if he could bring Hilde."

She took out a tissue and dried her eyes. "I'll tell her we're planning our own baby."

Relief showed in his face. "Ay so she won't come to the party. She and her mother will *have* to take the baby back to Germany. After that Hugh will be off to Africa, thank God." He laughed. "Mind, he did brighten up County Hall." With his arm still round her he drew her to the sofa. "All right, now, old girl?"

Maybe, she thought, as long you keep that appointment. Something must happen. I will make it happen, one way or the other. She nodded and he got up to switch on the television. "Catch the end," he said.

Like all the Victorian houses in Sutton Terrace Number Eleven with its long front garden and gracious reception rooms went to pieces at the rear. Eleanor, at the gas stove in the cramped kitchen end, trying to keep the fish-pie from drying up, looked through the small window into the garage that filled half the original yard space. Cathy was doing her homework at the long bench in the narrow breakfast room two steps up from the kitchen with a view only of rain streaming down brick walls. That jumble of a room was where much of their living happened. With its stove it was the cosiest place in the house.

Eleanor put on more coke. Cathy said, "It's not cold" and shifted nearer to the hall door which was open in case John called again. The thunder had frightened him.

Eleanor said, "Daddy had no coat. He'll be wet."

"I have something really special to tell Daddy."

Eleanor, returning to the kitchen end, looked round. "What is it?"

"It's for him first."

Eleanor bit her lip and said nothing. Her varicose veins were aching. If she sat down in the sprawling leather armchair that adjoined the bench she'd struggle to get out of it when she heard the car.

Cathy leapt up. "There's his hoot! I'll hide." She crouched down under the bench.

Eleanor watched the headlights swing round through the sheet of rain.

They lit up the garage shelves cluttered with tools, rags and oilcans. The shining body of the car slid past. Paul's face, in the light from the kitchen, hung briefly like a moon between clouds. Eleanor drew a deep sigh. It was the sense of restoration she always felt on his return.

"Don't bother him," she hissed back to Cathy. "He'll be tired."

"*He's* never too tired to listen to me." Cathy could certainly hurt in a few words.

They heard the bang of the car door, then the rumble of the garage door closing. Cathy was tense in her hiding place.

The backdoor opened and he was in the room, smelling of soaked tweed. He managed a half smile as his eyes met Eleanor's. She knew at once as he stepped up to the warmth of the breakfast end that he was not himself, but it was too late to stop Cathy.

She leapt out shrieking, "Daddy, I'm the brain of the school!" She stood before him smirking, with rare colour in her face.

He only looked at her in a sort of bewilderment and tossed his briefcase onto the armchair and his jacket after it. He swung a kitchen chair round from the bench, opened the stove door and sat right in front wrenching off his shoes and socks.

Eleanor looked sorrowfully at Cathy. There were days when he'd come in calling, "I'm home. Kill the fatted calf. I'm famished."

Cathy stood behind him, rigid with distress.

"Well, what was that supposed to be? News?" he said, not turning round.

"I don't know what it's about," Eleanor said. She knelt and squeezed the turn-ups of his trousers. "Darling, you'll have to change *everything*."

Cathy went out of the room without speaking.

"Well, what's the matter with her?" he asked, his voice flat and uncurious.

Eleanor took some old grey flannels off the clothes-horse in the corner. "These are aired. I don't know. But it must be something special." He took the trousers and changed into them. Even in front of the stove he was shivering. She pulled a jersey out of the basket of dirty washing. "Put that on and these socks." She went about the floor collecting his discarded clothes. The stooping made her sigh.

He said, "I'll be O.K. when I've eaten. I hope Cathy's not getting melodramatic."

She came in as he said it. In her arms was his best suit.

"What's that for?" Eleanor said.

"You said he had to change, didn't you?" Then she noticed that he *was* changed. A flash of anger crossed her face.

Paul said, "I only wear that for Appeal Cases or interviews."

Eleanor could tell he was making a huge effort to say even that much.

Cathy turned and marched out of the door again.

"Hang it up properly," he commanded in a sterner voice.

She slammed the door.

Eleanor shook her head. "*I* get that behaviour sometimes. You're usually so humorous with her that you never see it." She brought in the fish-pie.

He towelled his hair while she served him a great helping and poured the sauce. It eased down the hillocks of mashed potato like lava. He pulled up his chair.

"That looks great." Then he added, "I've met too much uncivilized behaviour today. I don't want it in the family the minute I come home." After that he ate in silence.

Eleanor made coffee and perched on the chair next to him to pour it out. Cathy came back in, passed behind them both and stood tensely the other side of Paul.

He looked up at her. "Did you hang up the suit?"

She shrugged and mumbled, "Of course."

"So," he said, "what's this news?"

"Oh" – she kept shrugging her shoulders – "it's nothing compared to *your* news and if I hadn't reminded Mummy she'd never have told you that."

Eleanor said quickly, "Daddy won't want to talk about the London job now. Let him have his supper. He'll not have had anything since lunch."

"I didn't have any lunch." He took a mouthful of pie. "And I'm not bothered about London."

Eleanor couldn't stop exclaiming. "Darling! Do you *really* not mind?"

Cathy snapped, "You said we weren't to talk about that."

Paul took her by the arm and his grip was severe. "Will you say what it is you want to say and stop snarling at everyone?"

"I can't now –" Cathy began and her lip trembled.

"We'll get no peace till you do."

Cathy leapt into the armchair, hiding her face. Paul's briefcase fell to the ground and some of the files slid out.

"Look what you're doing!" He slapped her upended rear.

She started up, her face scarlet, trod on the briefcase and gave it a kick. Then she snatched it up by the underside letting everything fall onto the floor.

Paul leapt to his feet and struck her hard across the face.

Eleanor cried out. His face was as flushed as Cathy's. She had never seen him look like that before.

The door opened behind her and John peered in. "I can't get to sleep." He looked at Paul. "Daddy, why did you leave your suit on the landing? I fell over it."

"So you lied as well." Paul's voice was drained of expression, his face white now.

"What's happened?" John came right in, round-eyed.

Eleanor got up. "Come on. Bed."

She trailed up the stairs, holding John's hand tightly. That blow would hurt Paul more than Cathy. Could it ever be wiped out? Would their happy, teasing relationship survive this? Hiding her tears she hung up the suit and settled John with a hug.

When she went back to the kitchen Cathy was hunched in the armchair, sobbing, her head on her knees. Paul was at the table, knife and fork in hand, not eating.

"It's some intelligence test," he began in an extra normal voice. "Her news."

"Oh." Eleanor tried to look brightly at Cathy. "Are you still practising them?"

Paul said, "The council do surveys on progress in the Eleven plus year."

Cathy gasped between sobs, "The paper had the City Crest on."

"Well, how did you get on, darling?" Eleanor asked.

Cathy slid off the chair and stood with her back to them. She sniffed hard. "I only had the highest score in our school."

"But that's marvellous."

Eleanor went to her and tried a self-conscious hug. Cathy half-turned, tears on her cheeks, and looked at Paul.

"I'm surprised they told you the results," he said. Cathy began to grin, reluctantly.

"They didn't. The paper was in Miss Day's desk. She told me to take some chalk to Class 3 so I had to open the lid. She was helping the dud readers so I had time to look. I was a lot of points higher than the next person."

Paul asked, "What sort of test was it?"

"Arithmetic and those pattern things. Matching up."

Paul reached for his briefcase, repacked and upright by his chair. As he bent down the light above him shone on the left side of his face. Eleanor saw the bruise.

"What –?" she began. If Cathy had thrown something – ? No, they were getting back to civilisation. It would be foolish to ask now. Paul took out a file. She hoped *Cathy* had put them back. He beckoned Cathy towards him.

"If you're so clever you can do something for me." He drew from the file two folded sheets and spread them on the table, crowding his plate to one side. Cathy darted forward and pulled a chair close to him. Eleanor looked over his other shoulder.

"They're plans of a house," Cathy said.

"Yes. You see this with the pencil marks on – that's the one the owner sent in. Neville Carr altered it. The man wanted an extension. There's the bathroom and bedroom over a sun-lounge. There it is in section and there it is in plan, upstairs and downstairs."

"I see, I see."

Paul slipped the other sheet over the top. "Now here's what Neville drew. He rearranged the upper storey to get most of the new bedroom into the existing space and so put the extension onto the gable end of the house."

"But what do you want *me* to do?" Cathy was all agog and wriggling with impatience as if her grief was forgotten. Eleanor felt bitter towards her. She thought, he's worn out, but he's so devastated with himself that he's desperate to make amends.

"I want you to find out the total area in cubic feet of the new extension."

"She couldn't do that." Eleanor tried to pull his plate towards him over the plans.

"But I can," Cathy shrieked. "Cubic feet is for boxes. It's only multiplying."

"You see, she gets to the heart of the problem at once." Paul pushed the plate back and pointed to Neville's neat figures. "Length and breadth in feet. Heights from the Section – there, for each room. Then you do a sum for each and add –"

Cathy dragged away the sheet, "I *know* – but I'll need some scrap paper."

"Oh write on the plan. That corner will do. There's a pencil in my jacket pocket."

"Now will you eat up?" Eleanor leant close to him as she put his plate in front of him again. She lightly touched his bruise and whispered, "She's been a very bad girl."

"Eh? She didn't do that."

Eleanor looked at Cathy. She was kneeling in the armchair, working at the end of the bench, her head bent over the page, black hair hanging forward, lips screwed up.

"Some fathers would have really walloped her for upsetting that briefcase."

"She's only got *this* one."

Eleanor kissed the top of his head. "This one's too good for her."

"I let her down." His eyes frowned with distress. "And myself."

"Nonsense." She caressed the wave of his hair at the back of his neck. She wanted him to be himself again. "What's this about anyway? What are you trying to prove?"

"Nothing crucial really." Cathy was still engrossed. "I told you Neville made a blunder. It came out today. That's partly why I was so late."

Eleanor drew her chair close and sat down. "Is this why he wants to resign?" She gave a small laugh. "Believe it or not, his wife called on me today. He'd been upset at lunchtime because you were cross with him. I don't know if that's why she called – to get a friend at court. She'd been up at the Grosvenor School getting herself a job."

"Had she indeed?" Paul spoke between mouthfuls. "She said she wanted one. She was waiting in the square for Neville when I left the office at lunchtime."

"How odd – us both seeing her the same day." Eleanor felt better now that Paul had eaten a large plateful. She poured him more coffee and decided it was too soon to mention Lena's invitation." She nodded towards Cathy. "What are you getting her to do? Find out if this house needed permission at all?"

"It did, in the submitted plan, but Neville reduced the scale of the extension yet he doesn't seem to have added it up anywhere."

"What *is* the limit? I've forgotten."

"Over one tenth of the original size or one thousand, seven hundred and sixty cubic feet, whichever is the greater."

Eleanor got up to put cheese and biscuits and fruit on the table. She peered at Cathy's workings. Cathy immediately put her arm across the plan.

"I'm just *finishing*. It's one thousand, seven hundred and twenty-four."

He reached for the plan. "Can it be right? You were too quick."

She put it behind her back. "It is. I always know if it's come right."

Eleanor said, "If it is, then it was permitted development. Let Daddy check it."

Cathy handed it over. "What if he adds it up wrong?" she grumbled.

Paul had it checked while Eleanor cleared away his plate.

"She's right." He stood up and carried his coffee over to the leather armchair. Cathy jumped off it and plumped up its cushion for him, her eyes searching his. He sank into the chair and stretched out his legs, wiggling his long feet in the old socks.

Eleanor studied him. "So Planning's not involved if permission wasn't needed."

Cathy giggled, tentatively. "It took *me* to find that out."

Paul eyed her. "Don't *boast*." She shook her head vigorously. Then he half-smiled. "It would have made all the difference at the time, but not now."

"For heaven's sake!" Eleanor said. "If you can't use it —"

"We'd have to crawl to the County Surveyor and say, 'That house where we made the mistake about the improvement line, it was permitted development all the time.'"

"Of course, I see. Lena never said — if she knew. So Neville should have done this sum at the beginning."

"Exactly. Now I'll have to suggest a new line but there'll be a furore over costs."

Cathy had stood on one foot listening in silence. Now she planted both feet squarely. "Why must I stay at school five more years? I'd be better than Neville Carr now. I'm not boasting — am I?" Then she noticed the pie-dish. "You said I could have supper with Daddy. There's hardly any —" She seized a spoon and began scraping it out. When she'd eaten a hunk of bread and jam as well she was ready to admit it was bedtime.

She went over to hug Paul, climbing on his knee, a thing she hardly ever did.

"Who gave you that bang?" she said, noticing it for the first time.

"Why should it be a who? It was a barn door actually."

"Mine wasn't." She touched the mark on her cheek where he had struck her.

"I know," he said. "I shouldn't have done that." Eleanor thought his voice shook a little when he said it. It was on the tip of her tongue to say, "*She was very naughty*," but Cathy, pressing her lips close to his ear, whispered, "I shouldn't have upset your briefcase. Or lied about the suit." Eleanor gave a sigh of gladness and went to wash up.

She heard Paul say, "Quits, then. All forgiven?" And Cathy echoed, "Quits."

Then she called out, "Night, Mummy. Don't come up. All those stairs you know with your varicose veins." And she was gone.

Eleanor came through and sat down on a kitchen chair. Paul began to get up to give her the armchair but she shook her head. "We'll go in the front room in a minute."

Somehow they sat on, the rain streaming past the windows, the stove glowing.

"No harm done," she said softly, "between you and Cathy. No offence taken."

"Offence!" He turned his head to her with that straight gaze she loved. "But there is, Eleanor, and much offence too." She could hear him saying it in *Hamlet* in the school production. He went on in painful earnest, "Today I blazed out at Neville, a subordinate – behaviour that I have loathed in others – and a few hours later I preached to a farmer who was eaten up by fury and frustration over a tiresome old woman. I thought, smugly, that *I* could have laughed off his problem, yet only a few hours on I have struck my own child."

"You were at the end of your tether."

"But I felt the farmer shouldn't *have* a tether. He should be free of anger. I wasn't."

"She was naughty and you were exhausted."

"I was. The last twenty minutes driving home my brain was whirring over the day's scenes like a film rewinding."

"You'd been acting the Pembleton Myth?"

"No, the Myth let me down or the demon within broke through. What horrible demon made me *strike* Cathy, not just rebuke her? Is that who I really am, not the suave, urbane Pembleton of the Myth? I saw Leonard King strike his son today and I was truly shocked." He told her about it.

"It sounds like King's habitual behaviour. You and Cathy are different."

"Yes, I was the teasing, benevolent father? Have I shown my true colours now? Do I know who I am any more?"

"It was a lapse from your true self."

He drew a long sigh and then said suddenly, "Maybe the farmer lapsed from his true self Today I slipped out of the Council Officer role and now I wonder if he struck the planning officer or *me*."

"*Struck* you? *He* did that, not a barn door!"

"He did it *with* a barn door. I *think* he did." He told her the tale. The truth of it lurked round a corner. The more he probed the less certain he would be. "It was *Mrs* Hodge's anxious face and the way he kept referring to the wind that made me wonder."

"But he must be stopped. If he's violent he's a danger to himself and the public."

"And how could *I* bring an action against him? I wouldn't want to even if I was sure. I understand him now. The inability to see with largeness. Today I was drawn in close, blindly, with Neville, Councillor Cranston, even with Ron Foggart's plots, and now tonight with Cathy. I was in, I was deeply engaged. I wasn't play-acting responses. The Myth was stripped away. Maybe the Myth was my Freudian Super-ego." He was half-laughing now.

"The thing with Cathy is over and done with."

He sat up and took her hand. "But I must face it." He described the afternoon, how he was stranded without his jacket and how Professor Smith, a man called Thomas, had helped him to find it. "So I deliberately invited Cranston to the farm. I was Paul and he was George and the farmer was Matthew. But it didn't happen like that at all."

"Of course it wouldn't. You had matters to discuss."

"That's it. They got in the way – but by what compulsion?"

"Darling, there are laws and regulations because we're all naturally selfish. You were just helping everyone see sense. Did he hit you for that – *if* he did?"

"*If* he did it was because I touched a raw nerve. I abhor violence. Yet Cathy tonight! Today has been a disaster, Eleanor. Am I not fit to do this job? Would I be more comfortable as a vicar? Derek suggested that."

He drew her down beside him and they cuddled together in the leather armchair.

"Vicar!" chuckled Eleanor. "I'm sure you'd be brilliant but you might have to believe in more than a sort of universal tolerance." She thought, maybe he does believe in something more. He comes to church so we can go as a family. What *does* he believe?

He said with his old twinkle, "It can't be *universal* tolerance – when I won't tolerate red brick in Dunford or unauthorised caravans. What do *you* think?"

"I think today you wanted to be an ideal planning officer as well as an ideal man before the bar of yourself and you were disappointed."

"Or was it before a higher bar? Perhaps I *am* moving that way. I knew that farmhouse needed a grand shower of perfect love and all they have had is a thunderstorm."

"I *hope* you're moving that way. But talking of moving, will you still be looking for other jobs now those fools in London failed to take you?"

"No, we'll stay." And he told her about the new job coming up in the office. "I know it's earmarked for me, just as Hugh Cole's job is earmarked for Neville."

"What! He gets promotion despite Lower Wooton?"

"Looks like it. Neville is the moral stalwart. No play-acting for him."

"Well never mind him. Will you like *your* new job? Not so many bad days?"

He laughed. "More perhaps and I won't get out into my lovely West Area – or not very often. I'll be negotiating with industrialists and fighting tangled Appeal Cases. And I'll have an office to myself where I won't be able to entertain the troops in my glass box, so I'll become a serious old Senior Officer of whom new recruits will be in great awe."

She kissed him. "You're already creating a new myth. *I'll* never be in awe of you and I'll never let you lose your sense of humour. You'll need it now when I tell you Lena Carr has invited us to dinner on Monday and I said yes, unless you have a meeting."

"You did, did you?" He eased her weight off his thighs a little. "I don't think I can cope with the thought of that *and* an elephant on top of me."

"Sorry. I'll tell you another thing. She's obsessed by you. She went through our photo albums for a sight of you and told me I was lucky to have you." So had Hilde, she remembered. Time enough to tell him about that episode too. "She was right of course."

He smiled. "Thank you for that. So we'll see them twice, Monday night and then Friday when Derek and Shirley are giving Hugh a farewell party. I shall be stiff and dignified on both occasions, on Monday to kill off Lena's infatuation, and on Friday to impress Bird that I'm ACPO material. I'll wear my best suit and have my hair cut."

She climbed out of the chair. "Shall we go and sit in the sitting-room to practise your new role?"

He shook his head, suddenly serious again. "Roles are out. I appalled myself tonight. I must find a better defence against the demon within than acting a role." He got up, smiling to reassure her as she began to say piteously, "Oh darling –."

Then he stretched his arms above his head and gave a huge yawn. "Bath and bed soon and if John wakes me at six again I'll get up and draw a new improvement line for Lower Wooton."

He followed her into the sitting-room, still warm from the day's heat and switched on a sidelight and the record player. Then he flung himself onto the sofa and put his feet on the coffee table.

"You know, Eleanor, the best part of every day is coming home to you."

Her eyes filled with tears. "That's the loveliest thing you've ever said to me."

"Is it? Well that's a good line to end on. Sit down and put your feet up too. We'll hear The Brandenburg Concertos. Then we'll go to bed."

Bach's notes came cascading into the room. They sat in the half dark, arms twined round each other, very still except for a stirring under her smock.

"Baby likes Bach as much as we do," Eleanor whispered after a while, her eyes turned to the bay windows where the curtains were still undrawn. A gentler rain slithered down the glass. Beyond was darkness except where stirring branches allowed a street light to peep through. When he didn't respond she twisted round to peer at his face. The lines were smoothed out, the eyes closed. He looked years younger, a mere youth. She nestled closer, satisfied, and listened to the music.

Lightning Source UK Ltd.
Milton Keynes UK
UKOW05f1809300617

304420UK00002B/63/P